# AUTUMN FROST

M.D. Schlatter

## DOT'S MICRO-PUBLISHING HOUSE

*Lebanon, Kansas*

*Seasons of the Heart Series - Autumn Frost, Book 1*

*Copyright 2008 by M.D. Schlatter Books*



Free Vector Art by Vecteezy.com

Character Drawings by Christopher Goedert.
   http://cpg-artportfolio.blogspot.com/



Dot's Micro-Publishing House books may be purchased for educational, business, or sales promotional use. For more information, please write the Marketing Department, Dot's Micro-Publishing House, 29051 200 Road, Lebanon, KS 66952.

Dot's Micro-Publishing House website: https://dotsmicropublishinghouse.com/

ISBN: 978-1-7321-7116-9

Printed in the United States.

1st edition

# Dedication

I dedicate this book to my children. To the dreams you have and the hope that you will never give up on dreaming them. I pray that you will understand that each of you has a God-given talent that He desires to bring to fruition within you.

I love each one of you so very much!

# ❧ Index of Titles ❧

Titles referenced here are associated with the Cannon Estate alone and are not always recognized in greater society circles.

<u>ASSOCIATE TITLES</u> - precedes the last name out of <u>honor and respect</u>

Lord - a man of character and honor - not dependent on wealth or social status

Lady - a woman of character and honor - not dependent on wealth or social status

<u>HOUSEHOLD TITLES</u> - precedes the first name of the <u>staff member</u>

LeDare - head of the household; Swedish for the leader (Anton)

Koka - head cook; Swedish for 'to cook' (Fiona)

Ménage - personal attendant; French for household (Becca, Eleanor, Deidre)

LeMiss - head of housekeeping; French for 'the miss' (Tonya)

Headmaster - head of gardening and grounds (Hubert)

Madame - an older woman of instruction; French for Mistress

Master - the chauffeur (Philip)

Miss - a female staff member

Porter - a male staff member; French for 'to carry'

# SEASONS OF THE HEART SERIES

## ❦ Preface ❦

**Seasons.** The world operates in seasons – winter, spring, summer, autumn – circulating predictably. However, it is not just nature that rotates in relation to seasons – matters of the heart can progress as well. Never before had the Lady realized how much the seasons of her heart matched the seasons of the world in which she lived. As she sat and rocked gently on the balcony swing, looking around her at the crisp autumn evening, she quietly reflected on this new revelation.

**Winter.** Distinguished by cold, dark and isolated days, this season is the harshest. And indeed the Lady's younger years had been a time that adequately reflected this season. She did not remember much of her earliest years, but those she did were plagued with sickness, death, and loneliness - with a lack of hope for anything better for which to look forward. Frozen. That is how she would describe those days that held no true joy, no true promise of life. Yet, for those who have hope in Jesus, those days – which may hold the very same elements – can still be arduous. However, unlike those despairing icy days without hope in Jesus, now she could see that even the coldest winter can bring a place of anticipation for spring.

**Spring.** True to the natural season, spring of the heart does not happen immediately. The Lady remembered how one spring season started off slowly and was a turbulent period for her. Slowly the ground of her heart started to thaw, and small blooms of promise and trust start showing up. New growth was all around – if one would only look. In the natural season, days grow warmer. However, there are still chilly nights and threats of potential late freezes. In this particular season, the Lady recollected how trust once was broken was the most chilling of experiences and can even bring freezing damage to relationships. However, the final work of this season is typically marvelous with all its splendor, color, and promises to come.

**Summer.** Though the joys and blessings of Spring are still in sight at first, soon the days are filled with walking in the heat of the day – causing some to stumble. The Lady remembered her struggles with her new-found faith and the times of testing that came in that season. The tests were more intense than they had been in the cooler spring days. Yet, she had to acknowledge that the warmth and trials of summer bring about the maturing of the seeds earlier planted. Though summer has its challenges of storms and strong winds, it also has joy and peace when the storms have passed. The season of summer definitely holds a bitter-sweet place in the heart.

**Autumn.** Then there is autumn - the natural season that brings shorter days, colder nights, and a deepening of the beautiful changing colors. In the heart, the Lady reflected on the fruition of the seeds planted in her own life – a harvest of the soul - her salvation in Jesus Christ. This season is usually associated with change, although it is also a time of preservation and establishing roots - roots that will sustain through winter and be the foundation for spring. In the heart this is a time of remembering - storing up the good things and if necessary bringing needed closure. It is also a time to focus on the sustaining power of thankfulness.

As the Lady rocked, she knew there would always be more changes, for, as with the natural world, the seasons do not stand still. However, she also knew that the faithful things would never come to an end.

Autumn

Edmund

Landon

Lady Cannon

Summer

James

Autumn DeBlue was eighteen and running. Trying to flee the life of pain and memories associated with her father's inattentiveness after her mother's death. In seeking escape, Autumn was always looking for a new job or some other way to foster her excuse to leave. She even once tried to attend college away from home. However, all of her efforts over the last year were always thwarted by either her father or merely the circumstances themselves.

Therefore, when she came across an ad in an exclusive magazine regarding a companion position in Michigan, she hastily sent in her application. Not truly thinking she'd even be considered for the opportunity since she had no previous experience as a companion, Autumn was surprised to actually get a response back asking for further information only a week later.

She had so rashly sent in her application, that she had not taken the time to consider the need for references. Or, for that matter, what other information would be required in pursuing such an offer. Therefore, she now intentionally took her time providing the necessary information.

Obtaining a copy of her driver's license was the hardest part, as her father held the original in the safe in his room. Since the legal age of majority was nineteen in Nebraska, Autumn had yielded to her father's demands to turn it over to him. Fortunately, Autumn was friends with the office assistant at work and was able to get a copy from her file there. In regards to the request for references, Autumn specifically decided to list only those she knew had no knowledge of her father. That whittled her list down to three rather quickly.

A week after she had returned her information, she received a letter from a Lady Doris Cannon requesting they speak over the phone. Autumn was dumbfounded, things were moving rapidly.

One day after work, Autumn made her way to the local mall to call Lady Cannon from a payphone there. She didn't want to make any calls from her house where her father would have a record of the call. The mall, though not popular anymore, was close to her work and still had pay phones. As the phone rang, Autumn tried to swallow the lump in her throat. "Hello, may I speak to Lady Doris Cannon, please."

The man on the other end of the line was sophisticatedly polite. "May I tell the Lady who is calling?"

"Umm...Yes, this is Autumn DeBlue. I received a letter requesting I call regarding the companion position."

"One moment please, I will see if Lady Cannon is available."

*What was up with the 'lady' reference? Is Lady Cannon some kind of royalty?*

Autumn had purchased a phone card to make the long distance call though she only had forty-five minutes of talk time. *I hope that will be enough.*

"Hello?" A sweet and gentle voice came over the line. "Miss DeBlue, I am so glad you called."

"Lady Cannon? Yes, I called as soon as I could. You wished to speak to me?"

"Yes, I have reviewed your application and spoken to your references. They speak rather highly of you; however, I have some concerns." Lady Cannon paused perceptibly. "Please tell me why a young lady of eighteen would be interested in becoming a companion for an old woman?" She sounded so refined and genteel, yet there was a strong sense of purpose in her tone.

Autumn paused; her heart pounding. *How could she explain without giving away too much information? Once again she had acted before thinking things through. I guess I'll try to stick as close to the truth as I can.* "A while back, my grandmother got ill and needed care. A young woman was hired to assist her, and I spent many hours talking with her about why she did her job. Helping the sick and elderly is something I've been interested in ever since I saw how much it helped my grandmother in her last days." Autumn was satisfied with her answer. The bonus was - it was true. She had looked into CNA classes at the local Community College, though she was unable to make the class schedule work with what her father required of her.

"Yes, well, I am thankful for openness, though I am sorry to hear about the loss of your grandmother. What about the rest of your family, your mother, and father? Have you spoken to them about your application?"

"No, Ma'am. My mother passed away a year ago, and my father is not involved in my life." Autumn wiped her sweaty palms on her jeans. It wasn't a lie, on the other hand, it wasn't exactly the truth either. Her father just didn't care about her unless it involved the farm or keeping her under his thumb.

Being pressed for time, Lady Cannon could not continue her line of questioning. Therefore, she inquired if Autumn could call again, specifying a more acceptable time.

Autumn agreed, growing excited about the possibility of actually obtaining a job in Michigan. Over the next several weeks, Autumn made several more calls - all from the mall. *I hope this is all worth the expense. If I don't get this job, it will take me months at the grocery store to earn back what I've spent on phone calls alone.*

In one of the last calls Autumn made, Lady Cannon again addressed the issue of her age and family. "Seeing that you are under age in Nebraska, I feel we need to have the approval of whoever is your guardian before I agree to hire you."

Autumn's heart leaped - a mix of thrill and nervousness. *She was actually thinking of hiring her?* "After my mother died, I started fending for myself. Since I am so close to the age of majority, no one really pays much attention to me."

Considering her personal knowledge of how the state of Michigan deals with minors, slight alarm arose in Lady Cannon. Not wanting to call Miss DeBlue a liar, Lady Cannon pondered her response. *Since the laws in Nebraska regarding the age of majority are different, maybe the way they deal with minors is different too. Or perhaps this young lady simply slipped through the system unnoticed since she was older. Unfortunately, it does happen.* With this reasoning, Lady Cannon chose not to press the issue. "I see. Well then, would you be able to arrange a trip to Michigan?"

Autumn's heart raced as she tried to contain her excitement. Before rational thoughts could catch up, she jumped at the offer. "Yes, when would you like me to come?" She was ecstatic that she had found a way to escape her father's dictatorial rule and a job to support herself at the same time.

"As soon as possible. Now, please understand this would be a preliminary meeting to see if you are qualified to handle the position. I have some unique and specific standards that go against today's modern ideas. I am not exactly sure if you will be able to handle all the restrictions that come with being my companion. I would like to meet you and see if indeed we are compatible."

"Yes, I understand." In Autumn's attempt to gain control of her emotions and speak more calmly - hoping to appear more mature - she wasn't really listening to all of what Lady Cannon was saying.

Therefore, it was with false confidence that she proclaimed: "I will make the appropriate arrangements as soon as possible."

"Good. Call me when you know your arrival date, and I will have my driver pick you up."

"Thank you, Lady Cannon. I will be in touch very soon."

As Autumn hung up the phone, she couldn't contain her enthusiasm anymore as she did a jig twirling and stomping her feet. It took several hours for the emotions to subside and the magnitude of the conversation to sink in. *How exactly was she going to get to Michigan? More importantly, how was she going to get to Michigan without leaving a trail for her father to trace? And what had Lady Cannon said about restrictions?* Dismissing the last thought by reasoning nothing could be as bad as what she faced with her father, Autumn focused on the thing she could do - find a way to Michigan.

Autumn had been able to set some money aside, even with her father's demands for rent and help with household expenses, though she'd used quite a bit of it on phone calls already. Even with that, what she had saved up wasn't enough for a flight to Michigan. She considered the bus. However, she had tried escaping that route, and her father had friends in the local stations who'd report back to him if they saw her. Plus, being the cheapest way directly out of town, she knew her father would search the bus stations first thing upon discovering she was gone. The only other way she could think of was to take the train, even though the train had its own difficulties. Looking at the paper in front of her in which she had outlined her options, Autumn rubbed her crinkled brow and sighed.

After a week of trying to work out various ways of transportation, Autumn was forced to call Lady Cannon again. "I'm really sorry, Lady Cannon, but the arrangements for coming to Michigan are being delayed."

"Oh dear, what has happened?"

"Well...because I'm a minor traveling alone, I've hit some snags."

There was no response.

Autumn somehow knew if she was going to keep her way of escape open, she had to be more honest with Lady Cannon. So, she mustered up the courage she needed to be truthful. "Traveling to Michigan is more expensive than I anticipated. I'm going to need more time to earn the finances for the trip."

Hearing this, Lady Cannon exhaled the breath she'd been holding. "How much additional money is needed?"

"Fifty dollars." In truth, that was only half the cost of traveling by train from Omaha, Nebraska to Kalamazoo, Michigan. She still had to **get** to Omaha and take a bus at Kalamazoo. Nevertheless, Autumn didn't want to come across as incapable. She knew Lady Cannon to be a wealthy woman looking for someone who could handle responsibility.

"Thank you for calling me. I still desire you to come as soon as you can acquire the necessary funds. Please call me weekly to inform me of your progress."

A week passed, and Autumn was about to give up on the idea. Her new boss was not overly friendly and definitely not in favor of Autumn. She had asked for overtime, but he ignored her request. At her current rate of income, it would take her another month to gain all the money she needed to travel even by train. Though Lady Cannon said she still wanted her to come, Autumn doubted she would wait that long. When all looked utterly hopeless, a letter arrived in the mail.

With a hand clasped over her mouth, Autumn read:

*Dear Miss DeBlue,*

*Please find enclosed an advance in pay for the sum of one hundred dollars. This advancement is to aid you in arriving promptly. Please use the extra finances for any unseen traveling expenses. Upon your arrival, we will discuss the repayment of this advance.*

*Sincerely, Lady Cannon*

*What luck! Now all she needed to do was find a way to Omaha, board the train, meet the connection in Chicago, reach Kalamazoo, board the bus to Grand Rapids, and call Lady Cannon when she arrived. If I make all my connections, I should arrive at Lady Cannon's late the day after I leave.* Easy. Well...once she got past her father. *Could she really pull this off?*

No matter how many times in the past she had tried to escape, her father always seemed to find her and bring her back. She never understood why he didn't just let her go. He had been so indifferent and uncaring ever since her mother had gotten sick. Shortly after her death, he made her drop out of school and find a job. Then, he began making her take over the farm chores. Eventually, he even took her driver's license away and restricted her movements to public transportation. And though Autumn had a job, her father made her pay rent and expenses, so most of it was gone before she got it. She had no social life and no extra money except the scraps of overtime she had saved. The oppression of what her father expected of her was too much to bear.

So the question still remained, *could she do it this time? Could she disappear into the darkness and never be found again?* That was her hope. Autumn was running, and this time she'd leave no trails behind.

# ♥ 2 ♥

*ONE MONTH EARLIER IN MICHIGAN*

Lady Cannon sat staring out the third story window of the law firm of Michaels, Douglas, and Thompson – one of the largest and best law firms in the greater Grand Rapids area. Lord Cannon, the Lady's late husband, had hired the firm nearly twenty years ago when he could no longer manage his growing estate on his own. The man now trying to get her attention, Landon Michaels, was a brilliant lawyer despite his youth - he was only twenty-seven and newly licensed.

"Lady Cannon? Lady Cannon?" Landon was leaning in toward her. "Do you understand what I have explained to you? In order to preserve your granddaughter's future inheritance of the estate, you need to find someone who can manage these affairs, and with the state of your health, the sooner, the better."

"Yes, Lord Michaels, I heard you." She turned to face him and made her way to the chair before him. "Regardless, it is not as simple as you make it sound. As you well know, the Cannon Estate is a large responsibility and to hold it for such a long period of time would take someone with incredible integrity. There are few qualified to handle the enormity of matters associated with the estate alone, not to mention someone who would uphold the standards we hold dear and teach them to Heiress Summer. I refuse to hand over the reins of my granddaughter's future to just anyone!"

Landon's shoulders fell. Over the years of their association, Landon had discovered the Cannon's to be genuine people despite the uniqueness of their beliefs. When Mr. Cannon, as he then knew him, approached Landon to inquire of his opinion on a matter of wording in a contract, Landon had been suspicious and guarded because he was still an intern and not normally consulted on such matters. However, a bond of respect and trust was established as those moments of inquiry increased, and Landon found Mr. Cannon not only receptive to his suggestions but following his advice. Yet, even with the awareness of that bond, Landon had been completely taken by surprise when after having passed the bar and deciding to stay with his father's firm, Mr. Cannon fought the senior members of the firm to have Landon named the head of council for the Cannon Estates.

The trust Lord Cannon had placed in him was an immense honor, and Landon felt the deep responsibility to aide Lady Cannon weighing on him. His brows furrowed with the effort to explain. "With time not on our side, if you choose to wait much longer, and heaven forbid something happens to you, Heiress Summer will lose more than her grandmother. There will be no need to find anyone with or without your standards or integrity because the State will appoint whomever they please as guardian and liquidate the estate!" Landon's voice had risen as the frustration built. Rubbing his forehead, he immediately regretted his harsh tone.

Lady Cannon shot him a sharp look. *How dare he threaten her like that?* Yet - she knew it was no threat – it was the truth. "I *do* understand the situation, Lord Michaels!" Throwing her right hand up in the air in exasperation. "What would you have me do, put an ad in the *Daily Times* and hire a ruffian?" She was joking, of course – the thought was ludicrous.

Landon brightened with an idea. "Well, actually, that might not be such a bad idea. It would be one way of gaining potential candidates." Lady Cannon's look of complete horror did not stop him from continuing to mull the idea over out loud. "You have asked your current staff and several of your social acquaintances with no success. If none of them are willing to accept the responsibility of Heiress

Summer and the estate, then finding someone outside of that circle could be our solution. Someone whom you can train to your standards." Landon liked the idea the more he thought about it. Now he just had to convince Lady Cannon that it could work. "I would not recommend a ruffian or the *Daily Times* though; we'd need to cast a broader net with specific guidelines to catch the fish we need."

Lady Cannon harrumphed; the thought was preposterous. *If no one who knew them well was willing to take on the colossal and long-term responsibility, why would a complete stranger want to help her out? Not to mention, how would she be able to trust a stranger, ruffian or not, with the one thing she valued above all others on this earth, her granddaughter?* Tired of going around in circles, she slowly rose and steadied herself. "Thank you, Lord Michaels, for your time today." Without further words, she started to make her way to the door.

Though his suggestion was rebuffed and no solution found, Landon was genteel enough to offer his arm and help her to the lobby.

The silence between them was deafening to Landon. Before he released her into the care of her chauffeur, he felt compelled to apologize. "Lady Cannon, I meant no offense. Surely you know how deeply concerned I am. I will continue to look for a solution."

Lady Cannon raised her hand to silence him. "You have not offended me; I simply cannot take anymore today. My head is starting to hurt. Let us pause in our debate and continue to wait on our heavenly Father. He knows the answers we need and when we need them."

Landon nodded in acknowledgment, though he had his doubts. He knew Lady Cannon had already been praying for some time with no obvious answer forthcoming. Therefore, he felt now was the time to take action, not to wait longer, even so, he kept his thoughts to himself out of respect. Relinquishing her hand with a nod of greeting to Master Philip, a long-standing member of her staff, Landon watched as Lady Cannon entered her car and was driven away.

As she rode home, Lady Cannon pondered her conversation with the young Lord Michaels. She knew things were getting more desperate and she hated to admit it. Her granddaughter was only four years old and needed special care. *Dear God, I know I need to find someone reliable and trustworthy. Please Lord, help me know what to do.*

As time and experience had already shown her, being reliable in difficult circumstances was a nonexistent character trait in people these days. In the short period of time since she had become the sole caretaker of her granddaughter, they had gone through a handful of nannies. Taking care of Summer, with her special needs, was a challenging position already without including what would be necessary if Lady Cannon was not around. Whoever was hired for the position would have the entire estate at their disposal once she was gone. She had to be certain whoever was chosen would not squander the Heiress' inheritance or mistreat her. The temptation would be great to use the estate for selfish gain - especially in the early years after the estate was settled and Summer was still a minor. This seemed an insurmountable goal. *Truly, who in this world would be so unselfish?* Lady Cannon was not sure she was up to the challenge of finding that one person - if they even existed.

As Lady Cannon sat in the back of her blue Cadillac being driven home by Master Philip, her thoughts drifted back to the years before the tragedy, and the health problems, to the best decision she had ever made – to marrying Thomas.

When Doris had accepted Thomas' proposal, he had been a young college graduate, who had dreams of being an investment banker and making a moderate income to support the family he had hoped would follow their marriage.

It took Thomas three years to get a solid foothold in the banking world. When he was finally placed in the investing branch of the Middleton National Bank, he rose amongst the ranks rapidly. Soon Thomas was the most successful investor in Middleton and began branching out to other cities and divisions. He became known for his discernment in picking successful investments and wisdom in dealing with financial crises. Throughout his climb in stature, Thomas continually credited his successes to God's grace and blessing. Despite some critics, Thomas doggedly stuck to Biblical principles and was monetarily rewarded. With his new-found wealth, he again looked to Biblical standards and made certain he gave back to God his first fruits and invested the rest - withholding only a small portion for a modest living.

Doris remembered the struggles she encountered during the years of increase. First, she had enjoyed her modest household and dressing conservatively. Therefore, she boycotted the high prices and revealing trends in the "elite" stores. Unfortunately though, the pressure to dress "appropriate to society" was hard to ignore and she feared she would embarrass Thomas when she accompanied him to his numerous social functions. Finding an appropriate balance was difficult.

Also, she had originally wanted to honor her husband – and God – by doing the work of a wife and a mother by taking care of the house and caring for her own child. However, as the fortune grew, she found Thomas trying to persuade her to hire servants and a nanny. Whenever she objected, he would gently argue that they needed to help those in the community by offering well paid and respectable jobs. This had remained an issue between them for months before Doris found a solution.

With Thomas' growing influence, Doris had also begun to find the growing task of hosting social events in her modest home with their modest income to be a much more daunting task. Several times, she was forced to host events in a rented venue, which only caused Thomas to again speak up about raising their standard of living for the betterment of all. Thomas had never wanted to live in excess, as general high society did; however, he often pointed out that they had been blessed and could use what was given to them to influence the world around them for the better.

Doris smiled to herself. She recalled one morning during these struggles when she had been prompted to read Proverbs 31. The end of that chapter in the Bible is about the *Wife of Noble Character*. Like many other women, Doris had often felt utterly inadequate to meet the perceived checklist of character traits this passage lists. Yet that day, as she read through the passage, something clicked in her understanding, and she realized it was not saying *she* had to perfectly perform all those duties, but instead said that she was *able* to do or manage the affairs of her life.

As Doris prayed for further understanding, a clear path was laid before her, one that allowed managing her household through servants, which would please her husband. She also discovered a way to establish a household where each person was valued for their service, which she felt would be glorifying to God. She made careful plans establishing a hierarchy of authority with titles to assure every servant, or staff member as she would refer to them, would be treated with decency and respect. This served two purposes. First, it organized the chain of command and second it reminded the staff to speak respectfully with each other, as well as, to respect themselves. Each member of the household **was** valuable. She wanted to make certain no one entrusted to her employ would ever be taken for granted.

Doris remembered that she had been especially nervous when she presented the plan to Thomas for his approval. However, Thomas had loved the idea, and Doris had begun implementing the changes immediately.

In the years that followed, Doris had so effectually accomplished her goals of valuing her staff that the Cannon estate rarely lost staff members. As word of the Cannon's household practices became known to society, the Cannon Estate became renowned for standing apart with its unique and old-fashioned standards. Even though these standards were highly irregular and contrary to "acceptable high society protocol," neither Thomas nor Doris caved to the pressures to relinquish their demands of respect for those in their service.

Chuckling to herself, Doris remembered the first time Thomas confronted a guest about his disrespectful tone with a staff member during an influential dinner. The guest, who was a well-known and highly placed judge, would not apologize because he was "above the servants." Thomas had escorted the highly placed judge to the door by the arm and informed him he was not welcome back into their house until he could behave inoffensively. The incident caused a societal scandal that lasted months. Nevertheless, in the long run, the Cannons were more highly respected for standing by their convictions than judged by their uniqueness.

Doris had also implemented conservative dressing standards for herself and the staff, as the fashions, even for servants, were not that of decency. This change led to the Cannons being sought out to host a myriad of social events and high society functions not always associated with Thomas' job. As Thomas continued to rise in influence, Doris continuously found herself entertaining exclusive guests from all over the country and was deeply distressed to discover society's decay prevailed as normal everywhere. She resolved to find a way that the changes within her home could be reflected outside of it as well - like a lamp on a hill.

The more interaction she had with the exclusive guests Thomas continually brought home, the more Lady Cannon discovered, with great relief, there were others - though few - who shared in her distaste for the debauchery in general high society circles. One afternoon, at a ladies tea, Doris had the opportunity to share her reasoning behind the titles given to her staff, and why they insisted these be respected by everyone, even guests in their home. Noting the importance of "simple respect," several of the ladies attending commented that this was what was lacking in their level of society. It was in that moment, Doris realized how she could potentially impact society with standards of decency.

She mulled over the idea she had gotten at that tea, tweaking and praying about it before speaking to Thomas. It was not her intention to establish a hierarchy within society; status seeking was already more of an issue than what was necessary. In fact, the opposite was needed: a respectful humbling or equalizing of people. Therefore, she determined only the titles of Lord and Lady would be used to eliminate the hierarchy and establish an equality between the people they associated with. Lord and Lady would be used by them as titles of honor that were meant to reflect the standards of decency, morality, and strength of character.

Receiving Thomas' support in this new endeavor, she bestowed the first title of Lord to Thomas himself. In return, he bestowed upon her the title of Lady. From that moment on, anyone indicating a like-minded opinion regarding respect and decency within their association was honored by them with a title. These were often offered to the honored party at a special dinner hosted by the Cannons. Once accepted, the titles were expected to be upheld by every guest or staff member within the Cannon estate. To assist with this, Doris had a banner of honor created that hung in the vestibule with the names of the honored.

The well-known reputation of the Cannon Estate was a large part of the current problem. Managing the Estate was not simply a real estate issue, it was carrying on the standards that had been established for over forty years. *Oh Heavenly Father, what am I to do? I need you. I need your direction. Please guide me and help me through this time as you have done so many other times in my life.*

Lady Cannon sat back and relaxed against the cushioned seats of the car. Though there was no immediate answer, she knew God had heard her and that she was in His hands.

# 3

For several days, Lady Cannon wrestled with what Lord Michaels had suggested – an advertisement of some sort. Finally, on the third day, when she was kneeling in her prayer room, pleading with God for His direction, the answer came. Lady Cannon rose slowly - if she rushed dizziness would settle in; however, she refused to stop kneeling before God as long as she was able.

As she reached the phone in her office area, a sudden peace washed over her. "Lord Michaels? This is Lady Cannon. After much prayer, I have decided to go ahead with your idea of placing an ad for help. I'd like it to be for a companion – not for Heiress Summer, but for myself. I want it in a reputable publication, only the best – aside from that you choose. And not too much information, I don't want it sounding like I am a decrepit plutocrat – I simply want a live-in companion for an elderly lady. Also, I'd prefer if it wasn't local, too many people know the Estate and me." She paused considering. "I think it best to have your office screen the applications. The ones that pass your approval I will interview personally."

Somewhat confused by the barrage of information, Landon took a deep breath praying for tolerance. "I understand, though, if I may, how does this help our situation?"

"Heiress Summer is my number one concern. She is too vulnerable to be exposed to potentially numerous candidates for guardianship while I try to test them for loyalty and compatibility. I need to be able to have our candidate working in the house under close observation so I can determine their genuine intentions. As a companion, I can restrict their movements around the house and limit the Heiress' exposure to them without too much suspicion until I am certain of my decision. A guardian would want to meet their ward, and an estate manager would want the full scope of their position outlined.

"Also, I believe an adequate first test will be finding someone willing to be a companion for an elderly woman. These days not many people have a heart of servanthood. By establishing them in my household as one of the staff first, I can test their loyalty and their true heart while they earn the privilege of knowing the truth. I hope to establish a lasting relationship with this person before my Father calls me home and they take over the responsibilities of the Cannon Estate and Heiress Summer's care."

Landon listened intently to all Lady Cannon said and readily agreed with her reasoning. "I'll start working on the ad as soon as we get off the phone. I'll email you the proof for approval before I submit it." With a sigh of relief, Landon hung up the phone. Maybe, just maybe, God had heard *his* prayers, and this situation would soon be resolved.

As Lady Cannon hung up the phone, she turned her back on the room and gazed absently out at the garden below. She wished Lord Michaels was able to do the job. He was probably the only one who was capable and trustworthy. Nevertheless, Lord Michaels said it was a conflict of interest, and legally he could not do both. She valued him too much as an advisor to lose him.

Over the last few years, Lord Michaels had grown in unreplaceable value to Lady Cannon. He was unique in his genuine care for his clients – not for their money, but for the people themselves, and efficiency was at the top of the many good qualities he possessed. Also, knowing Lord Michaels had proven himself worthy to the late Lord Cannon before he had even achieved the status of lawyer spoke volumes to Lady Cannon. Therefore, after her husband's untimely death, Lady Cannon had kept the Junior Michaels on because she trusted her husband's judgment completely.

Unfortunately, it wasn't long after Thomas' death that the senior partners at Michaels, Douglas, and Thompson, including Lord Michaels' own father, tried to convince Lady Cannon to revert counsel back to one of the more experienced partners. Under so much pressure, and still grieving, Lady Cannon decided to lay out a test of morality to help her decide. She used the example of King Solomon's decision in the Bible, concerning two women who each had a baby. In the night, one of them rolled over and smothered her infant. When she realized what had happened, she switched babies with the other woman. Except the other woman knew her child and petitioned King Solomon. King Solomon's verdict was to cut the living baby in half and give each woman one half. The wicked woman agreed to this because she felt that if she couldn't have a living baby, she didn't want the other woman to either. On the other hand, the true mother pleaded against this decision and was willing to sacrifice her own desires for the well-being of her child. Through this test, King Solomon was able to discern which woman was the true mother.

Using this story as a guide, Lady Cannon requested each lawyer draw up a proposed estate plan for the five years following Thomas' death, including their expected compensation rate. This was the 'baby' in the test. She then mixed up the proposals so that when she met with the partners, she could see how they responded to their proposal being attributed to another lawyer's work. The result was a chaotic backstabbing debate between the senior partners that opened Lady Cannon's eyes as to why Lord Cannon had chosen the junior Michaels in the first place. During the chaotic scene, Lord Michaels had sat quietly in his seat waiting for Lady Cannon to make her decision.

"Why are you not defending your own proposal like they are?" Lady Cannon waved her hand in the direction of the two specific partners currently in heated debate.

"As long as you pick my proposal in the end, I don't need to debate anything. It doesn't matter who gets the credit because I would know you would be taken care of as Lord Cannon had asked. That is all that matters. I would be keeping my promise to Lord Cannon."

That settled the issue of head council, and it was never again brought up, and Lady Cannon was indeed well taken care of as Lord Michaels had indicated.

Shortly after the test, Lady Cannon had invited the Junior Michaels to an honorary dinner where after explaining her reasons, she asked if he would receive the honorary title of Lord. She had never regretted her decision.

*Maybe I should come up with a test for whomever we find for this new position like I did with Lord Michaels? But what kind of a test would I need? Something to test loyalty and commitment. Hmmm...* As Lady Cannon pondered how to test the future candidate, she wished she had access to Lord Cannon's impeccable sense of character and uncanny way of discerning the truth in people.

A month went by with only a handful of acceptable replies to the advertisement for a companion. Those that made it through Lord Michaels' screening were turned over to Lady Cannon for inspection and approval. Unfortunately, the already limited applicants mostly turned out inadequate upon further investigation. That is, all except one – a reply from a young lady, Autumn DeBlue in Nebraska. Lord Michaels found her too young, she was only eighteen. On the other hand, Lady Cannon saw that as her shining feature. It would be easier to train a young and possibly naïve girl than a matron who was already established in routines and habits.

Lady Cannon instigated the first correspondence with this young lady requesting a telephone interview. She felt peaceful in her interactions with Miss DeBlue and believed it was God's leading that they found her.

Lady Cannon questioned Miss DeBlue numerous times. Still, she could sense there was more to the story than what Autumn shared. Something was holding Miss DeBlue back. One thought kept repeating in Lady Cannon's mind: *would she be taken advantage of by this stranger?*

In an attempt to reassure her heart and calm her thoughts, Lady Cannon personally checked all of Autumn's references a second time. And though they all spoke highly of Autumn, the questions still rang deep down in her heart. Lady Cannon then knew the only thing left to do was to wait and pray; she found herself once again on her knees in her prayer room.

Lady Cannon's prayer room was her favorite place. She spent many hours there working through the trials and sorrows of her life as she learned to lean on and trust in God. It was her foundational faith in Jesus Christ, that carried her through the deepest loss of her existence - the loss of her family and the responsibility of a traumatized grandchild. Jesus had faithfully stood beside her through those dark days, and she knew that once again, He would not leave her in her time of need.

As she prayed, Lady Cannon knew deep in her heart, that if she put her trust in Miss DeBlue, this young lady would in return be loyal. Therefore, taking a leap of faith, Lady Cannon took a step farther than she ever expected to and sent money to a complete stranger. Miss DeBlue was coming to Michigan, and Lady Cannon hoped she would indeed prove to be trustworthy. Lord Michaels would have been livid with this decision – had he known of it – therefore Lady Cannon decided informing him was not prudent and tucked away that knowledge.

As the courier took the envelope for delivery, she gathered all her concerns and thoughts and laid them at the foot of the cross until she could meet this young lady in person and determine for herself the promise within her.

# 4

Several days passed after Autumn received the letter from Lady Cannon before she was ready to leave for Michigan. In preparation, Autumn told her father she was going camping with the Nelson's for the weekend. The Nelson's were the *only* people her father trusted her to stay with. As she packed her two bags: a backpack and a small duffle, she was careful not to look overeager, or over-fill her bags for a weekend camping trip. Just in case her father questioned her as she left. She also tried to keep in mind that she would possibly have to carry everything she packed all the way to Omaha unless luck happened her way. She never considered what she would need once she was in Michigan – her thoughts were solely consumed with what she could reasonably carry.

As she looked around her room, she was devastated to realize two of her most precious keepsakes would have to stay behind. There was no way for her to pack the carousel from her grandmother or the antique doll her mother had given her. She would have to settle for her grandmother's ring and mother's locket to keep her memories alive. These four items were the only possessions she had worth any value – monetarily or emotionally. Autumn sat on the edge of her bed grieving the loss of these two precious items – if she were successful in getting away – she would not come back for them.

Standing in front of the carousel, she remembered back to when her grandmother had given it to her – she was eight. Grandmamma had taken her on a special trip to Ohio for her birthday. Their purpose was to tour the carousel factory there. Autumn watched as the delicate horses were blown from glass, decorated with colors of gold, blue, red, and green, and assembled into the carousel that now set before her. *How could she leave this?* Autumn stood in turmoil – she had no choice – it would never survive the trip, and there was no way to get it back once she left. She had looked into shipping it to Michigan ahead of her; however, she had decided against it for two reasons. One, it was very expensive to ship such a delicate item, especially considering there was no assurance it wouldn't get broken in transit. And two, she knew her father checked her room frequently, and if he realized it was missing, he would know something was going on before she was very far away.

Turning to the antique porcelain doll sitting beside the carousel, Autumn heaved a great sigh, as tears streamed down her cheeks. The doll was beautiful and in impeccable shape. Autumn's mother had received it from her grandmother – Autumn's great-grandmother. The memories tied to the doll were bittersweet. Autumn had received the doll for her sixteenth birthday; yet memories of her mother sitting with her, carefully appreciating the doll, went back to her earliest memories. During these times together, Autumn's mother would tell her stories of the family, leaving her a legacy – a legacy she now felt she was leaving behind. For a brief moment, Autumn debated whether life with her father was so terrible; still, she couldn't see any other way out. Her father would never let her go - especially after losing her mother - he'd always find some way to keep her tied to him.

Shaking those thoughts off, Autumn conceded the price of freedom was great; nevertheless, she had high hopes it would be well worth it. Her nerves were raw as she left the house that night. Pausing momentarily to look back at her father in front of the TV - his usual spot – another moment of hesitation passed. *Why was it so hard to leave? Had she not been longing and waiting for this day for what seemed like years?* She truly didn't understand the conflicting feelings she was struggling with.

Her father didn't even acknowledge her presence, or her leaving, and she didn't draw any attention to herself in hopes of avoiding any possible complications. She paused at the door. *I'll never come back here again now that I am free!*

As she walked down the road, the hesitations and moments of doubt were all lost as her heart filled with anticipation toward the first leg of her journey. She planned to walk to the Bogart's, a half mile away and ask for a ride to the bus station in Omaha – a diversion from the train station.

The Bogarts were new to the area, and Autumn knew her father would never go to them looking for her. They were Christians, and her father wanted nothing to do with any of those "religious people." Autumn met Mrs. Bogart almost six months ago when she was making her usual 2-mile jaunt to the public bus that took her to work every day. Her father had long ago distrusted her with a car and told her the exercise was good for her.

The Bogart's home was set back from the road with a yard and garden out in front of the house. Being a rural area on the outskirts of town, there was plenty of room between houses. Mrs. Bogart loved to garden, and she spent a great deal of time outside. Autumn had seen her at work as she walked past every day. After only a few days of this, Mrs. Bogart started waving to her with a pleasant, "Hello, beautiful day." Autumn usually nodded and kept walking.

One day, Autumn was on her way home when Mrs. Bogart walked to the edge of the road. Approaching Autumn in a way that she could not avoid her without being blatantly rude, Mrs. Bogart introduced herself, "Hello, my name is Penny Bogart. What's yours?"

Not really wanting to talk out of fear that her father would somehow find out, Autumn hesitated. Her father kept a strict account of her comings and goings. Though he never paid much attention to Autumn as a person, he was diligent in keeping her close to home. However, she had seen this lady every day and was curiously drawn by the kindness in her face. Finally, she gave in to curiosity. "I'm Autumn."

"I see you walk by here almost every day, where do you go?" Penny couldn't explain her fascination with this young lady as anything other than a nudge from God.

"Oh, I catch the bus into town for work." Autumn didn't know why she felt compelled to answer this woman against all her father's warnings, but there was definitely something about her that drew Autumn in.

"Why, that's a mile down the road." Penny looked down the country road imagining the distance.

Autumn ducked her head in shame. "Yeah, I know. But I have to get to work, so I walk it."

Penny's heart went out to the young woman who walked at least two miles a day just to work. Her mind raced with questions. *Was she supporting herself? Who took care of her? Where did she live? Where were her parents?* "Would you like to come in for a rest before you continue home?" She realized it sounded cheesy; however, Penny couldn't come up with anything else to say at the moment.

Immediately, Autumn's father's warnings sprung to her mind. "Umm...No thanks. I've really got to go." Autumn stepped around Mrs. Bogart and started off down the road again, this time at a quicker pace.

However, that simple conversation had opened the door for a budding friendship. A friendship in which Autumn was now hoping would aide her in her escape.

Mrs. Bogart started meeting Autumn on the road regularly with little treats and bottles of water. At first, Autumn tried to be pleasant and friendly yet aloof – she wouldn't trust this woman, whom she had so fervently been warned against by her father. Autumn never mentioned anything about home or personal life at all because if her father found out, he'd skin her alive. Autumn tried to keep the conversations centered around the garden, weather, or things in general, always keeping the conversations short as to not be late getting home.

It wasn't long before Mrs. Bogart brought up the subject of Jesus and faith in Him. Even though Autumn was not interested in "finding Jesus," she listened patiently because it was hard to dismiss Mrs. Bogart's genuine sense of caring and generosity. So, Autumn kept listening, not knowing when the relationship could become beneficial for her.

Autumn's father was constantly telling her, in his random rants, that Christians always wanted something in return for their kindness – usually money. Nothing was for free. In her mother's last years, she had become a Christian and started going to church. When Autumn's father found out, he had forbidden her mother to go back or to talk to Autumn about what she believed. However, Autumn knew her mother went to special meetings during the week when she was well enough to go, although she never attended church on Sundays. Her father was adamant that churches and Christians only wanted money – it was all a deception. He wanted nothing to do with any of them. However, all that her father said soon came into question.

Several months into their friendship, a time came when Autumn needed Mrs. Bogart's help, and she was thankful for the friendship she had. On that morning, Autumn had been running late, and she missed the bus. All she could do was wait for the next one, although it would take another 45 minutes, and by then she'd be late for work. Autumn's boss was not a compassionate man. *He'll probably fire me for being late. Still, what choice do I have?* Plopping on the bench and placing her head in her hands, tears began to stream down her face.

Though she had heard a car pull up behind the bus stop, Autumn had not paid much attention until Mrs. Bogart sat down beside her. "Miss the bus?"

"Yeah, and my boss isn't going to like it." Autumn put her head into her hands, trying to stifle the tears.

"Would you still make it on time if I gave you a ride?"

Autumn's head perked up, eyes wide with disbelief. "You'd do that?"

"I know how much you need this job." Shrugging her shoulders, Penny played with a string on the bottom of her shirt.

"You do?" *How does she know that? Does she know about my father? What else does she know about me?*

"Sure, why else would you walk over a mile a day to catch this bus? Come on, I'll drive you to work." Penny stood gesturing for Autumn to follow her.

Waiting for only a moment, Autumn jumped up and followed. She couldn't pass up the invitation. That day, Autumn began to realize the benefit of having people like Mrs. Bogart - someone genuine - in her life, even though she couldn't shake the words of her father either. *What would Mrs. Bogart want in return for this "salvation" trip to work?*

Autumn waited for the entire trip to town for Mrs. Bogart to say something about paying her back, yet she never did. She waited for something to be said over the next week, but nothing ever was. Finally, Autumn couldn't take the suspense anymore. "Umm, Mrs. Bogart, what do you want in return for driving me into town the other day?"

"Oh, honey! I don't want anything in return. I simply wanted to help a friend. And I hope the next time you need help, you'll feel free to ask me."

Autumn couldn't believe it, and Mrs. Bogart could tell.

"Look, Autumn, I know it is hard to accept that someone did something nice for you and doesn't expect something in return;

however, it is the truth. The world operates in an 'I scratch your back, you scratch mine' mentality, in spite of that, God works through love and kindness. Jesus, God's Son, came to this earth to serve, not be served; and He asks those that believe in Him to serve each other out of love. I've come to value you as a friend, and as my friend, I want to help you. Will you accept my friendship, no strings attached?"

Autumn thought about it for a moment and decided her father must have been wrong. "Yeah, but you know it doesn't really make any sense."

"Maybe not now, though I hope someday it will." Penny was pleased that Autumn had at least taken the first step toward truly trusting her.

*What a stroke of good luck!* Luck was the only thing Autumn could accredit her good fortune in finding Mrs. Bogart. No matter the cause, receiving such kindness and friendship – with no obligation – was a rare thing in Autumn's life. She decided she'd better not waste the opportunity trying to make sense of it. That was about two months ago, and Mrs. Bogart's kindness had continued, just as she said – no strings attached.

Autumn was now almost to the Bogart's home, and she hoped what Mrs. Bogart said about asking for a ride when she needed one still stood true. As she walked, she had determined to tell Mrs. Bogart she was going to visit her aunt on a short vacation and needed a ride to the bus station in Omaha, as the local bus didn't go that far. She hoped that would quash any suspicions.

Autumn knocked on the door and waited. The lights were on; still, no one was answering the door. *Where could they be?* She knocked again and tried to look through the windows to see if there was any activity inside.

Nothing.

"Great, now what am I going to do?" Autumn threw her hands in the air and turned around to walk off the porch. Her eyes landed on Mrs. Bogart's car parked off to the side of the driveway. *What if the keys were in the car?*

Autumn stood unmoving staring at the car debating with herself. *She could borrow the car and call Mrs. Bogart to come to get it when she was safely away. Surely, Mrs. Bogart would understand she tried to ask permission; however, no one was home. It **was** a desperate situation.* Autumn decided to check if the keys were there before she thought about it any further.

As Autumn walked over to the car, she glanced around her cautiously, looking left, right and behind her at the house. Being a rural area, no one was around. The doors were unlocked and there hung the keys. Quickly, Autumn threw her bags inside and climbed in after them.

Once again she halted. Sitting in the car, fear gripping her, a horrid thought hit her. *I'm stealing a car!* The thought rushed through her mind. *No! I am just borrowing it,* she rationalized again. Still, deep inside, she knew that taking the car without permission was stealing. After sitting there debating the dilemma before her, Autumn determined if she left a note, she wouldn't be stealing – only borrowing. Digging around in her backpack, she found a piece of paper and pen left over from her school days.

Writing a hasty note, Autumn ran it to the house and placed it in the screen door. Running back to the car, she started the engine and took off. *What a rush! What exhilaration!* The thought once again crossed her mind that she had just stolen a car. She pushed those thoughts aside, remembering her reasoning - *she was only borrowing it from a good friend - a friend who'd understand because she left a note.*

Despite her rationalizations, Autumn decided to turn north and take secluded roads to be sure no one saw her. Later she would wonder about that decision as surely she knew she was doing something wrong, or she wouldn't have felt the guilt and shame which drove her to the secluded roads. Nevertheless, maneuvering her way around the town she took the interstate-headed east. She had brought a map of how to get to the bus station in Omaha, just in case Mrs. Bogart needed it. Therefore, she felt sure she wouldn't get lost, even though now she was driving at night by herself.

The Bogart's, of course, noticed their car missing the minute they drove in. Henry, Penny's husband, was fuming and rushed right past the note in the screen door to see if anything else was missing. They had not received the most welcoming reception from their neighbors over the last six months, though they could not figure out what they had done to offend them. This was just another notch in the belt for some ruffian neighbor trying to get them to leave; he was sure.

For some reason, Penny was calm and not worried. Instead of rushing inside, she walked over to where the car had been parked and noticed the tracks on the ground. Whoever had taken the car had been to the house twice, and she followed the tracks back to the door. As she stood there staring, her husband called from within the house, that everything seemed to be untouched. She turned to go inside and noticed the note, which had dropped to the porch floor when Henry had entered:

> *Dear Mrs. Bogart, A desperate situation has come up, and I need to get away. I came to ask for help, but you were not here. I saw your car in the driveway and remembered you saying friends help friends. So I borrowed your car. I hope you can forgive me for not waiting around*

*until you came home but I didn't have the time to wait. I will call you tomorrow. Autumn*

Penny rushed inside and showed her husband the note.

"We should call the police."

"The police," Penny repeated after her husband.

"Yes. The police." Henry put his hand on her shoulder to brace her for what he was about to say. "Honey, the car was taken from our home without our permission, a girl is running from something desperate AND we can't aide a runaway."

Stunned by her husband's blatant declaration, Penny tried to rationalize. "No! The car wasn't *really* stolen. I mean, I did tell her if she ever needed help to ask, and that friends help friends, no strings attached. She came here for help, and I wasn't here." The expression on Henry's face was not softening. "She left a note, doesn't that count for something? I mean, how many thieves leave notes?" She threw her hands up in the air and turned away from him, her shoulders slumped and started slightly shaking. "Please, Henry! Autumn wouldn't just steal our car. Please give her until tomorrow to call and explain."

Shaking his head in disbelief at his wife's defense of the night's events, Henry answered her. "My darling, you are too soft-hearted, and I love you for it, yet I don't agree with people walking onto our property and borrowing our things without permission - note or not. We need to notify the police. What if she gets into an accident with our car? We would be liable. And the bottom line is – she didn't ask – even if she left a note, she didn't ask. Not reporting this could be doing her more harm than good."

His reasoning was sound, though Penny's heart was sure, so with new resolve, she mustered up a response she knew he couldn't argue with. "Henry, if Jesus needed our car, would you turn *him* into the police?" It was a bold declaration.

Stunned at his wife's audacity to throw such a question at him, he responded sarcastically. "If **Jesus** needed our car, **He** would have asked." Turning away from her, he contemplated her comment further. "Okay, we'll wait until tomorrow. However, if she doesn't call, we're calling the police."

"Thank you. She'll call. She said she would." Penny hugged her husband as her thoughts drifted to Autumn. She didn't approve of what Autumn had done, but she knew God would watch after her nonetheless. Saying a prayer for Autumn's safety and salvation, she turned in for the night.

When Autumn finally arrived at the bus station in Omaha, it was around midnight, and she decided to follow through with her plans to call information and get Mrs. Bogart's phone number. *What if she doesn't understand? What if she's really mad at me? Oh well, what was done was done.* Taking a deep breath, she gripped the phone tighter as someone answered the phone.

Sleepily, Henry reached for the phone. "Hello?" No one answered. "Hello, is someone there?"

Autumn was surprised to hear a man's voice answer. *Had she gotten the wrong number?* Just as he was about to hang up, she realized it must be Mrs. Bogart's husband. Autumn's voice shook as she whispered. "Um, hello, is Mrs. Penny Bogart there?"

All of a sudden it dawned on Henry who was on the other end of the line. He started to get riled up into a lecture about taking things that didn't belong to you when his wife reached over and took the phone from him.

"Autumn? Is that you?" The familiar voice rang across the line.

"Yes." Her voice was shaky and uncertain.

"Oh Honey, are you okay? What happened? Where are you? How can we help?" Penny's motherly instinct swung into full gear, and she forgot about her car being taken without permission.

Overwhelmed with the concern in Mrs. Bogart's voice, and the questions she was asking, Autumn stood silent for a moment. Finally, she managed to gather herself together enough to respond. "Yes, I'm okay." She knew she had to get this conversation moving and be on her way to the train station. The longer she stood in one place, the more likely someone was to remember her. "Look, I'm sorry I took the car. I came to the house hoping to get a ride, but when you weren't there, I panicked. The car is fine." She added the last part in hopes of softening the blow and any displeasure in her actions.

"I'm glad you are okay. Where are you now? How can we help? Can we meet you somewhere?"

"I couldn't ask you to do that, besides even if I wanted you to – it's too late. I have to keep on the move so he can't find me." She answered automatically, forgetting her previous plan to lie about visiting her aunt. "Do you have another set of keys?"

"Yes, my husband has a set here at the house, but Autumn, who are you running from? Maybe we can still help you?" Penny was pleading for more information, a way to help this girl she had been reaching out to and cared deeply for – her friend.

Autumn didn't know what to say, she started doubting again as to whether leaving was the right thing – a tumult of thoughts bombarded her and she was immobilized under the assault. Finally, she snapped to. "I'll lock the keys in the car. You can pick it up at the bus station in Omaha. I'm sorry for the drive. I'll never see you again. Thank you for everything you've done for me."

Sensing Autumn was about to hang up, Penny managed to add one more thing. "Autumn wait, there is a box under the driver's seat with some money in it. The key to the box is on the key ring. Take what you need." Penny had resolved that if she couldn't get Autumn to tell her more, then at least she could help her one last time.

Henry grunted at his wife offering money to this clearly unruly girl; however, Penny wasn't sure if Autumn even heard her. All she heard now was the dial tone. She stared helplessly at the receiver. After hours of prayer, Penny was confident that despite what Autumn had said, they would see each other again. She just didn't know if it would be here on this earth or in heaven. She hoped both.

# 5

Autumn put the receiver down, totally blown away by what she had thought she heard Mrs. Bogart say. She made her way back to the car and looked under the seat half expecting it to be empty. Instead, there it was – a metal box. She fumbled through the keys until she found the one that opened it and looked inside. Autumn's eyes grew wide at the sight of all the money. There were well over *three hundred dollars*. Still, Autumn couldn't bring herself to take any of it. She closed the box and sat there thinking about all she could do with that amount of money. After what seemed like hours, she reopened the box, took one hundred out, and wrote an IOU. She didn't know how she would replace it, yet she knew the extra cash would come in handy in her travels. Besides, she was starting to get hungry, and all the money she had was designated for train and bus fare. Autumn had figured she could handle a day without food, however, now that she had the means, she was going to use it.

Autumn locked the keys in the car and began walking down the street. She had chosen the bus station as a diversion to her actual destination - the train station - just in case her father did question the Bogarts. Autumn remembered seeing a Denny's Restaurant a few blocks, and she decided to get a bite to eat while she planned out how to get across town. By the time she reached the restaurant and took a seat, her stomach was growling fiercely, and she had a hard time focusing on the menu.

The waitress was friendly and warm, checking up on Autumn regularly and even having several small chats with her. Autumn sat there for an hour trying to figure out what her best course to the train station would be. *She could walk. She had the time, but it was the middle of the night in a strange town, and she was a single female. Not the best option. She could try to do a local bus, though she didn't have a schedule and didn't know how to get one. She could take a taxi - she had the money from Mrs. Bogart - so that could work; however, she didn't know how much it would cost and was leery of using all the money in one shot.* Using the payphone in the waiting area, Autumn called the local taxi service and inquired about the cost. She then determined taking a taxi was her best bet.

While she sat there waiting for the taxi, the waitress, Becky, approached her. "Where you off to now, Sweetie?"

"Just catching a taxi across town." Autumn didn't feel comfortable sharing too much information with a stranger, even a nice one.

"Mind if I sit and chat with you while you wait? It's my break time, and there's no one else here at this hour."

Autumn bit her lip but eventually nodded. *Did the waitress suspect she was underage and running away? What if she called the police?* After listening to the waitress, Becky, chat aimlessly for a few minutes, Autumn recognized something familiar in her. Studying her a little closer, a familiar peace came over Autumn, one like when she talked with Mrs. Bogart.

Sure enough, several minutes into the conversation, Becky started talking about Jesus and how He had changed her life. "You know, I pray every day before my shift for God to open my eyes to those I'm serving. It's been amazing how many different people sit in my section that I have had the opportunity to share my story with. Some I get to help, some just listen and walk away. Still, it is always amazing how God orchestrates those encounters. I feel like He brought you into my section tonight."

Autumn listened politely just like she did with Mrs. Bogart. She didn't want to offend anyone, yet she wasn't really interested in change right now either. There was too much happening to be thinking about making any more changes. Autumn saw the taxi pull up outside and stood. "Thanks for keeping me company. My ride's here." Autumn dug into her backpack for her wallet.

Becky put her hand on Autumn's. "Don't, Sweetie. Keep the tip. You may need it more than I do before you get to where you're going." Autumn shook her head as Becky simply walked away from her.

Taking her ticket to the cashier to pay, Autumn's eyes widened in astonishment as the cashier smiled back at her. "Your bill has been paid in full. Have a good night." Turning to look for Becky, Autumn was interrupted in seeking her out by the taxi driver behind her. Not wanting to wait for another one, Autumn let it go. *That was amazing luck! Who would have thought I'd get a free meal for just listening to some waitress tell her story.* Autumn shook her head - *unbelievable.*

The taxi driver took her to the train station without delay or incident. After paying him from the money she borrowed from Mrs. Bogart, Autumn proceeded into the train station. As she approached the ticket counter, the lady behind the window looked skeptically out at her. Autumn's heart began to race. *Would they sell her a ticket? Would they ask for ID? What if she couldn't get a ticket? What would she do then?*

Finally, the woman asked in a bored and tired tone. "Where to?"

Autumn realized she'd been standing there staring blankly. With a confidence she didn't feel, Autumn cleared her throat. "Kalamazoo with a Thruway to Grand Rapids."

"That will be one hundred twenty-four dollars."

Autumn produced the correct fair. "Thank you."

The woman handed over the appropriate tickets. "Your train is delayed and won't be departing until 8:00 a.m."

Her schedule had said 5:15 a.m., so, Autumn nodded her acknowledgment while carefully tucking away her wallet and tickets. *Well, at least she wouldn't be late. What was she going to do with seven hours in a secluded train station?*

Finding a spot that was close to the teller, yet out of the way of people, she decided to review her cash flow. With the money she had gotten from Mrs. Bogart and the train fare she just spent, she now had $73.85. *It was a good thing she had borrowed that money from Mrs. Bogart. Otherwise, she would have had to walk across town and who knows how that would have turned out.* Putting her money away, she decided to acquaint herself with the train station. As she wandered around, she found it wasn't a large building; however, it did have a small waiting room, a bulletin board with various local advertising, restrooms with lockers, a service desk, vending area, and a large route map. Maybe half a dozen people were sitting in the waiting area - some reading, some visiting, and most sleeping.

It didn't take long to explore the small station, and soon she found herself sitting in the corner again. *I wish I would have thought to bring a book. These chairs are not made for comfort, and definitely not for sleeping.* She twiddled her thumbs staring at the bags at her feet. *I'm getting tired, but I don't want someone to take my bags.* She glanced around at the others in the area. *They don't look like ruffians, yet you never know. I could put them in a locker so that I didn't have to worry about them if I did doze off?* Nodding to herself, she gathered her two bags and secured them in the lockers by the restrooms. Returning to her spot, she leaned her head back and closed her eyes.

*I wonder what time it is? It seems like time is at a standstill.* She tried opening her eyes; however, they felt gritty, so she left them shut. *Surely they will make an announcement when the train gets closer. She **was** exhausted after all the events of the day.*

Her head bobbed forward, and she jerked upright. She rubbed the kink that was now in her neck.

*Had she dozed off? What time was it now?* Shaking her head, she glanced around for a clock. She didn't see one within view. She shifted in the uncomfortable seat to take the pressure off her left hip which was putting her leg to sleep. *Wow. She was **in** Omaha, at a **train station**. I can't believe I've gotten this far.* She rubbed her eyes. *I've never gotten this far before. Was she actually going to make it?* She sat up straighter. *What am I going to do when I get to Michigan – I forgot to call Lady Cannon before I left.* She looked around again as if the answer would materialize. *I don't see any payphones here at the station. Why wouldn't they have at least one payphone? Surely travelers have to call for pick up.* Standing up, she walked around the outer edge of the waiting room trying to wake her leg up. She found a clock. *Four-thirty. I've still got three and a half hours before the train comes.*

She wandered back to her seat and sat down again, wincing. *I wonder what's taking the train so long? Why was it delayed? Was there an accident? Are trains safe? No, surely they are. Well, it's too late to worry about that now.* She leaned her head back again and closed her eyes against the harsh waiting room lights. *Maybe I'll have time to call Lady Cannon at the Chicago station. There is a layover, though with the train delay who knows how long that will be. I wonder if my Chicago train will be delayed too? What will I do if it isn't?*

Over the loudspeaker: "SECOND CALL.TRAIN 178 to CHICAGO."

*What!?* Autumn sat up and winced as she straightened. Her hand immediately massaged the kink that had returned to her neck. Limping as fast as she could - her leg had fallen asleep again too - she made her way through the crowd that had gathered around the doors to the tracks. *Where had all these people come from?*

"Excuse me, excuse me." Autumn finally reached the man in uniform at the door. "Is that the train to Chicago?"

"Yes. Last call for borders in five minutes."

"That's my train! But," She turned and looked at the lockers, then back at the man. "I've got to get my bags." She turned again and tried to dash back through the mob to the lockers.

She heard the man say, "Train leaves in seven minutes."

*Hopefully, that's enough time. Maybe stashing my bags in the lockers wasn't such a bright idea.* As Autumn reached the lockers, she dug into her pocket for the key. *It's not here! Where is the key?* Patting herself down, she tried to remember what she'd done with the key after removing it from the locker. *Okay, take a deep breath and think. I pulled it out, then walked over to my seat. I didn't put it in my pocket! I had it in my hand. I must have dropped it when I fell asleep.* Dashing back to where she had been sitting, she started looking around.

*Where was that dumb key?* She got down on hands and knees and looked under the seat. It wasn't there. Closing her eyes, she leaned her head on the seat and bit back tears. *What was she going to do? She'd leave the bags, except, not only was her money in them, but the tickets were too. She was stuck.* Completely at a loss, Autumn lightly banged her head on the seat a few times. Suddenly, her head perked up. *Did something just fall on the floor?* Shuffling back, she looked under the seat again. *THE KEY! Yes!*

"FINAL CALL. TRAIN 178 to CHICAGO BOARDING NOW."

Grabbing the key, she ran for the lockers. Fumbling, she had to try it a few times as she was shaking so bad. Yanking the bags from the locker, she gave it a quick once over to make sure she hadn't left anything behind and dashed for the doors pulling her ticket out as she ran. Fortunately, the mob had cleared away, and there was no one between her and the train.

The man who had been at the door was just boarding the train and waving at the engine to take off when Autumn rushed up behind him. "Wait, please. I've got a ticket."

He didn't look happy, and the train slowly started to grind forward, but he took her ticket and pulled her onto the train step. "Cutting that a bit close weren't you?"

"Yes. I'm so sorry. Thank you for letting me on." He nodded, and she followed him into the car where he directed her to her seat. Punching her ticket, he handed it back to her.

"Keep ahold of that. If you get off at any of the stops, you'll need it to get back on."

Autumn nodded. He turned and walked away frequently stopping to chat with this person or that. Autumn noticed this part of the train was not overly full. She took her two bags and placed them in the secure overhead compartment and found a small pillow and blanket. *Wow, that's nice. I had no idea they offered such luxuries in coach.* Shrugging, she sat down in her seat checking it all out: there was plenty of legroom, a little footstool, a fold-down tray if she wanted it, and a reclining seat that was far more comfortable than those waiting room seats.

She had happened to glance at the large watch the conductor was wearing as he returned her ticket. *Five-twenty. The train hadn't been late. She couldn't believe she about missed it because she had fallen asleep! And what about the nice man in the uniform, he didn't have to help her, yet he did. Wow. She was so grateful. She'd have to make sure she told him thanks again the next time she saw him. She was seeing a lot of luck coming her way on this trip.* Though she couldn't recognize these good things as anything other than luck, her heart was softening with gratitude.

Autumn took a deep breath. *She had escaped the clutches of her father!* With every mile between them, she became more certain her father would not be able to find her this time. Taking another deep breath, she leaned her head back again and reviewed the journey ahead of her. *This train would take her to Chicago where she'd have to change trains. She knew the Chicago station was larger than the one in Omaha; however, she hoped it wouldn't be hard to find her next train. That train would take her to Kalamazoo where she would board a bus called a Thruway. The Thruway would take her to Grand Rapids. Grand Rapids was where Lady Cannon said she'd have a driver pick her up; however, Autumn first had to contact Lady Cannon to let her know when she was arriving. Hopefully, she'd be able to find a payphone at the Chicago station.*

Autumn turned to the window and watched the sun rise higher in the sky casting beautiful colors all around. *Nine hours. She had nine hours on this train. That would put her in Chicago close to three o'clock this afternoon.* Digging out her Chicago train ticket, she looked for the departure time. *Five-fifty. She'd have three hours in Chicago to find her train track, call Lady Cannon, and hopefully get a bite to eat.*

Movement caught her eye, and she noticed a woman a few seats ahead closing a curtain around her. Autumn looked around and found she had one too. *Now, **this** is awesome.* Pulling the curtain around her, Autumn made herself comfortable and fell into a peaceful sleep.

When she awoke, they were well into Iowa. She watched the scenery pass by around her. *Who was this Lady Cannon and why did she put an ad in a national magazine? Why would she want to hire an eighteen-year-old girl? When they spoke on the phone, there was something so kind and warm about her – something that reminded her of her own grandmother. Unfortunately, there were many questions unanswered on both sides. I'm going to have to be prepared for any question Lady Cannon could pose. I can't afford to mess this up, not now, not after getting this far.*

As the train traveled along to this new place with which she knew nothing about and had no connection – she again started questioning what she had done. *What if it was some big hoax? What if she gets there and Lady Cannon doesn't hire her? She knew Lady Cannon was a wealthy woman, a woman of class and status, what if Autumn didn't fit into her lifestyle? Or, what if she wasn't capable of doing the job?* Autumn pushed the worrisome thoughts from her mind comforting herself with the idea that anything was better than Nebraska and it would all work out, *it had to.*

Little did she know that the life she was about to enter, the life of two people, one very old and one very young, would change **her** life forever.

The train ride from Omaha to Chicago was rather uneventful, and Autumn was very grateful. She was able to enjoy comfortable sleeping arrangements and the many beautiful areas she could see from the train. There were also opportunities to get off the train and stretch her legs at various stops, though the train stayed on schedule, so Autumn stayed close by to assure she didn't miss the boarding call. It was easier getting back on the train since the conductor (the man in the uniform) recognized her. He would always wave her on with a friendly smile.

The food in the Lounge Car was good; though, Autumn was thankful she had the extra money from Mrs. Bogart as it was expensive. She did manage to purchase some small snacks much cheaper off the train and bring them on board. She wasn't sure if she was actually supposed to do that though, so she kept them to a minimum. Autumn watched the others in her area make their way to the Lounge car for lunch. *I think I'll stick with my snacks and save the money I have left in case I need it. I wonder what the meals will be like at Lady Cannon's house. Will I eat with her or the servants? I hope it isn't all fancy stuff I don't know how to eat or won't like. If it is, hopefully, I'll have some time to get real food. I don't really know much about what I'm getting myself into since I was so focused on getting away. I should have asked more questions.*

Before she knew it, the conductor appeared at the front of the car announcing: "NEXT STOP CHICAGO. DEPARTURE IN TEN MINUTES".

As Autumn stood to gather her bags, the Conductor stopped in the aisle beside her and whispered. "The couple three seats up, directly in front of you, is also going to Kalamazoo. You might be able to follow them to your next train, though I know you have a layover, so that might not work."

Autumn looked at him with disbelief and confusion.

"I just wanted to make sure you didn't cut the next train so close. *That* conductor might not be so nice." He winked as he continued down the aisle smiling over his shoulder as he continued to make his announcement: "NEXT STOP CHICAGO. TEN MINUTES."

Autumn flushed.

Exiting the train, Autumn followed the rest of the departing passengers up the stairs to the main area of the station. Suddenly, she halted, gaping wide-eyed. The other passengers bumped their way past her into the station. *Union Station, Chicago was massive and busy. Very busy for three in the afternoon.* Frantically looking around, Autumn spotted the couple the conductor had indicated, just a short distance to her right and decided to be bold.

Autumn hurried after the couple. "Excuse me." She touched the woman's arm. "Excuse me, but I was wondering if you could help me?"

The woman - she was probably in her late forties - looked to her husband whose crinkled bushy brows gave the impression he'd rather not. However, the woman turned back to Autumn and gestured for her to follow them to the side out of the main flow of traffic.

"How can we help you, dear?"

"I, umm, I've never been in such a large city, and I don't really know where I'm going. I'm supposed to catch the next train in three hours to Kalamazoo. I…uh…overheard you might be going that direction, too?" Blushing she looked down at her feet.

"You *overheard* that, did you? I'd say it's more likely that a certain nice young conductor said something." She raised her brows.

Autumn didn't answer.

"Well, we **are** going to Kalamazoo, and you are welcome to join us as we wait. We travel from Princeton to Kalamazoo frequently to visit our grandchildren. Peter knows that and probably pointed us out. He's such a nice young man."

"Peter?"

The lady started walking across the large station, so Autumn followed. "Yes, the conductor - his name is Peter. He's done this before, you know. Found a young person who needed a little more guidance and connected them with us. We are happy to help, and he knows it." She smiled. "Union Station can be very overwhelming if you don't know your way around. Lots to see." She gave Autumn a knowing look. Autumn hadn't stopped staring wide-eyed since they met and began winding their way to the Boarding Lounge that matched their tickets.

The lady's husband sat down as she put her carry-on bag in a seat next to him. She gave a short verbal tour. "This is the Boarding Lounge for the train to Kalamazoo. You can wait here with us if you'd like, though we may go walk around the station to get some exercise after sitting for a while. Down that way," pointing to the left, "are the stairs that lead up to the food court if you're hungry. Go past the stairs, and you'll find the bathrooms. If you have other baggage that needs to be claimed, it's back the way we came down that main central area to the left. If you need anything else, please don't hesitate to ask me. If I don't know, I'll try to help you figure it out. They are very friendly here." She smiled again.

"Um...I need a payphone?" Autumn had been looking around as they walked; however, she had not seen any nearby.

"Ah, yes. Payphones are in that large central area by the Passenger Services sign."

Autumn nodded. "Thanks. I need to make a call, and then I'll be back." She started to walk off but stopped. She looked the lady in the eye. "Thank you. I really do appreciate your help. It made being here much less scary." The lady nodded and turned to talk to her husband.

As Autumn walked away, she came to the awareness that she felt calmer, and even though the station was still huge, she didn't feel so alone. *I don't even know these people's names, and yet I feel like they are friends.* Shaking her head. *That's just crazy.*

Before she called Lady Cannon, Autumn wanted to be sure the Kalamazoo train was on schedule. Fortunately, there was a huge arrival/departure board by Passenger Services that Autumn actually understood. Seeing that indeed it was on schedule, she called Lady Cannon.

"I just wanted to update you on where I'm at. I've made it to Chicago, and I'm now waiting for the train to Kalamazoo. It's on schedule, and if everything continues as planned, I should be getting to Kalamazoo around nine this evening. Then I'll catch the Thruway bus to Grand Rapids. I should be arriving around eleven. Will it still work for you to have a driver pick me up?"

"I am very pleased Miss DeBlue. I had no idea you would be arriving so quickly."

"I'm sorry. I forgot to call you yesterday when I left Nebraska, and this was my first opportunity with a payphone where I knew my train wouldn't be delayed. If it doesn't work for tonight, I understand." *Though, I don't know what I'll do if you don't come get me.*

"Did you say you'd be arriving in Kalamazoo at nine?"

"Yes."

"Why won't you be in Grand Rapids until eleven? Do you have a layover waiting for the bus?"

"My ticket says the Thruway leaves for Grand Rapids at ten o'clock."

"Hmm...I think Master Philip could meet you in Kalamazoo and return home more quickly than having you ride the bus to Grand Rapids. I will have him plan to be at the Kalamazoo train station no later than eight-forty-five. Master Philip will be wearing his chauffeur's uniform and will have a sign so you can recognize him. Since you will be arriving so late, I will not see you tonight; nevertheless, I will make sure the staff is aware of your arrival. I will see you first thing in the morning."

*What could she say to that but okay? There was no arguing with the boss, right?* "Thank you, Lady Cannon. I look forward to meeting you tomorrow."

*Well, what's done is done. I wonder if I could get a refund on the Thruway ticket?* Walking back to the Boarding Lounge, Autumn found the lady that had been so kind and asked for help. They spent the next hour trying to get a refund on the Thruway ticket. In the end, it just wasn't worth the hassle and Autumn decided to let it go. *I guess I wasted that twenty dollars.* She was feeling very discouraged until she realized that technically that money had come from Lady Cannon. Therefore, if Lady Cannon wanted to waste it by not using the ticket, that was her decision and didn't reflect on Autumn's responsibility. *After all, she was just obeying directions from her boss. Right?*

Shaking off her discouragement, Autumn passed the time walking the station with the couple whom she discovered to be Mr. and Mrs. Danvers and flipping through some of the magazines she found lying around. Maybe she was more relaxed, or maybe she was getting used to waiting for the train, either way, the three hours passed quickly. Unfortunately, not everything was going to continue so smoothly.

As the time for the train's arrival approached, Autumn gathered up her two bags - this time she kept them both with her - and got in the growing line at the gate behind the Danvers. However, even though the call for boarding came over the loudspeaker, the passengers were not being let down the stairs to the platform. Chatter started reaching Autumn about the police searching the passengers for a missing girl. The Danvers looked at Autumn but didn't say anything.

Soon, Autumn noticed there were no less than eight police officers around the Boarding Lounge and Gate. One of the officers spoke to the ticket master as two others began walking down the line of waiting passengers. Autumn's heart started pounding. *Had her father figured it out? Were they looking for her? What was she going to do?* She felt the blood draining further from her face, and she began to feel light headed as the police officers started going through the line one by one looking at a photograph they had in their hands. *No, no, no...this can't be happening. I'm so close!*

Autumn stood paralyzed, palms clammy, head throbbing. *She could try to get out of line and wait it out, although if they were sure the person they were looking for was boarding this train, they would be watching until it left – possibly even delaying it as they searched the passengers further.* She hiked her bag further up on her shoulder and wiped her hands down her jeans. *She could try to find a different way - maybe a bus - however, her money was scarce, and she didn't even know if that was possible at this late hour.*

Autumn looked around trying to see if there was any indication that a bus was available, of course, she couldn't see anything from the Gate. *Besides, if her father had tracked her all the way here, he had to have tied her to Lady Cannon. The police would be watching for her to arrive in Grand Rapids or even Middleton. In fact, they would have probably contacted Lady Cannon for details. No, they had to be looking for someone else, there just wasn't any way her father could have traced her to Lady Cannon, especially not this soon. After all, she was still supposedly camping with the Nelson's. He probably didn't even know she was gone yet. She'd take her chances and stay in line.*

It seemed like each second was in slow motion as the police officers got closer and closer to her. Mr. Danvers kept glancing uneasily over his shoulder which only increased Autumn's anxiety. She tried to look less guilty by smiling and attempting conversation with Mrs. Danvers, but she feared worry was written all over her face. The officer that had been speaking to the ticket master began generally scanning the line as the others went one by one. Abruptly, his gaze, which has skimmed over her, came back and locked with Autumn's.

*I'm going to puke.*

He charged past several people, his gaze never leaving hers, and came directly at her.

Autumn held her breath, willing herself not to vomit.

"You." He pointed straight at Autumn. "Step out of line."

The world spun, and Autumn fainted.

When she came to, Mrs. Danvers was waving a bottle of nasty smelling stuff under her nose. One police officer was by her side, while the one who had pointed at her stood above her, arms crossed glaring.

Not waiting for any niceties, he demanded. "What's your name?"

Shaking her head to clear it, it took a moment to respond. "Autumn DeBlue, sir?"

"Where'd you come from?"

"Umm…Omaha, sir." Autumn's head was beginning to pound again, and she saw stars.

"I'm sorry sir, but I think she's gonna pass out again." This came from the officer beside her.

"What's wrong with her?" The gruff officer looked at Mrs. Danvers.

"I'd say she was dehydrated and exhausted. I haven't seen her eat or drink since we met on the train here, though she might have had something I didn't see."

Gesturing to another officer nearby, the gruff officer commanded. "Make sure the others are still watching, and get this girl some water and a sandwich."

Autumn laid back and stared up at the ceiling of the train station. *They actually have some pretty cool lights up there.* She chuckled at the absurdity of the thought. *If they are looking for me, I might as well get it over with.* "Who are you looking for?"

He ignored her question. "Do you have ID and proof of where you boarded?"

Sitting up, she reached for her bag. Another officer she hadn't seen before grabbed it from her. Autumn gasped and raised her hands in the air. "My tickets and ID are in my backpack. There is a black wallet. It holds everything you need."

Taking that as permission, the third officer unzipped her back and rummaged through it. *I'm glad I didn't have anything private in that bag.* He found the wallet and handed it over to the gruff officer, who opened it and examined what he found inside. He shook his head. "She's legit. This isn't our girl." He immediately dismissed her and went back to intensely searching the other passengers. The third officer dropped her backpack and wallet in her lap and hustled after the gruff officer.

The officer that had been sitting by her, on the other hand, had more compassion. "Sorry for the scare. He's been after the suspect for months and is pretty intense about the case. Here's the bottle of water and sandwich. You need to take care of yourself, especially when traveling." At that, he got up and left her sitting on the train station floor with Mrs. Danvers on a seat not far away.

"Well, that was interesting. I thought for sure you were done in." Mrs. Danvers winked at her and rejoined her husband in line.

*What did that mean? Honestly, she didn't care right now.* Autumn put her stuff back in her bag, opened the water and took a long drink. ***That*** *was too close. I never want to experience anything like that again.* She opened the sandwich and took a bite. It was dry on one side and soggy on the other, even so, she ate the whole thing. After a few moments, she did feel better and managed to stand up. Rejoining the line behind the Danvers, she proceeded to wait with the other passengers for another thirty minutes. *She'd be delayed in getting to Kalamazoo.*

Finally, the ticket master started clearing passengers to advance to the platform where they would board the train. Two police officers stood on each side of the gate watching while others monitored both the lounge and platform below. One by one the passengers presented their tickets and headed for the train. When Autumn finally found her seat, she collapsed into it with an intense sigh. She wasn't sitting near the Danvers, as they had first class seating and Autumn's tickets were for coach. She had been astonished to discover Peter had sat her in first class on the first train despite her coach tickets. Mr. Danvers further surprised her by checking to make sure she was okay before finding his own seat.

With all the excitement at the last station, Autumn decided to simply relax in her seat and enjoy the ride - not venturing off the train at any of the stops. These seats weren't as plush as the first ones. Still, there was plenty of legroom, and the seats swiveled to face the windows. Not having a curtain for privacy, Autumn turned toward the window hoping for peace and quiet.

Eventually, Autumn closed her eyes, and simply dozed off and on, always listening for the next stop's call, so that she didn't miss Kalamazoo. Finally, her stop was next, and she once again gathered her bags.

The Kalamazoo station was a quaint little stop made of red brick. Its turrets and peaked roof made Autumn think she was exiting into a fairytale. *I can only hope this turns out half as favorable as a fairytale ending.* She immediately began looking for a uniformed man with a sign; however, she didn't see one on the platform or when first entering the station.

Mr. and Mrs. Danvers said their goodbyes, and Autumn once again stood alone. Looking around the station, she discovered there once again were no payphones. *So I can't call Lady Cannon. Now what?* With the delay in Chicago, the train didn't arrive until almost nine-forty-five. The station was clearing out, and it didn't appear that anyone was waiting for her. Not knowing what else to do, Autumn found a seat. *What was she supposed to do? The Thruway leaves in fifteen minutes. I still have my ticket, and I could still go to Grand Rapids. However, Lady Cannon said she'd have her driver pick me up here. Is he late or did he leave because I wasn't here at nine like I had hoped? Kalamazoo seemed rather small whereas Grand Rapids would give her more options for possibly finding a way to Middleville. Why couldn't this have just been easy?*

Caught up in her thoughts, Autumn didn't see the man rush through the main entrance while frantically looking around. Finally seeing Autumn in the corner, as most people were now gone, he approached her tentatively. "Excuse me, are you Miss DeBlue?"

Autumn looked up to see a tall, handsome man, though a bit disheveled, in a black suit standing before her. He had a sign that read DRIVER FOR MISS AUTUMN DEBLUE, though it was tucked under his arm. His hair was messed up, and he didn't have a hat on like she expected of a chauffeur. She pointed to the sign. "Who do you work for?"

Standing up straighter, the man sniffed. "I am Master Philip, and I am employed by Lady Cannon of Middleville."

Autumn exhaled in relief, then smiled. "Thank goodness. I was really hoping you hadn't been conked on the head by some ruffian who was now trying to abduct me."

Master Philip snorted. "Not likely in Kalamazoo, Miss." He sobered. "I do apologize for not being here when you arrived. The ticket master said the train was delayed. The car seats are far more comfortable than the benches here, so I went to wait in the car. Unfortunately, I fell asleep and didn't hear the train arrive." He bowed. "I do hope you will forgive my tardiness and not report me to the Lady."

"I'm not the tattling type, Master Philip. I was a bit worried, but now that you are here, let's get on the road. I'm ready to have this trip over with."

# 6

Edmund DeBlue was pacing the floor. Autumn said she was going camping with the Nelson's for the weekend. It was now Sunday afternoon, and there was no sign of her. He had tried to reach the Nelson's, but there was no answer at their house. *Could they just be late getting in from the lake? He had made a BIG mistake by not verifying Autumn's story. He had thought they were past all this.*

Edmund paced back and forth again pondering as to whether to try the Nelson's again or what his next move should be. He knew the police would do nothing until she was missing for twenty-four hours and though she technically had been gone for two days, they wouldn't start counting until he could verify when she had actually gone missing. He needed to confirm whether or not she was with the Nelson's over the weekend. Hesitating in his pacing, he decided to call the Nelson's once more and leave a pleading message to call immediately upon their return. With that done, there was nothing more he could do except wait.

He sat down at the kitchen table with a beer in his hand and the case nearby.

It was two hours later when the phone rang waking him with a start from his drunken dozing at the kitchen table. Desperately he reached for the phone, "Hello…Hello! Autumn?"

"No, Edmund, it's Dave. Dave Nelson. We just returned home from a long weekend of camping at the lake and got your message. Is everything alright?"

"Oh, hi Dave. So you *did* go camping?"

"Yes?" Dave responded hesitantly, startled that Edmund would know this.

"Great, well, will you tell Autumn that I will be there shortly to get her. I'm sure she was planning on taking the bus home, but I need to come to get her." Relief surging back to his panicked heart.

Dave faltered in his response, not understanding. "Um, Autumn isn't here Edmund."

"She isn't? Well, where is she?" The blood drained from his face again. He worked hard to keep the anger at being made a fool from seeping out.

"Sorry, I don't know. Jessica was just saying this weekend she was worried about her. Autumn hasn't returned any of her calls for a while now, and we haven't seen her around for nearly a month." Concern filled his voice.

Edmund couldn't hold it back any longer. He stood and pounded his fist on the table toppling the half-filled can he'd been drinking. "What?! She told me she was going camping with you this weekend, *and YOU JUST SAID YOU WENT CAMPING!*" He was trying to make sense of it all, but the pieces just weren't fitting together in his buzzed brain.

Dave remained calm and did not react to Edmund's outburst. "We did go camping; however, it was just our family. I don't know how Autumn knew we'd be gone though. I'll check with Jessica to see if she by chance knows anything."

As Dave put Edmund on hold to talk to his daughter, Edmund took a few calming breaths as he sank into deep despair. This was not good news - it was extremely bad news. In the past, Autumn had a tendency of isolating herself before running away and had he been paying attention he might have noticed the storm coming before it hit. As it was, he was blindsided.

Dave came back on the line. "Edmund? Jessica said she ran into Autumn at the grocery store last week. That's how Autumn knew we were going camping. Other than that, Jessica hasn't heard anything from her. Sorry, man. If you need any help in tracking her down, I can come over."

"Thanks, Dave, but it's too late. I'll have to call the police. She's been gone for two days." Edmund hung up and angrily swept his arm across the table, knocking the various cans to the floor. Sitting back down at the table, he put his head in his hands and tried to think.

Dave and his family had been good friends after the death of Autumn's mother, Sue. Edmund had been so lost in grief he could barely function. Alcohol became the numbing agent that got him through his days. When Autumn started running away, Edmund couldn't even reason what needed to be done. Dave, being an ex-police officer, had been there and was a great help in locating her. Dave's daughter, Jessica, also reached out to Autumn trying to befriend her and offer some support. Yet, nothing seemed to reach through the wall Autumn had constructed around her after losing both her mother and grandmother so closely together.

Edmund knew from what Dave had shared with him that Autumn painted a very different picture of their home life to Jessica. To Autumn, Edmund was a tyrant - a controlling and demanding taskmaster. For a moment Edmund sat at the kitchen table, head in his hands, wondering what he was doing wrong. He knew he had gotten drunk a few times during those early months, but that didn't seem to explain Autumn's persistent drive to get away. He could never remember what had happened when he woke up, but since Autumn never complained, he assumed he just blacked out and slept it off.

Sue had always been better at dealing with Autumn. He simply didn't know how to relate to a teenage girl. He *had* implemented several strict rules after her first attempts to run away, but those had been for her own good. *Now, what was he supposed to do?* He had already been watching every move she made and restricted her access to the car. *When would she realize that he was doing the best he could? That everything he did was for her best?* No matter how much he wanted to, he couldn't bring back her mother or grandmother. *Why couldn't she understand this?*

Though his heart was racing with anxiety, he kept telling himself he wasn't overly worried because she had never gotten far before. Letting the anger settle in usually focused his thoughts on what needed to be done, this time though, all he could see was the hassle and embarrassment. *Why couldn't Autumn just do her part and stay out of trouble? Didn't she realize he was grieving too? Didn't she know this hassle of chasing her down all the time was wearing him down?* Before he knew it, the kitchen chair he had been sitting on was being thrown across the room splintering into dozens of pieces.

Maybe he should just let her go. If she hated him that much, maybe it was for the best. No, he couldn't do that. Sue would never even consider such a thing. He'd go after her and find her. Then they'd have a serious heart to heart. However, in the past, he had been on top of things and caught her disappearance within hours of her leaving. This time she was two days ahead of him. With this sudden realization, he sat down. Hitting the floor with a thud, he grabbed his aching head. He had forgotten he'd just thrown his chair. Clenching his teeth in anger, Edmund got up and called the police.

As he waited for the detectives to show up, he cleaned up the broken chair and scattered beer cans. Then he tried to piece together as much of the story as he knew to this point. He also gathered the few things he knew they'd ask for: a recent picture of Autumn and a full description. Then he ventured into her room and looked around. He was startled to see that everything looked pretty much in place - he often did a room check to keep an eye on things. He couldn't even tell if she took any clothes. What really boggled him was that Autumn's two most prized possessions were still in her room. Every other time she had run away, she had taken them with her; this brought on a new sense of alarm. *Could it be that she hadn't run away but had been abducted? No, that couldn't be. Why else would she lie about going camping with the Nelson's? Surely that indicated forethought and planning.* Yet, he jotted the observations down, as to not forget to mention them to the detectives.

Once he had gathered all he could think of, he sat down on the couch to wait. Autumn had two days in her favor, and he hadn't a clue where to start. If any of his buddies at the bus station had seen her, they would have called, so he knew she hadn't taken a bus. He had to admit to himself that he had gotten lax in watching her. After Autumn started running away so frequently, he had made a habit of checking her room every couple of days and keeping close tabs on her, always following up on where she went. It had been over six months since the last attempt, and he hadn't checked up on her in a week or so. She seemed to be accepting life the way it was, just her and him, or at least that was what he had thought. Apparently, he was once again out of touch with the reality he was living. And now, because of his lack of attentiveness, he was utterly clueless.

It was 4:19 p.m. when the detectives finally showed up at his house. He offered the two detectives a cup of coffee and invited them into the living room for what he expected to be a long interrogation taking several hours. Accepting the coffee, they declined the living room and took seats around the kitchen table. The older one seemed to note the missing chair and smell of beer, yet said nothing.

The two detectives introduced themselves as Harper and Thornton. Harper was the younger of the two and Edmund presumed he was the rookie with Thornton being the experienced veteran. Harper got out a notepad as Thornton began asking questions.

What was the full name of the missing person? Please give a full description of the missing person including age, height, weight, hair and eye color, and a picture if you have one. When was the last time you saw the missing person? Have you contacted the missing person's friends, associates, and other family looking for her? Where did the minor attend school? Did the missing person have a job outside of the home? Was the missing person involved in any extracurricular activities? Was there anything else missing? Is there any other information that could be useful in finding the missing person?

Edmund did his best to answer all the questions. Thornton was suspicious and kept looking at him skeptically. When Edmund explained that Autumn didn't attend school, he quickly added that she had tested for her GED and passed with flying colors. Edmund knew he'd be high on the suspect list if they suspected foul play and judging by the way Thornton was looking at him, he was a suspect. Thornton's expression grew leerier when Edmund mentioned the carousel and antique doll that still remained and how on previous attempts to run away Autumn had always taken them with her.

"So Autumn has run away before?" Thornton inquired eyeing Edmund threateningly.

"Yes, right after her mother died a year ago. We went through about four months of various disappearances and run away attempts. However, she always took the carousel and doll with her. This time they are still in her room."

"So do you think she ran away again or do you think she has gone missing?" This question came from Harper. Thornton eyed him harshly as if reprimanding him for speaking, but then turned to Edmund for his answer.

"My first thought was that she had run away again, mostly because of the lie she told about going camping with the Nelson's. However, when I saw the carousel and doll still in her room and none of her clothes obviously missing; plus the fact that it has been six months since she last attempted anything like this…I guess I'm a bit unsure." He dropped his head into his hands on the table. "I thought we were settling into a good routine." Looking up his shoulders still sagging. "She even mentioned once something about taking some classes at the Community College after work." He was being honest; still, this was all too much to bear again. And with the way Thornton was looking at him, he was struggling to keep his emotions in check.

Harper perked up, ignoring Thornton. "Well, did she?"

"Did she, what?" He was so lost in his own thoughts he didn't even realize what he had said.

"Did Miss DeBlue take classes at the Community College?" Harper clarified.

"No. I don't know what happened."

Thornton exchanged a glance with Harper that Edmund didn't like, then they asked if they could take a look at Autumn's room, which he had no objection to.

"Did Autumn have a boyfriend?" Harper was looking at a picture, one that Edmund had not seen before. In it, Autumn was sitting on the lap of a young man with her arm around his neck and cup in her hand like she was at a party.

Edmund was stunned. "No, at least not that I was aware of."

"Do you know this young man in the photo?" Harper pressed.

"No, I have never seen the boy or the photo before now." Edmund was starting to realize there may be a lot more he did not know about his daughter. And apparently, he wasn't the only one thinking that as Thornton harrumphed as he continued searching Autumn's room.

"Can we take this?" Harper continued.

"Sure, I don't see why not." In hopes of showing that he did know something about his daughter and to get off Thornton's bad list, he offered. "Jessica Nelson was as close to Autumn as she would allow anyone to get. She might be able to identify the boy."

It aggravated Edmund greatly that Thornton would suspect him of anything nefarious. Edmund readily admitted he should have been paying more attention. Though many parents don't pay attention to their kids - especially when they are almost nineteen and basically on their own - it didn't mean he was an evil person. He was justified in not knowing a few things about his daughter. *Wasn't he?*

By 6:30 p.m. the detectives were gone, and Edmund sat back down on the couch with his case of beer, too exhausted to do anything else. *How could he go on with his daughter missing and knowing it was his fault? He hadn't kept a strong enough grasp on reality.* Over the last few months, he'd let the leash he had harnessed his grief with slip. Maybe he was too hard on Autumn, but it was for her own good. Sue had always known how to talk to her. How to get her to open up the wall she constructed after her grandmother passed away. Once Sue was gone, that wall was impenetrable to him, and he had no clue as to how to deal with her. He took a drink of the can in his hand and tried to forget.

After half the case of beer and hours of staring at the ceiling, wishing this was all a dream, blaming himself over and over again, replaying every detail of the last months that he could remember, and somehow wishing he could make it right again, he was finally overtaken. Edmund drifted off into a drunken stupor.

It was midmorning when Edmund came to and realized he missed going to work. He was an independent sales representative for an insurance group and had a lot of freedom in his job. He slowly got up and called the office stating he was sick and would need a few days. He justified that it wasn't really a lie, he was sick from guilt and blame, as well as the hangover he had. He had to shake this drudgery off, get out there, and start looking for Autumn. He knew the police were investigating. Still, he couldn't just sit back and do nothing. He had to get out there and help. Besides, he wanted to be the first one to find her.

Edmund headed to the pickup and determined to go through Autumn's routine the best he knew stopping to talk to anyone who might have information along the way. He knew she walked to the bus for the trip into town because he wouldn't let her take the car. He had told her she could have her driver's license back when she proved responsible enough to handle it. Ironically enough, Edmund had contemplated giving it back just last week. Pounding the steering wheel of his pickup, he shook his head at how duped he had been.

Driving along the route to the bus stop he took in each detail of the road. They lived on the outskirts of town and enjoyed the benefits of country life with the convenience of having public transportation still close by. There were only three houses in the one and a half miles to the stop, and he knew two of the three families. Edmund decided to stop off at the Johan's house which was their closest neighbors along this route to inquire if they'd seen Autumn anytime recently. The Johan's were a young couple trying their hand at farming. The wife worked in town at nights and stayed home with the baby during the day. The husband worked the farm during the day and was often in and around the yard doing things.

Sure enough, as Edmund drove up, Mr. Johan's met him in the yard. "Hey Edmund, what's up?"

"Have you seen Autumn?"

"No. I can't say that I have, though I've been working calves, so I've been a bit preoccupied."

As they were chatting, Mrs. Johan came out with the baby on her hip. "Hi, Edmund. Usually, I see Autumn on her way to the bus in the morning as I'm coming home. But, the baby was sick all weekend, so the last time I saw her was Thursday."

Edmund thanked them and continued down the road.

The next house he came to was the Bogart's. He drove right on by as he had told Autumn many times to steer clear of them. They were known for being religious fanatics and were not well liked in the area. Even though Autumn questioned him on many things, this was one thing he knew she would not have crossed him on. So, he proceeded down to the Humphrey's to inquire of them.

Mr. and Mrs. Humphrey were an older couple, and they didn't get around much anymore, not even on good days; however, they were kind, and he knew they had taken a liking to Autumn. When they were together, Autumn often asked if they could stop by and visit with the Humphrey's, and Edmund didn't stifle her kindness. Today as he stopped to visit, he found they couldn't help either - they hadn't seen Autumn since he last brought her by over a month ago.

At the bus stop, he parked the truck and waited for the bus. When it arrived, he asked the driver if he'd seen Autumn, but the driver said he didn't have time to answer questions and started to shut the door. Thinking fast, Edmund hopped on and paid the fee to ride the route. It was a good waste of two hours and the cost of the fare.

The driver knew Autumn by the picture Edmund showed him, yet could only say that she boarded at the 109, rode to the 112, and about 9 hours later she boarded at the 112 and got off at the 109. The driver said she never talked to anyone on the trip and kept to herself if someone sat by her. When Edmund had exhausted his questions, the only thing he knew was that Autumn was faithful in her routine. Edmund stared out the window for the remaining of the route back to his truck, planning what he'd do next.

When he finally got back to his truck, he proceeded into town to the 112 stop. It was only three blocks to the grocery store where Autumn worked. He drove around several of the blocks noting the businesses - a lumber yard, a department store, the old mall, an office store, a couple restaurants, and some residential blocks. Nothing seemed to strike him as to a lead of where Autumn would go, so he headed to the grocery store and asked to talk to the manager, Tom.

Edmund had spoken to Tom after Autumn's last runaway attempt. He had requested to be informed if Autumn was ever late or didn't show up for work, though he hadn't heard anything from him for a while. Unfortunately, Edmund was told that Tom no longer worked there, and that about two months ago a new manager took over. Disbelieving his misfortune and getting frustrated with himself for not knowing, Edmund asked to talk to the new manager. The new manager was *not* as friendly or cooperative as Tom.

Reaching his hand out, Edmund introduced himself. "Hi, I'm Edmund DeBlue, and I'm Autumn's father. I previously spoke to Tom about my concerns with Autumn's behavior and was wondering if you could tell me if you've noticed anything going on with her."

Clearly put out by the interruption to his work, Steve, the new manager, ignored Edmund's hand and snapped. "I've already spoken to the police this morning, and all I can tell you is that Autumn DeBlue no longer works here."

"Since when?"

Steve sighed and put his hands on his hips, planting his feet with a strong stance. "I will fully cooperate with the police, but I have no intention of giving out personal information to private individuals no matter who they claim to be."

This last statement angered Edmund, and he clenched his fists. "I am her father and guardian. Legally you have to cooperate with *ME* because she is a *MINOR*." He yelled at the man.

Leaning in, Steve got right in his face. "I have no proof of who you say you are, and no record of Miss DeBlue having a father listed as a contact. I will not be responsible for giving out information that could affect the well-being of a young lady susceptible to the whims of men."

"Susceptible to the whims of men…what the heck are you talking about? I am her FATHER!"

"So you said. I think this conversation is over. I gave all the information I had to the police. You can talk to the detectives in charge if you want to know any more." Steve turned and walked into his office, closing the door firmly behind him.

Infuriated, Edmund stood there debating knocking the door down; however, he decided he didn't need to make any more of a scene or have the police called against him. He definitely didn't want to get on the bad side of the investigating officers any more than he already suspected he was. So he turned dejected to leave. As he crossed the front of the store, an elderly woman wearing a checker's smock cautiously approached him.

"Excuse me, sir? I couldn't help but overhear you talking about Autumn."

"Yes." Edmund turned hopeful that maybe someone would actually have information that would help him.

"Is she okay? I worry so much about her." The older lady confessed.

Turning on all the charm he could muster while simmering with residual anger, Edmund confessed. "I'm not sure ma'am, the last time I saw her was Friday evening, and no one seems to be able to give me any helpful information. If I may ask, why are you so worried about her?"

"Well, that young man, Marcos, just wouldn't leave her alone you know. At first, he would come in and sit at the tables, drinking coffee, waiting for her to get off work; but Tom put an end to that. That was before he was fired, of course. Then we'd see him pacing outside the doors waiting for her; so Stan, the carryout, started walking her to the bus stop after her shift when he could."

Edmund attentively listened to all the elderly lady told him, awed that he knew nothing of anything she said. "After a few weeks of that he disappeared for a while, and we thought he'd finally given up, then Thursday afternoon he was back looking for her. She wasn't here with Thursdays being her day off you know, and then on Friday, I saw him talking to her again after she got off work. He walked with her as she headed for the bus stop as Stan wasn't able to go with her. So you see when she didn't come in on Saturday at her usual time, well, that is when I got so worried about her."

Edmund stood stunned. He didn't know that Autumn had every Thursday off. She left the house for the bus stop every day of the week except for Sundays when the store was only opened for a few hours and didn't need her to work. "The manager said she wasn't working here anymore. Do you know anything about that? You said she worked on Friday, right?"

"Oh my, no. I had no idea. Yes, yes, Autumn was here Friday until about four o'clock when she gets off. It was payday and all, you know. Did Steve fire her? That scoundrel." The elderly lady shook her head. "Things just haven't been the same since they fired Tom."

"Did you tell this to the detectives that were here earlier?" Edmund queried.

"No, I haven't seen any detectives."

"Could you identify this man if you saw him again?"

"Oh yes, yes indeed. I've seen Marcos enough, yes I could."

Edmund reached back for his wallet and took out a picture similar to the one the detectives took last night. After they left, he looked deeper into Autumn's drawers and found several more pictures that looked like they came from a party she had attended, though when or where she had attended it was unknown to him. "Is this the man that you are talking about?" Edmund extended the photo to her.

She reached out to take the picture and studied it. "Yes. Yes indeed. That is him. That is Marcos."

Edmund looked down at the ladies name tag and said, "Thank you so much, Dottie, for talking with me. You really have been a great help, and I do hope to find Autumn very soon. Can I ask a few more questions?"

"Sure, sure, anything I can do to help Autumn. She is such a dear, you know."

"Yes, she is. Do you know, did Autumn work here every day? I mean every day other than Thursdays of course."

"Oh no," the woman looked surprised at such a suggestion. "After Tom left Steve cut everyone's hours. No, Autumn only worked Monday, Wednesday, and Friday the early shift and then Saturdays the afternoon shift."

"Did Autumn ever mention having to get another job when her hours were cut?"

Dottie thought back, "No, but I do remember her saying something one day after her shift about having to hurry to the mall."

Edmund was trying to be patient as Dottie was giving him such useful information; however, his mind was racing, "One more question if you will. What times are the early and afternoon shifts?"

Again Dottie looked at him as if this was such common knowledge he should know it. Still, she responded nonetheless. "The early shift is from 8-4 and the afternoon shift is from 2-10."

"Dottie, you have been a huge help to me. I am going to share what you told me with the detectives that are investigating Autumn's disappearance. Can I tell them you'll confirm what you've told me here?"

"Oh yes, yes. In fact," Dottie walked back over to her register and started feeding a receipt from the register. "Here is my address and phone number. I'd be happy to help Autumn in any way even if they fire me."

Edmund didn't know why they would fire her for wanting to help Autumn, but his head was rushing with so much new information that he couldn't stay there any longer to press the issue. He thanked Dottie again and rushed to the truck where he headed straight for the police station.

He entered the building and asked for Hardy and Thornton. He was directed back through a corridor and to the left where he entered a large open room full of desks. About halfway back and by the wall he saw Detective Hardy sitting at his desk. Thornton was nowhere to be seen. Quickly, he made his way back to Hardy and greeted him. Surprised, Hardy stood and shook Edmund's hand and offered him a seat next to the desk in the aisle way.

Edmund proceeded to tell Hardy about his conversation with the clerk at the store, Dottie and gave him the paper with her information on it. Hardy gladly accepted it and finished writing his notes on what Edmund had told him.

"So, what now?"

"Now, we verify what you have told us, and we try to find this Marcos guy to question him. Thornton is at the school right now talking to Jessica Nelson. We will see if she can give us any insights." Hesitantly, Harper tapped his notepad as if he was wrestling with how to say what came next. "I have to tell you Mr. DeBlue that Thornton won't be happy you are out investigating on your own. You need to let us professionals do our job."

Noting the warning, Edmund asked, "Well, what do you expect me to do, just sit around the house and twiddle my thumbs while my little girl may be out there hurt somewhere or worse?"

"I understand how you feel Mr. DeBlue. I'm simply making you aware that Thornton won't like it. Are you now thinking she is missing again over being a runaway?"

"I don't know what to think. With every turn, I'm finding out more and more that I have no idea who my daughter is or what she has been up to. It worries me that this Marco guy shows up again right before she disappears."

"I'm sure you *are* concerned, and I promise we will look into every lead we have."

Edmund thought Detective Hardy was trying to reassure him; nevertheless, it didn't really come across very hopeful. Nonetheless, Edmund thanked him and got up to leave. He turned to go. "Please keep me posted, and I'll let you know if I find out anything else useful."

"You do that, Mr. DeBlue," Harper gave him a half-smile.

As Edmund left the station and climbed back into his truck, he tried to figure out what to do next. It was getting rather late now, and instead of trying to pursue the mall lead tonight he decided to wait until morning. Not really thinking about what he was doing he started the truck and drove off slowly not having a clear direction. After a few blocks, he found himself looking at a beautiful park as the sun was getting ready to set. Not wanting to go back to the empty house, he decided to go for a walk and think things through.

For a while he did just that – walk – eventually, he found himself sitting under a tree looking out across a little pond with a fountain in the center. As he sat there, he was reminded of a time when he had done this very thing with Sue, his beautiful and loving wife.

# 7

To ease her heart and the turmoil of her mind, Lady Cannon often visited her granddaughter's suite to watch her play. Proceeding to the second story of her magnificent home, Lady Cannon stopped to look at the family portraits that hung along the wall in the east wing. *How she missed her family - Thomas, Brian and Brian's beautiful wife, Vivian.* They had shared so many wonderful memories that were now turning into vague recollections in time. *I need to make sure these memories are preserved for Summer. Once I am gone, no one will be here to tell her the stories of how her parents met or all the good things they accomplished before they were taken from us. I wonder if Lord Michaels knows of a good historian with whom I can share these stories with and put them in a book or video collage for her?*

Adding the task of speaking to Lord Michaels regarding a historian to her mental to-do list, Lady Cannon continued down the corridor to the second door on the left. Pausing outside, she tried to listen for Summer playing. Lady Cannon loved to catch her unaware and watch her play unobserved when possible. *There is such sweetness in the innocence of children's play.* Not hearing any noise, Lady Cannon eased the door open and peeked inside.

Heiress Summer wasn't in the main area. Stepping into the room, Lady Cannon scanned the areas Summer enjoyed playing in the most. Still no Heiress. With concern starting to creep into her heart, Lady Cannon began a more thorough scan of the room, pausing at the slight sound of a sob. Following the sound, which was followed by another one and a hiccup, Lady Cannon discovered Summer curled up in her blanket tucked into the corner behind the rocking chair.

Lady Cannon carefully eased down beside her and shifted the small child onto her loving lap, securely wrapping her in a stable embrace. "My dear Summer, whatever is wrong? Why are you crying?" Lady Cannon began rocking side to side against the wall as she sat on the floor holding the child.

"I want Mommy," Summer softly cried.

"Oh, Sweetling. I miss your Mommy and Daddy, too. Don't cry, Summer, I am here with you. Granny is here."

Trying to comfort Summer in these times was so difficult. *What was she supposed to say? How could she possibly ease the pain of losing both parents at such an early age? The one thing that brought comfort to Lady Cannon was the knowledge that she'd see her family again one day in heaven. How was she to convey such thoughts to a four-year-old in a way she'd understand?* Lady Cannon often spoke to Summer about Jesus and heaven, though she wasn't sure the child understood. Most of the time, she quietly sat staring into space while Lady Cannon talked. It left her feeling very much like she was failing in her ability to reach her grandchild.

Even now her efforts to comfort the child were to no avail. Lady Cannon felt she did not know how to talk to Summer. She had had only one child, and she never catered to Brian. From early on she spoke to Brian as she would any other person, and though she held him and loved on him often, there was none of the silliness she saw in other mothers' interactions with their children. She had never seen the point in it. She loved Summer to no end and would do anything for the child. Still, Lady Cannon never felt that she connected with that love. Perhaps it was the situation in which they were thrust together; one would never know for sure how circumstances had changed their relationship.

Lady Cannon continued her rocking, hoping something she did would ease the sorrow Summer felt. Softly, she began singing. "Jesus loves me this I know, for the Bible tells me so. Little ones to Him belong, they are weak, but He is strong. Yes, Jesus loves me. Yes, Jesus loves me. Yes, Jesus loves me, the Bible tells me so." She repeated this until Summer stopped crying and eventually fell asleep. Lady Cannon sat in the silence, eyes closed, pondering, and remembering.

It was two years ago that the accident that took both of Summer's parents away had occurred, and Lady Cannon had figured that Summer would have forgotten her parents by now; after all, she was only two when they died – a mere babe. She knew nothing more than living with Lady Cannon and her staff, yet here she was crying out for the mother she barely knew.

The episodes of silent rocking had lessened over the years, coming and going on waves of grief. Slowly, the rocking turned into isolated crying where Summer would hide and cry. Though better, both situations still occurred frequently enough that Lady Cannon worried she may never fully recover from her feeling of abandonment. On the night of the accident, Summer had been left with Lady Cannon while her parents and grandfather had gone to a social dinner. Lady Cannon would have gone as well; however, as circumstances happened, she had come down with a severe headache - unknowingly the start of her illness - and did not feel up to socializing. As if she sensed something amiss, Summer had been nearly in hysterics when they had tried to leave. Unknowingly, Brian and Vivian had *promised* to return in a few hours. That was never to be.

Though obviously tired, Summer had not wanted to be left alone, so Lady Cannon had agreed to stay with her. Soon that was not enough, so Lady Cannon took Summer downstairs to play in the vestibule while they waited. Thomas had said they would not stay late and Lady Cannon had expected them home half an hour earlier. It was unfortunate that because of this, Summer had been present when the police officers came to the door. Before Lady Cannon could give the order for the child to be taken upstairs, an officer was explaining there was an accident.

Even at the age of two, Summer had instinctively known there was bad news. She had immediately sat down, curled into a ball, and started rocking. No tears, no cries, just silent rocking. The poor traumatized child barely ate and Lady Cannon was forced over the course of time to seek all types of advice and help for the child from physicians and psychiatrists. Nothing seemed to work and the only answer consistently given was time.

Lady Cannon eventually hired a nanny to care for Summer as it was more than what she could handle day in and day out with her declining health. Unfortunately, good help was hard to find, especially with such a severely needy child. Summer would come out of her silent rocking occasionally, but, unfortunately, it was still a trial to get her to eat. Many nannies passed through their lives in the first six months. This constant change only caused more confusion and difficulty in Summer's delicate state.

Finally, Lady Cannon found a young lady named Tinny, who worked well with Summer and stayed with them for nearly a year and a half. Lady Cannon was of high hopes as Summer's episodes seemed to lessen with each passing month and recently had almost disappeared completely. However, when Lady Cannon approached Tinny regarding becoming a guardian for Summer, Tinny confided that she was engaged to marry and had been trying for months to find a way to ask leave of her position. Summer was devastated. Shortly after Lady Cannon had given Tinny leave, the episodes of crying and rocking returned on a regular basis.

For the time being, they were making due with the assistance of the housemaids and current staff, yet the stress on Lady Cannon's health was starting to show again, and Summer was often left alone for short periods which Lady Cannon did not like with her in her current state. Without some help soon Summer could once again go through another major loss – that of Lady Cannon, which would result in a loss of her inheritance as well. The trauma that would occur to the child without a guardian or living relative would be substantial for she would be turned over to the state as a ward until she turned of legal age. The mere idea of where they would put a traumatized child, such as Summer, was enough to sicken Lady Cannon further.

When she had been made aware of the grievous mistakes in the wills of her loved ones, Lady Cannon had insisted Lord Michaels search for any way to assure her granddaughter's inheritance and stable future. Unfortunately, there was little that could be done to undo these travesties.

Knowing Lady Cannon did not like the responsibility of financial decisions, Lord Cannon had designated in his will that all his estate was to be held in irrevocable trust for the use of his wife upon his death; and upon her death, anything remaining was to be distributed to charities. Brian had already received several installments through his life with his final share of inheritance when he married. There apparently was a will in the works to include an inheritance for Lord Cannon's grandchildren; however, it had not been finalized before he had died.

The estate had not actually been given *to* Lady Cannon; it was more accurately placed in trust *for* her. She was given rights to designate through the trustees' - one of which was Lord Michaels - access to a certain amount of funds for as long as she was living. Everything else was handled by the trustees, which was a very thoughtful thing for Lord Cannon to do - except in a situation such as this. Lady Cannon technically had no money of her own. Therefore, she could only gift a certain small amount to Summer every year due to tax laws. The main estate and true financial security would be liquidated and given away upon Lady Cannon's death.

Lady Cannon had wanted to somehow add a codicil or clause to the trust documents to cover Summer. Unfortunately, the trust documents were drawn up under a different lawyer before Lord Michaels was involved in the estate affairs. Written in an irrevocable clause, buried in legalese, it stated if she tried to change the trust in any way without written consent from Lord Cannon she would forfeit any and all claim to the estate. Therefore, with Lord Cannon deceased, there was no leeway for Lady Cannon to include her granddaughter in the trust provisions. When Lord Michaels discovered this, he was livid and argued against it in court based on Lord Cannon's character and past examples, yet the documents were solidly legalized, and the judge would not overturn it.

To complicate things further, Brian had not established a new Will upon his marriage to Vivian and, therefore, the old Will Thomas had insisted upon back in Brian's college days, was enforced. That Will absorbed everything back into the Cannon Estate, so once again Summer was unprotected and provided for.

Lord Michaels had informed Lady Cannon the only way around the trust restrictions was to appoint a guardian for Heiress Summer *before* Lady Cannon's death and then she could rightfully designate through the trustees a transfer of funds to a new trust for the Heiress. This was the only way to circumvent the ill-fated clause to assure Heiress Summer's inheritance. The resulting problem, of course, being: who does one trust with such a large estate and hefty decisions regarding the life of such a precious child? Moreover, Lady Cannon was more concerned about the overall welfare of the child than the money she would inherit.

Turning her attention back to her granddaughter, Lady Cannon prayed quietly - seeking God for His answer and a way to help her traumatized granddaughter. Suddenly out of the depths of her heart, after sitting there for nearly an hour with Summer in her lap, she heard the small still voice of her Heavenly Father speak to her.

*My child, as you love the little one in your arms, so I love you with even greater love. And as you are embracing this child, I am embracing you in this time of waiting. Remember My goodness and have My peace as you wait for the help you seek. For surely I tell you My promise of help is on its way.*

Lady Cannon stopped rocking in awe of this revelation and received instant peace within her heart and mind.

"Granny, what's that?" Summer's soft voice broke through Lady Cannon's thoughts.

"What sweetling? What are you asking?"

"What is on your face?"

"My face? I don't know, what do I have on my face, my dear?" Lady Cannon reached up to wipe at her cheek as if she had a mark or smudge on it.

Not knowing what it was she saw in Granny's face, Summer explained. "You were sad like me, but then you changed. Your face became different - not so sad." Summer tilted her head to the side looking at Lady Cannon with intensity.

Lady Cannon was stunned speechless for several moments. "Well, Summer, what changed on my face was the peace of Jesus. When you are sad and missing your mommy and daddy, and Granny can do nothing to comfort you, it grieves my heart, and I become very sad, too."

"Granny is also very worried about the future, about who will take care of you when I no longer can." Lady Cannon often tried to speak gently of her death to her granddaughter to prepare her for the inevitable time when she would no longer be with her here on earth. "However, when I am sad, I talk to Jesus – asking Him to help us – and He told me that help was on the way. When He spoke to my heart, I had peace and was filled with His love. That peace and love from Jesus was apparently the change you saw on my face."

"I don't like to eat, peas."

Lady Cannon smiled at the small child. "It's not peas, as what you eat. It is peace - as in quietness or harmony within your heart. When you trust in Jesus, you know He is in control, and you don't have to worry anymore. So you become at peace."

"Ooohhh...can I have peace? When I'm sad, will Jesus help me?"

"Yes child, you can have the peace that Jesus offers and be filled with His love. You simply ask Him for it. However, He only gives His peace to those who choose to believe in Him."

"How Granny?" Summer asked attentively.

"The Bible says that we have all done wrong. No one is perfect, except Jesus. And who is Jesus, Summer?"

"God's son who came to earth and died for me."

"That's correct. So, since you believe in Jesus, you simply talk to Him and say you are sorry for doing wrong. Then, ask Him to forgive you and to give you peace."

Illumination crossed Summer's face. "Like when I disobey Becca, and you make me say sorry to her?"

"Yes." Lady Cannon was touched by the innocent grasp of the truth and by the desire she clearly had to have the peace she so desperately needed. *What if Summer is too young to understand what she is doing though?* Lady Cannon prayed with Summer nightly and would love nothing more than to see her trust in Jesus and accept His free gift of salvation. *Surely it couldn't hurt to encourage prayer and repentance? God is the only one who can judge the heart's readiness to receive Him and maybe, just maybe, this was the time for Summer.* "Would you like to ask Jesus for His peace and forgiveness now?"

"Oh yes, Granny!" Summer rapidly clasped her hands together in front of her and bowed her head. Then she hesitantly looked up at Granny and said, "I...I want to do it myself."

"Of course, dear." They both bowed their heads again as Summer began to pray.

"Dear Jesus, Granny says I need to tell you I am sorry for doing wrong. Please forgive me - and everyone else who does wrong. Granny says you gave her peace. Can I please have some? I'm sad a lot, and I want to be better." At this Summer opened one eye and looked up questioningly to see if there was anything else she needed to say.

Lady Cannon smiled down at Summer and said, "Amen."

"Amen," repeated Summer.

"I don't know about you; however, I feel much better now."

"Me, too. Can I have a snack?"

"Yes, go see what Koka Fiona has for you in the kitchen." At that, Summer hopped off her lap and skipped across the room.

Lady Cannon sat there slowly moving her feet to regain the feeling before she rose steadying herself with the chair. It seemed more necessary with each passing day to rise slowly so that the blackness didn't settle in. Once up, she slowly followed her granddaughter down the stairs to the kitchen. Upon glancing in on Summer and seeing that Koka Fiona was taking good care of her, Lady Cannon retreated to the Library to call Lord Michaels about finding and hiring a historian.

As Master Philip turned and led the way to a very nice navy blue Cadillac, Autumn exhaled once again trying to calm her nerves. The chauffeur set her bags beside the trunk of the car and opened the back door for Autumn to get in. Though she was utterly exhausted from all the travels, she could hardly contain her excitement at being chauffeured. *This would never happen to me in Nebraska.*

Master Philip finished loading her bags in the trunk and Autumn sat back trying to relax. *She had made it! Virtually untraceable and by herself - well, not including the extra money from Lady Cannon and Mrs. Bogart, which she'd pay back. She had accomplished the greatest feat of her life so far.*

Precipitously, she sat up tall in the back seat of the Cadillac, enough so that the chauffeur glanced at her in the rearview mirror. She was going to start a new life – putting Nebraska, and all that died there to rest – and she knew if she was going to make this work, she had to think more highly of herself. Not being proud but realizing she was more than a poor, stuck, and helpless girl. Sitting in the back seat, watching the scenery pass her by, the nerves began rising in her stomach to the point of nausea. *Can I really pull this off? Can I socialize with wealthy people and not come across like a country bumpkin?* She straightened her spine once more and set her jaw. *If rubbing elbows with wealthy people doesn't come naturally then I'll act the part until it does. I'm **going** to make this work!*

As exhausted as she was, she couldn't sleep with all the thoughts, questions, and nerves running through her, so she stared blankly out the window. After a few miles, Master Philip quietly turned some music on in the front of the car. Autumn was not familiar with the songs, but she began to relax and rested her head on the back of the seat.

The time went much more quickly compared to the train with all the stops. Before Autumn knew it, she saw a sign indicating Middleville city limits. Master Philip drove straight through the town as Autumn studied her new surroundings from the window. *I'm surprised the town isn't bigger. I guess I figured that since Lady Cannon is so wealthy, she'd live in a city. This seems like a nice, clean, small town.*

Autumn was even more astounded when Master Philip continued out of town on the other side of Middleville. The town lights were still in view - though not directly - when the car stopped at a set of ornamental black wrought iron gates. Master Philip took what looked like a phone out of the glovebox and dialed a number which apparently opened the gates as they shortly began to move. Turning down a long lane lit with old-fashioned black lamps, Autumn found herself watching the gates close behind her. When Autumn turned back around her eyes widened, and jaw went slack at the sight before her.

A massive mansion with white pillars and trim stood three stories high before them. Virtually every window on the first floor was illuminated with some type of light, and though it wasn't Christmas, white twinkle lights were seen around the exterior in places. The majestic house towered over her as the chauffeur stopped at the front steps and opened the door for her to exit.

Feeling small and completely out of her realm of comfort, Autumn took a moment to gather what courage she could muster before exiting the car. As she ascended the main steps between the two center pillars, she paused to take another deep breath. Reaching her hand out to knock, she jumped as the doors swung open before her. Standing in the doorway, she could see the enormity of the dazzling entry and the refinement of the man who had opened the door. She was not able to fully take in the whole glittering sight though, for as soon as she entered, her attention was captured by the middle-aged gentleman in formal wear who bowed. "Welcome, Chatelaine DeBlue, I am LeDare Anton, Lady Cannon's head of household. We have occasionally spoken on the phone."

Autumn nodded as she recognized his voice.

"I am sure you are exhausted from your travels. If you follow me, I will show you to your suite."

*Suite – she was going to have a suite!* Her stomach flipped, and she felt nausea rock her to her core again. Not knowing what to say, Autumn nodded again and quietly followed LeDare Anton up the left-hand stairs to the second floor. "Your suite is in the west wing." LeDare Anton gestured as he turned left at the top of the stairs and proceeded down the corridor to the first set of double doors on the right from the stairs. LeDare Anton opened the doors and stepped back, waving Autumn into the room before him. *Could this be right? The room is not only enormous, but it's gorgeous as well.* Hesitantly, she glanced in uncertainty at LeDare Anton who was still behind her.

Seeing her uncertainty, LeDare Anton took compassion on the young woman whom the Lady hoped would be the solution to her difficulties and the future of the Estate. Though the entire staff had been told to portray Lady Cannon as a strict and particularly eccentric - in hopes of determining the young woman's true commitment - it was also outside of their nature as a whole to not show kindness. Therefore, they were instructed to offer her assistance and help her feel at home. "Are you hungry Chatelaine? Our cook, Koka Fiona, would be happy to provide something."

Without waiting for a response, LeDare Anton stepped more fully into the room and continued. "Lady Cannon has already retired for the night; nonetheless, she wanted me to personally see you settled and assure that you feel free to make yourself at home." He gestured to the room again. "Is there anything you need?"

*Need? Heavens no, she didn't **need** anything. This was far more than she expected to get - a small cot on the third floor in this house would be more than she deserved.* Autumn quickly scanned the room, there was no bed visible, yet there were several doors. Walking over to the couch a few feet in front of her, she felt the luxurious fabric. *Am I dreaming? Could this be real? I've never even seen fabric like this before.* Suddenly she realized LeDare Anton was watching her and waiting for a response to his questions. Folding her hands in front of her to keep them steady, Autumn tried to answer LeDare Anton's questions. "A small dinner would be appreciated, but I don't need anything else other than my bags and time to get acquainted with my new surroundings. Is this a guest room?"

LeDare Anton smiled kindly. "These are **your** rooms, Chatelaine. Lady Cannon has assigned these rooms to you for your personal use for the duration of your stay with us. Please, make yourself at home."

*How long was Lady Cannon expecting me to stay? If this is how she treats her employees, no wonder everyone is so nice. I wonder though, why does LeDare Anton constantly refer to Lady Cannon as 'Lady'? And is LeDare his first name? And what was a chatelaine? Why does he keep calling me that? I thought I was to be a companion.*

Reigning her thoughts in, Autumn acknowledged LeDare Anton's affirmation that she was supposed to be in these rooms with a firm nod.

"Our Lady also asked that you be instructed to meet her at eight a.m. in the Library before breakfast. I will have one of the maids wake you and assist you in preparing for your first meeting with the Lady."

Again, Autumn simply nodded.

"If there will be nothing else Chatelaine, I will go see to your dinner."

When LeDare Anton did not move to leave, she realized he was waiting for her dismissal. "Um, yes, thank you. I don't need anything else. Thank you for your kindness."

LeDare Anton bowed again with a smile on his face. "Very well, I will see you in the morning Chatelaine." He stepped back into the hall, closing the doors with him.

Autumn turned to begin looking around the large room she was left in – she would come to know this room as her Great room. The room was twice the size of her living room in Nebraska - the only thing she had to compare it with - and was shaped like a backward 'L.' It was very nicely decorated with matching furnishings all in shades of royal blue with accents of gold.

Immediately to her left was a lavish sitting area with two plush couches, two plush barrel chairs with throw pillows and something Autumn had never seen before – it looked like a loveseat yet smaller – around the chair-and-a-half were more throw pillows. Autumn walked around the furniture, feeling the different leathery fabrics and admiring the modern blue and gold patterns on the pillows. *Whoa, this furniture is all covered in the most heavenly fabric.* She sat down on the couch, sinking into its plushness, and wrapped her arms around a pillow. *This is heaven. I could stay here for the next week and never move.* Not daring to sit down too long for fear of falling asleep, she made herself get up and examine the rest of the room.

Her attention was drawn to an enormous painting on the wall by the door. All the furniture was arranged in the sitting area in a way which would allow for optimal viewing of the exquisite meadow of yellow jonquils, yet also foster intimate conversation for those who sat there. *It makes the room feel more comfortable and like a home, not a hotel.*

As Autumn was standing there admiring the picture, it suddenly phased out and changed to a mountain scene with woods and a waterfall. Intrigued, she stepped closer. *Unbelievable. I can see all the paint strokes, yet it's digital - a flat screen TV in a frame - almost like a framed projector screen.* She looked up at the ceiling and the back wall to see if there was indeed a projector, but there wasn't. *It must be a large digital picture frame playing a slideshow instead of a TV.*

Standing in front of the picture frame, she again looked at the sitting area. This time, she noticed the oak chest and bookcases which were housed on the opposite wall from the TV behind the chair and a half. Walking over to examine these, she determined the center chest was actually an entertainment center with DVD capabilities. Autumn turned the DVD on to see what would happen. Sure enough, the mountain scene changed to the DVD prompt screen. *So it is a TV as well as a digital picture frame.* Three remotes were lying there, but Autumn decided to wait until later to figure out what they all did. The two bookcases were full of books, movies, and delicate glass figurines. *These remind me of grandma's carousel.* Tears threatened to fall. She took a deep breath and brushed them aside to continue her exploration.

Walking around the corner into the longer part of the room, Autumn noted the wall of windows at the far end with fine draperies of royal blue and silken gold. On a raised platform in the center of this area was an oak desk and bureau that matched the entertainment center and bookshelves. The platform effectively created an open yet separate office area. Approaching the desk for a closer inspection, Autumn fingered the filigree of the wood as she passed. The matching bureau behind the desk was filled with all the necessities a modern office would need. And there was a luxurious leather office chair which Autumn sat in and spun around a few times laughing.

Coming to a stop facing the desk, Autumn looked over the computer. The wireless mouse beckoned to her on the desk – she loved computers, and her curiosity won out over any trepidation. As she anxiously watched the screen come into focus, she was startled to read the greeting: WELCOME CHATELAINE DEBLUE. Jumping back, she looked around the room as if someone was watching her. She felt a bit silly at her reaction as the screen transitioned to a normal desktop. She felt like she was doing something she wasn't supposed to, yet LeDare Anton had told her to make herself at home. *And it **did** say welcome. Surely they wouldn't mind if I just looked it over a bit.*

Autumn quickly maneuvered around the computer and discovered the available software – no expense had been spared in selecting the latest programs and installing more than enough memory to run them. *I love this computer. It is so much more advanced than the ones at school or the library, but it's gonna be awesome to work on.* The one thing her father had agreed to allow her in regards to higher education was computer classes, which were offered in affiliation with the library; she had loved every one of them.

Exploring enough of the computer for one night, Autumn looked around the large room again, noticing the round oak table tucked into the corner at the right of the door. It was surrounded by four wooden dining chairs in the same ornate oak as the desk and decorated with a fine blue satin cloth. A gorgeous crystal globe trimmed in gold and holding blue candles sat at the center of the table. *I wonder if this is where I'm supposed to have my meals? Will I always be eating alone? Is it like a hotel where I order room service? So many things I simply don't know. I should start a list.* Pulling out a sheet of paper from one of the drawers in the desk she had earlier noted, she did just that.

Standing at the edge of the platform, Autumn could see four doors: the double doors that led to the hall, one door directly across from the desk, and two on the long wall running between the desk and table. She decided to start with the closest one - the one across from the desk.

Autumn tentatively opened the door and peeked into the room. It was a room a quarter of the size of the great room, and it adequately housed the largest bed she had ever laid eyes on. The bed went from one wall to the other with a small walkway on either side. She had never even imagined such a bed existed – it was topped with what seemed to be hundreds of pillows and was draped with satiny gold canopy curtains at each corner bedpost. The bed covering, a down-filled duvet, coordinated with the blues of the great room.

At the sight of the pillows, Autumn could not resist running and flinging herself on the bed. After laying there for a moment in pure comfort and awe, she sat up to take in the rest of the room. At the head of the bed on each side, stood oak nightstands each containing a golden lamp with blue shades - both currently on. In the far corner from the door, a large plush chair with a small table provided for a more private sitting area. The wall opposite the bed appeared to have windows as the draperies ran from wall to wall. However, had she looked, she would have found sliding glass doors instead of windows that went to a private balcony. This room was her boudoir or private chambers.

Autumn lay back on the bed again in a state of dreamy awe. *Could all this be real? Was she dreaming? What would she have to do to earn such luxuries? Are all companions - or chatelaines if that's what I'm to be - treated so well?* She obviously did not know what she had signed up for when she agreed to come to Michigan, still, could she make this somehow work out for her benefit? If this is how she'd be treated, then she'd do everything in her power to do the absolute best job ever. *Anything Lady Cannon asks I'll do it!* Before she knew it, Autumn had dozed off.

Suddenly waking to a noise her sleep-deprived brain couldn't process, Autumn drug herself off the bed and decided to finish looking in the other two doors. *I wonder how long before the cook brings food, or my bags arrive. I'd really like to go to bed.* Shrugging her shoulders, Autumn headed for the first door just off the platform across from her bedroom door. It opened to a huge closet slightly smaller than the size of her bedroom in Nebraska. It was broken into sections by ornate oak panels. Each section had partially filled racks of shoes, and rods of clothes with accessories.

The chauffeur had brought her bags and had sat them on the floor. *That must have been the sound I heard that woke me. This is everything I own in the world, and it looks pathetic in comparison to this lavish closet. I wonder what all these clothes are doing here. Surely Lady Cannon doesn't need this space for storage in this large house.* Adding this to her list of unanswered questions, Autumn continued to look around the closet. At the far end of the closet was a small window covered in a smaller version of the same blue drapery in the great room.

As Autumn turned to leave the closet, she saw a door to the left of the one she had come in. Curiously, she opened it and discovered it led into a bathroom. *Wow, how awesome that someone can go from the bathroom into the closet without being seen.* Stepping into the bathroom, she first saw the tub to her left. It was a large corner tub that was actually sunken into the floor. It had real plants around it and was illuminated by a wall of panels that lit up with a soft glow like stars. Self-consciously, she looked down at her garments which she had worn for nearly two days and felt she desperately needed a bath. However, upon further examination, she discovered that she didn't know how to turn it on. It didn't have a normal knob and spout, although it did have several push buttons. Not wanting to break anything, Autumn decided to wait until someone could show her how to use the fancy tub.

Turning away from the tub, she noticed the large double sink and mirror continuing down the wall. Coming to the other end of the room, she paused and contemplated the two fixtures beside each other – both looked like toilets, yet one did not have a seat and looked to have some type of sprayer nozzle on it. She had no idea what it was.

Going with what she knew, Autumn determined the 'odd toilet' was for men and used the elegantly seated toilet with great relief.

Further exploration of the bathroom revealed luxurious linens nicely displayed around the room at convenient locations and all in hues of blue. The bathroom was lavish with ivory tiles and golden fixtures. A remarkably comfortable stool was placed before another large mirror and vanity which was situated across from the sinks. Brushes, curling irons, and various other hair accessories were neatly arrayed on the top of this vanity. Seeing another door to the right of the vanity, Autumn exited back into the great room close to the table and chairs at the front of the room.

Her thoughts were interrupted by a knock on the door. Upon answering it, she found a rather rotund middle-aged woman with a cheerful grin. She greeted Autumn as she entered the room. "Hello Chatelaine, I'm Koka Fiona th' cuik of th' hoose. LeDare Anton said ye waur a wee bit hungry." Autumn smiled at the woman's Scottish accent as she opened the door wider to allow her in. *Why does everyone in this house have strange titles before their names?*

Watching as Koka Fiona took the silver tray she was holding over to the table in the corner, Autumn followed curiously. Koka Fiona uncovered the dishes. "I'm sorry hen, it isn't a foo meel boot it will tide ye over till mornin'." She turned and looked at Autumn. "If thaur be naethin' else Chatelaine, I'll be off."

Autumn snapped to from her perusal of the food. "Oh, of course, thank you, Koka Fiona, I really appreciate you providing this for me at such a late hour."

Koka Fiona nodded with a genuine smile. "Yoo can laev th' tray oan th' table when yoo're dune. One of th' maids will brin' it doon in th' mornin'." At that, she slightly curtsied and made her way towards the door. "Oh, an' ever'one calls me Koka, please dae th' sam."

Autumn nodded in acknowledgment as she stood there overwhelmed by everything she had encountered so far. As Koka

Fiona reached the doors, it finally occurred to Autumn to ask about the tub. *She seems nice enough. Hopefully, she won't mind helping me even though she's the cook.* Taking a deep breath, Autumn spoke before the cook could open the door. "Koka? Could I ask a favor?"

Curious, Koka turned and nodded to affirm her willingness to help.

In her best wealthy person imitation, Autumn straightened her shoulders and lifted her nose. "After traveling all day, I desperately need to bathe before bed..." *What am I doing? You can't haughtily proclaim your ignorance.* Changing her tone and letting her shoulders fall in submission, she continued. "I'm not certain how to run the bathtub. Would you be able to show me?"

Autumn wasn't sure how to interpret the expression on Koka's face - was it amusement or pity. Not being bold enough to ask, Autumn simply followed as Koka Fiona turned and proceeded to the bathroom.

The cook explained the waterfall mechanism that filled the tub and the new water jet system. "Lady Cannon jist had these installed in aw th' second fluir bathrooms thes pest summer. Th' place needed a bit of tooch up efter sae many years, ye know. We're raither prood of them ye see, not e'en th' gov'ner's mansion has tubs like these uns."

Autumn listened, nodding and pretending to understand the significance. "Thank you so much Koka, this was very helpful."

Satisfied that she'd done what was asked, Koka turned once again to leave with another curtsy.

Following Koka Fiona out of the bathroom - and unwittingly leaving the water running - Autumn approached the tray of food almost forgotten by the distraction of the tub, to see what Koka Fiona had brought her for dinner. There were two big fluffy rolls stuffed with chicken and something that resembled a grape and rice stuffing. Next to the plate of rolls sat a large bowl of mixed fruit with whipped topping and another bowl with a garden salad and strawberry vinaigrette. All of which was beyond delicious. Koka Fiona had also brought her a cold glass of milk and a pitcher of water.

She had enjoyed her meal so much she had forgotten the water was still running until she entered the bathroom once again. Fortunately, being so large, it had not overflowed or made a huge mess. Breathing a sigh of relief that she didn't have to confess to a messy mistake her first night, Autumn figured there was enough water to bathe in and turned it off.

Despite her exhaustion, Autumn took her time savoring the luxuries of the bath with the scented soaps and shampoos, which were neatly arranged on a shelf at the back of the tub discreetly hidden by some foliage. As she finished her bath, she wrapped the extremely large plush towel around herself and used the adjoining door to enter the closet. Sifting through her bags, she quickly found a clean pair of sweats and a t-shirt which were her usual sleepwear. Not knowing what to do with her dirty clothes, Autumn simply set them beside her duffle on the floor and wrote down to ask about laundry tomorrow.

After dressing, she returned to the bathroom to brush her hair and teeth, using what she had brought with her even though there were plenty of supplies already on the counters. *I can't believe how soft my hair is after using the shampoo and conditioner. And my skin feels soft, too. I could really get used to this. If I'm not careful, I'll get spoiled and not remember how hard life can be.* She smiled in the mirror at herself. *Then again, why should I try to remember the hard times? I'm moving forward, and I'll do my very best to keep this good thing coming.*

Finished in the bathroom, she turned off the lights she could find and crossed the great room into the bedchamber. She wasn't sure how to turn off the great room lights, so she was forced to leave them on. She felt guilty, yet still didn't want to bother anyone at the late hour to help her fix it. It was only moments after her head hit the pillows that she was sound asleep – completely exhausted from traveling and the emotional thrill of arriving in Michigan.

# 9

The next morning, Autumn awoke with a start at knocking on the door to the bedroom. In the minutes it took her to gain her bearings and remember where she was, the door was gently opened, and a young woman entered. "I beg your pardon Chatelaine, but it's time to get up. We need time to get you ready to meet with the Lady."

Autumn blinked her gritty eyes and rubbed them a few times. "Oh, right. Of course, I'll be right there." Autumn sat up and stretched remembering where she was. "Um, What time is it?" She looked around the room and didn't see a clock and the room was still very dark. She could only see a little bit of light around the edges of the shut draperies.

"It is six a.m. Chatelaine; and our time is very short. I tried to let you rest as long as I could. Please join me in the walk-in closet. We will get you dressed and prepared as quickly as we can." The maid exited and headed for the closet, not really giving Autumn a choice.

*Dress me? What am I a two-year-old that can't dress myself? And why is two hours such a short time to get dressed? I'm usually up and going in no more than 30 minutes.* Shrugging her shoulders, she guessed the only way to find out was to follow the woman. Autumn made a brief detour to the table which still held the tray and leftovers from last night. She filled a glass with water and carried it with her into the closet.

Entering, Autumn found the young woman going through the clothes at the back of the closet. Upon seeing Autumn in her sweats and t-shirt, the maid stood agog in what Autumn interpreted as clear horror at the sight. Unsuccessfully, the young woman tried to pull herself together. "I apologize for my inappropriate response, Chatelaine. I hope you will not take offense, I was unprepared for the...uh...casualness of your attire."

Autumn looked down at her sweats and t-shirt. *What's wrong with being casual when you are sleeping?* However, before she could respond, the young woman was continuing on with her introduction.

"My name is Ménage Eleanor, and I will be your personal attendant. Are you a size 8 or a size 10? I can't quite tell with your..." Eleanor paused as she eyed the sweats and t-shirt again, "sleepwear." She ended in careful thought.

*Why do I need a personal attendant? I definitely don't want to get on the bad side of someone I have to be around all the time. Plus, I may need her help to navigate all this new territory.* Autumn was still unsure as to what was wrong with her 'sleepwear;' however, she decided she wanted to be pleasant and make the most of an awkward situation. "I'm not easily offended. I'm not sure what's wrong with my sleepwear, but I didn't mean to catch you off guard. How about we start over? I'm Autumn DeBlue." Autumn reached out her hand in greeting.

Eleanor paused for a moment considering, then smiled taking her hand. "I'm Eleanor. And when we are private like this, it's okay to call me just Eleanor, but anywhere else in the house, you'll need to use my title. Lady Cannon is very particular about her titles."

Autumn nodded. "Thanks. I wear mostly size 10 because I don't like my clothes tight though I can fit into an 8 if I have to. I have my own clothes here." Autumn turned to where she had left her bags the night before except they were not there. She turned to Eleanor with panic in her eyes. "Where are my bags?" Her heart was racing. It wasn't much, yet it was all she owned.

Distracted at looking through the clothes on the racks, Eleanor did not notice Autumn's panic. "They have been put away,

Chatelaine. You will not need the clothes you brought as the Lady is very particular and she has purchased a wardrobe for you. What doesn't fit will be replaced with pieces that do once your position has been established."

Not fully registering what Eleanor had said in the midst of the continuing rise in the beating of her heart which pounded in her ears, Autumn became more insistent, almost shouting. "Where are my things. Where did they get put away? I want to know." Everything she owned in the world was in those bags – her money, her personal records, her clothes. Not to mention her mother's locket and grandmother's ring, which she had taken off for her bath. It was not much; nevertheless, it was hers, and in case things didn't go so well, she wanted to know where they were.

Shocked by the outburst, Eleanor sheepishly walked over to the far left section of the closet and opened several drawers. "Everything is right here. I didn't mean to upset you; I was only trying to be helpful in getting you settled, as I was directed by my Lady."

Autumn rushed over to the drawers and began looking through things. Yes, everything was there. It was only then that she became embarrassed by her actions and mistrust. Everyone had been so kind so far. "I'm sorry. I...I shouldn't have gotten so upset. I'm...I'm not used to others handling my things." She took a deep breath and exhaled it to calm her heart rate. "I'm...I'm sorry for being so harsh?"

Eleanor curtsied and turned back to the clothes. Autumn wasn't sure if things were okay between them or not as Eleanor simply jumped right into the next thing. "Yes, Chatelaine. We must hurry now; we don't have much time to dress and ready you." Picking out a striking rose-colored dress with matching shoes, she handed them to Autumn. "You will have to use your own undergarments for now. Here, put this on." Normally, Eleanor was supposed to help put the dress on, holding it out to keep it from wrinkling; however, this time she felt slightly panicked herself. This was a huge responsibility and chance for advancement for her, and she didn't want to mess it up on the first day by not being ready. Handing the dress to Autumn, Eleanor went to the section of the closet that held the accessories. Finding what she was looking for, she went into the bathroom – leaving the door open.

Autumn quickly shucked off her t-shirt and threw the dress over her head. It was a gorgeous gown though not formal by any means. The material was a blend of something stretchy and soft yet strikingly refined. Upon pulling it on, she realized it went all the way to the floor. Hiking up the skirt – wrinkling it some – she pulled her sweats off and slipped on the shoes.

She was trying to button the back when Eleanor reentered. "Let me. Just stand straight."

Autumn obeyed. After buttoning the back of the dress, Eleanor evaluated it and determined it to be a bit too long for the matching flat shoes and instructed Autumn to change with a cream pair that had a slight, yet sturdy, heal. Pleased with the adjustment of shoes, Eleanor literally took Autumn by the hand and led her into the bathroom to fix her hair. Seeing what was about to happen, Autumn hesitated, and Eleanor impatiently directed her to sit in front of the vanity. Autumn obediently sat; nevertheless, she was instantly and involuntarily swept back in time.

When Autumn was a little girl, her mother loved to fix her hair in all types of styles, and Autumn fondly remembered hours shared with her mother in the bathroom in Nebraska or sitting in the living room watching movies. But once her mother became sick, it drained her too much, and Autumn stopped asking her to even brush it. No one had touched her hair since her mother passed away. Having no idea of the turmoil going on inside of Autumn, Eleanor began to brush her hair gently but determinedly, and the tears Autumn so valiantly fought off started rolling down her cheeks.

When Eleanor finally noticed, she was alarmed and deeply concerned, stopping immediately. "Chatelaine, what's wrong? Am I hurting you?"

Autumn choked back the tears and tried to gain control. "No, Eleanor. You were very gentle. My mother used to brush my hair, and I was just overwhelmed with memories. No one has touched my hair since she passed away."

Eleanor quietly nodded and proceeded to brush her hair more gently than before. "You have lovely hair, very strong and beautiful, but...if I may ask...why are the ends so roughly cut?"

Autumn blushed. "I cut my own hair several times for various reasons. But, thank you. I've always liked my hair." Autumn slightly smiled at Eleanor who returned the smile through the mirror.

"If you are okay with it, we can have it fixed tomorrow, so it's more evenly trimmed. I'm sure the Lady will approve of that."

Autumn simply nodded. *I'm putting the past where it belongs. It's time to move forward.*

After brushing her hair, which was just below Autumn's shoulders, Eleanor began braiding two panels of hair at the nape of her neck and wrapped them up and around the top of her head making a crown of braids - the ends barely met in the middle. Securing the braids with pins that had either large diamond-like jewels or ribbons that matched the dress perfectly, Eleanor smoothed the rest of Autumn's hair straight down her back.

When done, Eleanor said, "This will be your daily hairstyle which I will do for you, unless the Lady specifies differently. I know this may all seem very different to you; however, the Lady will explain everything to you later. Now, please do whatever morning toiletries you need here in the privy and meet me in the great room straight away. We still have much to do." Eleanor left, and Autumn used the toilet - trying not to wrinkle the dress - washed her face and brushed her teeth – being careful not to get anything on the dress or mess up her hair. *Tomorrow I'm going to have to ask to do all this before I dress so I don't have to be so careful.*

Looking herself over in the mirror, Autumn thought something was missing. With further reflection, Autumn went back to the closet where her stuff had been put away and retrieved her makeup bag. Making her way back to the vanity she took out the locket and ring she had placed there last night. Then she applied a light base foundation and a neutral lip gloss. When she was done, Autumn exited to the great room for whatever Ménage Eleanor had next.

Up to this point, everything was moving so fast that Autumn had not thought much about asking questions; however, as she entered the great room, she couldn't hold back the need to ask them any longer. "Eleanor, why do you call me 'Chatelaine' and Lady Cannon 'Lady'? And how did you know how to fix my hair, or what dress to pick? And why is it that Lady Cannon is so particular about what I wear?" She had many more questions, yet suddenly stopped when she noticed there was another woman in the room with Ménage Eleanor.

Ménage Eleanor curtsied to Autumn. "Chatelaine, may I present Madame Hue. She has been instructed by the Lady to start your preparation for employment."

Madame Hue gestured for Autumn to take a seat which she did - plopping more than sitting. Madame Hue cringed.

"Now in regards to your questions, please allow me to briefly explain what I can. The Cannon Estate was founded on respect, and everything within it is geared around that respect. Lady Cannon is the head of this house, and out of respect she is addressed as "Lady." She has her own reasons for requesting such a title, which I will leave for her to explain if she desires. You are referred to as Chatelaine because the Lady instructed you be given that title of respect – it is the French word for the position in which you are being groomed. You will notice everyone in the employ of the Estate is given a title of respect. Again, the Lady can explain her reasons if she desires, your job is to respect those titles and their position within the Estate."

"Lady Cannon is also a woman of great stature in the community, as well as the state, and often has visitors stopping by – some being unannounced. For this reason, she requires everyone in her employment to be dressed to her standards at all times outside of their rooms. Therefore, the Lady took the liberty of arranging a wardrobe for you. You can consider this your uniform for employment with the Cannon Estate. It may be an unconventional uniform. Nonetheless, that is what it is."

Autumn involuntarily nodded as if in understanding. Madame Hue gestured to Eleanor and breathlessly continued.

"Ménage Eleanor has been instructed by Lady Cannon as to what is required of her to continue as your personal attendant. She went through training on how to complete several of Lady Cannon's preferred hairstyles and was entrusted to pick the style that would best compliment the Chatelaine and meet the Lady's preferences based on your hair length and facial structure." Madame Hue paused to take a breath.

"I am an instructor of etiquette, as well as a dear friend of Lady Cannon. I have been requested on numerous occasions to help give instruction, to maintain the standards of the house which are important to Lady Cannon. It will be my personal goal to instruct you in such a way as to equip you to meet Lady Cannon's specific standards for a long-term position with the Cannon Estate." She kept speaking more rapidly as she went so that she again had to pause for a breath.

"Now, for your first lesson – we are running out of time, so it will be quick. In meeting with the Lady, you should first know that you are to curtsy." Madame Hue stood and demonstrated the curtsy again. "She is the only one you are required to curtsy to in this house at this time. It is always appropriate to curtsy to guests or visitors as a sign of respect; however, you will receive more on that later. Let me see you try again."

Autumn stood and repeated what she'd seen Madame Hue do.

"Good, now make sure your right leg always goes back behind the left. And be sure to slightly bow your head as you bend your knee. Yes, very good."

"After curtsying to the Lady, she may ask you to sit. Please *do not* plop – as you did a moment ago – rather lower yourself with control and grace, placing yourself in the chair, tucking your right leg gently behind your left at the ankle. And gracefully place your hands on your lap. Now, let me see you sit."

They had to practice this a few times until Autumn could hold her balance while dipping and Madame Hue moved on. Knowing time was running out, she again began speaking rapidly to get in all the instruction before time was up.

"Never sit before the Lady. It is rude to seat yourself before that of someone higher in respect. Remember never to speak first, yet always answer when spoken to. When the Lady asks you a question, answer freely though concisely. When the meeting comes to an end, wait for the Lady to rise before you do. The only exception to this is if the Lady needs help, then you may assist her without offending. If you are to accompany her somewhere, follow behind the Lady and slightly to the right or if still in conversation to the right of her but not in front. Never walk in front of the Lady – or anyone of higher respect – unless opening a door or pulling out a seat to assist. And when it comes time for you to leave her, remember to curtsy again."

Madame Hue was speaking faster and faster as she glanced at her watch and Autumn's head was spinning with so much to remember. "Can you remember all of that?"

"I will try." This was all that Autumn could manage to get out.

Eleanor who was now standing by the door interjected. "It is time; I will take you to the Library."

Still dazed at the mountain of information thrown at her in such a short time, Autumn followed Eleanor with glazed eyes not really paying attention as to the path they took. When they finally stopped before a set of large double doors, Autumn snapped out of it as Eleanor gave her a last look over.

Timidly at first, Autumn entered the room looking all around. The room was empty. She glanced back at Eleanor who was still in the door. "Wait here for Lady Cannon."

With a few minutes to gather her thoughts, Autumn tried to remember all that Madame Hue had told her; however, she was soon distracted by the books and decorative furnishings of the room. Autumn began walking around taking in the surroundings.

Autumn noticed several sitting areas. There were two cherry wood tables surrounded by chairs across from each other diagonally. A smaller sitting area to the right of the tables contained two black leather chairs and an end table. On the end table was a black lamp with a deep red shade. The largest sitting area was more to the center-left and contained two small deep red couches facing each other and two black leather chairs at their ends. In the center of this sitting area was a cherry wood coffee table. On the table, Autumn could see there were several recent periodicals and magazines.

The two side walls of the room were lined with shelves of books from top to bottom, and each side had a ladder that ran on a track along the top of the shelves the full length of the wall. On the sides of the double doors, Autumn had entered were two smaller bookshelves that appeared to have children's books and above them were two portraits. Above the right bookcase was a portrait of a man and woman, whom Autumn guessed to be Lady Cannon and her husband in their thirties. Above the left bookcase was a portrait of the same couple in their fifties with another couple who appeared to be in their thirties holding a little girl of maybe one.

Turning around to look at the rest of the room, Autumn moved more toward the larger sitting area as she noticed the two narrow windows that ran from floor to ceiling in the wall opposite the doors. These windows had long red sheer drapes and golden hooks and hangers. Between the windows, on the wall, hung a large painting of a man standing at an old looking door poised to knock. The man wore a long white robe with a blue sash, and his hair and beard were long. What drew Autumn into the picture the most was the man's eyes. It was as if he was looking at her yet he wasn't. Tearing her eyes from the man, she noted below the picture on a delicately carved table, lay a large book with golden edges opened somewhere in the middle. The pages of the book were illuminated by a gold lamp hanging from the wall directly above it.

This was apparently a very special book – having a very special place of honor in the house. Autumn started to reach out and touch it when the doors behind her opened causing her to spin in surprise and shame for wanting to touch such a treasured item of the Lady's house.

 10

Seeing Lady Cannon enter and take only a few steps into the room, Autumn nervously approached her and curtsied a little shakily.

Lady Cannon was impressed at how well the young lady had remembered what Madame Hue had instructed. "Well done, and with hardly a quiver of nervousness." As Autumn straightened, she saw a warm smile come over Lady Cannon's face. "Now tell me, what had you so intently interested that you were surprised by my entrance."

"I was admiring the painting and the book, my Lady." Autumn gestured to the far wall. "They seem to be of great value to you."

"Yes, yes indeed." Lady Cannon moved slowly, yet gracefully, over to one of the leather chairs in the larger sitting area. "Come, let us get acquainted."

Autumn moved to join her although she remained standing as Lady Cannon did not sit. Once at the chair, Lady Cannon turned to look at the young woman before her. She was indeed young, much younger than she had pictured in her mind and very beautiful. She was not petite though not large boned either, a good middle ground in her frame. She had large caring blue eyes that Lady Cannon felt allowed her to look straight into the depths of the young lady, where she saw a lot of reservations and walls guarding her precious heart. *That insight is from above and not my own perceptions, I'm sure. Yet, even with the reserved nature of her heart, the young lady seems willing enough to do what was asked of her. After all, look what I put her through this morning and there were no complaints.*

Autumn tried to stand still while she was being evaluated and waited for whatever would be asked of her next. While she waited, she decided to do a little evaluation herself. Lady Cannon was definitely a woman of grace and elegance. Even in her so-told sickly state, she beamed of beauty and strength. To Autumn, she did not look sick at all, she was older, maybe late sixties, though she did not have that thin, sickly look that her grandmother had when she became ill.

The thing that baffled Autumn the most was the contrast of how Lady Cannon was portrayed since her arrival - that of a strict, unforgiving, eccentric - and the gentleness Autumn encountered whenever she interacted with Lady Cannon. Autumn couldn't remember even the slightest harshness coming from her in any of their previous conversations, and even with Autumn's lack of knowledge, she was received warmly by Lady Cannon. Despite what Ménage Eleanor or Madame Hue said, Autumn felt completely at ease.

After a moment of careful evaluation, Lady Cannon sat, and Autumn tried to gracefully follow. "So Miss DeBlue, I know that you are eighteen, that you are from Nebraska, and that you have been caring for yourself for the past year. I have seen from your resume that you have worked at a grocery store for most of your young life and have no other work experience. I also know that you have stated you desired to help someone else as you saw another young lady do for your grandmother. What else can you tell me about yourself?"

Autumn sat in silence trying to think of something else to add. Lady Cannon eyed her suspiciously while she waited. Finally Autumn confessed. "I don't really know Lady Cannon, I mean…my Lady." She blushed as she was unsure what to actually call Lady Cannon, "That seems to really sum up my life, and I can't think of anything else to share."

"Really? Well, then I will have to ask my own questions. Why are you not in school? Being only eighteen you should be in your senior year of high school, enjoying the events and outings such a year brings to a young life. Why did you choose to get your GED and not finish high school?"

That was *not* a question Autumn had prepared for. However, she was used to thinking fast to cover her steps to avoid difficulties with her father. "Well, my Lady, after my mother died and my father no longer cared what I did, school was no longer an option. I had to do something useful with my life." *Might as well make use of those quotes my father was always throwing at me.* "So I opted to take my GED, which I passed with high scores." She was trying to turn what she saw as a negative into a positive.

"Yes, I saw that. Do you like to learn? Did you ever want to go to college?"

"At first I was just focused on living. But recently, before I applied for the position of *companion*, I was considering the Community College there locally. Unfortunately, my initial inquiries were met with roadblocks that seemed impossible."

"But if you were given the opportunity, you would like to get a college education?"

"Yes, my Lady, maybe someday."

"And where did you live while in Nebraska, after your mother died and your father was no longer involved as you say."

"The small farm that my family lived on belonged to my mother. She received it from my grandmother who passed away just six months before my mother. The executor of my mother's will made allowance for me to stay there for as long as I wanted." Autumn did not say that the executor was her father.

"And what happens now. That is, if you stay here with me, what will happen to your mother's farm?"

"I'm not sure, my Lady. I wasn't told the contents of my mother's will, but I do know that as long as my father is still living nothing will be done regarding my mother's land and house. A week after my mother's death I received two things from her and was told that would be all I would get. I assume the executor will probably make other arrangements for the care of the property, but I don't know. I don't see how my mother's farm affects any of my future decisions as the land and house hold no benefit to me."

"What of your things? Surely you had personal possessions. I was told you brought only two small bags with you."

"Yes. I only brought a few changes of clothes as...my Lady...made it clear this meeting was tentative. I really don't have much anyway and what I left behind will be stored for me until I return or send for it." *Actually, I don't know what father will do with my things, he very well may trash them all out of spite. Good thing I already said goodbye to everything I left behind.* Autumn refused to think of the carousel or doll.

"I see." Lady Cannon had not missed the tinge of pain that flashed through the young woman's face at the end of that statement. *I wonder what she is not telling me. What did she leave that would cause her pain?* "Well enough about that for now, I would like to know about your interests. Do you have any hobbies? What do you like to do with your free time?"

This was also not a question Autumn had prepared for. "I honestly have not had much free time between working and living."

"Well, what did you fill your days with?"

"In a usual day, I would wake up at five-thirty to do the farm chores and get ready for work. I walked to the bus stop where I would ride the bus into town. I would work a full day and sometimes take on additional hours for the extra cash it would bring. After work, I would run any errands that I needed to do in town – groceries, household items, things like that – then I would ride the bus back to the stop by my house and walk home. I learned quickly to shop frequently, so I didn't have to haul large quantities of items on the bus. Often, I wouldn't get home 'til late afternoon when I had to do evening chores. By the time I was done, I simply wanted to eat some dinner and go to bed. On my days off, I spent my time taking care of the house, doing laundry and occasionally I would cook up meals in advance for the week so that I wouldn't have so much to do when I got home from work. I really didn't have time for extra activities."

Feeling pity for this young lady who worked so hard so young, Lady Cannon's heart broke. "What about before your mother died? Surely life wasn't as hard before she died, what did you do for enjoyment then?

"Well, my mother was sick for five years before she died. At first, we still had a somewhat normal life, but within the last few years, I pretty much took care of my mother. I was eleven when she first became ill. Whatever interests I may have had, long faded away."

Autumn was starting to feel uncomfortable as her life was very depressing and she really didn't want to talk about all that she had left behind. She wanted to know what was ahead of her. In silence, she stared down at her hands.

Lady Cannon noticed the uneasiness and paused in her questioning. In silence, she simply observed the young lady before her for several heartbeats. "Is there anything you would like to ask me dear Chatelaine?"

At this Autumn looked up. "Um, yes, well...I actually have so many questions I don't know where to start."

Seeing the flicker of interest in Autumn's eyes, Lady Cannon was pleased to simply wait for her questions.

"You don't look sick to me. Why are you looking for a companion? Why do you call me chatelaine if I'm a companion, and what do you expect from me?" Autumn ducked her head to hide the blush from being so bold.

"Those are very good questions." Lady Cannon affirmed and was pleased when Autumn again looked up. "The older I get, the more my health will deteriorate. I was given counsel that I needed to have someone in mind whom I could trust my future health care needs to and someone who could handle the business of my estate when my health does finally give in. I am told that if my illness advances far enough, I may become less than competent to make decisions. Therefore, I determined that I would rather find someone now when I have a sound mind and a capable body than to wait until I am too far gone and someone else is given the ability to pick an incompetent person for me."

Lady Cannon paused and looked Autumn straight in the eye. "Of all the applicants I chose you. My intentions in selecting someone so young are simple. I plan to train you in the ways I prefer to have things done. Since you are so young, you do not have previous knowledge of how to run an estate – everything will be new to you. Hopefully, by the time I am incapable of making my own decisions, your training will be complete, and I will be able to rest assured in the decisions you make because you will have earned my trust."

"With the aid of my legal counsel, we have established a two-step process to test our compatibility. To start off, you will be my companion. As such, you will join me in my interests and activities. You will dine with me and spend time with me talking. We will endeavor to learn about each other and build trust through a relationship. You will be given the respect of the next position under me, though you will have no authority as of yet. That is why I have given you the title of Chatelaine and not Lady."

"I am fully aware that you have no social background, so we will start off slowly training you how to be a lady - one of heart not status. Although your training will include etiquette, manners, and society's protocol as well as dancing, entertaining, literary understanding and the arts, it will also include character training. I would also like to see you pursue a college education. We can discuss in what area of interest another time. It is important for a lady to be educated. You will also be introduced to the general running of my estate though again, you will have no authority to make decisions until farther along in the process."

"When I am confident that you are ready to take the next step, I will formally present you to my friends and associates. At that time, you will go from being my companion to my aide, and your title will be changed to reflect your position. You will be given limited authority and be instructed in the more detailed business of my estate. As you show yourself faithful, you will be given the opportunity to earn more authority and trust. You will not obtain full authority until I am completely incompetent."

Lady Cannon paused to let all that she said sink in. Autumn sat in stone seriousness at the revelation of the magnitude of what was being asked of her. This was no light matter; Lady Cannon was offering her a life beyond what she could ever have hoped for.

"Autumn, I am not offering a grocery store nine-to-five minimum wage job. I am offering you a new life. You will not get paid in monetary sums to perform certain duties for a set time. If you accept my offer, you will agree to a long-term commitment to my estate and to me. A commitment where the benefits of living are the compensation."

"You will become equal with me in my house. Your job will not be complete until my estate is settled at the end of my life. Truly, I am asking for a commitment from you for the duration of my life." Lady Cannon paused. "If you do not think you can commit to the long term, I need to know now. I have very little time in which to find someone willing to stay the course."

In all seriousness, Autumn pondered what Lady Cannon was offering. "If I will not receive any monetary sums for this commitment, then how am I to pay you back for the money you advanced me? And how am I to live or prepare for the day my job is done?"

Lady Cannon was impressed with her attentiveness and desire to know all the details of the arrangement before committing herself to such a weighty task. "In regards to the money I advanced you, your acceptance of my offer will be payment enough."

"As far as how you will live, you will receive everything you need to live and perform your duties as my *companion* provided from my estate. You will have no need to worry about paying for anything as everything from your meals, clothing, healthcare, education, and even social activities will be paid for by my estate for as long as you stay in your position. At the end of my life, you will be given all you have possessed during your time with me, and I will assure you have enough to survive until you find another position. However, if at any time you break your commitment to me, all possessions acquired will remain in my estate and your compensation will only be the training and education you have already received. If a need so arises, I will consider a monthly allowance, although I do not see the need for that at this time."

*That is way more generous than I expected. It seems too good to be true. Why would Lady Cannon give so much to someone she barely knows? Lady Cannon has a lot more at stake in this than I do.* Forgetting about her posture, and everything else Madame Hue had hastily taught her, Autumn threw herself back on the couch with a sudden harsh exhale. "Why such generosity?"

"To promote loyalty, my dear. By giving you so many reasons to say yes, it promotes staying with your commitment as to finding something better down the line. Of course, I would also ask that you sign a contract which outlines the details of your position to protect us both from any unforeseen legal or tax complications."

Autumn sat absorbing what was laid before her. *A new life is what she was seeking. But it was hard to fathom that she was being offered one so extravagant and on a silver platter. Was there a catch she wasn't seeing? A pitfall she could be blinded from? She needed to see it on paper, to be able to pore over the details to make sure she wasn't trapping herself into something she couldn't get out of.* "Can I review the contract and get back to you? Would that be okay?" *I hope she doesn't think me ungrateful.*

"Of course dear, considering the magnitude of the commitment on your part, I would expect nothing less." Lady Cannon stood shakily. "I will have Lord Michaels put the finishing details in the contract immediately although as it is a Sunday, we won't have it until tomorrow morning." She extended her hand to Autumn. "Shall we go get some breakfast?"

And with that, the meeting was over. Autumn followed Lady Cannon to the dining room. At first, Autumn walked on the left of Lady Cannon and then remembering what Madame Hue had said she switched to the right.

With the switch, Lady Cannon smiled to herself.

They were met at the door of the dining room by LeDare Anton. He escorted Lady Cannon to the end of a large oak table while Autumn followed behind. The table had twelve matching oak chairs around it with a hunter green and gold runner down the middle. There were two golden candlesticks each capable of holding three candles, though they did not have candles in them presently. Above the table in the center of the room was a fabulous gold and crystal chandelier. Other gold and crystal sconces were hung at various distances along the walls to illuminate the dining hall.

The room had two large windows facing east. At the center of these windows was a double glass door that led out to a patio. Autumn could see a beautiful yard and garden area just beyond the cobbled patio. The windows were covered with the same type of drapery as was in Autumn's room, only in the deep green with gold trims. Autumn was beginning to realize that every room had a theme and everything within the room was furnished with the same color or style to match that theme.

Autumn also noticed at the far end of the room was an elaborate oak corner hutch with an attached buffet on each side providing for a continuous serving area from one end to the other. The glass front of the upper hutch showed off white china plates, platters and various serving pieces all trimmed in gold. There was a green and gold runner that went the length of the serving area.

LeDare Anton pulled the end chair out for Lady Cannon to be seated and another man in uniform pulled out the chair on her right for Autumn. Autumn watched carefully to assure Lady Cannon was settled before she took her place. After seeing the ladies seated, the man in uniform brought the fine white china plates with gold trim filled with delicacies Autumn had only heard of before. Autumn took a tentative bite of one of the pastries. It melted in her mouth, flooding her taste buds with an almond sweetness. *It would be wonderful to eat like this all the time. Was this the usual breakfast fare or something special because she was here?*

"Is the breakfast satisfactory?"

"Yes, quite delicious." Autumn paused, deliberating how bold to be. *You won't know unless you ask.* Autumn could almost hear her grandmother's words echo in her mind. "Is this what you eat every morning?"

Lady Cannon chuckled softly. "No. Though this is my typical Sunday breakfast or treat as it may be. My weekday breakfast is usually fruit, bagel or muffin, and juice though they come in many varieties." Lady Cannon was pleased that Autumn was getting more comfortable with her. "Though I suppose we will need to add a bit more substance now. I don't need much to keep going these days;

however, I still remember what it was like to be young and need that energy."

Autumn just nodded and took another bite of pastry.

After breakfast Autumn was escorted back to her room by LeDare Anton while Lady Cannon attended to her own affairs. Still being new to the house, Autumn wasn't at all sure she would have found her way without LeDare Anton's help.

Once back in her rooms, Autumn had time to catch up on some sleep and think things through as Lady Cannon would be gone for most of the day. *Why wasn't she given a tour of the house? I suppose I'm still a guest here until I accept the position. What was Lady Cannon doing now? Why hadn't Autumn been invited to go with her? I'm sure everything will become more clear once I sign the contract.*

As Edmund reflected back to the first time he took Sue to the park and sat under a tree with her, tears began to fall down his cheeks. He loved his wife very much. Sometimes the pain of her death was so intense he could barely breathe.

His life had been coming around to near perfection before she got sick. After some rocky early years in their relationship where he forced poor decisions and was so self-focused - trying to find his niche in the world - he had finally found a job he enjoyed and the desire to spend time with his family. Little did he know when he took the insurance job he'd need the flexibility to take care of his sick and dying wife. He could still remember six years ago when he accompanied Sue to the doctor. *Was it really six years ago already?*

After months of struggling with extreme fatigue, and skin that was abnormally pale and bruised easily, they finally decided Sue needed to find out what was going on. The doctor asked all sorts of questions and ran what seemed to be every test available. Finally, the word came back: hemolytic uremic syndrome, probably acquired from some type of *E. coli* infection.

HUS is an extremely rare disease, and it could be life-threatening due to complications with the kidneys, especially if untreated. However, the doctors were optimistic in Sue's case because the diagnosis was made early on. Though the treatment was long and intensive, Sue had a good chance of recovery. Her kidneys had shown no signs of damage, and with treatments starting immediately, hopes were high. There would need to be diligent follow-up care as relapses were common, but there was no indication Sue was at risk for the worse complications.

It took several weeks for the magnitude of what was happening to sink in. Autumn took the news the hardest being only eleven at the time. Sue was utterly exhausted from the constant visits to the doctor and looked sickly from the treatments. When Sue took a leave from her job as a teacher, Autumn seemed to panic and became obsessed with spending time with her. Sue had always hoped to go back to work once the treatments took effect. Still, Autumn interpreted her leave of absence to mean Sue had given up trying.

Edmund had been consumed with taking Sue into town twice a week for the plasma exchange treatments, keeping his job, and trying to manage the small farm they lived on. They had been told the first treatments, though numerous, were vital, and that as time went on, they would become less frequent, so Edmund focused on trying to get through the initial craziness of the diagnosis. Unfortunately, the house and the irrational fears of his daughter were not on his priority list. In fact, with Sue so sick, he insisted Autumn take on the main responsibilities of the house, hoping the two problematic issues would work themselves out.

Looking back, Edmund could now see that in Autumn's irrational way of thinking, she began to harbor resentment toward him way back then. Autumn blamed him for not spending more time at home with her and Sue during those first months. Being a child, she couldn't see that he had to work to pay for the massive medical bills that were accruing. And the resentment deepened each time he forced Autumn to leave her mother to do anything – be it school, chores, or even eating. She was so attached to her mother and paralyzed by fear that any separation was torturous for her.

As the months wore on with treatment after treatment and no obvious improvements in Sue's condition – preventing her from returning to work – Autumn became very sensitive to any change she faced. The extreme irrationality of her behavior irritated Edmund, and he often lost patience with her. Sue tried to bridge the gap encouraging him to breathe deeply before dealing with Autumn and to remember she was just a child, but more times than he would like to admit, he lost control trying to rationalize with her. In his attempt to avoid confrontation, he found himself spending more time working at the office.

What Edmund couldn't see at the time was that Autumn's irrationality was a child's way of coping – though be it through denial. Autumn came to believe that any change would be the end change and so as long as things stayed the same, she wouldn't have to face the change of not having her mother with her. Sue tried to comfort her as well. Still, Autumn was stonily convinced the only way to keep her mother alive was to not change a thing. It became so bad that Autumn refused to go to school. When they finally got her to go, she could not cope with even a substitute. The entire family was grateful when summer vacation finally came because they didn't have to fight to get Autumn to go to school. She could be with Sue all day.

Edmund remembered the one time they managed to convince Autumn they could all go on a family vacation. The doctor had graciously written a note 'prescribing' some relief from the chaos and treatments that ensued upon the discovery of the HUS. They had gone for a week to the YMCA in the mountains; however, when they came home, it was discovered the disease was no longer responding to the previous treatments. They would have to start another form of treatment called platelet transfusion. If that wouldn't have been devastating enough, within a week of this news, Sue's mother was diagnosed with untreatable cancer and only given a couple of years to live.

They tried to keep the news from Autumn for as long as they could. When she finally found out, she wouldn't tolerate a weekend at the lake or even an evening away from the house. Daily life became a prison for Edmund, with no way to escape the pain and burden of a sick wife, mounting bills, and an irrational daughter.

After several months of the platelet transfusions, the doctors thought things were going well, so Sue was put on a maintenance schedule to keep things going in the right direction. Life seemed to get back to a more normal form of living with only a few doctors' visits here and there. This allowed Sue to start teaching again as a substitute, and she gained enough strength which enabled her to take care of her mother as well.

Thankfully, even with her grandmother being ill and deteriorating visibly, Autumn began to relax as she saw her mother living more normally. Edmund was even able to get them to the lake occasionally with the Nelson family, which relieved some of the pressure of bondage on him. As the months progressed, Autumn began to thrive in school again becoming more social and active with friends. It seemed that things were looking up.

Sitting under the tree now as the sun was hitting the horizon in front of him, Edmund shook his head in disbelief. He never seemed to see the storms *before* they came. *Why was it that he was always blindsided by the tragedies of his life? Why could he not see the warning signs, which in hindsight, were blaring their sirens at him?*

Turning his thoughts back in time again, Edmund remembered that Sue had been so happy when Autumn came home and asked if she could be in the school play. Sue had been so eager to see Autumn enjoy her high school years that she volunteered to help with the curtain call – her health wouldn't allow for her to do more, though she was doing well. That was almost two years ago during Autumn's sophomore year.

Two months after play practice began, Sue's mother passed away. Sue coped by throwing herself into settling the estate and play practices. Edmund thought she needed to slow down and tried to convince her that someone else could run the curtain for the play, but

Sue insisted she needed to do this for Autumn. It wasn't long before it became too much and in the midst of rehearsal one evening, Sue collapsed. She was rushed to the hospital, and it was determined that she had an intestinal blockage with her kidneys failing.

Dialysis was started immediately with the intention that the assistance to her kidneys would allow them to start functioning again, yet she had to take it easy. Though Autumn tried to protest, Sue insisted she stay in the play and follow through with her commitments. Edmund didn't know how Sue had convinced her, but Autumn finally agreed with much trepidation.

That was the beginning of the end. Over the next six months, Sue deteriorated rapidly. She was almost unable to see Autumn in the play that she had so strongly insisted on. Finally, on the last night, she mustered up enough strength to go. The stress on her body put her in bed for two weeks, and Autumn grew more unsettled with the passing days, refusing to go back to school, even though the year was almost done. She would not leave her mother's side for more than a few minutes at a time – even sleeping in the same room on a cot – caring for her every need and willing her to get better. But no amount of willing would prevail; Sue's body couldn't take the stress of her failing kidneys, and she passed away with Autumn at her side.

Edmund visually shrunk as he sat remembering that day. He had been at work when Sue died, and he knew Autumn never forgave him for not being there. The wound of his absence was deep - she hadn't even called to tell him when it happened. He found out when he got home that night. Autumn was in the kitchen fixing dinner, as she had grown accustomed to in those last few months; being five years older she was handling the responsibilities of the house with much more maturity. When Edmund asked how Sue was doing, Autumn didn't reply, so he headed into the bedroom to see for himself. He found her lying with her hands gently folded over her body bluish grey and still. The reality of what he was seeing took several minutes to sink in and then he sat weeping for hours. When he finally gathered himself together, he found Autumn robotically cleaning up the dinner that no one had eaten. He had asked Autumn why she hadn't called him, and her reply was, "You didn't care enough to be here, and once she was gone, there was nothing you could do."

The first days after Sue's death, Edmund had been so preoccupied with making arrangements, and processing the discovered secrets of the estate, that he didn't really have time to grieve, let alone think about Autumn. Really, the first few weeks were such a blur that he couldn't even remember who had taken care of her or what she had done. He realized now that this inattentiveness combined with not being there when Sue died, brought back the resentment in full force that started when Sue had first become sick.

Edmund straightened next to the tree as the realization of his neglect for his daughter sank deep into his being. The sickness in the pit of his stomach grew as he grasped the concept that Autumn had first run away only days after Edmund had given Sue's clothes to the local mission store. He remembered they had had a huge fight over it, as Autumn wanted to keep everything right where it was down to Sue's toothbrush. Edmund had thought she was being so childish and berated her for it, saying some very harsh things in his anger and need to bring her into reality – her mother was gone! Now he saw the situation so differently – she **was** a child – a hurting child, that needed her father to help her grieve and understand what was happening. But between his own grief and the issues that they'd had for years, Edmund hadn't been willing to see it. Edmund shuttered in recognition that when Autumn needed him the most to assure her, love her, and give her security, he had been too consumed and preoccupied with selfish tasks and his own grief.

By the time Edmund started to resurface from the blur after Sue's death, Autumn was in full rebellion. Feeling utterly out of control and unable to deal with his unruly teenager, Edmund sank into depression. With the frustration of what he discovered in Sue's will, the grief for a wife he dearly loved, and the rebelliousness of the daughter Sue left him, Edmund's prison returned, and he ignored Autumn completely. It wasn't that Edmund didn't love Autumn, it was the issues of the past that clouded his ability to fully embrace her.

When Autumn began running away, he was tempted to let her go; however, the guilt to honor his wife's dying sentiments urged him to keep pursuing her out of obligation. He could see now that he had been so cold-hearted toward her, Autumn's running away was a cry for help. She was only trying to get the attention he so neglectfully did not give her. Edmund could see it all now: how much she had needed him, how much she had needed to be allowed to be a child, and not forced to be a grown up with so much responsibility.

When she started rebelling, Edmund had forced her to drop out of school and get her GED. She was neglecting her classes anyway and ruining her GPA. The hope of her attending college was diminished as the possibility of her gaining a scholarship had been obliterated with several failed classes. After gaining her GED, even with high scores, he found she milled around the house all day doing nothing particular of value. Therefore, he forced her to get a job.

Unfortunately, this only brought more resentment from her and further rebellion. Trying to gain some ground through tough love, he insisted she paid rent – trying to bring home the concept that nothing is for free and hopefully, earn respect for the things he did provide her. He justified his tough love by putting all the rent money into a savings account for her with the hopes that maybe someday she'd be able to go to college, but she didn't know that.

On top of forcing her to get a job and pay rent, he forced her to work around the house and farm to teach her responsibility. He thought that was the real reason for the rebellion; Sue had spoiled her too much. He also wanted to teach her how to take care of things because someday, if all went well, the land and house would be hers. Because of his discoveries in Sue's will, Edmund had not told Autumn of her inheritance just in case complications arose in the future. Looking back at it all now, he wondered how he could have been so blind to his treatment of her – his only daughter. How terribly he wronged her. *Why had he not seen any of this before; before it was too late?*

The park was now dark, and the little walkway lights illuminated the path back to his truck. Deep in thought, Edmund wondered what he was going to do now. So much had been made clear to him under that tree. The most daunting was that Autumn had been biding her time to make the perfect escape from *him* and the prison *he* had created in his selfishness. What made it even more devastating is that his actions had caused her to unknowingly walk away from the hope of a good future. He now knew more than ever before, if they did not find her soon, that she would be gone forever. And with that, came the burden of what he would do with his wife's dying wishes if he never found their only daughter again.

Worn out and exhausted from the last two days events, Edmund slowly drove back to the small farm he called home. Unfortunately, upon his arrival, he realized that chores still had to be done. He was so accustomed to Autumn doing them, that he barely knew what needed to be done or where Autumn kept things. He managed to finish the chores in about an hour and headed into the house for dinner. Once there, he had to rummage through the cupboards for something edible.

Autumn had taken on making all the meals after Sue died, and she regularly made meals ahead on Sundays. But since she hadn't been there, he had eaten all the meals she had prepared. Sitting down to a cold can of expired ravioli he found stuck in the back of the pantry, Edmund tried not to sink into the depression weighing heavily upon him. *What had he been thinking?* He took Autumn for granted far too much. He had to get a grip on his life. He couldn't live like this, under so much guilt.

The next day, Edmund decided that before pursuing the mall lead, he had to get things at the house under control. Such things like chores, laundry, meals, and even house supplies needed to be addressed in case it was a while before Autumn came back home. He wouldn't let himself think that maybe she never would. These tasks took him most of the morning, and as he walked around grumbling about how inconvenient this was, something unfamiliar inside him checked his attitude. This was exactly what he had forced Autumn to do every day, and she never complained to him about it. Though he could imagine that it was part of the reason she wanted to leave so badly.

During lunch, which he rummaged from the back of the freezer, he made a list of things the house needed so he could get them while in town. Leaving the dirty dishes unrinsed in the sink, he headed off to investigate the mall lead – even though Harper had warned him not to. He soon found that it was a dead end, at least to him – no one would cooperate with him. He went into every store asking if his daughter had worked there and was met with the judgment of being an uninformed deadbeat father from most. Comments like, "If she is your daughter, shouldn't you know where she works?" were way too common. And after last night's revelations, he couldn't disagree with their judgments of him.

Defeated and with no other leads, he returned to the farm after a frustrating trip to the grocery store. *How had Autumn kept everything straight with so many brands to pick from? And the prices? When had food gotten so expensive?*

Once home, he called several friends who worked at places like the bus stations and taxi companies. Still, they had no help for him. He then wrote out all the details that he knew and tried to see if he was missing anything. They were all dead ends. All except the Marcos guy and he couldn't do anything with that one. He would have to leave that trail to the detectives. With another day gone and another inadequate supper – burnt frozen pizza – he headed to bed and collapsed without even checking his messages.

# 12

Edmund awoke at six-forty-five the next morning to his phone ringing. Totally disoriented, it took him several rings to answer. Finally, half asleep and head swimming, he managed to pick up the phone; yet, he still had to try a couple of times to make an audible sound. "H-He-Hello."

"Edmund? It's Lisa. Hey, how are you feeling? If you could make it in at all today, we've got some major issues here that we need you on." There was a pause. "*Can* you make it in today?"

It took Edmund a few minutes to remember who Lisa was and what she was talking about. Being so consumed with finding Autumn the last few days he had totally dismissed his work responsibilities. Lisa was the secretary at the insurance office he worked for. She was saying something about leaving several messages yesterday but never getting him. With nothing left for him to do in finding Autumn, and needing to keep his job, Edmund told her he'd be in though it wouldn't be until nine. He still had to do chores and get cleaned up.

Over the next few days, Edmund had to confess the distraction of work was a welcomed relief. He was able to pour himself into fixing the substantial problems that surfaced in the two days he was away. However, his reprieve was short-lived as soon as he was faced with the difficulty of keeping up with the farm and his job.

The farm had several acres of crop ground that were usually rented out. In line with everything else in Edmund's life crashing, the renters bailed on him after harvest and left the ground needing attention. And though he was still concerned about finding Autumn, these other issues took precedence in his thinking. Besides that, he had been calling the detectives every day for an update, so they had stopped taking his calls. Whenever he called the front desk would simply recite the same message: "We'll let you know if we have any developments."

With so much weighing on him, Edmund decided to see if he could hire a farm manager and not find another renter. He put an ad in the local paper for someone experienced, offering a small salary and a room if desired. After several days with no response at all, Edmund was starting to get worried. He talked to several of his neighbors and friends who were farmers, and they advised him that the benefits were too low for even a farm hand, let alone a manager, and no one took rooms anymore.

He was back to square one. He couldn't afford to offer more, not right now – though he did consider offering a portion of the crop income – he determined that now was not the time to get into a partnership. When he was about to give up hope, he received a call from a young man of twenty-two named James McCurry. James stated he didn't have any experience solely managing a farm, but he had worked for other farmers his whole life – efficiently expressing knowledge of the farming cycles - fertilizing, working the ground, planting, harvesting. Having the time and willingness to do the job and knowing how to run the appropriate equipment was key. However, the most important thing to Edmund at this point was that he was willing to accept the advertised pay.

Furthermore, he shocked Edmund in declaring he wanted the room. When Edmund inquired why, James told him it would be more cost-effective if he lived on the farm instead of traveling back and forth to town every day. So Edmund decided to give the boy a try. *What do I have to lose?*

In finishing their conversation, James asked for a couple of days to tie up some loose ends with his previous job. Edmund didn't mind as that would give him some time to get the basement ready for occupation. Sue had insisted they finish the basement of the farmhouse as guest quarters because one never knew when they would be needed. Edmund guessed she had been right in this. The finished basement would provide James with his own bed, bath, sitting room and entrance. They'd have to share the kitchen, though.

When James arrived two days later, Edmund thought he looked familiar but couldn't place seeing him before. He was a few inches taller than Edmund and had blond hair, brown eyes, and tanned skin. He had very masculine and rugged features as was fitting to a farm hand, yet he was poised and polite. He wore the standard farm attire – a plaid shirt, jeans, and boots. Edmund thought he seemed a bit nervous and as they toured the farm, Edmund watched as James took everything in with wide interested eyes.

James asked many questions, some of them surprising Edmund. "So…umm…who owns this land?"

"I do." Edmund saw no need complicating the issue by explaining his wife's estate to a stranger.

"Did you buy it from the previous owners? I mean…is it a family thing or did you just acquire it?"

"The land was inherited by my deceased wife from her mother. So, yes, it's a family thing."

"Is there someone you plan to pass it on to? Or will it eventually come up for sale?"

Edmund looked at the boy long and hard. *What was the purpose of this line of questioning?*

James sensed the tension. "I'm only asking because I'm looking to put down roots on a piece of my own land, so I can stop working for other people. If you don't have someone to pass it onto, I was wondering if you'd consider working something out with me."

Though Edmund admired the boy's honesty and respected his desire to make his own way, he was also cautioned by this proclamation. "I've got a daughter, Autumn, and she will inherit *everything* once she turns 19."

"Well, that's great that you have a daughter to pass things down to. Does she live here too? Will I get to meet her?"

Again Edmund's suspicions were raised. Not knowing how much to tell this curious and strange young man, Edmund's reply was simple and evasive. "She's not available at this time."

However, this request not only made Edmund uncomfortable, but it also angered something deep inside him. He was angry at Autumn. *She should be here to claim what is rightfully hers.* Then that unfamiliar sense of reason checked him again. *She would have been if* he *had not been so selfish.*

Sensing a sore spot in Edmund and not wanting to rock the boat, James decided to back off the subject of Autumn. He needed to build trust in Edmund and give this new situation a chance to solidify before pressing too hard about the future.

After the tour of the farmland and equipment, Edmund showed James to the basement and his rooms. They discussed the job arrangements and the shared usage of the kitchen. Edmund informed James that he'd try to keep the kitchen stocked, but if he wanted specific items, he was welcome to keep them in the fridge in the basement. And any smoking or chewing must be done outside. James seemed to have no qualms about such rules.

With James hired to take care of the farm, the demands of his insurance job keeping him busy, and trying to get updates from the detectives every few days, the days simply plodded on, turning into weeks.

Then one morning, Edmund was awakened by the phone.

"Mr. DeBlue." The voice on the other end of the line sounded familiar.

"Yes, this is Edmund DeBlue." He sat up in bed trying to place the voice.

"Mr. DeBlue, this is Detective Harper. We need to speak with you. Can you come down to the station right away?"

"What is it? Have you found her? Is she okay? Yes. Yes, I'm on my way." A surge of panic and hope ran through Edmund. He threw on some clothes and headed for the door. Only, as he approached the landing, he found James standing there – disheveled and obviously dressed in haste himself.

In the past few weeks, James had noticed that there was no Autumn around the house. The only people that lived in the house were Edmund and himself, though Edmund kept referring to Autumn as if she had just gone to town for an errand or short trip.

One day, when Edmund was at work, James decided to snoop around the upstairs and found a bedroom that was evidently that of a teenage girl. He also found several pictures of a young girl and a woman who was obviously her mother. James studied these carefully. For James' own reasons he had to determine if this girl, Autumn, was still around and well before he made his true intent for taking this job known. However, getting Edmund to open up and tell him the truth was proving to be very difficult. So, when James heard the phone ring and Edmund's responses – the floor was rather thin and had several vents – James headed upstairs to confront Edmund and see if he could gain any new knowledge.

"Is everything okay, Edmund? I heard a portion of the conversation. Is it your daughter; is she okay?" James saw no reason to keep his eavesdropping a secret; surely Edmund knew how sounds traveled in his own home.

Taken back, and in a hurry to get to the station, Edmund responded without much thought. "I don't know. Autumn has been missing for several weeks now, and the detective just said he needed to speak with me. I have to go!" And with that, Edmund pushed past James and headed out the door.

James stood stunned. *Missing? That was the big secret. Autumn was missing, and Edmund didn't want James to think that the land was up for grabs, so he kept insisting she would be back soon. Either that or he was in denial that Autumn may be gone for good. But what had happened? Why was she missing? Was it foul play or a runaway?* The protective instincts in James began to rise, and he determined that when Edmund got back, he would confront him about this one way or another. There was too much at stake to play innocent for too long.

Arriving at the station, Edmund did not check in at the desk but went straight back to the detectives. When Harper saw him, he stood, though Thornton stayed seated reviewing the document before him.

"Mr. DeBlue, thank you for coming so quickly." Detective Harper was saying as he gestured to the seat by his desk.

"Of course, what is it? Have you found her? Is she alright?" Edmund was beside himself. He wanted to know everything. Now.

"Well, we have been following two possible leads. One is not good, Mr. DeBlue, and the other doesn't look hopeful."

At this, Edmund slumped back in defeat. They hadn't even told him yet, and he knew Autumn was gone for good.

"We felt you should hear what we have found out first hand and then we will need you to confirm, if possible, our latest findings."

"And what are your latest findings?" Edmund didn't really want to know. He did not want to hear this.

Thornton finally spoke. "Mr. DeBlue, we have just discovered the body of a teenage girl dumped in a ravine just three miles from your house. She partly fits the description you gave us; however, we could not fully identify her by the photo. We need you to look at the body and determine if it is your daughter."

A body? A *body*. Edmund couldn't breathe. *This couldn't be happening.* He never expected this – in all his rationalizing and soul searching – he never imagined he'd have to identify his daughter's body! Something pricked inside him – *no, Autumn was not dead, she just ran away. She was coming home again.* Edmund just could not grasp the idea of anything different. After several moments of uninterrupted whirling thoughts battling within him, he sat up completely in control. "What happened, how did she die?"

Thornton and Harper looked at each other and then Harper, who was far more compassionate, answered. "This girl, who still may not be your daughter, had been raped and murdered."

NO! No. No. No! It could not be Autumn. It couldn't be. Edmund was sick to his stomach, and the room began to spin. This could not be happening.

Knowing that this was a difficult time for the man, Thornton and Harper let him sit for several minutes not saying anything. Finally, Thornton spoke up in an uncharacteristically tender tone. "Mr. DeBlue, will you come with us please."

Edmund got up and followed them to the morgue which was housed in a separate yet attached building. Upon entering they approached a table with a body on top covered with a sheet.

"We need you to look carefully and determine if this is your daughter. I know this is not easy, but it is necessary. Take your time and be sure."

Edmund nodded.

"Are you ready?"

Edmund nodded again, swallowing the lump in his throat. *I just might be sick.*

Harper removed the sheet for Edmund to examine the face of the girl.

Edmund looked at the girl on the table for quite a while, struck with relief and pity at the same time. It was obviously *not* Autumn. There were several features different in the girl's face - even her neck was different from Autumn's - and the hair was more blonde. Edmund was certain, and it wasn't just denial. He exhaled in an air of gratitude. "It's not her."

"You are certain?" Thornton asked.

Edmund nodded.

After answering several questions from Thornton, until he was satisfied with Edmund's identification, or lack thereof, they left to go back to the detectives' desks.

"Thank you again for coming and going through that difficult situation. With that door closed in Autumn's case, the only other lead we have at this time is with Marcos." Harper said.

The man identified in the pictures as Marcos L. Delagatos had been found in the United States illegally and was scheduled for deportation to his own country by the end of last month. Upon further investigation, they found that he had fled to Mexico two days after the disappearance of Autumn, and was supposedly with a young woman close to - but not exactly matching - Autumn's description. The young woman was described to be eighteen or nineteen with dark brown hair and a little taller than what Autumn had been described as.

Knowing that hair color could always be changed, and the other details not strong enough to eliminate this possibility, they were pursuing this lead in Autumn's case. Their informant had told them Marcos intended to marry the girl and make a new life somewhere in Mexico. It was not clear if the young woman had wanted to leave or if she was forced to go with Marcos. At this time, neither Marcos nor the young woman, have been located, though they were working with the Mexican authorities and the federal government since a minor could be involved.

Though this was still not good news, Edmund had to agree that this sounded much more likely than the other case. And Edmund was beyond grateful that it had not been Autumn on that table, though a part of him was grieved for whoever's daughter that was.

There were no other leads as to where Autumn would be if she were not with Marcos in Mexico. Basically, the detectives told Edmund that if this lead runs cold, there was nothing more to investigate. Of course, they'd keep the file open for a while longer, but eventually, without new evidence, it would be put in the unsolved files. If Autumn were discovered to be with Marcos, she would be brought back to the U.S., and they would take it one step at a time.

Edmund left the station.

When he arrived home, Edmund was relieved to see that James was not at the house. He called Lisa. "Hey, I won't be coming into the office today."

"Is everything okay? You sound a little shaken."

"I was called into the station early this morning to identify a body. They thought it might have been Autumn. It wasn't her, but I need some time to process all that happened and what they said about her case."

"Of course. I'm thankful it wasn't your daughter, Edmund. We'll see you tomorrow."

With the rest of the day to himself, he plopped down on the couch to think about the options he had ahead of him.

He had about two hours of quiet time before he heard James drive in with the tractor. Hoping James would go onto something else, Edmund lay still on the couch. *Maybe if he doesn't see movement or hear any noise, he won't pursue any questions and just get back to work.*

But that was not to be. When James saw Edmund's car in the driveway, he immediately proceeded to the house, having several hours to work up his courage and plan out his speech.

Entering the house James went straight through the kitchen door as he made his way into the living room. "Edmund? Edmund, are you home?"

Reluctantly sitting up, Edmund turned to James as he approached the couch, "Yes, I am right here."

James jumped back and stumbled a little - his confidence shaken with being startled by Edmund's sudden appearance. However, just one thought of Autumn emboldened him again. "What happened? Is Autumn okay? Where is she?"

Edmund didn't know why - maybe it was a need to talk it through again or just the satisfaction of sharing it with someone else who for whatever reason seemed to care - he felt compelled to tell James everything. Edmund invited James to sit down and told him what he knew. James listened intently to every detail, exhaling deeply when Edmund revealed the dead girl was not Autumn. When Edmund was done telling James the facts of Autumn's disappearance, he went on to confess his new revelations of neglect, guilt, and selfishness. James noted the deep regret and sorrow that he saw in Edmund's eyes and could tell Edmund's heart was being changed.

As Edmund finished, silence fell between the two men, and James sat quietly determining what his next move should be. He had originally thought he'd have to reveal his hand to get Edmund to talk to him, but now, maybe he could keep his secret for a bit longer. At least until they could determine if Autumn would be coming home. Everything was so uncertain, and with the new turn of events, James wondered if Edmund was starting to trust him, maybe even like him. If so, James didn't want to risk any chance of losing the ground he had gained by revealing his hand too early.

With so much to think about, the two men continued to sit in silence, taking in the deeper thoughts that lingered between them.

# ♥ 13 ♥

The next morning, Eleanor did not come to Autumn's room until eight in the morning. Autumn had been alone in her suite for the whole day prior. She had explored the TV remotes, played on the computer, and slept a lot. Meals had been delivered by different staff members, yet Autumn had not seen Eleanor until bedtime. She helped Autumn unbutton the dress and directed her to wear a very comfortable cotton nightgown. Then she disappeared, and Autumn was on her own again.

*I guess when I asked for time to think about it, my request was taken literally.*

It was with great relief when LeDare Anton was at her door two hours later carrying a large manila envelope in his hands. He had an approving smile on his face. "The Lady would ask that you review the enclosed contract and if everything is satisfactory, she will meet you in the Library to sign it."

Autumn took the envelope he offered, and he bowed to her. She thanked him, shut the door and quietly walked over to the desk.

Her hands were shaking as she took the contract out of the envelope and began to pour over it. She found there were a few words she did not understand, and quickly searched them out using the computer. It took her nearly an hour to make sure she understood and agreed to the conditions of the contract. Basically, Lady Cannon was offering to house, clothe, train and educate her in exchange for being a loyal long-term administer of her estate. Put in those terms, Autumn thought she would love the challenge of it. It was a straightforward contract. Autumn could determine nothing to be underhanded or tricky in the wording, and who wouldn't want the opportunity to live like royalty?

So, she gathered up the papers, placed them back in the envelope and headed downstairs to meet with Lady Cannon. As she came out of her room and glanced down the hall into the right wing of the second floor, Autumn thought she saw a little girl hiding behind a statue watching her; however, when she looked harder, she didn't see anything. *Apparently, I'm either seeing things, or there was a trick of the light with the statue.* She shrugged. *Oh well, I don't want to keep Lady Cannon waiting any longer.* As she came down the stairs, LeDare Anton met her and went immediately to inform Lady Cannon that Autumn was waiting in the library.

Autumn entered the familiar room and this time sat down at one of the tables, glancing up at the portrait of the family. *Hmm...I thought I saw a little girl upstairs. I wonder if it could be the same one. That is if I saw a girl at all. No one has said anything about anyone else living here, other than Lady Cannon. If I did see a little girl, she's probably just visiting anyway. We never talked about Lady Cannon's family. I assumed she was all alone or she wouldn't be trying to hire me.*

When Lady Cannon entered, Autumn rose and curtsied, forgetting her previous train of thought. As strange as it was, curtsying to Lady Cannon simply seemed like the correct thing to do. Autumn liked the idea of respecting Lady Cannon by offering her deference. They hadn't known each other long; nevertheless, Autumn felt they somehow shared a connection.

"Well, my dear, what do you think? Is it acceptable?"

"Yes, my Lady. I am ready to sign and accept your generous offer if you are willing to accept me in my humble state." Somehow, Autumn felt empowered, be it through the elegant words of the contract or the confidence that Lady Cannon placed in her, she did not truly know.

"Oh my dear, I am so relieved." Lady Cannon placed her hand over her heart and breathed deeply. "Yes. Yes indeed, I do accept you just as you are." At this, Lady Cannon reached out and embraced Autumn in a show of affection that surprised Autumn as well as warmed a portion of her heart.

"Now dear, should we sign this and get on with things?" They both signed. "I'll have Lord Michaels prepare you an official copy, and it will be delivered to your suite later today."

Once that was done, Lady Cannon wished to discuss Autumn's schedule for the next several weeks. There was so much for Autumn to learn yet she didn't want her to be overwhelmed and have no fun either. It was also Lady Cannon's hopes that she would stay busy enough that she would not notice the Heiress for at least a little while. Lady Cannon wanted to get to know Autumn better before she subjected Heiress Summer to the changes and a new acquaintance.

It was determined that Autumn would have etiquette and protocol lessons every morning from eight to eleven as they were the most critically needed training, to begin with. From one to five every day, she would have various other lessons. On Monday's she would have art classes, computer classes on Tuesdays, literature on Wednesdays, business-estate training on Thursdays and dancing on Fridays.

Breakfast was to be delivered to Autumn's suite each morning, Koka would make those arrangements with Autumn. Lunch and dinner were to be eaten with Lady Cannon in the dining room. Autumn was to dress nicely for dinner as they often had company for evening meals.

After dinner, Autumn would spend time with Lady Cannon until eight when Lady Cannon usually retired. Autumn could then have free time until curfew, which was 10 p.m.

Saturdays would be outing days, where she would do various activities with Lady Cannon depending on weather and interest. On Sundays, Autumn was to attend church with Lady Cannon in the morning; however, after lunch, she was free to do as she pleased until curfew.

"I've never attended church before."

Lady Cannon gave a dismissive wave. "It matters not. Attending church is a mandatory requirement for me. Do you object to this?" *Maybe we should have talked all this through before we signed the contracts. Well, at least if this is going to be an issue, we know now and can shred the signed contract if need be.* Lady Cannon waited anxiously for Autumn's response.

Before Autumn's friendship with Mrs. Bogart, Autumn would have ended the arrangement right there based solely on her father's convictions of Christian people. Now, however, Autumn was curious to see what church was. Mrs. Bogart had invited her several times, but she was never able to figure out how to keep it from her father. At this moment though, he wasn't here, and attending church was mandated by her employer. How life had changed so quickly.

"No, my Lady, I don't object. But I do want you to know that I'm not familiar with what church is."

Lady Cannon nodded in understanding, and they moved on to the next topic.

Lady Cannon felt the need to put a few restrictions on Autumn such as the curfew; where the lights were to be turned out, and she was to be in bed no later than 10 p.m. every night. This would be handled on the honor system unless there was an obvious problem.

Autumn was also restricted from the second floor right wing. "These are my private suites, and I'm not quite ready to share them as of yet. I've got some sensitive memories and precious items that I'd like to share with you in time as we get more acquainted and build trust between us."

This, of course, peeked Autumn's curiosity; nevertheless, in realizing she had her own secrets to keep in her heart, she never entertained the thought of going against Lady Cannon's wishes.

The only other restriction was that Autumn was not to leave the grounds of the house without Lady Cannon's expressed permission - for a time. This was for her safety, as well as, Lady Cannon's reputation.

Autumn felt the schedule and restrictions were acceptable, and Lady Cannon seemed pleased.

When it was lunchtime, the two of them headed to the dining room where LeDare Anton again greeted and escorted the Lady to the table. This time, Autumn simply followed to her place at Lady Cannon's right.

The conversation quickly turned to their afternoon activities for that day as lessons would not start for a few days while preparations were made.

Even though she knew a wardrobe was to be provided, and Madame Hue told her to view it as a uniform of sorts, Autumn was still taken back when Lady Cannon told her they would be shopping for more clothes. Ménage Eleanor had determined that only three of the dresses previously provided would work for Autumn's shape and size, and two of them - including the rose dress she wore yesterday - needed alterations. Therefore, Lady Cannon determined there would be no time like the present to get Autumn fitted with her wardrobe.

But this grieved Autumn enough that she could not refrain from objecting. "Excuse me, my Lady, I don't want to seem unappreciative, but what of all the dresses I already have? Surely we could simply have them altered or something. It seems such a waste to simply discard them." *We could probably feed a third world country for the cost of those dresses. Well, maybe not a whole country, but still, that's a lot of money.*

"Oh dear. Did you think we'd throw the clothes away? Oh, no. No, they will be returned. I have a favorite little store in town that was gracious enough to allow me to borrow various dresses to have on hand for you. No. They will not be discarded at all, that would indeed be very wasteful."

Autumn was relieved by this and so thankful she'd spoken up because now her mind could be at ease.

They were to leave immediately after lunch, and Lady Cannon sent LeDare Anton to summon Master Philip for the car and tell Ménage Eleanor to have the dresses sent down and be ready to accompany them.

At the mention of Master Philip, Autumn perked up in interest as to what was being said.

Lady Cannon did not seem pleased with this indicated interest. "Does something about Master Philip interest you?" She wasn't harsh or judgmental, but Autumn noticed a tone she had not heard before, almost a caution.

"No, my Lady. It was just a familiar name as Master Phillip was the first person I met in Michigan, and I have not seen him since the night I arrived."

"Hmm...that reminds me, I supposed meeting the staff and receiving a tour of the house needs to be the next thing we accomplish. Remind me to tell LeDare Anton upon his arrival that it needs to be done upon our return."

"Yes, my Lady." Autumn felt as if she had done something wrong, though she did not know what. So she did as she always had done at home when she wanted to avoid conflict, she made as little noise as possible to avoid drawing attention to herself.

Lady Cannon went back to her meal and Autumn did the same. She did not have to remind Lady Cannon, for in moments LeDare Anton had re-entered the dining room, and Lady Cannon informed him of her new directive. In moments they were finished with lunch, and LeDare Anton escorted Lady Cannon with Autumn following on the right out the front doors and to the car waiting in the drive.

They rode in silence for quite a while before Lady Cannon spoke. "I wish to explain my tone earlier. I have lost the service of several female staff members to marriage. They fall in love and move away with their husbands. Though I do not begrudge them for finding love and pursuing it, when I saw your interest in the mention of one of my younger and more handsome staff members, I was concerned. Would I invest all this time in you only to lose you as well to a husband? You are a young woman, and I foolishly had not thought of your potential interest in marriage until that moment. And to be honest, it worried me that we had not addressed the issue previously."

*Marriage?* Autumn had not thought of marriage either. Though her parents had been happily married before her mother got sick, seeing how horrible it was to lose the one you committed your life to was too much. Autumn had determined she never wanted to go through that. Marriage had never played into any of her plans for her future.

She let her eyes shift to Master Philip who briefly met her gaze in the rearview mirror indicating his understanding of the conversation. Autumn blushed. She could see how it would be a concern for Lady Cannon. To reassure Lady Cannon this was not an issue of concern, and to end whatever hopes this conversation might bring Master Philip, Autumn made a decision. "Could we add a clause to the contract? Something that indicated that I agree of my own free will to not marry until my position with you has ended?"

Lady Cannon looked shocked. "Why would you want to do such a thing?"

"I have no intention of marrying. Ever. Right now, I am far too young and have no such interest. And later on, I have no desire to give my heart away only to lose those I love. I'm perfectly content without being married."

"Do you *never* wish to marry?"

This question had a sense of sorrow mixed with disbelief, and it confused Autumn. *Wasn't the issue of me getting married the whole point of why Lady Cannon was upset in the first place? Which is it? Is she upset I might marry or upset that I never want to?* Not knowing how to proceed in the conversation, Autumn decided to jest a little and hope for the best. "Why would I want to marry when you are providing me with everything my heart desires - safety, security, and companionship? No. Marriage is not an option for me."

Lady Cannon remained thoughtful, dismissing the jest. "At this time, perhaps, nonetheless, there may be a time in the future when you change your mind and wish you could. I do not want some clause in a contract to cause you to begrudge your service to me later on."

"Yet you do not wish to lose me to marriage either. Surely your lawyer could find a way to word the document to satisfy both sides?"

Lady Canon quietly pondered this suggestion. *It would give her much more guarantee and assurance of Autumn's loyalty, and if she does want to marry, Lady Cannon could possibly help influence her in whom to pick. Still, was this fair to Autumn? Was it the right thing to do?* She needed to pray about it. "I will think about this more and will let you know what I decide."

They rode the rest of the way to their destination in silence.

For the next two hours, Autumn was primped and pranced about in dresses and shoes and accessories. She had never in her life been through so many clothing changes and alterations. It was all exciting and yet very tiresome.

When Lady Cannon had selected at least ten daily dresses which would also work for attending church and several formal gowns all with shoes and accessories, she instructed Autumn to be fitted with new undergarments and sleepwear as well.

To Autumn's bewilderment, she was fitted with bloomers and bodices instead of her usual underwear. She had never imagined such simple garments could feel so wonderful and be so luxurious. The cotton was so soft and flexible it was almost like it wasn't there, yet the ribbons and stretchiness allowed for support. In wearing them, she noticed they made her feel more like a lady and less like a farmhand.

Finally, they were done, and though several of the dresses would need to be altered and delivered later, Master Philip loaded several bags into the trunk of the car.

LeDare Anton met them at the door when they arrived. Autumn would learn later that the gates had an alarm system that notified the kitchen when a car passed through its gates. With help from Master Philip, Ménage Eleanor unloaded the trunk of the car and started putting away the treasures in Autumn's rooms, while LeDare Anton took Autumn to meet the staff and tour the grounds.

Lady Cannon retired upstairs until dinner.

# ♡ 14 ♡

Autumn already knew LeDare Anton, the head of household, Koka Fiona, the cook, Master Philip, the chauffeur, and Ménage Eleanor, her personal attendant. In the kitchen where the staff gathered for various meetings and meals, Autumn met LeMiss Tonya who was LeDare Anton's wife and head of housekeeping and two housemaids whose names she could not remember. Autumn was also introduced to Ménage Deidre and Ménage Becca who were introduced as Lady Cannon's personal attendants. There were also half a dozen kitchen aides, both male and female, that Autumn acknowledged but did not try to retain their names all bearing titles of Porter or Miss. And though she did not get to meet him, Autumn was told that Headmaster Hubert was the gardener and he had three additional hands.

"This is all of the regular staff for the Cannon Estate. On occasion when Lady Cannon entertains, we may bring in additional staff members to assist us. Lady Cannon always addresses us with our titles; however, as we are very much like a family here, some prefer either title or name alone. They will each let you know their preference. I am always LeDare Anton."

Autumn nodded and turned to those gathered around. "Thank you. It is a pleasure to meet each of you, and I hope as time goes by, I will have the opportunity to get to know you all better." Autumn had never had any siblings, and the idea of a large extended family was fascinating to her.

After this, LeDare Anton took Autumn on a tour of the first floor of the house. She had of course seen the dining room and the library and now the kitchen. LeDare Anton showed her where the laundry, the storage, and pantry were off the kitchen and the first-floor staff bathroom which was also located in the kitchen area.

"As you can see, the kitchen is the center hub of the house on the first floor. Though the guests never see it, this is where everything originates."

LeDare Anton led Autumn back out to the main entrance area. "This is the vestibule. It serves three basic needs: a place to wait while the household gathers to leave, a place to visit during gala events, and as a meeting place for those that stop in whom the Lady does not wish to make comfortable." This last statement was said with a gleeful smirk.

Autumn couldn't help but chuckle. "Are there many visitors that Lady Cannon doesn't wish to make comfortable?"

"Not as many now as there were in the early days after Lord Cannon passed on. The vultures were thick then."

Autumn nodded in some understanding as she remembered various people stopping by after her mother died asking about the land, and she had felt the same way about some of them. *I guess I know now why the entrance has a fireplace and couches. And why it's so large. I wonder what it will look like at Christmas? It would be gorgeous with red ribbons and white twinkle lights.* Autumn shook her head, what in the world made her think of Christmas now?

Dismissing her wayward thoughts, Autumn followed LeDare Anton into the next room. She stopped in mid-step, and her jaw dropped. It was a magnificent ballroom. It was a huge room with a wooden floor and three chandeliers - one central one with two accented smaller ones that matched what was in the dining hall. There were only two windows on the west side and a large window facing the front of the house. The colors in this room matched those of the dining hall only with more gold than green. At the far end were two luxurious guest bathrooms to accommodate the needs of those being entertained. In the outside corner of the hall was a slightly raised platform with a grand piano and space for various other instruments. However, what caught Autumn's eye were the wooden benches scattered all along the walls. They had ornately carved arms and feet, yet still had plush covered sitting areas. She couldn't help but try one out just to see what they were like.

LeDare Anton tried to hide his smile, though Autumn saw it. Strangely, she didn't feel self-conscious at her curiosity. Lady Cannon accepted her just as she was and so everyone else didn't seem to matter.

After viewing the ballroom, LeDare Anton took Autumn up to the west wing on the second floor to show her the various other suites in her wing. There were six suites in total; two larger suites, one of which was hers, and four smaller suites where the bathrooms and walk-in closets were combined. The main rooms of the smaller suites also seemed smaller and did not contain the raised desk areas or the same amount of furnishings. Yet, each room had its own color theme: Plum, Burgundy, Deep Sage, Royal Blue, Biscotti, and Wild Berry.

Though she knew she couldn't enter the east wing, she couldn't help but ask LeDare Anton a bit about it. "Are there the same number of suites in the east wing?"

"No. The east wing only has three suites."

"And Lady Cannon is the only one who lives over there?"

LeDare Anton lifted his eyebrows at that question, as if it were impertinent. "The east wing has ALWAYS been the family wing."

And with that, the conversation was closed as he led her to the stairs at the far end of the hall.

The third floor was split into two areas by a door in the central hall. The rooms on the west were for guests. Autumn noticed that the guest rooms did not have theme colors like the suites on the second floor. They were all decorated with a warm neutral hue and had only accents of color. There were twelve guest rooms each containing a private bath that reminded Autumn of a very nice hotel.

The rooms on the east were reserved for the staff members who lived on the estate. Several of the household staff drove into work each day, though a few chose to live upstairs. There were two larger rooms with private baths for LeDare Anton and Tonya - being married - and Koka Fiona. Then there were twelve smaller rooms - which reminded Autumn of the college dorms she had seen when she visited the campus last year that consisted of two rooms sharing one bathroom.

"The south staff rooms used to be reserved for the men and the north was for the women. This is basically true today, except Ménage Deidre, who wanted a room of her own - and my wife. And because we don't require everyone to stay on the estate like in the olden days, Master Philip, Ménage Becca, and Ménage Eleanor don't have to share their bathrooms. Times have changed considerably in what is required of a household staff member; nevertheless, it would be a shame to let all these rooms go unoccupied. So Lady Cannon gives every staff member an incentive to live here, though several have chosen otherwise for their own reasons."

"That makes sense. Does the gardener and his helpers all live off the estate?"

"No. Headmaster Hubert stays in the Garden House, although all of his hands do live off grounds."

LeDare Anton took Autumn back downstairs and out the front doors. Briefly, he showed her the large patio off the dining hall and the gardens beyond. There were actually three gardens. LeDare Anton said she'd have time later to explore them more fully on her own and so he just brushed past the paths that led to them. He then showed her where the orchard and pond paths were and emphasized that the pond was not for swimming, though they did have a paddle boat.

By the time they finished the tour, there was only a little time left for Autumn to catch her breath and freshen up before she needed to rejoin Lady Cannon in the dining hall.

As she entered her great room, she threw herself down on one of the couches and heaved a huge sigh. *It has been quite a full day. I never knew shopping and touring a house could be so exhausting. I wonder if the other staff members will resent having to listen to someone much younger than most of them? Especially one who obviously has more privileges than they do. I'm going to have to be very mindful not to get conceited.*

Her thoughts were interrupted by a crash and muttering coming from her closet. Autumn had not noticed Eleanor was still putting things away when she had entered earlier. Getting up to see what had caused the crash, Autumn discovered Eleanor on the floor frantically picking up accessories from a fallen drawer. Autumn rushed over to help her out.

"Oh no, Chatelaine, please, you do not need to help me. You should be getting ready for dinner."

"Nonsense, if we both work at it, it will get done quicker." Autumn gathered her skirts and knelt down to help. Eleanor just stared at her in awe for a few moments before going back to the mess she had made. They worked companionably for a time until Autumn decided to venture the question that she had been mulling over. "Eleanor, do you despise me?"

"Despise you? Oh no, Chatelaine. Why would I despise you?" Eleanor was clearly surprised by such a thought.

"Oh, I thought maybe you and the others might because Lady Cannon, or…the Lady put me here in this nice room and you are all on the third floor sharing bathrooms. Not that your rooms aren't nice, but they aren't the suites either. And compared to most of you, I'm really young. I don't want anyone to hate me or begrudge me being here."

Eleanor chuckled. "No one will despise you. Lady Cannon offered your position to most of us before she started looking for you. No one wanted the magnitude of responsibility you will carry. Plus, we all still have our freedom."

Autumn was taken aback by this statement. *What did she mean by that?* "You don't think I am free? That's strange to me because I feel freer now than I've felt in my entire life. Can you explain why you see my position as so restrictive?"

Eleanor shrugged unconvincingly. "We get paid a wage to perform a duty. We are not under contract and at any time that we *want* to move on or try something else, we are free to quit our job or marry whomever we'd like, and it doesn't affect anyone's life but our own. The Lady treats us well, and for the most part no one wants to leave; however, we wouldn't trade our *choice* to do so no matter how good we had it. No. No one will despise you for your luxuries knowing what you are choosing to give up to have them."

They finished picking up, and Eleanor looked at the clock. "You'd better be getting downstairs now, Chatelaine."

Autumn nodded and rose, pondering what Eleanor had said. *I don't think I agree, but I'll tuck it away to ponder later. Maybe there is something there I'm not getting right now. To me, I'm gaining so much more than I'm supposedly giving up.*

Before she left, Autumn turned back toward Eleanor. "Eleanor? I know you were assigned to serve me and maybe for you it's just a job, but I hope we can become more than that, I hope we can be friends."

Eleanor nodded. "I think that would be nice."

Autumn turned and hurried down the stairs to the dining hall.

The next few weeks were a flurry of lessons and learning. Madame Hue was impressed with how much Autumn retained in the etiquette she taught and even the monotony of the protocol. Autumn absorbed it like a sponge, and even Lady Cannon started noticing differences in her actions.

Lady Cannon had hired special instructors for the dancing, literature and art lessons. Autumn found literature to be boring, and she didn't really understand the interpretation portions of the art classes, although the drawing was fun. But dancing...she *loved* the dancing.

Autumn didn't need the extensive computer lessons Lady Cannon had originally planned because once the system had been explained to her, she excelled at understanding them. Computers seemed to come naturally to her. Therefore, the business-estate classes were increased to two times a week which sped things along much faster. Though some of the material was very dry and boring the instructor, Madame Tanner, made it fun by giving Autumn mock estate's to manage using real data. Autumn quickly learned what she could do with the resources that would eventually be given to her to manage.

Through all the courses, Autumn couldn't help but notice all her tutors were women. *I wonder if that has anything to do with the fact that Lady Cannon has not mentioned the marriage clause again. Maybe she's still concerned that if I have a chance to meet a man, I'll be tempted away.* Since she was growing more familiar and comfortable with the Lady, Autumn decided to casually bring it up in their next conversation -which was at lunch.

"My Lady, may I ask a question?"

"Absolutely, dear. What is on your mind?" Lady Cannon delicately picked through her salad looking for the craisins and oranges.

Autumn smiled. *She always eats the fruit first then finished with the spinach. I wonder why she doesn't just ask for the fruit?* Bringing her thoughts back to the issue she wanted to discuss, Autumn took a deep breath. "I can't help noticing all my tutors are women. Is that because you are still concerned about me marrying someday? Because, if it is, I am still very willing to add a clause to our contract."

Lady Cannon looked up in surprise. "Oh no, dear. That is not why all your tutors are women. I chose most of them because they are associates of mine; however, I do find that the best way to avoid temptation is to simply remove it from being present."

Lady Cannon was silent for a while. Autumn waited as she sensed Lady Cannon was deliberating something.

"My dear, I am not certain what to do regarding the marriage clause you suggested. I...I want to be fair to you, and I am not convinced a clause would be binding anyway. Nevertheless, it would give me comfort to know that your commitment lies with me and not that of the whims of a teenage heart."

"Have you spoken to your lawyer? What does he say?"

"I confess I have not spoken to him. Are you really certain you'd like me to pursue this?"

"Yes. I have never met a man who could hold my interest for very long, and as I said, I determined long ago I did not want to put my heart out there." Putting her hand over Lady Cannon's, she met her eyes. "I truly am content being your companion. You have given me so much. And even if I met a man tomorrow, I would not leave you for him. I'm committed to you."

Lady Cannon was so moved, tears came to her eyes. Though she still doubted what the right thing to do was, she nodded in agreement to talk to Lord Michaels.

They sat companionably in silence, each lost in their own thoughts. Unexpectedly, Autumn asked. "My Lady, may I inquire why you bestow titles on those around you?"

Lady Cannon looked to her in surprise - it seemed so disconnected from their previous conversation. Yet, she realized she had never shared her reasoning and thought now was as good as any. "Years ago when the Cannon estate was first growing, my husband, Thomas, wanted to hire staff members. We had never had staff members before, and honestly, I was not impressed with what I saw in others who had them.

"As you know by now, I am a strong believer in God and talk to Him on a regular basis. I wrestled with the idea of staff members for several weeks, every day getting on my knees in our bedroom before my heavenly Father. I sought His direction regarding this, as I questioned how we could have staff members and honor Him at the same time.

"As I prayed, God began to move deep within my heart. He first recalled to my mind a scripture in Daniel that says: *'He changes times and seasons; he sets up kings and deposes them. He gives wisdom to the wise and knowledge to the discerning.'* I determined from this that God was changing the season of my life to incorporate servants as He had blessed us with wealth. Still, my heart grieved as I saw so many around me who had been trapped in the lure of self-righteousness and pride - I did not want that for my future and legacy.

"A few days later, a phrase began running through my mind – it was not a whole verse – just a phrase: *the LORD bestows favor and honor.* It kept repeating in my mind, perplexing me as to why I would recall just that phrase. Later that day, I was working in my study, and I found a scrap of paper with 1 Peter 3:5-6 written on it. *'For in this way, in former times the holy women also, who hoped in God, used to adorn themselves, being submissive to their own husbands; just as Sarah obeyed Abraham, calling him lord...'*

"When I read that verse and placed it with the phrase ringing in my mind, I garnered God was directing me to be submissive and obey Thomas. Even in his desire to have servants; yet more than that, I was stirred deep in my heart by the phrase *calling him lord*. Sarah, of the Bible, called her husband, Abraham, lord or master. I mulled this over in my mind for days trying to decipher what it meant to me. I concluded it would bestow a great honor on my husband to call him Lord of our house and would remind me to remain submissive to his leadership. Therefore, I resolved, to call Thomas, Lord Cannon, out of submission to his God-given authority.

"I felt this resolved the issue of self-righteousness as I would constantly be reminded to be submissive. Still, I struggled with how to keep from falling into the pit of pride at having servants under me – taking them for granted - which I saw so many of our associates did. A few days later, I was casually looking through my Bible – I wanted to read, yet didn't have a direction as to where. Turning the pages, I stopped on Isaiah 45; I read the whole chapter, though verses four through six jumped off the page at me."

Lady Cannon slowly rose to retrieve a Bible. Autumn had noticed that there were few places that Lady Cannon went where she did not have one close by. Turning to the appropriate page, she read:

❖ *4 For the sake of Jacob, my servant,*
*of Israel my chosen,*
*I summon you by name*
*and bestow on you a title of honor,*
*though you do not acknowledge me.*

❖ *5 I am the LORD, and there is no other;*
*apart from me, there is no God.*
*I will strengthen you,*
*though you have not acknowledged me,*

❖    *6 so that from the rising of the sun*
     *to the place of its setting*
     *men may know there is none besides me.*
     *I am the LORD, and there is no other.*

"Did you notice in verse four that God *summons you by name and bestows on you a title of honor?*" She glanced at Autumn who had an intrigued expression on her face.

"I genuinely revere God's word and desire to never take it out of context, so I fully acknowledge that this passage is not directly speaking to my issue of servants. Yet, it did stir within me an audacious idea – what if I bestowed titles of honor to those in my house? I will never claim God instructed me to do this. Still, I do believe the idea is pleasing to Him. And I have found it to be a way to keep from falling into the pit of pride – for each person is special and not to be taken for granted."

Autumn was in awe that Lady Cannon would be so bold as to implement such an idea. "How did you become Lady then?" It seemed highly unlikely that Lady Cannon would be so proud as to declare herself a title.

Lady Cannon smiled fondly. "That was my dear Thomas' idea. He insisted if he was to be Lord of the house, then I was to be Lady of the same. The first titles bestowed upon us."

*Of course, what other title would Lady Cannon have?*

"As the years went on, whenever someone gained favor with my husband or myself – be it a friend or business associate - they were given a title of honor. Usually, the title was of 'lord' or 'lady,' though some requested a different title like Madame Hue. All these titles were used while they were within our house or when we associated with them, even in public. We soon found that even the slightest title gave people a feeling of respect. And those who received titles related more amiably to each other and became more dependable. We saw this happen from the lowest servant to the highest of society."

"But, aren't those titles already used by those in current society circles? If the estate was growing, wouldn't you have achieved those titles anyway?"

Lady Cannon shook her head. "Back when we started bestowing titles, they were not commonly used by society here. And as you know, there are few places across the country where titles are used even in today's society."

Autumn looked at her in disbelief. "So you started all this?"

"Oh, heavens no. I would never want to take responsibility for how society has taken something meant for honor and turned it into another ladder climbing, status seeking classification."

Still not fully understanding, Autumn persisted. "So how did current society come to use the titles then?"

"Several of the highest in society saw how the use of titles affected us by giving us favor in return and decided to follow suit. For some, they wanted to incorporate the honor system we had established. Unfortunately, there were those that wanted the benefits of bestowing titles for selfish gain and the status it gave them. Therefore, the purpose of using titles to bestow honor and doing so with God in mind was forgotten over the years, and they often excluded their servants. Still, in this house, titles are only given or honored in conjunction with our original purpose. Someone may have a title in society, yet I do not always acknowledge them as such, just as society does not always acknowledge my titles – such as my lawyer, Lord Michaels."

Autumn nodded. *I guess that all makes sense. Though, it is amazing that one lady could start something that would end up impacting so many people. Despite what she says, it sure seems that what Lady Cannon implemented impacted society. I never thought one person could make a difference.*

The next day Autumn was surprised to have her morning protocol lesson interrupted by Lady Cannon herself.

"Lord Michaels sent this over this morning. I've looked it over, and I cannot argue against what it says; however, I'd like to hear your thoughts on it before we proceed." Lady Cannon looked grieved.

Autumn reverently took the envelope Lady Cannon offered her and removed the document inside. As she had done before, Autumn took it to her desk to read while Lady Cannon sat and talked with Madame Hue.

The document read:

**AMENDMENT TO CONTRACT OF COMMITMENT**

**AS OF** the below signed date, the **CONTRACT OF COMMITMENT** between the following parties:

**LADY DORIS CANNON**, Principal Party,

and

**AUTUMN DEBLUE**, Minor Party,

will be amended.

**THE FOLLOWING** section titled "**MARRIAGE AGREEMENT**" will be added to the original contract as follows:

In regards to the marital and relational state of the above mentioned Minor Party, the Minor Party has requested this Amendment, and it is entered into of her own free will.

It is therefore agreed between the Principal and Minor Party that the Minor Party will abstain from pursuing or engaging in any relationship for the duration of her service to the Principal party without the express consent and an Amended Approval of Exception from the Principal Party. If the Principal Party is not able to give consent due to her health, the Minor Party agrees to notify the law offices of Michaels, Douglas, and Thompson and wait six (6) months after that before engaging in any such relationship or risk breach of contract as stated below.

It is agreed upon by both Parties, that should the Minor Party decide to pursue or engage in a relationship without the express consent and approval of the Principal party, the Minor Party will pay back a portion of the investment of the Principal Party in monetary sums of fifty thousand dollars ($50,000.00). To be paid through the law firm of Michaels, Douglas, and Thompson as penalty and breach of contract.

**THESE CHANGES** are the only changes to the original contract. The entire remainder of the original contract remains in full force. This Amendment shall be immediately in effect upon signatures of both parties below.

*Fifty Thousand Dollars! Whoa, that is a lot of money. Good thing I don't plan on breaching this contract because there is no way I could come up with that kind of money. But, I can see that there has to be some consequence, and that is a good one.* Autumn looked over to see Lady Cannon watching her.

"I'm ready to sign. I have no problems with adding this to our current contract."

"Are you certain? You do not have to sign this, dear."

"I'm certain. Besides, you left me a loophole I didn't ask for."

Lady Cannon nodded, and both parties signed the document.

Weeks soon turned into months and Autumn was thriving. Madame Hue had stopped her lessons, and in her free morning time, Autumn accompanied Lady Cannon to her appointments and on more of her outings. They were growing closer together, and Autumn started seeing Lady Cannon in more of a grandmotherly role than as an employer. Autumn could even say she was starting to trust and admire Lady Cannon in ways she never thought possible. She wasn't sure she *loved* Lady Cannon; however, she was getting attached to her.

Autumn had been attending church with Lady Cannon faithfully as was mandated and was finding that she enjoyed it. At first, Autumn's curiosity was almost a distraction. She watched everything with such great intent, yet as she learned more of the etiquette and appropriate behavior of a lady, Autumn actually started paying attention to what was being said up front. She even began recognizing some of the songs and singing along with them.

*Was it this Jesus they believed in and talked about what gave people like Mrs. Bogart and Lady Cannon such peace and joy in life? Was having assurance in Christ something that could really make a difference in how a person lived?* These were just a few of the questions that started surfacing in Autumn's idle times.

Lady Cannon was pleased with Autumn's progress and ability to learn quickly. And she felt that their friendship had developed nicely. Lady Cannon was positive that attending church each week had opened Autumn's eyes to new truths and wisdom, and she prayed daily for Autumn's salvation.

Yet even as their relationship deepened, they each held their secrets close.

Lady Cannon could not believe that Autumn had been with them for six months now. Autumn had embraced all of Lady Cannon's eccentric standards with zeal and seemed to truly enjoy her new skills and talents. And as Lady Cannon pondered the road ahead of them, she felt it was time to take their relationship to the next level. Unfortunately, she hesitated because even though they had broken through so many walls, and Autumn had grown by leaps and bounds, Lady Cannon knew Autumn was still hiding something, and she wasn't sure if their relationship could survive the revelation of the secrets they each kept.

One day while Lady Cannon was in her prayer room seeking God for direction, she heard her Heavenly Father gently reprimand her.

*How can you expect Autumn to trust you if you do not trust her? You are holding on to your own secrets and hiding the truth from her behind your own walls. Until you are willing to let go and give Me full control of the future neither your walls nor hers will ever fully come down.*

With that still fresh in her mind, Lady Cannon went to make new arrangements.

# 15

Lady Cannon had spoken to her granddaughter about Autumn frequently when she visited with her. Therefore, Summer knew Autumn was hopefully, going to be the one to help them out when Lady Cannon could no longer oversee things on her own. And though Summer knew about Autumn, the reverse was not true.

Lady Cannon was sure that Autumn had suspicions about what happened in the east wing though she never said anything, nor asked any questions. At first, Autumn had been so busy with lessons and training that Summer wasn't very restricted; nevertheless, as Autumn gained more freedom, Summer was more confined.

Now the time had come for them to meet and Lady Cannon was nervous that Autumn would feel betrayed. *Would this set them back to mistrust and closed-off hearts? Would Autumn try to leave? Would she understand?*

Lady Cannon gathered all her thoughts and decided it was time to see what God had in store for all three of them. What happened next would be the true test of Autumn's loyalty, and determine whether or not she was ready to start handling some of the authority that Lady Cannon needed her to take on. Though she liked Autumn very much, Lady Cannon wished she had more time with her.

As Autumn came down the stairs for breakfast one morning, she heard childish laughter coming from the dining hall. Her curiosity was peaked, and she slowly approached the doors to look in unnoticed. There sitting in Autumn's chair to the right of Lady Cannon was a young girl of about five. Autumn immediately recognized her from the painting in the study though she was years older now. Autumn had also thought she had seen her in the east wing a few times though not being allowed to go there could never be sure. Autumn had pondered this and never understood why Lady Cannon would want to hide this little girl from her.

In the months since she had joined Lady Cannon, Autumn had learned that the seat to Lady Cannon's right was one of privilege and honor. When guests came to visit Lady Cannon, Autumn was often moved to the left or further down the table depending on how many guests were present and who they were. So it should not have bothered Autumn to see this little girl in her seat, but it did, greatly.

She hadn't stood there long before LeDare Anton noticed her and gestured her to enter. LeDare Anton always announced those entering the hall after Lady Cannon had already been seated which gave Autumn great motivation to make sure she was early to meals especially when guests were present. However, no one had told Autumn they had a guest this morning, so as Autumn entered, LeDare Anton announced her.

"Chatelaine Autumn, my Lady."

Lady Cannon looked over and rose to greet Autumn with a hug and kiss on the cheek, something they had recently started. "Good morning my dear, how did you sleep?" Lady Cannon asked as if nothing was amiss.

"Well, my Lady, and you?" Autumn's response was automatic as her mind was whirling and her eyes were on the child in *her* seat. *Why am I so jealous of this little girl? I don't even know anything about her. Yet, I still feel threatened somehow.*

"Very well, thank you. Ah dear, may I introduce you to *Heiress* Summer Cannon." Lady Cannon turned and gestured to the girl. "My granddaughter."

Summer stopped giggling and cautiously scrutinized Autumn. It would have been proper for Summer to stand or even nod in acknowledgment of the introduction, however, she didn't. Autumn was certain it was intentional.

*If Lady Cannon put all this effort to teach me - a stranger - about her standards, I'm certain she would teach her granddaughter.*

Still, Summer sat there with a stern look in her eye judging Autumn. So Autumn - forgetting her training - sized up the Heiress in return. Lady Cannon stood there in utter anxiety at the tension between them.

Finally, Autumn remembered herself and gave a slight curtsy. "Welcome to our table Heiress Summer." Then she moved to the place that had been set for her to the *left* and waited for Lady Cannon to be seated again.

Summer continued to eye Autumn as she sat and was served breakfast. The rest of the breakfast conversation was thick and restrained with Lady Cannon not explaining anything of Heiress Summer's sudden presence or introduction.

After breakfast, Lady Cannon directed the Heiress to her suites and requested Autumn join her for a walk in the garden. Though fall was in the air, it was still nice enough to enjoy the fall flowers with a light coat. As they exited the dining hall, Lady Cannon expressed how she would miss getting outdoors once the cold set in, and then they walked in silence.

Within minutes of walking with Lady Cannon, Autumn's defenses let down, and she felt more like herself, the self that had grown to love this woman like a grandmother.

*Yes, she did love her. Maybe that was it. That was why she was so hurt and bothered by the sudden appearance of an unknown granddaughter. Summer's presence puts into question the security I've found in my position with Lady Cannon. To me, Summer threatens the bond we have formed. Also, I don't want to share Lady Cannon with anyone else. Yet, if there is anything that I've learned about Lady Cannon, it is that she is fair and has a large heart. She is fully capable of spreading her love and attention around, even if it means shared time with Summer now.*

With this revelation, Autumn was the first to speak. "My Lady, I need to apologize for the way I greeted your granddaughter and for my behavior in the dining hall. I must confess I was jealous and fearful of losing your attention and affection. It was childish and foolish of me, can you forgive me?"

*Ah, the truth.* Coming from Autumn, this truth showed she was maturing and yet still vulnerable. "Yes dear, of course, I can forgive you, though you must know and understand that everything I do and have done over the last year has been for the benefit of my granddaughter. She is my heir and first priority. Things are about to change for us."

These words stung. Though Autumn should have known Lady Cannon's actions over the last few months had not been for her benefit alone, to hear the truth spoken so bluntly hurt deeply. Deep inside, Autumn felt a small voice she was not accustomed to, whisper to her heart that she was facing a choice. She could embrace this pain and accept what Lady Cannon had for her - whatever it was - or she could turn her heart away and lose the good things she had gained with Lady Cannon. Autumn knew the right answer, yet struggled with being afraid: afraid of the pain and of what it meant.

As Autumn was working through these things, Lady Cannon found a bench and sat down, patting the spot beside her. "Let me tell you about my granddaughter." And with that, Lady Cannon told Autumn of her only son Brian, his marriage to Vivian, the struggles they had trying to have a baby and the joy of the arrival of Summer. She told Autumn of the car accident and the terror that overtook her granddaughter.

With the need to be completely honest with Autumn, she even ventured into Lord Cannon's will and the need for a guardian for the Heiress so that her inheritance would be secured and she would not be taken as a ward of the state upon Lady Cannon's death. If a guardian were not found, Heiress Summer would lose everything her father and grandfather had worked for. When she was done revealing everything to Autumn, she sat still with tears in her eyes waiting and praying.

Autumn took in the entirety of what Lady Cannon told her and marveled at the bareness of the heart before her. *What a gift this is, this trust.* She now understood the restriction of the east wing. Lady Cannon felt she had to protect her granddaughter until she could be sure Autumn was the one to take over the reins. Autumn was also in awe at the thought that Lady Cannon planned to entrust one of the most precious things in her life to the care of Autumn. *She must trust me greatly.*

And yet, Autumn was hurt. She thought she could trust these people and that she had become a part of their family. Instead, they had kept a huge secret from her. Not only Lady Cannon, but Ménage Eleanor and the entire household staff. *How could she ever trust what any of them said again? They had all lied to her - though mostly through omission and most from a sense of duty to their employer - still, they had lied for the last six months?*

With this hurt in her heart that felt very vulnerable now and in the protection of that same heart from potential other lies, Autumn summarized what she had heard from Lady Cannon rather harshly. In doing so, she constructed a thin layer of hardness between them. "So, you hired me, trained me, and spent all the efforts trying to make me a lady, building trust in me not to be your *companion* after all. You did all of this so that you could test me to see if I would pass for an appointment as Heiress Summer's guardian. Thus enabling you to die with a clear conscious knowing your granddaughter would be taken care of?"

With the situation cast in such a light upon the lies she had been living; and the probability that she had just alienated the trust she had built in Autumn; Lady Cannon stared straight ahead as her shoulders slumped just slightly under the weight of her burden. "Yes."

Seeing the visible toll of what Lady Cannon said weighing down on her and remembering that little voice that said she had a choice to make, Autumn changed her tone. "You must love your granddaughter very much to go to such extremes for her."

Lady Cannon met Autumn's eyes. "I would die for her if it would help her, instead, I have been asked to live, that is until I can prepare you."

"Are you so sure *I* am the right one for this appointment? What are you going to do now, just give up and die instead of fight to live? Surely you do not think now is the time for me to take over. I am not ready! And *you* are not ready to die. So why have you chosen now to expose this farce we've been living?" Autumn didn't mean for her tone to change towards the end; nevertheless, the hurt and anger inside of her demanded some ventilation.

The harshness of the words mixed with Autumn's baldness caused Lady Cannon to look at her sharply. "Indeed you are not ready." Then she softened her tone. "And neither am I." Exhaling, as if in defeat, she sat quietly for a moment. "Nonetheless, now **is** the time to see how you and Heiress Summer get along. She can be quite the handful, and I am getting worn out trying to care for her myself. I apologize for the deception; it was the only way I knew how to be certain of your intent, character, and loyalty. Nevertheless, I acknowledge it was unfair to you, and I sincerely ask you to forgive me for deceiving you in my purpose. Still, I need your help. I need your youth. And more importantly, I need Heiress Summer to trust you and you to trust me."

That last statement struck Autumn deep within. *Did she trust Lady Cannon? And if so, how much? Enough to tell her about her father or what she left behind in Nebraska? No, I'm not ready for that; however, I do trust Lady Cannon. I trust her to know what was best for her granddaughter and even for myself. Furthermore, I know Lady Cannon trusts God and that she would let Him guide her and lead her. Even more importantly, I'm beginning to understand that even though I do not know this God of Lady Cannon's, I have seen Him work enough now in Lady Cannon's life to know that He is trustworthy. So, if Lady Cannon says this is the time, I will do what Lady Cannon requested.*

After several minutes of contemplation on the issue of trust, Autumn turned to Lady Cannon, bowed her head in respect and submission. "I do trust you in this and acknowledge the goodness of your heart in all you have done to this point. I acknowledge I was harsh in my words and tone, will you forgive that as well? What is it that you require of me in this new endeavor? And if I may, how does this change our previous contract?"

Lady Cannon noted the acknowledgment of trust in *this* issue, though not sensing the time to push trust in *all* issues, she addressed the question. "The contract was written with this transition in mind. Your service is still to me, not Heiress Summer. The way the contract is worded my turning over the estate to you, even on behalf of the Heiress, is covered under the current contract."

Autumn made a mental note to look back through the contract in light of this new information.

Lady Cannon continued. "As far as what is required of you now, since your lessons have nearly ended in all things except the business-estate lessons, you will start spending your new available time with Heiress Summer instead of with me."

Autumn visibly shrunk in defeat. She loved their times together and did not want to give them up.

"We will still have our Saturday afternoons to ourselves and in the evenings after Heiress Summer is in bed. I would miss our times together dreadfully if we did not still have some of them, though we may need to be more flexible as to when they occur. And of course, you will still join me in church on Sundays as usual. You will also maintain your current free times, as I am sure you will need time to yourself."

Autumn felt some relief in knowing that she would still have some time with Lady Cannon, even though it was a drastic cut in that time.

"Your focus now will be trying to build trust with Heiress Summer. I have spoken with Madame Tanner as to switching your lessons to the mornings so that they align with the Heiress' tutoring hours. Unfortunately, Madame Tanner needs time to rearrange her schedule to accommodate this change; therefore, your lessons will be postponed until next week."

"Heiress Summer isn't going to school? I thought maybe that is why I haven't seen more of her around the house? Isn't she old enough for school?" Autumn interrupted Lady Cannon out of surprise.

"No and yes. Heiress Summer is supposed to be in kindergarten this year. Unfortunately, she is too insecure and unstable. I tried to take her to tour the school and prepare her for the transition; however, she cried in hysterics the entire time - she just wanted to come home. We did not even finish the tour, and Master Philip had to carry her to the car. As you have noticed, she does not even accompany me to church on Sunday's because of her fear of change. And you know how serious I am in attending church."

Indeed she did. But something stirred within Autumn at the mention of being afraid of change. That was exactly how Autumn felt after her mother died.

"I have hired a tutor to start her schooling here in her suites. She has not warmed up to the idea yet, and I am afraid I will have to find several tutors before she embraces the idea. Still, she must have schooling. Anyway, I'd like you to spend the afternoons with her. We will have meals together as usual with Heiress Summer joining us now. Becca will tend to any of the Heiress' needs in dressing for the day, preparing her for her lessons in the mornings, and will again tend to her after dinner. You will have charge of her care from after lunch until dinner every weekday. And you will now have the freedom to enter the east wing and see her whenever you wish. Do you have any questions?"

"Only one, what is it you desire for us to do from lunch to dinner? I mean, do you have any specific guidelines or tasks for us to accomplish?"

"Build trust. That is your sole goal. I do not have any further restrictions or instructions for you other than what I have already placed within the service of your contract and that of which you are accustomed to."

"Yes, my Lady, I will do what I can." Autumn had no clue what she was going to do with Summer to build trust or fill the hours of time they were going to be spending together. She had never been around young kids.

Lady Cannon rose and slowly walked back to the house. "Come with me; I will show you the east wing."

Autumn was thrilled to see the secret chambers. She had wondered about them for so long, yet never dared to push for information as she had her own secrets. She followed Lady Cannon up the stairs and to the right. As they walked along the corridor, Autumn noted the family portraits hanging on the walls telling the story of the lineage of the family. She stopped to look at them now knowing the story behind them.

Lady Cannon waited patiently, admiring the portraits herself and touched that Autumn would care so much to see them. "I've hired a historian to put together a book for Heiress Summer. It will contain stories, pictures, and the history of our family. With the Heiress being so young, I felt it important to have a way to pass down our heritage after I'm gone."

"That is a wonderful gift. I wish I had my grandmother's stories and recipes written down somewhere."

Lady Cannon nodded, and they continued down the corridor. Autumn noted there were only four doors in the hallway on this side. At the first door on the right, Lady Cannon opened the door to reveal her private suites. Autumn marveled at the size and lavishness of the rooms. *I thought I was used to the fineness of the house.* The rooms had all the components of her own, only with more living area. Lady Cannon's rooms were coordinated in a lovely rose and green combination. They perfectly matched the delicacy and gentleness of Lady Cannon's personality.

Lady Cannon then took her across the hall to the first door on the left, which was an empty suite identical to Lady Cannon's, only in a more subdued blue and white; it reminded Autumn of the sky. "These rooms were Brian and Vivian's suite. I had left them exactly the same for Summer, including the clothes in the closets. She does not remember much of her parents; nevertheless, I often find her napping in their bed or reading in one of their chairs. I know from my own times in these rooms, the clothes still hold a bit of their scent."

This moved Autumn greatly as she remembered her own father not being so sensitive when he got rid of her mother's things just weeks after she died. Autumn noticed an extra door in the bedroom and decided to ask about it.

"That door goes directly into Heiress Summer's suite. It was put in when they discovered they were expecting and would want the next room for the nursery. They did not want to go all the way around to reach her in the night."

Autumn nodded.

After this, they proceeded to Heiress Summer's suite where she was studying with her tutor. Autumn noticed that Summer was just staring at the young woman who sat across from her, not paying any attention or participating in any way with what the tutor was doing. Upon their entrance, Summer did look at them, and Lady Cannon directed her back to her studies.

Heiress Summer's suite was decorated in the prettiest pinks and whites, as a princess' room should be, with a canopy over the bed and another over a corner reading area. A school area had been set up where the office spaces were in the other rooms.

After leaving the Heiress' suite, Lady Cannon continued down the hallway to the fourth door. "This is my most sacred room. When I am in here, I put this ribbon on the door. Under no circumstance am I to be interrupted when in this room unless Heiress Summer's direct well-being is at stake."

Autumn was stunned at her sternness and the gravity with which she referred to this room. She could not imagine what would be inside that would hold so much importance to Lady Cannon, and for a moment, she doubted that Lady Cannon would show her.

But then, Lady Cannon opened the door. Around Lady Cannon, Autumn could see a beautifully lit room with stained glass windows and pews like at church. As Autumn gazed around this room, Lady Cannon stepped to the side to allow her access.

"This is my prayer room. I come here to seek out God's will and comfort in my life's journey here on earth."

Autumn glanced back at her amazed. *Her prayer room was the most sacred room in the house?* This peaked her interest even more in Lady Cannon's faith.

Directly across from the door they entered, standing on the ground - or at least appearing to be - was a beautiful yet rugged wooden cross illuminated from above. Several feet away from the front of this cross were several pews with room to walk completely around them. In the corner to her right was a raised platform with cushioned steps and railing as if for kneeling and to her left was a sitting area with several books, a table, and two chairs.

There were three doors, one Autumn assumed to be direct access to Lady Cannon's suite as in Heiress Summer's room. Lady Cannon showed her that the second door led to a bathroom directly connected to the prayer room. However, nothing was mentioned about the third door. Autumn noticed it had several locks on it and decided not to ask.

"What do you do in here? Why do you have this room?"

"As I said, I come here to pray and seek out God's will and comfort. I also study His Word and spend time with Him here."

"And does it work?" Clearly Autumn did not understand the whole concept for such a room.

"Yes. God meets me here; though He would meet me wherever I sought Him." Lady Cannon wanted to be sure to make the point clear that God was not restricted to this room or any room. "Do you know why I showed you this room?"

"No."

"I showed you this room because it is vital in our lives to be connected to our Creator and the only true God. We cannot even imagine how much we desperately need Him in our lives. Because of this truth, I am going to open this room to you. You may come and use the room with reverence whenever the ribbon is not on the door."

"What would I do in here?" Autumn was sincerely touched that Lady Cannon would share her most sacred room. However, she really had no idea what she was expected to do in it.

"You can sit and pray, think or even talk out loud to God." She gestured to the right corner area. "You can kneel and pray." Turning to the table, she continued. "Or you can read His Word and study it. You may find that the stories of the Bible, like Ruth and Esther, especially interest you."

Feeling the need to acknowledge the magnitude of this offer, Autumn curtsied. "Thank you, my Lady, for allowing me such a privilege."

"Use it wisely, for if you abuse this privilege, you will lose it and many more." Lady Cannon said this sternly enough to sink in the gravity of the warning and cause a shiver to go up Autumn's back.

Autumn gravely nodded her understanding.

Once they left the prayer room, Lady Cannon had a meeting to attend in the Library leaving Autumn on her own until afternoon. Autumn went back to her room to attempt to absorb the changes in her responsibilities and what she had been told about Heiress Summer.

Autumn had stored the contract she had signed with Lady Cannon at the back of the closet where she kept her meager belongings. Figuring no one would think her stuff worth messing with, Autumn reasoned that was the safest place to keep anything important.

Back at her desk, Autumn poured over the contract looking for changes or restrictions she had not seen before in light of the new information she possessed. Lady Cannon had been right; the contract was worded clearly to cover her duties even as a guardian to Heiress Summer. The contract had taken the two positions and woven them together into a single unit seamlessly. Considering all the new information Autumn had been learning about estate business and contracts, Autumn was impressed. Whoever wrote the contract was a master of terminology and had a comprehensive understanding of the estate world.

# 16

Months had now gone by, and Edmund sat at the kitchen table warming himself with a cup of coffee. He sat there, deep in despair since hearing the latest news from the detectives. They had found Marcos in Mexico and Autumn was not with him. Marcos had told the authorities that he had indeed seen her the Thursday before she disappeared, though only long enough to tell her good-bye.

Marcos had been an employee at the grocery store and had befriended Autumn. He confessed he had wanted their relationship to go further though Autumn had said no. The pictures of the two of them had been taken at the store Christmas party the year before. Tom, the manager Edmund had initially talked with, had been fired upon the discovery of Marcos' illegal status. Marcos confessed that he had tried to convince Autumn to leave with him; however, she had refused him each time he offered. That was all Marcos knew.

With that door closed because of no new evidence, the detectives had no choice except to put the investigation on the back burner. And Edmund was forced to face the fact that Autumn wasn't coming back.

James entered the kitchen, got himself a cup of coffee, and sat down across from Edmund. He knew the latest news regarding Autumn and his heart was sick as well.

After Edmund had finally shared everything with James, the two men had become friends. Though Edmund did not understand it, he sensed that James genuinely cared for Autumn's well-being, and appreciated the support from James during the months of waiting. Edmund no longer saw James as a threat to what was rightfully

Autumn's, but instead as a friend and companion during these hard times.

And to his great surprise, over the course of those months, Edmund discovered that James was one of those dreaded Christians. If it weren't for the fact that Edmund needed James, he would have fired him and kicked him out immediately. As it was, Edmund had come to rely on James considerably and knew he couldn't afford to lose him. Therefore, Edmund sternly told him to keep his beliefs to himself, which he respectfully did. James was the first Christian Edmund had known who used such restraint. That mixed with how hard James worked and how genuinely he lived, Edmund came to respect James -if not his beliefs - all the more.

With the floors so thin in his old house, Edmund knew that James prayed regularly. Late at night or early in the morning as he lay in bed, Edmund could sometimes hear James talking. Though he could not always hear what was being said, it was clear what he was doing. Edmund thought about asking him to stop as it was disruptive, but then he had heard James praying for Autumn and figured it couldn't hurt.

Now though, sitting across from this *praying Christian* and seeing no good in it, Edmund was angry and wanted some answers. "I know you pray. I've heard you. You've even prayed for Autumn...so why in the hell has your God not heard you? Why hasn't he brought her home? Why can't I find her?" The anger was simmering at the edge of his control and Edmund fought to keep it together. He hadn't lost his control since that night in the park. He had been doing good.

James looked up from his cup at Edmund's outburst in surprise. He was caught off guard, not only by the topic - which he had been forbidden to talk about - but by the tension radiating off of Edmund. James tried to respond honestly, yet keeping in mind Edmund wouldn't actually receive anything he said at this moment. "Yes, I have been praying for Autumn's safety and well-being. But...God is not a vending machine. I can ask all I want; still, if it's not in His will,

He won't answer it in the affirmative. He only does what is in His will and what He deems best. Praying is more like a father who listens to a child and lovingly considers his request. There is no guarantee the answer will be what you want, but you can rest assure that whatever the answer is, it's the right one. Maybe wherever Autumn is, she is better off there for the time being?"

That was it, the trigger that sent Edmund over the edge. Kicking his chair back as he stood, he banged his fists on the table, spilling the coffee in his cup as he yelled. "Well, *I* am not better off with her gone. Why haven't you prayed for her return, not just her safety? I want my daughter back!"

James was not a perfect man, and so he had to get control of himself before he answered. Still, the truth in his heart seeped out. "I am not God! If I were, *I* would bring her back. I *have* prayed for her return *if* it's God's will, but apparently, it isn't. And if this is how you treated her when you got upset, I don't wonder why." Realizing his tone was getting louder, and his grip on his temper was slipping, James quieted his voice and took a deep breath, speaking more to himself than Edmund. "I don't have all the answers, but I know He does. I *have* to trust in that."

"Well, I don't." Edmund barked, hitting his hands on the table again, further spilling the coffee, as he turned to leave.

James reached for a towel to start cleaning up the spill. "Hey! Where are you going? We need to talk this through."

"For a walk to cool off. Is that okay with you, *DAD*?" Edmund mocked and spat back at him.

James let him go - they both needed to cool off. He knew it wasn't anything personal - just a hurting man venting his frustration and lack of understanding - but he wished he would have handled that better.

Edmund walked down the road that led to the bus stop, ranting in his head. *What in the world? What is the point of having an all-powerful God if He doesn't answer your requests? What's the point of talking to Him if He isn't going to listen? AND who says God knows best? There are a lot of things that HE lets happen that I see no good in. Granted, I've done my fair share of wrong things, but surely there is nothing wrong with wanting my daughter home. How can being away be better for her than being here where she belongs? I shouldn't have lost my temper with James. I know he isn't to blame. Still, I don't understand why God doesn't help. He's probably the only one that can now.*

About half a mile down the road he looked up to see Mrs. Bogart mulching her flowerbeds. He didn't really feel like talking to anyone, especially another Christian. Yet maybe this was an answer to James' prayers, and she had seen Autumn. *This might be an open door. She might hold a new clue.* Edmund hesitantly approached her.

Having not seen Edmund approaching, Penny was a bit startled when he spoke. "Excuse me. I'm sorry; I didn't mean to startle you. I was just wondering if I could ask you a few questions."

"About what?" Penny didn't recognize the man, and she had learned to be leery of strangers in this area, especially after the news of the abused girl found just a few miles away.

"Allow me to introduce myself, my name is Edmund DeBlue, and I live just down the road." He paused to see if she would introduce herself in return. She didn't. "I have a young daughter named Autumn. She used to walk past here on the way to the bus each day. I was wondering if you remember seeing her?"

Penny recognized the name right away; however, she was cautious to say anything as she knew Autumn had run away from something or someone. *What if this man is abusive? What if he wasn't Autumn's father at all? What if by talking to him, it puts Autumn in danger?* She decided to tread carefully in what she disclosed. "Yes, I saw Autumn often, the poor thing having to walk so far each day. She's very fortunate that nothing serious happened to her like that other girl." She couldn't help the distaste she felt show in her tone. Yet, his response shocked her.

"Yes, we are very fortunate that was not Autumn. Look, I've come to see that I have made many mistakes - for many years now. But, well, I don't know what has happened to her. She's simply gone; gone for good probably, and I can't even tell her how wrong I was." Edmund hung his head and kicked his foot in the dirt. He hadn't meant to share all that; he was still off-kilter from earlier.

Penny wasn't sure what to make of his confession, but she sensed a broken heart in need of true healing, a healing that could only come from above. So as he turned to leave, she ventured, "I spoke with your daughter many times right here on the side of the road. We became good friends, and I even helped her a few times when she missed the bus and needed a ride to town."

The change was shocking. Instantly, Edmund was angry that Autumn had disobeyed him.

The look in his eyes caused Penny to step back and refrain from telling him anything else. *This is a dangerous man.*

"She stopped here and **talked** to you!" As the anger built in him, he shouted. "You gave her rides? Where to?"

Penny took another step towards the house as she heard her husband come out to see what the commotion was. Not wanting to endanger Autumn but wanting this man to leave, she answered his question. "Y-yes, once or twice she missed the bus and would have been fired had she not gotten to work on time. So I gave her a ride to the grocery store." As understanding settled in, Penny grew in confidence knowing her husband was not far off. "I see now why she was so afraid of talking with me."

Edmund tried to gain control, yet it was no use, the blood was pounding in his head as he demanded answers. "When was the last time you saw her?"

"Months ago, I don't remember when exactly. Autumn was heading home."

"Are you sure?" Edmund took a menacing step forward but stopped when he heard the cock of a shotgun. Looking over, he saw whom he assumed was Mr. Bogart come around the bushes carrying his shotgun. *Some Christian example you are.*

"Yes, the last time I saw Autumn she was headed home."

Edmund nodded and turned to leave, but something stopped him even through his haze of anger. "Thank you for befriending Autumn; she needed all the friends she had. If you hear anything from her, will you let me know? The police have hit a dead end in finding her."

Penny nodded, and Edmund left. Looking over her shoulder, she saw Henry standing with his gun, and she shook her head. *What is that man thinking? I seriously doubted he needed his gun.* She was glad though that he had been there *and* that he had not heard the last of what Mr. DeBlue had said. She hadn't really thought about the secret she held and wasn't sure what her responsibility was now; other than to spend a lot of time in prayer.

Obviously, the situation was very complicated in Autumn's family life. Penny had not heard from Autumn since that last phone call, nor did she expect to.

Edmund thought about the contrast of James and Mr. Bogart. Granted, he didn't really know Mr. Bogart, but he was sure James would never approach a stranger with a shotgun like that. Then again, James was very protective and would defend what was his. *Maybe that was what Mr. Bogart was doing; defending his wife? If a stranger had approached Sue like that and started yelling, wouldn't I have done the same? Especially now, with those men still at large who attacked that girl.*

Even so, it made him appreciate James' calm demeanor and respectful attitude. James put up with a lot as Edmund mocked his beliefs and his God, yet he'd never responded with hostility. Edmund determined he had better apologize when he got back.

James received the apology, and Edmund felt the tension disappear, though there was a reservation about Edmund's temper and what it meant in Autumn's disappearance. He told James about the conversation with Mrs. Bogart and of Mr. Bogart's actions with distaste.

"I've met the Bogart's. They have had some rough times since moving into the area. Random vandalizing, things stolen from their yard. It hasn't built much trust in their neighbors."

Edmund had no idea they had suffered such ill. He readily admitted to not welcoming them and even blatantly ignoring them; still, he had not heard of how badly they had been treated by others. It gave him a new understanding as to why Mr. Bogart acted the way he did. He **was** simply protecting his wife - as any man should.

James started noticing changes in Edmund, after the revelation of the Bogart's troubles. He still grieved over Autumn, but he was accepting her absence more and more. The big difference was that Edmund was walking down to the Bogart's more frequently. Taking them food, supplies, or simply offering them help with whatever they needed. James wasn't sure why he was doing this, but he felt this was a good change for Edmund.

It wasn't long before Edmund began asking more questions about James' belief in God. He tried to answer all of Edmund's questions the best he could; nevertheless, Edmund never seemed to be satisfied with James' answers, coming back with more questions each time. Finally, James bought Edmund a Study Bible of his own and told him if he'd read it each day he'd start to have a better understanding. And to James' surprise, he did.

Several more months passed and the days became usual. James handled the farm; Edmund worked at the insurance office. They ate supper together and talked about what Edmund had just read in the scriptures. Then they went their own ways, James downstairs and Edmund to his room to read.

James was starting to wonder when he should make his intentions known to Edmund but kept getting a "wait" from God when he inquired. James understood this. With so much happening in Edmund's heart, what James had to say could quickly turn it cold again, so he waited.

Thanksgiving came and went, and Christmas was rapidly approaching. With all that Edmund had been experiencing and his new openness toward God, James ventured out and invited Edmund to church for the Christmas program. His church put on a dramatic presentation once a year at Christmas with a large cast, live animals, and elaborate costumes that covered the entire salvation message from the birth of Jesus to His ascension.

At first, Edmund declined, though the more he thought about it, curiosity got the better of him.

The night of the program Edmund heard James preparing to leave and joined him at the door wearing black slacks and a blue button-down shirt. Surprised, James stood unmoving.

"Umm...Is the uh, offer to go with you, um, still open?"

James was stunned almost into dumbness. "Yes. Yes, indeed. You, You are most welcome."

Edmund gestured to his clothes. "Well, is this appropriate or do I need to change? I have never been to church before."

"You look great. I'm only wearing jeans because I have to help haul in the hay bales."

Edmund nodded, but still felt uncomfortable. "I'll go put jeans on. I can help unload bales, too."

James went to get the pickup, and they headed out into the snowy night. James was elated, and Edmund was as nervous as a schoolgirl on her first date.

James drove to the church, and they proceeded to unload the hay bales. Having something to do helped alleviate the nervousness, though not totally eliminate it. Everyone was nice and welcoming, but Edmund was still uncomfortable. He suddenly saw Mr. and Mrs. Bogart enter the foyer of the church and raised a questioning glance at James.

"I told you I'd met the Bogart's. I just didn't tell you it was at church."

Edmund shook his head, but let a small smile out nonetheless.

When Henry and Penny saw Edmund standing in the foyer, they were pleasantly surprised and went to greet him immediately. They invited him to sit with them, and since James had gone to move the truck, he went ahead and joined them. Once seated, Edmund made sure there was room for James in case he wanted to join them later.

Edmund took in the church, all bright and cheery with lights and greenery. There was a cross up front on the stage and an organ. He could see the windows were stained glass but couldn't really see the designs in the dark. Henry made small talk with Edmund, and soon the music started. Edmund looked around for James, yet still didn't see him. The pastor was now in front welcoming everyone, and the lights were dimmed so the program could start. Moments later James slipped in beside Edmund and he let out the breath he had been unknowingly holding. He felt less vulnerable with James there.

As the program progressed and the story unfolded from the miracle birth of Jesus to his unjustified death, Edmund watched completely taken in. Edmund was familiar with parts of the story as he had been reading his Bible, though seeing it now played out before him filled in several of the lapses in his understanding. A tear slipped down his cheek as they depicted Jesus' gruesome death.

The room went completely black, and everyone sat in darkness and silence. Edmund knew the certainty of death and assumed the play was over. Edmund's shoulders sank in the realization that the hope he had been searching for was dead. *He didn't understand. If the Messiah they had been waiting for had come and then died, why did James and the Bogarts still believe?*

Unexpectedly, bright lights flashed up front, and there was a horrific noise. Edmund's head jerked up, and he stared in awe and confusion at what was going on. The tomb where they had laid Jesus was open and the soldiers were fallen on the ground. Edmund earnestly watched as the rest of the story was told - how Jesus defeated death and rose again. How he died and became the sacrificial Lamb for the sins of the world. And then, He showed Himself to many people before ascending to heaven. Edmund had read about Jesus' resurrection, but it had never been real to him - not like this. Now the tears were really streaming down Edmund's face as he finally understood what he had been reading all along. He had hope, and he needed this Savior, Jesus.

James and the Bogarts watched Edmund in growing excitement. When the time came at the end of the service for the pastor to give a chance for acceptance of this Savior, they were sure Edmund would respond, but he didn't. Disappointed and confused, they finished out the service and joined the others in the fellowship hall for cookies and cider. Edmund was quiet and reserved though polite and obviously moved.

The drive home was silent, and James had to admit to God he didn't understand. As they headed into the house, Edmund stopped him. "James, would you mind joining me upstairs for a moment?"

Intrigued and hopeful, James followed Edmund into the living room. Once there, Edmund sat quietly for some time. "I wanted to thank you for taking me tonight. And for your patience and endurance over these last few months. I again realize how harshly I treated you in your beliefs."

James nodded and continued to listen.

"I know you have indicated before that you have forgiven me but do you think that God could forgive me as well - knowing things about me that are even worse than how I have treated you and other Christians?"

"I have no doubt. The sacrifice of Jesus was for all sin, and in God's eyes, sin is sin - separating you from Him. Be it a lie or murder - both can be forgiven by the blood of Jesus. Think of the two criminals on the cross with Jesus, all it took for the one to be welcomed into paradise was his acceptance of Christ as his Savior."

Edmund was taken back by the mention of those two particular sins together as that was exactly what Edmund was asking. One of the deepest secrets he possessed was the decision he made to force Sue into an abortion before they were married.

Edmund had convinced Sue to move in with him, even though they weren't married, while she finished out her student teaching. They had plans in place to get married that following summer; however, within months of her moving in, she became pregnant. Edmund didn't think they could afford a baby off of his meager salary alone and insisted that Sue abort the baby. They fought over it for months. Finally, Edmund gave Sue an ultimatum. Unfortunately, that ultimatum drove a wedge between them, and Sue left him. When she moved back to the area over a year and a half later, Edmund pleaded with her to forgive him, and they began to rebuild their relationship, eventually marrying two years later.

Edmund knew God could forgive him for the lies he had told, and even the bad decisions of his past, but what he didn't know was if God could forgive him for forcing his wife to kill their first child and drive away their second?

James waited patiently as Edmund absorbed the truth of the forgiveness being offered to him. "James, I want to accept Jesus' forgiveness and his sacrifice. Will you pray with me? "

James wanted to jump for joy and shout from the mountaintops. He never thought he'd see this day, let alone be a key part of it, but containing his joy as to not lose the moment; he knelt with Edmund and prayed.

# 17

Autumn entered Heiress Summer's suite and found the girl curled up in the corner rocking. She was not crying, just sitting there. Over the last several days, Autumn had tried to observe and get to know this little girl; however, the Heiress did not respond to Autumn's inquiries. Autumn's heart broke for the pain she was suffering. Autumn knew it well. Nonetheless, she never actively dealt with her own pain. Therefore, she did not know how to help Heiress Summer with hers. Autumn sat down on the rocking chair across the room knowing the Heiress had seen her enter.

This was the routine they had gotten into. After lunch, Heiress Summer ran upstairs to sit in the corner under the canopy and rock while Autumn sat in the chair across the room. The two of them sat there in silence for the whole four hours. Eventually, Autumn began to bring books to read. On occasion, she would read out loud, and Heiress Summer would respond by venturing out a bit to play, yet when Autumn stopped reading, she was right back in the corner.

Autumn didn't bring anything to read today. Instead, she sat pondering what she could do to build trust in this troubled little girl. It wasn't that she was afraid of Autumn, as Heiress Summer would respond when she had to; nevertheless, the Heiress would not instigate anything herself. Not having any real experience with children, Autumn did not know what to do with her. Thinking about this, Autumn tried to remember what it was that she had wanted to do when she was a little girl. *What was it that she needed most when going through the grief of losing her own mother?*

Things like security, love, and attention came to mind, though Lady Cannon had provided all of these things for Summer. In fact, Heiress Summer had been given pretty much everything Autumn could think of. Yet she was still detached – reclusive. *What was she missing?* Autumn sat trying to figure it out when suddenly from deep within her she heard that unfamiliar voice again.

It said *fun*.

*Fun?* Autumn pondered this.

Heiress Summer had everything a child could ask for regarding security and love: toys, clothes, a room filled with whatever her heart desired, and staff members at her beck and call. All of this was so conveniently located within the walls of the house that she was never taken outside of these walls for anything other than business.

Heiress Summer also had the attention from numerous caretakers who would do whatever she commanded of them, but they were there to fulfill a job, and the Heiress knew that.

What Heiress Summer didn't have was friends: no playmates.

Autumn suddenly sat forward. "Summer?" The little girl skeptically looked at Autumn from across the room as no one addressed her so casually in the house except Granny. "Have you ever had any other little girls over to play?"

Summer looked shocked at the idea and then replied in a very sad and quiet tone. "No."

Autumn sat quietly again, deep in thought. Of course not, she had been surrounded by adults all her life; she probably didn't even know any other little girls her age.

No wonder the school was terrifying to her, so many little people – people she could not command or dictate to, the only social skills she possessed. Summer literally did not know how to have fun or make friends. She had been taught from infancy how to dictate orders, fulfill the protocol requirements of being an Heiress, and entertain herself - which were necessary skills, but not what she needed now. She was never given the opportunity to interact with other children. That fact, compounded by the reality that everyone she did manage to bond with, eventually abandoned her, left this little girl reclusive – not wanting to venture out to be hurt again.

Autumn stood in indignation at the revelation and looked over at the little heiress.

Summer noticed the movement and cautiously stopped rocking to watch her.

Autumn began to pace. *Would Summer respond to having fun with her? How can I engage her interest so much to override her reservations?* Autumn determined she would find a way to be Summer's playmate and she would do everything within her power to never hurt this little girl.

Like a flood, ideas began pouring over Autumn regarding all the things they could do together. She began to get excited thinking about taking Summer out on various outings to places like the park and maybe even the zoo. She stopped herself. First, she would need to make a plan and then she would need to convince Lady Cannon the plan would work. Autumn spent the remainder of time hatching out her plan.

That evening at dinner, she requested permission for Master Philip to take her into town. She had spoken to Lady Cannon earlier about her revelations that afternoon, though not going into specifics as to how she was going to address the situation. Though Lady Cannon had agreed to let her try, Autumn could tell she was doubtful.

Lady Cannon granted permission, and as soon as Autumn was free, she had Master Philip take her to the big toy store where she purchased a child's stroller, some princess accessories and a few other fun items for them to play with. Once back at home, she decorated the stroller and prepared a story for Summer because tomorrow they were going to start having fun!

Autumn could hardly get through her lessons and lunch in anticipation for the day she had planned. As Heiress Summer ran ahead to her room, Autumn went back to her suite, retrieved the newly designed carriage, and proceeded into the Heiress' suite pushing it ahead of her.

As soon as Summer saw her, she scooted to the edge of the canopied corner to get a better look.

*That's encouraging. Come on Summer, come to see what I've got planned for you.*

"Have you ever seen an elf maiden carriage before?"

Summer shook her head.

"Well...let me tell you about the elf maiden who stopped by my room last night. She brought me this carriage. It had been created especially for a little girl with the name of a season to ride in; a little girl the elf maiden had lost."

Gaining more interest from Summer, Autumn continued to tell the story she had made up. She hoped to get Summer to sit in the carriage and eventually go for a ride. "The elf maiden told me that when a special little girl with the name of a season was found, and she sat in the carriage, she would become the bravest of all the princesses and live happily ever after."

"You have a season's name." Summer eyed Autumn suspiciously.

"You're right I do. Let's see if I fit, shall we?" Autumn went to the front of the stroller and pretended to try to sit in it.

Summer giggled. "You're too big."

Autumn pretended to pout. "I guess it's not for me then. Do we know of anyone else with the name of a season?" Autumn tapped her finger on her chin like she was seriously pondering this.

After a few minutes, Summer scooted closer and ventured in a shy voice. "I...I...have the name of a season."

"You do? Are you sure? Maybe we should name the seasons just to be sure. Do you know what they are?"

Summer shook her head no.

"No? Well, then how do you know your name is a season?"

A sad look came over Summer's face. "Granny says my mommy used to say 'Summer is the best season because that's when she got her *Sunshine.*' Mommy used to sing that song to me when I was a baby - *You are my Sunshine, my only Sunshine.*" Tears threatened to overcome her, but Summer just rocked them away.

Autumn didn't really know what to do with that information. It broke her heart. Deciding distraction was the best answer, Autumn tried to regain Summer's attention to the carriage. "Since your name is a season too, would *you* like to see if maybe *you* are that special little girl the elf maiden lost?"

Summer sheepishly nodded, and Autumn gestured for her to come and sit in the carriage.

*Thankfully, Summer is a small child.* Encouraged, Autumn fastened the belts around her. "The carriage won't work without the belts." Then Autumn started pushing Summer around the room. Soon they were doing turns and swerves all over the room. "Do you want to go into the hall and see what we can do out there in the elf maiden carriage?"

Excitedly, Summer nodded yes. So they ventured into the hall. They started off slowly swerving back and forth down the hallway from one end of the east wing to the other end of the west wing. Soon they were laughing and zooming up and down the halls as Autumn ran behind the carriage doing all kinds of tricks.

The ice between them had begun to crack.

Hearing the commotion, Lady Cannon opened her door and stepped out into the hall indignant at the disruption. She had never heard Summer laugh like that and did not realize that was who was making such a racket. At the sight of Autumn and Summer laughing and playing, tears began to form in her eyes. Before she was noticed, she quietly returned to her room as to not disturb their play. *And so it has begun.*

Later, Lady Cannon asked Autumn about the stroller, and Autumn explained her idea to build confidence in Heiress Summer slowly by first riding in the stroller around the house making it fun; hoping that eventually, the Heiress would be confident enough to go to the park or other places as well. Lady Cannon was impressed with the creativity and concept, though she was not certain it would work. Autumn wanted to give it some time, and Lady Cannon agreed.

After several days of playing and riding around the house in the elf maiden carriage, Autumn decided to take the next step. Entering Summer's suite, she had a coat instead of the carriage.

Summer was obviously disappointed.

"Would you like to ride in the elven maiden carriage today?"

Summer nodded.

"Excellent. The elf maiden visited me again last night and told me about a special tree in the garden. I thought we'd go see if we can find it. There's supposed to be a special surprise underneath it. What do you think?"

At first, Summer wasn't so sure and didn't look convinced of the idea.

"That's fine; you don't have to ride in the elf maiden carriage today. We can sit quietly and read instead." Autumn put down the coat and got out a book as she sat in her chair.

That was not what Summer wanted. However, though the ice had begun to melt between them, Summer rarely spoke more than a few words to Autumn. So Autumn sat still, pretending to read her book while Summer debated what she wanted to do.

"I guess we could try...to find the tree. If Granny says, it's okay."

"Oh good! I've already talked to your grandmother, and she granted us permission to go exploring as long as we don't go too far."

Summer nodded and eagerly put on her coat.

Together they walked hand in hand down to the vestibule where LeDare Anton had the carriage waiting. Autumn started venturing around the house on the patio by the dining hall. After a couple of times around the edge, Summer actually wanted to see more. So, even in the cold winter air, they began exploring the garden paths, the orchard and walked around the pond looking for the special tree the elf maiden told Autumn to look for.

The elf maiden carriage idea was working better than Autumn anticipated. Summer was really opening up and getting excited about seeing more than just her suite and the inside of the house.

Autumn also started doing other fun and creative things with Summer as well - especially when the weather was not nice, or they had worn themselves out with the carriage. One day she came into the room with two cans of silly string, and they had a silly string war. Another day, they made play dough down in the kitchen.

Summer was still struggling with the tutor and doing school work, so one day Autumn brought a can of shaving cream, and to Summer's horror started spraying it all over the table. Then she went through the whole alphabet and drew shapes in the shaving cream. Soon they were having a shaving cream war, and were covered from head to toe - but they were having fun!

Autumn found herself spending her free time researching more ideas for games and activities to do with Summer. She even gave up her reading to plan out and shop for the next day's activities. Autumn began to realize that in playing with Summer, she was getting to relive the childhood she missed because of her mother's sickness. Healing was taking place within her own heart. New seeds of hope and promise were beginning to sprout.

One day Autumn told Summer she had a very special surprise from Granny. As Autumn led Summer to the reading corner under the canopy, Summer excitedly bounced up and down. "This is a very special book made just for you. It is the first book of your family history that your grandmother had made for you." Autumn showed Summer the picture on the front cover of her grandmother, grandfather, mother and father with Summer in their arms. Summer started crying and shaking her head back and forth - indicating she did not want to read the book.

At this, Autumn decided to tell Summer a different story. Putting the book aside, Autumn pulled Summer into her lap and started to tell Summer about a little girl who had a wonderful life with her Mommy and Daddy. The little girl and her family would go to the lake, camp, and go on long trips to see places far away. Her Mommy spent hours baking with the little girl and playing games with her, and they all loved each other very much.

Taking a deep breath, Autumn told Summer that one day the little girl's Mommy got really sick and could no longer do any of those fun things, which made the little girl very sad. This little girl watched as her Mommy got sicker and sicker, and eventually, her

Mommy died. The little girl was so sad and lonely and became afraid of everything. The little girl was so afraid she didn't want anything to change because she thought she would forget about her Mommy. Then the little girl's father gave her a beautiful little locket with her Mommy's picture in it so she would never forget her. Eventually, the little girl grew up and moved away and found a new family. One that she grew to love just as much and the little girl, who was now grown up, lived happily ever after with her new family.

As Autumn told Summer this vague version of her own personal story, tears welled up in her eyes.

When she was all done, Summer was looking at her intently. "Was that little girl you?"

"Yes, Summer. You see, I understand the pain of losing your Mommy and Daddy because even though my Daddy isn't dead, he left me all alone too. Now though, I have you and Lady Cannon as my family. Though my story is sad, it is important to remember the good stories and fun times we had with the people we love."

"Is that why you always wear the locket?"

Autumn was astounded at her observation. "Yes, I never take it off except to bathe. And that is why Lady Cannon had this book put together for you. She wanted you to be able to remember the good stories of your Mommy and Daddy. We don't have to read it right now, but one day when you are ready, I'll read it to you okay?" Summer agreed and then put her arms around Autumn in an embrace that melted Autumn's heart.

Leaning back Summer asked, "If Granny and I are your new family, why do you still call her Lady Cannon?"

"Out of respect, sweet one." Autumn recited a protocol that she knew Summer would remember. "One should always address those older with respect until given permission to do so otherwise."

That night at dinner, Summer brought up the topic again. "Granny, since Autumn is now a part of our family, I want her to call you Granny like I do. But she says she can't until you say so. Can you give her per...per...What was that word?"

"Permission, sweet one." Autumn smiled at Summer's insistence.

Confused, Lady Cannon turned to Autumn for interpretation. Upon understanding the request, Lady Cannon granted permission for private use within the family.

As the days grew into weeks, Summer became a different little girl, especially when Autumn was around. Lady Cannon was so relieved at the changes in her granddaughter that when Autumn asked if they could venture out to the local toy store one afternoon, she agreed.

Lady Cannon mandated that Master Philip was to go with them - even into the store - in case it was too much for Summer and they needed to leave. With great anticipation, Autumn had Master Philip load the carriage in the car, and she went in search of Summer.

"I've got a surprise for you today!"

After the last surprise of the family book, Summer was a bit more reserved in her enthusiasm.

"Granny gave us permission to go to the toy store. We can go see all the new things and pick a few of them to bring home for us to play with. Doesn't that sound like fun?"

Summer eagerly nodded and went to get her coat.

When they arrived at the large department store, Summer was once again reserved and unsure she wanted to get out of the car.

Master Philip brought the carriage around as Autumn tried to encourage her. "Remember, when you are in the carriage, you can be the bravest of princesses."

Summer conceded.

As Autumn pushed Summer into the store, she marveled. *I can't believe this is working so well. I feel like I've won the lottery and it's a simple matter of a little girl learning to trust. Each time she opens the door a little more, I feel like I've somehow conquered the world.*

They spent over an hour looking around the store and picking out a few things to take back to the house. As they were walking around, Summer noticed a play area with a ball pit, rope climbing and various other activities. Every time they passed it, her head would stay fixed on the kids playing until she could no longer see them.

Finally, Autumn decided to venture the unthinkable. "Summer, would you like to go to the play area?"

Summer nodded eagerly.

Once there, Autumn looked very sad. "I'm sorry Summer. The elf maiden carriage is not allowed in the play area. See the other strollers parked here. If you want to go in, we have to leave the carriage here. Do you still want to go in?" Autumn held her breath.

Summer contemplated the fun the other kids were having and the security of her carriage. Finally, she looked up at Autumn. "Will you go with me?"

"Absolutely."

They spent another hour playing in the play yard. At first, they avoided all the things that Autumn couldn't do because of her size. Eventually though, Autumn convinced Summer that she could do it with Autumn standing at the other end or on the other side. As Autumn promised, she never left Summer's side as Master Philip watched attentively from the sidelines.

"Oh, Summer. I need a break. All this laughing and climbing is wearing me out. Can we go sit on the side for a moment?"

Summer's brow wrinkled, and she looked over to the side where Master Philip and other adults were sitting. "You can go sit down. I want to keep playing."

Stunned, Autumn just stared at her a moment. "Are you sure? I told you that I'd stay with you."

Summer nodded. "It's okay." She thought for a moment. "Just stay with Master Philip where I can see you."

Autumn smiled at her little command - *we will have to work on more appropriate social interactions* - and went to stand by Master Philip, inquiring of the time, while Summer continued playing on her own.

After a minute of silence as they observed Summer playing freely, Master Philip leaned over and with obvious affection said, "You are amazing."

Autumn blushed and turned to look at him. "Thank you."

Their faces were very close as Master Philip had not pulled away and Autumn breathed in. *He smells good.* Master Philip smiled as if he could read her thoughts and a gleam shone in his eye. Autumn smiled in return and took a step back, still smiling.

She had no intentions of seeking Master Philip's affections - especially not with the information Eleanor had been sharing with her in the evenings as they gossiped and giggled like school girls. Master Philip was notorious for his playfulness and lack of commitment in relationships. It was rather surprising that Lady Cannon kept him around.

Besides, she felt nothing for Master Philip - no spark of interest, no flutter of the heart, no turning in her stomach. She didn't even know if these things existed in real life; nonetheless, it was only these things that would cause her to take a second glance at any possibility for a relationship.

In hopes of reiterating her stand of friendship only, she patted him nicely on the shoulder. "I appreciate the compliment, but it is Summer who is doing all the work. She's the amazing one. Thank you for accompanying us here. Let's not get personal though."

Summer started requesting more outings. Knowing that Lady Cannon would prefer that Summer attend church, and eventually, school one day, Autumn elicited leverage from Summer's enthusiasm. She promised to ask for more outings *if* Summer started going to church on Sunday mornings - and she cooperated with her tutors. Summer thought that was too much to ask, but Autumn stood firm.

"You know Granny, sweet one. Attending church is very important to her. She will not grant permission for more outings if they are more important than church."

That next Sunday as Lady Cannon and Autumn stood in the vestibule waiting for the car, Summer came bounding down the steps in a pretty pink dress.

Lady Cannon was shocked speechless for a moment. "My dear, what are you doing?"

"I want to go to church with you Granny." Summer replied as if it should have been obvious.

Astonished, Lady Cannon looked at Autumn who just smiled. "Are you certain?"

Looking down at her feet, Summer answered. "Yes, if I can take my carriage."

Flabbergasted, Lady Cannon again glanced at Autumn for help. She could not bring herself to discourage Summer's willingness to attend church; nevertheless, it would be inappropriate to take the highly decorated elf maiden carriage into the sanctuary. Lady Cannon stood silently debating what to do.

Autumn sensing the difficulty bent down to Summer's level. "You can ride the carriage from the parking lot to the doors of the sanctuary, but the carriage must stay outside of the sanctuary, out of respect for others there to worship God. Okay?"

"Will you stay with me?" Summer asked Autumn.

"Yes, just like when we went to the toy store."

Summer perked up and started bouncing. "Okay, then I want to go."

Completely in awe, Lady Cannon nodded. Due to this enormous accomplishment, Lady Cannon did, indeed, grant permission for more outings, and Autumn was able to take Summer to the museum, the inside zoo, and even to the art gallery. Unfortunately, the weather was getting colder and all their activities - although fun - were geared towards the inside. Autumn couldn't wait until spring when she could take Summer to the park or fishing like her mom used to do with her.

Lady Cannon found herself spending more and more time in her prayer room thanking her Heavenly Father for the miracles she saw almost daily. If anyone had told her seven months ago that Summer and Autumn would be inseparable, she would have called it impossible. If anyone had told her that Autumn would become like a daughter to her, easing the loss of her only son, she would have never hoped.

Now, they were just one month from Christmas, and the only thing Lady Cannon could wish for was Autumn's salvation, and perhaps, her trust. Lady Cannon knew there was still something lingering in Autumn's past that was holding her back. She wished and prayed for full disclosure to put these things to rest before the next phase of her plan was complete.

With so many things falling into place, Lady Cannon went ahead with preparations for Autumn's formal introduction. Autumn had completed the courses and requirements necessary to get her Estate License and now there was only the guardianship of Summer to finalize. Once that was complete, Autumn would start taking over more of the decisions and obtain more authority, allowing Lady Cannon to be able to enjoy the end of her days on this earth.

# ❦ 18 ❦

Autumn's excitement was mounting as the preparations for the Christmas ball were taking shape. Lady Cannon had allowed Autumn to be in on the planning of the gala event. The Cannon estate hosted five balls over the course of the year. The Christmas ball would be Autumn's first. It was going to be spectacular, like nothing Autumn had ever imagined she'd ever be a part of, let alone be featured in.

With all the hustle and bustle of the house with decorations, food preparations, and visitors, there was never a quiet moment to be found. Except in Lady Cannon's prayer room. It seemed to be the only place to find peace and quiet.

Autumn had not availed herself of the privilege before the busy Christmas season. Now, Autumn found herself sitting in the quiet room almost every day in search of peace - not really praying or reading - just being. Strangely to her, it seemed to rejuvenate something deep inside her to simply be there.

She had been listening to the sermons in church for months now and was gaining knowledge of God and church. But as of yet, Jesus was not personal to her. She had to confess the warnings of her father held much influence over her, even though Autumn knew her mother had gone against them and believed in God. Though they were not allowed to talk about it openly, her mother had shared many things with Autumn about her faith in those last days. Things Autumn did not understand at the time, yet was coming to understand now.

And she could definitely feel God's peaceful presence in the room as she sat and reflected on the events of the past several months.

If Autumn was truthful, she had to confess His guiding hand was apparent in several situations throughout the last year. She was even starting to realize that the small voice she kept hearing was His.

Christmas week was upon them, and the mayhem around the house was at its climax with packages being prepared for delivery to the children's home, scores of guests arriving by the moment, and the gala rapidly approaching on Christmas Day. Autumn was in awe as she watched Lady Cannon directing the mayhem, knowing one day it would be her job to do the same.

*What strength she must possess, not in the physical sense, this will take its toll on her body, I'm sure - but in her character and leadership. How gracefully she makes the decisions and conducts herself. How can she stay so strong and grounded in the chaos? She's surrounded by people everywhere demanding her attention, and yet, she stands alone - strong.*

Every year, the Cannon Estate sponsored a gift drive for the local children's home nearby. Various elite guests had been invited to spend Christmas week at the Cannon Estate. This was a tradition Lord Cannon had started years ago. Some even expressed Christmas wouldn't be the same without the Cannon Christmas Gala.

Taking advantage of this opportunity, Lady Cannon had started the tradition that every guest who accepted the invitation was assigned a child to purchase a gift for - this was beyond a monetary donation - it was personalized. Then, Lady Cannon organized transportation for the whole group to deliver these gifts to the children. It was a tradition that was steeped in love and charity. So much so, that there were those that continued to help the children even though they were not attending the week-long events. This started the monetary collection, all through December, for gifts and supplies to be purchased and delivered.

*These guests consist of doctors, lawyers, politicians, and other very influential people who are yielding to the influence of one woman to be hands-on in their charitable giving during the holiday season. It's simply amazing. Why would they even listen to her - she's one woman?*

Hours before they were to leave for the children's home, Autumn found herself once again in the prayer room's quietness. *I simply cannot stay away from this room. This truly has to be Lady Cannon's secret for maintaining calm during the chaos. Without these moments of solace, I would be completely overcome with the responsibilities before me. Didn't she say something about staying connected to our Creator - how vital it was?*

*I don't know how connected I am, but I know I can't do all this alone. It's simply too much. Not the work - that I can handle, it's the weight of always being alone in the crowd. When I'm leading, I don't get to interact with people because I'm supposed to be holding it together. If I slip in my leading, everyone involved could falter. When I'm organizing something, I'm so busy keeping it going that I don't get to experience the event. It's over, and I wonder how it went? It's hard to be the one carrying the load, and I simply cannot do it alone. What am I going to do?*

Autumn ventured up to the second pew and sat looking at the cross, draped with a red satin sash for the season, feeling the burden weigh on her shoulders. She didn't notice the Bible sitting beside her until she shifted in her seat and her hand knocked it to the floor. As she leaned down to pick up the book, she saw a verse underlined and read it.

**"Here I am! I stand at the door and knock. If anyone hears My voice and opens the door, I will come in and eat with him, and he with Me."**

*Why does that sound familiar? It's like I've heard that before, yet I know I haven't. There is something about it though. What is it?*

Suddenly, she stood and made her way to the library downstairs. In her haste to get there, she was not looking ahead of her. Swinging herself around the end of the staircase, she ran into a hard wall of a man. "Oh, excuse me. I'm so sorry." She didn't look up to see who it was, embarrassed by her behavior - she didn't want to know.

The man brushed off his impeccably tailored suit, as if bumping into her had gotten him dirty. "Quite alright. You might try slowing down a bit though." The man stepped around her and continued on his way.

Autumn ducked her head in shame and continued to the library hoping it was empty.

Entering the room, she walked to the far wall and stood transfixed on the picture. Drawing even closer, she once again felt the eyes of the man in the picture peering straight into her, and she knew this man was Jesus, God's son.

As she stood there immobilized, she heard that small voice inside her repeating the words of the scripture, only this time more personally: ***Here I am Autumn! I stand at the door of your heart and knock. Hear my voice and open the door to Me, and I will come in and eat with you and you with Me for eternity. You will never be alone again.***

The magnitude of what those words meant crashed down upon Autumn and she collapsed to her knees in tears and recognition of how real Jesus was. *He sees me. ME! He sees me and knows me. And He wants me. Wants to be with me for eternity. Whoa!* Just as she was going to accept this offer, thoughts of her father, the lies she had told, and the pain of her past rushed like a flood upon her. *Whoa. He sees me - sees all I've done - all I haven't done. How can I receive such a grand invitation from God! I'm so unworthy and must be so dirty in His eyes. No. I can't. It's too hard. It's too late for me.* Autumn sat there in a heap on the floor in defeat and grave despair.

This is how Lady Cannon found her when it was time to leave for the children's home. Autumn had been looking forward to this trip for weeks. Now so heavy with regret and feeling ashamed of her filth, she only wanted to hide. Nevertheless, Lady Cannon had allowed Autumn to take charge of the children's home event, and with so many people depending on her, Autumn had no other option than to follow through. So, with deep sorrow in her heart, she arose and wiped her eyes.

*I don't know how I'm going to get through this, but I'll have to find a way. I want to accept God's invitation, but I can't. There has to be another way.*

Lady Cannon knew immediately something was wrong, yet she could not figure out what could have happened in the few hours since she had last seen Autumn. She approached Autumn, who was crumpled on the floor. "My dear, whatever is wrong?"

Autumn simply shook her head as she gathered herself together.

The guests were in the vestibule waiting for them. "Do you need to stay home? I'm sure the guests will understand you are under the weather." Autumn's countenance was indeed gloomy.

Autumn just shook her head again, took a deep breath and walked to the vestibule. Lady Cannon watched as Autumn regained her composure and firmly placing a mask of false joy on her face, took charge of organizing the guests into the vehicles. Though she fooled many, Lady Cannon knew something had happened to turn Autumn's heart frosty cold.

Despite her bone-deep sorrow, Autumn enjoyed seeing the bright faces as they delivered boxes to the sick and suffering children. She almost forgot the pain of not being able to receive God's invitation amongst the little children, though upon returning to the house, the pull of the cross and the intensive need to accept the invitation resumed.

*I can't. I simply cannot. There is no way.*

In her distracted state, Autumn forgot that she was to be announced at dinner. She absently took the arm of LeDare Anton's second in charge as he escorted her to the table and was taken back when LeDare Anton announced behind her. "Chatelaine DeBlue, Lady Cannon's aide."

Furthermore, she was astonished, when she was seated at Lady Cannon's right hand. They had thirty guests, all of whom were due to higher respect than Autumn, so as was custom, she should have been moved down the table. Also, Summer usually sat at Autumn's right hand during guest dinners and was moved when she was to honor guests. However, Autumn noticed Summer was not at her right and immediately began looking for her. Surprisingly, Summer was at the head of a smaller table which had been set up further down in the dining hall for the younger guests. This was a testament to how well Summer was gaining social skills now.

As Autumn stood behind her seat waiting for Lady Cannon's entrance, she quizzically looked at LeDare Anton standing by the door. She couldn't interpret his expression other than to see he was pleased. She then took note of those who were seated around her. She tried to smile at each of the guests; however, one man down the table was looking at her with what Autumn perceived as a scowl. *I bet that is the man I ran into. I suppose I really should apologize again, though he doesn't look very friendly.*

As Lady Cannon entered and was escorted to her seat, she took note of Autumn at her side and nodded in affirmation. As they were sitting, Autumn tried to inquire why. "Lady Cannon?"

She did not respond, yet gave a glance that indicated now was not the time to have this conversation. Though Autumn had her answer, she could see the concern in Lady Cannon's eyes and knew she was keeping Autumn close.

After dinner, there was musical entertainment planned in the ballroom. Autumn yielded to her desire to hide. "May I be excused to my suite, my Lady. I am afraid I am not up to entertaining this evening."

Lady Cannon nodded, granting her permission. Her concern was still evident as she continued to the ballroom.

As Autumn reached the top of the stairs, she glanced back over her shoulder at the guests entering the ballroom. That same man was standing in the doorway watching her ascend the stairs. When she met his eyes, he gave her a slight nod. *Who is that man? And why is he watching me so much?* Autumn turned away and went to her suite. She tried to dismiss the man from her thoughts. Still, they would wander back to him if she didn't tend to them. *Better thinking of that man than dwelling on my insufficient unworthiness.*

Christmas Eve came with a flurry of last-minute preparations. The dining room was busting at the seams with guests and delicacies, and yet Autumn found no joy in them. The pull to answer God's invitation grew with each passing day, making it difficult for Autumn to focus.

*Every conversation, every reference seems to bring me back to Him. I know in all rationality that is not true, but I can't get away from the tugging of my heart. Yet, how can I face HIM? How can I bring my filth before Him and expect to be welcomed?*

Finally, it was time to go to the Christmas Eve program, and with reluctance, Autumn donned the gorgeous gown which had been made especially for this evening. *What a hypocrite I am. Dressed in riches while filthy inside. I don't want to go to church. That is His house. How can He even allow me to enter His sanctuary without striking me down? I'm a fake. Sure, I look nice on the outside, yet inside...I'm rotten.*

Lady Cannon, Autumn, and Summer were to greet and lead the mass processional to the church program. As she descended the stairs to the vestibule, several of the guests, who had already arrived, looked up from their conversations to watch her descend. She noticed that same man was there again. *Who is he? He's not staying at the house, or I would have met him. He must be someone local whom Lady Cannon has invited to participate in the holiday, yet I haven't been introduced yet.* This time though, the man did not turn to watch her, even though several in his group did. For some reason, this blunt refusal to acknowledge her bothered her more than the looks of intrigue from the others.

She quickly brushed away those thoughts and tried to refocus on the purpose of the night. This was supposed to be a joyous season and a miraculous time for Autumn, yet she could not get past the despair in her heart. There was no hope within her.

Summer, on the other hand, was brimming with hope and life as she excitedly bounced all around the vestibule. Summer had told Autumn she loved the story of baby Jesus and couldn't wait to see it played out at the church. Autumn knew the basics of the story, although she had never actually read it before and previously had been anxious to see the Christmas play. Now, she simply wanted to hide.

Autumn sat through the program and was moved by the telling of God's son coming to earth and His provision for Joseph and Mary through the wise men. Still, she completely missed the purpose of Jesus coming in the first place. When it was all over, Summer stood in line with the other children to get their oranges and candy bags before the Cannon Estate procession headed back to the house.

*Overall, that was a successful event. Summer managed to go the whole evening without the elven maiden carriage which was a huge accomplishment. Everyone enjoyed the program, and now I can go hide in my room until tomorrow when I have to face everyone again.*

Though it was typically Becca's job to get Summer ready for bed, tonight Summer wanted Autumn. "Please, Autumn. Please! I want you to tuck me in tonight." Summer tugged on Autumn's arm as she begged.

Being so very proud of Summer's accomplishment, she agreed to help settle Summer in bed. Hand in hand they skipped down the hall to Summer's room. Once Summer was in bed, she patted the spot next to her for Autumn to sit. "Didn't you love the story of Jesus?"

Autumn nodded. "It was a very nice play."

"Yes, but what about Jesus. You know Christmas is all about him right?"

"Yes, sweet one. Jesus is the reason for the season."

"No." Summer sat up displeased with Autumn's rote reply. "No. Not that. Christmas is about *JESUS*...God's son...and how He left heaven and came here for us...to be our Savior...you know...to clean us of our mistakes...the bad things we do." Summer tilted her head as if she was trying to make Autumn understand. "Don't you know *JESUS*?"

Autumn couldn't answer. She didn't know Jesus. She knew *of* Him, as God's son, but nothing about Him.

Summer smiled and patted Autumn's hand. "It's okay. I didn't know Him either for a long time. But Granny says that Jesus came here so that we could be forgiven. Cuz, without Jesus' forgiveness we can't go to heaven. So, you need to know Him, okay? Cuz I want you to go to heaven with me."

Autumn smiled and nodded, confused more than clear about what Summer was saying.

*Surely there is more to it than a five-year-old knows. It's not just about forgiveness, it's about correcting my mistakes. And there is no way to make what is in the past right again.*

As Autumn left Summer's room, she could no longer fight the pull to be in the prayer room. She **had** to face Him and explain why she wasn't worthy because she could not go on in her present state.

Not seeing the ribbon hanging on the outside of the door, she opened it and blindly moved to the foot of the cross. Sinking to the floor, tears began to fall down her cheeks as she gave in to the pull on her heart. "Oh God, I can't do this anymore. I am a filthy liar and full of deception, yet I cannot resist you anymore. You can't possibly want someone like me. I know you see me. You see it all, and I don't understand why you won't just let me be. I'm telling you, God, You don't want **me**." Autumn's shoulders shook with her sobs.

"Yes, He does." A voice from behind Autumn jerked her to her feet.

Seeing Lady Cannon standing at the back of the room, Autumn went pale. "M..m..my Lady, I am so...so sorry, I had no idea you were here. I beg your pardon." Curtsying dramatically, she then turned for the door. *Stupid, stupid, stupid. Now, what am I going to do now? She heard, she heard it all, and I'm going to lose it all. It's over.*

Lady Cannon stepped into her path and looked Autumn straight in the eyes. "Stop running, Autumn. Now is the time to stop running."

Autumn halted in place and tears overcame her again. She put her face in her hands and wept. Lady Cannon gently put her arms around her and embraced Autumn in love and support. For a long moment, Lady Cannon stood there holding her.

Finally gaining some control, Autumn again tried to apologize. "I'm s..so..sorry. I d..didn't see the r...r..ibbon."

Lady Cannon led Autumn by the hand to the back pew and gestured for her to sit. "My dear, why don't you tell me what has been happening in your heart. What has God been saying to you?"

Again Autumn broke into tears. Through sobs, she tried to explain. "He...He has been drawing me here. To the pr...prayer room. To just sit with H...Him." She told of what happened the day of the children's home outing and the despair and sorrow in her heart at not being able to accept the invitation of God.

"My dear, why do you feel that you cannot accept His invitation? What is keeping you from him?"

A little shocked, as she thought it was obvious, Autumn tried to explain. "Because I'm filthy. My life is full of lies and deception that clings to me like filth and makes me unworthy of His invitation. I wouldn't dare come to your table in dirty rags, how can I even possibly consider coming before the God of the universe?"

To Lady Cannon, this explained more than just Autumn's spiritual struggles, but also her avoidance of the esteemed guests in the house. Autumn had been hiding from everyone because she felt so filthy on the inside. She had been running from God because she could not bring herself to deny His invitation, yet also felt she could not face Him in such a filthy state.

"I just couldn't take it anymore. The pressure of avoiding God was just too intense. And then Summer said I needed to know Jesus and..." Autumn threw her hands up in the air as if that explained it all.

"Fighting against God is a futile endeavor. I know this from years of experience." Lady Cannon patted Autumn's hand. "Summer is correct, you know. You do need to come to know Jesus in a personal way. Can I tell you about Him?"

"I know He is the Son of God, who miraculously came to earth. What more is there?"

"Oh my dear, there is so much more. Do you know why Jesus came to earth?"

"Summer said it was so that we can be forgiven and go to heaven. Surely there is more to it though; simple forgiveness will not make right the wrongs I've done."

"You are correct. Forgiveness is a part of the process, though not the solution. No, Jesus came to earth to die for you."

"Die for me? Why would He do that?"

"Because He loves you so very much. You see, it all goes back to Adam and Eve. They brought sin - separation from God - into this world. God is perfect and holy, and He cannot be associated with anything less. You know this, which is why you have been struggling. What you have yet to learn though is that God had a solution for this separation. He sent His only Son to earth to be the ultimate sacrifice. Do you remember hearing tonight about how the Israelites had to make sacrifices at the temple?"

Autumn nodded.

"Well, they did that to make amends for their sin - their wrongdoing. God gave them the Law to follow, and yet no one could follow it perfectly, so they had to atone for - or make right - their sin through offering sacrifices. God knew though, that this process would become a ritual and meaningless, and could not go on forever; it was not perfect, and therefore, wasn't enough to satisfy His need for rightness. So, He sent His Son to live the perfect life and become the perfect sacrifice. And whoever believes in Jesus, and accepts *Him* as their Savior, is washed clean from all their filth by His blood."

"But if He died, I don't understand why you believe in Him today? I mean, if He's dead then why do you talk to Him?"

"That is a very good question. Jesus died on the cross; He was crucified - a terrible death. He did this to take on all the sin of the world; past, present, and future. But Jesus did not stay dead, because

He is fully God and fully man, He rose again and is living today. He lived among His followers for forty days after His death and then He went to heaven. And He still lives today. That is why I believe and talk to Him."

Tears began to flow down Autumn's cheeks again. "So there is a way. A way to be clean and accept God's invitation to dine with Him?"

Lady Cannon nodded. "There is much more to walking with Jesus, yet all you need to be clean is to say 'yes' to Him. The Bible says in Romans 10:9-10, *If you confess with your mouth, 'Jesus is Lord', and believe in your heart that God raised Him from the dead, you will be saved. For it is with the heart that you believe and are justified, and it is with your mouth that you confess and are saved.*"

The way to freedom had been before her the whole time; she just had not understood it until now. She wanted to be clean and free, yet she was still afraid. Afraid that if she accepted the invitation of Jesus, He would require her to reveal the secret of running from her father and she would be forced to go back because she was still a minor in Nebraska.

Lady Cannon watched Autumn struggling within and sensed this was the time to press for the truth. "Autumn, I want to help you; however, I can do nothing unless you tell me the truth. You have become a daughter to me, and it grieves my heart to see you so tortured. Why won't you trust me? Don't you know there is nothing you can say that will change how I feel about you? How God feels about you? He already knows everything. Why won't you tell me what is holding you back from embracing Him and the new life He has given you?"

"I don't want to lose you or what I have here. I am so afraid if I tell the truth, I will be forced to leave you and Summer."

"I don't understand. Who will force you to leave?" A bit frustrated, Lady Cannon paused to say a prayer. "Do you remember the day when you first met Summer? I told you she was so important to me that I'd die for her if it would help but instead I had been asked to live?"

Intrigued as to where this was going, Autumn said, "Yes."

"I have come to feel that same way about you. I don't know what you have been hiding, yet I will do everything within my power to not allow whatever it is to separate us. I would die first, or if need be, live long enough, to gain assurance that we'll be together, if not here on earth - in eternity."

Lady Cannon paused long enough to let what she was saying sink in. "Autumn, you know Jesus feels the same way about you because He *did* die for you. He died so you wouldn't have to be afraid anymore. He died so you could have the assurance of eternity in heaven with Him, and with us, if you will believe in Him and accept His salvation. If you put your trust in Him, we would have all of eternity together no matter what we face on this earth."

At this truth and assurance, the walls of Autumn's heart collapsed. *How could she refuse such love, such promise?* "Lady Cannon, I want to accept Jesus' invitation. I want to receive the cleansing of the Blood of the Lamb so that I can dine with Him and you in eternity. Will you help me?"

Lady Cannon let out the breath she was holding and grasped Autumn's hands. "Yes, my dear, first let's pray and then we can talk." Lady Cannon's heart was overflowing as her prayers were being answered this very hour. *How marvelous was her Heavenly Father in all He did?*

Lady Cannon led Autumn in a simple salvation prayer, emphasizing that Autumn could repeat the words, though the meaning of them had to come from her heart. At the end of Lady Cannon's prayer, Autumn added. "Lord Jesus, I'm scared. I do thank you for making me clean and forgiving me, but I don't' know if others will be as forgiving. Please help me and provide the strength I need to be honest. Amen."

Autumn was amazed at how she felt freer, cleaner and more loved than she had her whole life - it was an immediate sensation - full of joy. And there was such peace in her heart - until she turned to Lady Cannon. "I have to tell you the truth now." And she did. She told Lady Cannon the truth of her father and her running away. She also confessed her fear that if her father knew where she was, he'd make her go back because she was still a minor. Though Autumn at times thought about her father and wondered how he was, she did not want to leave Michigan or Lady Cannon.

"This is definitely an issue of concern. I think I need to speak with Lord Michaels and determine what needs to be done on the legal front. You are of legal age here in Michigan, though I do not know how that affects the situation in Nebraska. You will be nineteen in a month. Still, I don't want to be deceptive. Also, tomorrow is Christmas, and the various offices we would need to consult are closed. So let's get through the commitments of the holidays before delving too far into the issue of your father."

The house was full of guests, and there were hundreds of people counting on them tomorrow; not to mention, in just one week they had the New Year's Eve Ball. With so much to do and so many guests, Lady Cannon could see now was not the time to stir up potential trouble.

"However, I do not like the idea that your father does not know if you are dead or alive. You need to call him and let him know you are safe and will be getting in touch with him after the holidays."

Though she had prayed, Autumn was still afraid. *Lord, I don't want to call him. I'm not ready. Isn't there another way?*

**Mrs. Bogart.**

Autumn then told Lady Cannon about Mrs. Bogart and their friendship. "Could I call Mrs. Bogart and have her deliver a message to my father? I'm just not ready to talk to him yet." Plus, Mrs. Bogart would want to know Autumn had accepted Jesus' invitation.

Lady Cannon approved of the idea, so it was determined Autumn would do that first thing in the morning.

With all the uncertainty, Lady Cannon brought up the issue of her coming out ball tomorrow night. "I'll need to speak with Lord Michaels about that as well. I think it best if we wait to announce you as guardian and estate manager until later. I know this is a disappointment; nevertheless, we need to do this correctly and make sure there won't be any complications down the road."

Autumn agreed, knowing it was the right thing to do.

"Autumn, before we leave, I hope you understand that you will need time to heal. Jesus forgives us immediately, but it may take time before you are able to forgive your father for the way he treated you. Pray for his salvation and try to remember he is as lost as you were a few hours ago and with no hope. Therefore, please remember that though you are saved, there is still a long journey ahead of you as you learn to walk with God and receive His healing."

For the first time, Autumn saw her father in a new light. She was grieved for the pain he must be in, and she determined to pray for him right then. Lady Cannon joined her, adding her own prayer for a softening of his heart and understanding.

As they parted, well past curfew that night, Lady Cannon assured Autumn that no matter what happened with her father, she would not face it alone. Having the burden lifted from her, Autumn felt as free as a songbird. She slept the most peaceful sleep she had ever experienced, knowing when she awoke it would be Christmas, the first true Christmas of her life, and it was going to be glorious.

# ❤ 19 ❤

Autumn lay wide-eyed on her bed, staring at the ceiling, marveling at all that had happened the night before. There was gratitude so deep within her she wanted to go to the balcony of her suite and proclaim the love of Jesus with all her strength, yet knowing there were guests still sleeping, she refrained. Instead, she uttered thanks and appreciation to her Heavenly Father and prayed for her earthly one.

With so much excitement and many tasks to be tended to, Autumn got up to start her day. Opening her door, she met Ménage Eleanor in the great room of her suite.

In surprise, Eleanor exclaimed. "Good morning, Chatelaine. I hear a most marvelous thing happened last night."

Autumn nodded in wonder as to how she found out. "Yes indeed, dear Eleanor. But how did you know?"

"Oh, we have been praying for some time, and Lady Cannon could not sleep until she had informed me, knowing how close we have become."

Autumn shook her head; Eleanor never failed to amaze her with what she knew. They would often stay together in the evenings, and Eleanor would fill her in on the happenings around the house. Autumn requested that Eleanor take a few moments now to sit and talk with her before the mayhem of the day swept them away.

As the two friends sat sharing stories and celebrating in Autumn's salvation, Autumn was surprised when Eleanor presented a gift. "It is not really a Christmas gift; it is more of a birthday gift."

"A birthday gift, but my birthday isn't until next month?"

"Not your physical birthday; your spiritual one. You are now a new creature in Christ Jesus."

Autumn opened the gift and saw Eleanor had purchased a Bible with her name on the cover. Eleanor leaned over and opened the front cover. "I went ahead and wrote in it the day of your new birth in Christ Jesus so you will always be able to remember when you made your commitment to Him."

"But how...how did you have this?"

"Like I said, we have been praying for a long time, and I bought it out of faith. I knew you would come to see your need for Him and accept His free gift of salvation. I just didn't know when."

Autumn embraced Eleanor in such appreciation; they both were in tears.

"Now, dear Chatelaine, it is time to ready you for Christmas. We have much to do, come and wash up as I get your dress ready."

It was not long before Ménage Eleanor had her dressed and ready for breakfast. For the morning and early afternoon, Autumn wore a lovely green satin dress with a hint of golden shimmer. Autumn's hair was done in the usual daily manner with a little more flair and a few more ribbons.

As Autumn dismissed Ménage Eleanor to inquire when breakfast was being served, she sat down at her desk to make the call to Mrs. Bogart as she had promised. Once again she had to call information, though she recognized the number given to her. With shaking hands she prepared to dial the number, then stopped, deciding to say a prayer for God's leading first. Calm came over her, and she was able to make the call with confidence.

One ring, two rings, three rings, Autumn was about to hang up when she heard Mrs. Bogart's voice. "Hello?"

"Mrs. Bogart. It's Autumn."

"Autumn! Oh Autumn, where are you? Are you okay?" Penny was in shock.

"I am doing very well, Mrs. Bogart. God has been so good to me. I wish I had all the time in the world to tell you about the wonderful things He has done. Unfortunately, my time is limited, and there are two reasons for my call."

Penny's heart leaped inside her. "Oh Autumn, so much has happened since you left. You really need to know what has been happening with your father."

"My father?" Autumn's heart dropped to the pit of her stomach. "You know my father?"

"Yes. We met a few months ago. Edmund, James, and my husband, Henry, have become quite good friends, but I am getting ahead of myself. Can you tell me where you are? Your father has been so upset over your disappearance. I'm sure he will want to know." Penny was determined to find out as much as she could while she had Autumn on the phone.

Autumn tried to change the subject while she processed what Mrs. Bogart was saying. "First, I wanted to let you know that I have accepted Jesus Christ as my Savior. I knew you'd want to know right away. I can't even begin to tell you how He has been working in my heart and life, and I know He started it through you. Thank you so much for your friendship and for showing me His love."

Penny couldn't help but shout out. "Praise you, Jesus. Oh, how I have prayed for you."

Autumn smiled. "I also called to request a favor. I realize this may be awkward for you, especially with your new friendship with my father, and I have already asked so much of you. Could I impose upon you once again?"

Penny paused, only because of how Autumn had phrased the request. She was more refined than the girl Penny had known on the side of the road many months ago. She was intrigued as to what Autumn would ask of her. "Well, I suppose I can consider another request, but I have to say, if you are going to ask me to keep any secrets from your father, I cannot."

"Actually, I was going to request that you let him know that I am alright."

"Of course, honey, I would be happy to tell him. But...why don't you call him yourself?"

Autumn did not know what to say at first. She could have called him just as easily as she had called Mrs. Bogart, then Autumn remembered. "Honestly, Mrs. Bogart, I am afraid. I am sure he is furious with me for lying to him and for running away. He never really understood how horrid it was living with him. Anyway, I'm not ready yet to face him, though I will soon, after the holidays, I promise."

'Oh, but Autumn, he has changed. You should know that, just by the fact that he has become friends with us. He truly has come to see his neglect of you and wishes to make it right. Won't you give him that chance?"

"It doesn't make sense, Mrs. Bogart? Why has my father befriended you? He forbade me to even speak to you, and I disobeyed him on even that. What happened that he would change so much?" Autumn was confused.

"Let me start at the beginning. A few months back after the police had come to a dead end in searching for you, your father was walking on the road and stopped to talk to me just like you used to. When I told him I had helped you on occasion, I saw immediately why you ran away; he was instantly enraged and dangerous. However, shortly after that first conversation, he started coming over to talk with Henry, my husband. It did not take long for us to realize this was a miracle from above. The more he stopped by, the more he asked questions about our God. We soon found out that a fellow believer and church member named James McCurry was employed by your father and lived in his basement. After several months of visits and a lot of prayers, we all become friends."

"That truly is a miracle knowing my father and all that he believed about Christians." Immediately, Autumn was alarmed. "Did you tell him about me borrowing the car?" Though Autumn had noted Mrs. Bogart's earlier comment about the police, she did not know if their search had included this information.

Penny was ashamed. "No. We have not told him anything about the car, but we probably should especially under the circumstances."

"What circumstances?"

"Well, that is another part of the story. As I told you, your father asked us many questions about God and Jesus. Finally, James bought him a Bible and told him to read it, and he did every night. Then he and James would discuss what he was reading. We thought last night, at the Christmas program, might be the time he would give his heart to Jesus. But when the time came, Edmund did not respond. We were all disappointed, though knew God had to do the work, not us. Henry and I decided to pray when we got home. About two hours later, James called and said once they were home, Edmund asked some questions and decided he needed Jesus' forgiveness. Autumn, your father accepted Jesus last night."

Autumn was completely dumbfounded. *Her father! Last night?* Autumn was trying to process all of this when she heard that small voice she recognized as God. ***All things are possible with Me. I work in mysterious ways to men, but I have your ultimate good in mind.***

Autumn was very quiet.

"Autumn, are you still there?"

"Yes, yes I am. I am just so stunned. Who is James?"

"Oh, he is the man your father hired to help run the farm. Shortly after you left, things started to fall apart on the farm, and Edmund needed help, so he hired James. He now lives in your basement."

"You know, Mrs. Bogart, I am beside myself with the understanding that our Heavenly Father would orchestrate such a night as last night for our good. Did I mention that it was last night that *I* accepted Christ?"

"No! You mean you *and* your father accepted Christ on the same night?"

"Yes, and He ordained it that I should call this very morning."

"Autumn, your father really has been so worried about you and has changed so much. He has told us so many times he wishes he could make things right with you. Can you not call him yourself and tell him these things?"

Autumn was pondering this when Ménage Eleanor entered the room. Autumn tried to get her attention before she spoke. Unfortunately, it was too late. Thinking Autumn was in another room, Eleanor proclaimed rather loudly. "Chatelaine, breakfast is being served in ten minutes, you really must hurry."

Trying to cover the receiver on the phone, Autumn answered. "Thank you, Eleanor, please go ask our Lady to pardon my tardiness as I finish this call. I will be there momentarily."

Eleanor blushed as she curtsied, and rushed off with the message for Lady Cannon.

"Autumn, Autumn are you there?"

"Yes, Mrs. Bogart, I am still here, but I need to go. Please tell my father that I will be in touch with him after the New Year and the holiday mayhem has subsided."

Trying to get more information before she hung up, Penny pressed. "Who were you talking to? What is a Chatelaine? Was she talking to you?"

Autumn grimaced. "I am so sorry, Mrs. Bogart, I cannot answer your questions right now. I really need to go. Please tell my father that I am being taken care of, and I will call him when I can. I really must go now. Will you tell him?

"Yes. I will tell Edmund, but I still think you should call him yourself."

"I will after the holidays, I promise. I must go. Good-bye and God Bless you, Mrs. Bogart."

"And you, Autumn."

Penny hung up, checked her caller ID and immediately called Edmund.

# ♡ 20 ♡

Autumn hung up and took a deep breath. She quickly reflected on what Eleanor had said and tried to think if there was any way her father could figure out where she was by what was said. She was not trying to hide anymore, yet if a reference had been made she would need to advise Lady Cannon right away. She determined the only references were "Chatelaine," "Eleanor," and "Lady" which could be anyone. Hurriedly, she stood and made her way to breakfast where upon entering LeDare Anton announced her presence and escorted her, personally, to her seat.

She curtsied to Lady Cannon and acknowledged the rest of the table seated below her. Her eye caught that same man watching her intently, yet she dismissed it as Summer scampered up to greet her with a hug and kiss.

"It is good to see you happy again." Autumn smiled and squeezed her hand before she went back to her table.

"Pardon my tardiness, my Lady, I was making the phone call we discussed last night." Lady Cannon met her eyes, quietly questioning. "Everything is taken care of, and I have news to share with you when you have a moment to spare."

"Good news, I hope." Lady Cannon inquired.

"Yes, in fact, most astounding news." Autumn's eyes beamed, and Lady Cannon wondered what news from Nebraska would bring Autumn so much joy.

After breakfast, the guests were to visit in the vestibule and enjoy carols sung by various artists brought in by Lady Cannon. Several tasks needed to be tended to and guests to be mingled with. Lady Cannon had requested that Autumn make a special effort to avail herself to the guests, especially after the last few days of avoiding them. So, with Summer by her side, they made their way to the vestibule sitting area to play games, puzzles, and dolls.

At various times, Lady Cannon would bring guests over to meet Autumn, and she would visit with them until they were satisfied or found other guests to visit with, then she would return her attention back to Summer. Autumn was having Summer pick up their latest game, as it was almost lunchtime, when Lady Cannon approached them with the man she kept seeing.

Autumn's stomach dropped, and her heart began to beat harder as she stood to greet him. *Finally! I have been wondering who you are for days now. I know I shouldn't care, but you intrigue me.*

Seeing him up close, she realized he had deep brown eyes with gold flecks. He stood a good six inches taller than she did and he had broad shoulders - something she remembered from running into him. He wore an expensive black tailored suit that accentuated his fine build with a green tie that surprisingly matched her dress. He was quite handsome. *No. Stop it, Autumn. You are not interested. You cannot be interested.*

She also noticed he was working his jaw. *Is he angry? His eyes don't look angry, but I don't know anything about him, so he could be upset about our last encounter. Why else would he be working his jaw like that?*

She was so distracted with her observations of the man that she almost missed Lady Cannon's introduction. "Chatelaine, may I introduce you to Lord Landon Michaels, our legal advisor, and counselor."

*Legal advisor? Counselor? THIS was Lord Michaels? Oh, no....no...no...no...this cannot be Lady Cannon's lawyer. I have to get a grip. I should not be thinking anything remotely interesting about this man, especially not if he is Lady Cannon's lawyer. UGH!* Realizing she was belated in her response, Autumn curtsied and bowed her head ever so slightly in respect. "Lord Michaels, it is a great pleasure to make your acquaintance, and I sincerely apologize for my inattentiveness the other day."

Landon reached out and took the newly introduced Chatelaine's hand - though she had not been offering it to him. Slowly bringing it to his lips, he pressed a soft kiss to the back of her hand and had to keep himself from gasping. That slight kiss caused his lips to burn, the electricity sparked from the contact was more than simple shock. *How did this woman affect him in so many different ways? Intrigue, confusion, lust, nervousness. It was impossible to think straight with her looking at him like that.*

He struggled to get his thoughts back in line. "Our run-in was a pleasant distraction to the day." He smiled teasingly with genuine charm radiating from him. "Though at the time, I did not have the pleasure of knowing who was running into me." Landon could not bring himself to relinquish her hand, though he knew he should.

Autumn blushed and again dipped her head. She was not at all sure how to respond to such a comment, and he was still holding her hand, which was sending tingles up to her elbow.

Trying to bring the conversation back to a professional level, Landon forced himself to release her hand, and tucked his own behind his back to keep them from reaching for her again. "I have heard so much about you over the last several months. Lady Cannon has never passed up an opportunity to sing your praises - gracious, kind, loyal, dedicated, inventive, compassionate. I find that I feel very much like I already know you, though we haven't been introduced before. I see though, that our Lady neglected to inform me of how lovely you truly are." Landon glanced at Lady Cannon who was watching their encounter intensely. "Though, I would say your greatest accomplishment is how excellently you have handled your newly acquired position." He shifted his glance to Summer and then back to Autumn.

Autumn noted his reference and nodded her thanks. *How can this man be so bold? Taking her hand without her permission - and right in front of Lady Cannon. He must be very confident of his position within the estate - or maybe he is simply kind, and I'm misinterpreting his attention due to my own interest. I've* **got** *to stop thinking about him.* Autumn sheepishly glanced at Lady Cannon who simply smiled in response. *What is that supposed to mean? Does she approve of how Lord Michaels is interacting with me? I'm so confused.* "Thank you, Lord Michaels, your admiration is very kindhearted, and it pleases me exceedingly to know our Lady is satisfied with my performance. I value her opinion above all others."

*All others. Ouch! Was that a hint?* Leaning in toward her, Landon decided to test the waters further. "My admiration is more than kindhearted, and please, call me Landon."

That got Lady Cannon's attention. She had never heard him request to be addressed so informally - not even with her after so many years of service. Still, Autumn was indeed lovely - especially today - the glow around her was nothing short of radiant and she was an especially gifted young woman. *A possible match between these two would be most beneficial. And the way Lord Michaels is looking at my Chatelaine, I would say the possibility was not too far-fetched. The real question is, would Autumn be open to such a match? Or if she even should be interested in a match at this new time in her life?*

Autumn blushed again ever so slightly and shifted back just a hair as to not be rude. "You are indeed gracious, though I fear so informal of address would be disrespectful of your esteemed position with our Lady."

The Chatelaine's smile was so sweet, Landon barely registered the refusal as he struggled to keep his knees locked under him. He turned to Lady Cannon for help. "My Lady, do you have any objection to my request? We will, after all, be working closely together on estate business."

Lady Cannon thought for a moment. "No, if it is what you would prefer, I give my permission for private conversation. Though, I would prefer your title be used when in conversation with others."

Autumn could not believe it. *What is she thinking? This has been a foundational standard in her home. Why is she changing this now? What is she up to?*

"There, that settles it. Landon, it is every time we are in private conversation. Now, if our Lady will permit, would you take a sleigh ride with me, Chatelaine?"

In the planning of the Christmas day events, Autumn had suggested providing the guests with sleigh rides around the premises of the estate. Lady Cannon thought the idea marvelous and arranged for two sleighs with horses dressed in bells to provide the entertainment in the late morning and all afternoon.

They both turned to Lady Cannon who nodded in approval.

Autumn had promised to take Summer on a sleigh ride; therefore, when she heard that Autumn was going, Summer started to accompany her. However, Lady Cannon redirected her to the puzzle she had been putting away. "The Chatelaine will take you another time. This one's for Lord Michaels." Reluctantly, Summer sat back down with Lady Cannon and finished picking up her puzzle.

Upon seeing this, Landon was thankful for the forethought he had had to request permission from Lady Cannon to speak with the Chatelaine in private ahead of time. Though his motives were a little mixed. Though he definitely wanted to spend time with this woman, his main reason was to be sure they were completely open and aware of where each person stood. In the future, they would, indeed, be working closely together within the estate.

LeDare Anton assisted Autumn with her coat and then she took Landon's offered arm as he escorted her to the waiting sleigh. They were seated rather closely and wrapped in warm furs for the twenty-minute ride. Autumn did not have to look to know he was looking at her.

Trying to think of something to say, Autumn spouted the first thing that came to her mind. "Lord Michaels…ur...Landon, may I inquire as to who in your office wrote the contract between Lady Cannon and myself?"

Landon was taken back by this question, as it was not what he was thinking, or even considered they would talk about. "I did."

Turning abruptly to face him, Autumn was astounded. "*You* wrote the contract?"

"Yes. I personally handle all of Lady Cannon's legal affairs. Was there something wrong with the contract? I had not been told of anything amiss."

"No, nothing at all, in fact, I was very impressed with it. I reread the contract after being apprised of the change in my position to incorporate Summer. It was remarkable how you entwined the two positions into one - a marrying of sorts. Truly, it was inspiring."

Landon laughed. "Now it is you whose admiration is so gracious. What I did was simply a playing of words. However, I can counter your high praises in that it is truly *you* who are remarkable."

Autumn saw the admiration in his eyes, and it made her look away. "Me? There is nothing remarkable about me." And she believed this wholeheartedly. She was a simple country girl who had been blessed - nothing more, nothing special.

"I beg to differ. When a young woman makes her way halfway across the country by herself with little money, to give herself in service to an eccentric old woman she does not know, that is remarkable. When that same young woman then discovers she had been deceived in her original appointment, yet finds forgiveness and embraces a troubled child, that is remarkable. And then, that same young woman discovers the key that unlocks the child from her misery and restores peace and joy back to the household she recently joined - that's beyond remarkable. And none of those even begins to mention the numerous lessons you had to undertake, or the fact that not only did you do them, but excelled at them.

"Besides, here you are just months into your endeavor and not a person in the house would be able to tell you were not raised in high society, nor would anyone question that you belong here. So, I guess you are correct; you are not just remarkable, you are phenomenal."

Autumn was not comfortable with all the praise being thrown at her, and therefore, decided to defuse some of it with a jest. "You forgot, a young woman who also can be found playing with dolls in the vestibule during a Christmas gathering."

Landon laughed. "Exactly, and very graciously I may add."

There was a pause in the conversation as they enjoyed the scenery.

*He seems to know everything about me? He'd get along splendidly with Eleanor.* Autumn chuckled to herself. *Why has he taken such pains to know so much? Is he simply watching out for Lady Cannon? What do I know about him? Maybe I should be looking out for Lady Cannon too, though Lady Cannon has known Lord Michaels a lot longer. Didn't she mention testing him once to prove his loyalty? So, if Lady Cannon trusts him, what does that say about him?*

Autumn pondered this as they rode. *In order for Lady Cannon to hold him in such high regard, not only would he have to be a great counselor and trustworthy, but he would have had to prove himself to be kind, compassionate, intelligent, dependable, and loyal.*

Landon watched her, trying to decipher every expression. *I want to know everything there is to know about this woman. I want to be able to tell if she is sad or hurt, joyful or excited. I want to know what makes her smile, and how she came up with her ideas with Summer. I want her to trust me, not only like Lady Cannon trusts me with the estate, but with her heart. She has completely captured my interest. She intrigues me with her abilities and choices, she challenges me with her correct manner, and she stirs desire in me simply with her touch.* Since that first encounter at the stairs, he had not stopped thinking of her. *The way she openly loves and cares for Lady Cannon and Summer stirs my heart. How can someone love strangers so openly?*

He had been receiving regular updates on her progress with the classes and responsibilities since her arrival and had already established a high regard for the person she was - one he had doubted in the beginning. However, what she had achieved with Summer was simply miraculous. He had also been watching her the past few days as she helped host the Christmas events. He had observed her actions and reactions; therefore, he knew something was going on within, despite the happy mask she wore. Things simply did not accurately reflect what he had come to know of her. Even with her obvious distraction and avoidance of the guests though, he could tell from his observations she was gentle, kind, and sweet-hearted. Therefore, he was not surprised when Lady Cannon informed him of her personal struggles and conversion.

Sitting beside her now, his heart was pounding like it had never before. He had been in other relationships, yet never before had he been this swept away. He truly did not understand his feelings, and he wanted her to know there would be no secrets between them. His affections were honorable and true, even knowing the truth about her past, though he would not act on them with her being so young.

Landon reached over and took Autumn's hand under the blankets. Immediately, the tingling started moving up her arm, distracting her. She tried to focus on what he was saying nonetheless.

"Chatelaine...may I call you Autumn?"

Autumn nodded dumbly. *Why not? Lady Cannon gave permission for her to be informal with him.*

"Autumn, I'm going to be very straightforward with you. I know about your past. I know about your father, about the lies, and I know about your salvation last night." His blood was pumping hard through his chest at the feel of her hand in his. "I realize that from your perspective we just met; however, *I've* been learning about you for months. I would now like *you* to know *me*. I don't want there to be any secrets between us - we will have to work closely together and have a very open relationship. I know you trust Lady Cannon, and Lady Cannon trusts me, but what I need to know is...can you trust me?"

It was hard to focus with him holding her hand. *Could she trust this man that she knew nothing about simply because Lady Cannon trusted him? What was she trusting him with? She knew she was attracted to him like she had never been to any other man before, even though they had just met. And she knew she could not pursue a relationship with him - if that were what he was asking. Everything seemed to be getting complicated and confusing. What was she supposed to say?* She sent a silent petition up seeking for guidance on how to answer this question.

Peace washed over her and Autumn felt she had an answer. Autumn knew it was not beyond God to bring people into her life, after all, look at Mrs. Bogart, Becky, and Lady Cannon. God had used each one of these people in her life for His glory. She did not know what purpose Landon would fill, yet she had no doubt God was in control.

"I'm not certain what exactly you are asking of me, but yes, I believe I can trust you; and I would like to get to know you better - as acquaintances."

"That's a start." In his heart, Landon prayed. *Lord, if you will grant to me the heart of this precious woman, I will guard her with my whole being until the day I come to be with you.*

Autumn was exhausted. After delivering Summer to her suites for a period of rest after lunch, Autumn retired to her own as well. She knew she needed a break. After a few hours of peaceful resting, Ménage Eleanor woke her to start dressing. Unfortunately, it was at that time that Autumn remembered she had promised a sleigh ride to Summer, and she could not break that promise.

"Eleanor, please go see if Summer is awake yet. If she is, we'll take a quick sleigh ride before getting ready."

"Chatelaine, we have much to do, and it is already late in the day."

"Then I suggest you hurry to see if Summer is ready. I will not break my promise to her. I'll meet her in the vestibule."

Before entering the sled, Autumn instructed the driver to make an abbreviated trip as she had no intentions of stressing Ménage Eleanor any more than she already had. Summer did not notice the ride was cut short and the girls had a splendid time, laughing and singing. Autumn realized she would remember it forever and was grateful she took the time to keep her promise.

Upon entering her room, Autumn found Ménage Eleanor pacing frantically. "I am here, Eleanor, and I'm all yours. I will not prohibit you from your duties again."

With great relief, Eleanor flung her arms around her.

With all the hoops, skirts, buttons and fabric, it was an ordeal to dress, though Ménage Eleanor - with the assistance of another maid – accomplished it in short order. However, the hairstyle Ménage Eleanor had practiced for weeks consisting of braids, spirals, and pearls, took considerably more time. Ménage Eleanor determined between the exquisite gown, and the fabulous hairstyle, Autumn would be the most stunning woman at the ball - even surpassing Lady Cannon.

The regal gown that had been specially made for this occasion was a shimmering off the shoulder ruby red sateen ball gown with yards of fabric that was very well-fitted. The fit made the dress flattering without restricting movement or breathing, which was what Autumn had feared. Somewhere, she had gotten the idea that all ball gowns had to be uncomfortable, so when she accompanied Lady Cannon to acquire her Christmas gown, she requested comfort as a priority. She was pleased to discover, if well-made, any gown could be pleasant to wear.

Being so nervous about her first ball, Autumn sent for Lady Cannon to come and approve of her dressing and appearance before she even dared to step out of her suite. By the reactions of both Ménage Eleanor and Lady Cannon, Autumn knew she would draw attention at the evening's activities, and it unnerved her slightly, yet she could hardly contain her excitement.

With so many things to arrange and attend to, Autumn was in the dining hall when LeDare Anton started announcing guests in the vestibule. Knowing Lady Cannon expected her to be present, she made her way there in hopes of quietly joining the guests unnoticed.

Landon had been in the library enjoying some peace and quiet when he heard LeDare Anton start announcing guests. Knowing he needed to be present as well, he had made his way to the vestibule, only to be pleasantly surprised by seeing Autumn ahead of him in the hallway. His pulse raced as he caught sight of her. Never in all of his years of service to dignitaries had he seen a woman so stunning, so incomparably beautiful - and it was not only the outward beauty he saw.

Autumn heard someone approach behind her, stopping a respectable distance away, though she did not turn immediately to see who it was. Yet, even with the distance between them, she still got goosebumps, and her stomach flipped at the familiar voice coming from behind her. "Chatelaine, your beauty outshines the brightest star in heaven tonight."

Turning, she saw Lord Michaels bowing. She curtsied in return. "You are indeed a master of words, Lord Michaels, but do you always exaggerate?" She teased him.

Her smile made his heart leap. Leaning in slightly, he whispered. "I am not exaggerating. Every woman will be jealous, and every man will be intrigued. I promise you that. Truly, you are lovely. And it's Landon, if you please." He winked.

Autumn raised her brows at his bold proclamation and blushed at his compliment. Not having a reply for him, she simply turned back around to look at the crowded vestibule as he joined her and offered his arm in escort. The vestibule was abuzz with the additionally hired staff members carrying trays of hors-d'oeuvres and wine glasses for the guests to enjoy while waiting for dinner to be served. Autumn soon found that it was a maze to get just two feet, and she was appreciative of Landon's escort, even though he led her around the vestibule like a proud peacock assuring everyone saw her on his arm.

Dinner was called, and Landon immediately led her in a course toward the dining hall entrance. As he did, one of the servers carrying a tray of wine glasses stepped wrong and began to lose his balance. Seeing the catastrophe in motion, Landon quickly put himself between her and the server protecting her from the collision.

Consequently, Autumn unexpectedly found herself in a face to face embrace, just in time to avoid a collision that would have ruined not only her dress, but perhaps, her entire evening.

The server regained his footing and begged their pardon as he quickly retreated, though neither of them heard a thing. Landon stood holding her, regretting that he'd have to let her go as her eyes met with his. He was certain she could see the depth of admiration within them. He would need to clarify his intentions with Lady Cannon very soon.

Gently freeing herself from his embrace, Autumn remained close enough to whisper as she looked up at him. "Surely you remember the clause added to my contract, and the consequences of breaking it."

He continued to hold her gaze and knew his intentions were indeed clear to her. "I am *fully* aware of that clause, but it does not change the matters of the heart."

She nodded slightly in acknowledgment. "Unfortunately, I am naive in matters of the heart."

"Then I will tread very carefully in my endeavoring." He tenderly took her hand again and continued to lead her to the dining hall.

All through dinner, Autumn was distracted by what was happening in her own heart concerning Landon. *What made him feel so strongly about her? And what was she feeling in response? Whatever it was thrilled her and scared her at the same time.* It wasn't but five months ago that she told Lady Cannon marriage was not for her. Landon knew of this, yet he obviously did not care. These feelings and thoughts were all so new to her, and nothing she had been taught by Lady Cannon had prepared her for them.

Lady Cannon was very pleased with Autumn and how she was handling herself - despite being a bit distracted at dinner. She was stunningly beautiful and held the attention of everyone in the room. This would have been the perfect occasion to introduce her as her estate manager and Summer's guardian; nevertheless, that was not to be at this time. *I wonder how Autumn was holding up under the pressure of so much attention? Though deep in thought, she is still pleasant and conversational.*

Glancing at Lord Michaels sitting two chairs down, Lady Cannon saw that he was making conversation with those around him, and yet, keeping an eye on Autumn as well. Lady Cannon had seen the episode in the vestibule with the server and the intimate conversation that took place afterward. She prayed. *Lord, is this of you? Please protect your new daughter and keep her safe from false affections and ill-will. I know Lord Michaels is a good man. Still, Autumn is very young. If it is your will, provide the way.*

Lady Cannon made a mental note to speak with Autumn about Lord Michaels' attention and the influence of a lady when the ball was over, and some of the guests had left. She chided herself for not having the foresight to prepare Autumn in advance.

After dinner, the guests enjoyed socializing in the vestibule and ballroom as more guests arrived for the dancing. Autumn had already received several offers to dance and was having a hard time keeping track of whom she had pledged dances to. She could definitely see the benefits of dance cards as in the past and tried to make a mental note to consider such a thing for the New Year's Eve Ball.

Just before the dancing was to start, Lady Cannon stood on the raised platform in the ballroom to make a wonderful welcoming speech acknowledging Autumn's assistance in the festivities though proclaiming nothing more about her position with Lady Cannon. Autumn's heart sank a bit at the realization that this could have been her 'big' night of introduction. Still, another part of her was thankful that she had some more time to learn the ropes and get things settled first.

She noticed Landon move to her side, his arm gently placed at the small of her back – it was a very protective stance. As Lady Cannon finished her welcome and the music started, Landon took her in his arms. "May I have the first dance?"

As he had already claimed her in his arms, Autumn thought the question was a moot point. However, she didn't protest to his bold claiming of her either, and willingly, let him lead her to the dance floor.

After several turns, he commented. "You have learned well; you are an excellent dancer."

"Thank you, Landon, I have thoroughly enjoyed learning the art of dancing."

They were on their second dance and Autumn was beginning to think he was not going to relinquish her to dance with anyone else she had committed to when he was tapped on the shoulder. He hesitantly, yet graciously, stepped to the side. After that, Autumn was passed from one suitor to another, until finally, she lost count as to how many times she had been passed. Winded and needing a break, she spotted Lady Cannon off to the side and excused herself to join her.

"You are quite the popular lady tonight." Lady Cannon teased Autumn with a sly smile. "Especially with a certain man who is quite jealous of your attention." She nodded over to where Lord Michaels was visiting with a group of men, and he glanced their way. Autumn dropped her gaze and blushed yet again. "Are you having fun, my dear?"

"Immensely, but I do need a break to catch my breath. I had hoped that by coming to you, my suitors would leave me alone for a moment." She let out a little laugh, and Lady Cannon joined her.

Autumn's plan worked, and she was allowed to rest for several minutes. She enjoyed visiting with Lady Cannon and those around her. Several dances had passed, and she was beginning to wonder what she should do to indicate her desire to dance some more when Landon was by her side again. She was starting to think he could read her mind.

This time, words were not even spoken as she took his hand and he led her to the floor. They danced until she needed a break, and then Landon would escort her around the room, visiting, hand gently at the small of her back in a protective stance until they danced again. Once or twice another offer to dance came along, and he would reluctantly relinquish her to another partner; otherwise, he never left her side.

When it was time for Summer to retire for the evening, Landon graciously escorted the two to the top of the stairs and returned to the ballroom. As Autumn and Summer walked the east wing to the Heiress' suite, Autumn sensed something was troubling her.

"Did you enjoy the ball?"

Summer nodded.

"What was your favorite part of the night?"

"Watching all the ladies dance."

"Was there anything that happened that you did not like?"

Summer just shook her head no.

Once in Summer's suites, Autumn inquired more directly. "Sweet one, please tell me what is wrong."

At first, Summer did not want to say anything, but then Autumn got her to confess. "I don't want to lose you."

"Lose me? How are you going to lose me? I'm not going anywhere."

"Lord Michaels looks at you. Pete looked at Tinny, too. I don't want to lose you like I lost Tinny."

Autumn marveled at the perceptiveness of this child. "Sweet one, you are not going to lose me like you lost Tinny and I'll tell you why. I have a contract with Granny; it's a written agreement that is enforced by the law. In it, I chose you and Granny over anyone else. Even if I did want to get married someday like Tinny, I would not leave you or Granny. It's a part of the contract that whomever I married would have to choose to become a part of our family. Okay?"

Though Autumn thought she was too young to fully understand, Summer seemed to grasp the significance and security the contract offered. Autumn made sure she spent the time necessary with Summer to help her understand she could not lose Autumn in marriage or any other way, save death and then they would have eternity together. Still, Summer did not want Autumn to return to the ball, so she stayed until she fell asleep, which was only moments after reading a book.

Returning to the ballroom after being gone for quite some time; Autumn briefly and quietly explained to Lady Cannon why it had taken so long to settle Summer. Landon had approached immediately upon seeing her enter the ballroom and stood at her side hearing the conversation. Upon Lady Cannon's approving nod, Landon embraced Autumn and whisked her onto the dance floor envious of her attention.

It did not take long for Autumn to forget her concerns regarding Summer as Landon briskly spun and turned with the lively music. At the beginning of the evening, Landon had kept the steps simple as to not embarrass Autumn, though he soon learned she was fully capable of the more lively and complicated steps in which he enjoyed leading her in now.

Autumn was thoroughly enjoying the challenge of keeping up with Landon and his obvious talent in dancing. However, she also wanted to take advantage of the opportunity to gain a better knowledge of this man who was not afraid in the least to show his affections for her. Therefore, she proceeded to bombard him with questions as they spun around the floor.

Where did he live?

How long has he been a lawyer?

Where was his office?

What was his favorite food?

Did he like to read?

What was his favorite kind of music?

Did he have any siblings?

Did he work for people other than Lady Cannon?

Did he like sports?

After a tumult of superficial questions to which he responded pleasantly, Autumn couldn't think of anything else and fell silent - content to simply dance.

Landon was pleased with all the questions Autumn asked as it confirmed within him a mutual interest - even if only as acquaintances - yet he couldn't deny to himself that he wanted a deeper relationship. *This woman is my future. I don't know how, and I don't know when, but I know it in my bones. I'm certain - these last few months of watching her confirms it - she is the one.*

The night finally came to an end, and exhausted beyond comprehension, Autumn made her way to her suites. *How in the world am I going to get out of this dress by myself? I may just sleep in it and let Eleanor deal with it in the morning, though these hoops will*

*be nasty to sleep in.* She was pleasantly surprised to see Eleanor waiting for her. As she undressed, Eleanor chatted endlessly about the gossip of the night, as was their custom.

Finally, Autumn turned to her dear friend. "And what of me? What is the gossip regarding me?"

Eleanor paused and debated saying anything. Still, Autumn insisted. "It is said that by the end of next year, you will be married to the young Lord Michaels. He made his interest very known tonight, and it would be a splendid match for the Cannon Estate."

A little shocked and very concerned, Autumn countered. "I'm not getting married and certainly not matched."

"Why not? Our Lady is for it. It would be a good thing for everyone, including Summer. Everyone except for Master Philip that is, though if he is truthful with himself, he has known he had no real hope with you." Autumn glanced up at Eleanor's confession of Master Philip's affections. "The real question is how it will come about?"

Autumn was tired, confused, and at a loss. In her emotional state, she responded harshly. "That is enough. We will not discuss Lord Michaels further."

"Of course, Chatelaine, I will take my leave if there is nothing further you need."

Eleanor started to leave, and Autumn sank to the couch she was standing by. "Oh, Eleanor, I'm sorry." Autumn put her head in her hands. "I truly do not know what I am going to do."

Eleanor rushed back to Autumn and embraced her. "He is a good man, Autumn; you will not find any better. It would be a good choice to pursue this relationship."

"But that is just it; I agreed *not* to pursue *any* relationship with *any* man. I fear I have already started to give him a portion of my heart; still, I cannot in good conscience, pursue a relationship with him."

Eleanor nodded thoughtfully. "Then maybe you should simply let him pursue you." And with that, she took her leave.

As Autumn crawled into bed, she thanked God for His provision and His salvation. She said a prayer for her father, Lady Cannon, Summer, and finally, for the situation with Landon.

*How quickly things have changed! Several months ago, I was worried about whether this job would even work out. Just a few weeks ago, all I had to think about was what to do with Summer and preparing a few things for the holidays. The last few days have been life-changing, in themselves, with my salvation and accepting God's invitation. Now, I'm faced with what to do with my future? Everything keeps changing. When will it settle down and just be simple?*

Autumn took a deep breath. God was the only one who knew what lay ahead for any of them. She'd trust in Him.

# ♡ 21 ♡

Edmund awoke Christmas morning with hope in his heart. Not so much a hope of finding Autumn but a hope that wherever she was, God was big enough to take care of her. James had prayed with him last night, and he reaffirmed that prayer again this morning.

Edmund was so relieved and full of joy, he bounded out of bed to make breakfast. He had never really experienced joy and peace of soul before, and he intended to enjoy every minute of it now, just in case it didn't last.

Edmund was dressing when the phone rang. "Hello, Edmund here." He had gotten used to identifying himself, even at home, because people often confused Edmund and James on the phone.

"Edmund, it's Penny, you won't believe what just happened."

Edmund listened intently as Penny relayed Autumn's message, that she had accepted Christ as her Savior last night as well and all that she knew from the conversation. "It's amazing, Edmund. I hardly recognized her. Her voice is so much more refined, and she apparently had some type of a servant." At least that was Penny's interpretation of what she had heard. She also gave Edmund the number from her caller ID.

"Thank you, Penny, for calling me so quickly with this information."

"But Edmund, there's more." Knowing Edmund had so recently accepted Christ and that his temper had a tendency to flare, Penny hoped Edmund wouldn't allow her confession to ruin their friendship. Whatever happened though, she knew she had to tell him. "I have a confession to make. Autumn borrowed our car the night of her disappearance. We weren't home that night, so I didn't see her or talk to her, but when we got home, our car was gone. She left a note saying she was borrowing it and then left it at the bus station in Omaha."

The hope in Edmund's heart, which had swelled to almost overflowing at the news of hearing from Autumn, immediately evaporated. In frustration and hurt, he demanded. "Why didn't you tell me before? You knew how much I wanted to find her."

"I know. I'm so sorry, Edmund. I should have. Please try to understand, when we first met, I didn't know you. All I knew was that Autumn had run away from something she felt was drastically wrong. I thought I was protecting her. Then this morning, I realized I wasn't protecting her anymore. Now, I was only selfishly trying to save face. I was wrong Edmund - on many counts - and I humbly ask you to forgive me."

Edmund's fury had been growing within him, and he started to see red at the edges of his vision. *This information could have helped me find her so long ago.* But then, he heard the word "forgive." Instantly, the anger was quashed as he knew he had no right to be upset with Penny. He had been forgiven, just last night, for things far worse than this. And he knew, if he could not learn to forgive others, he could not rightfully walk in his new relationship with Jesus Christ.

Taking a deep breath, Edmund calmed his heart - James had been helping him learn how to manage his anger issues. "Thank you for telling me the truth, Penny. I am upset at not getting this information sooner, but I do forgive you for lying to me. I really wish you would have told me, but as you know, I've come to learn that God is in control. James has told me many times, and I'm starting to believe it myself, that maybe there is a purpose to not knowing this before now."

Penny let out the breath she was holding; she had been bracing herself for the explosion of Edmund's temper. "Thank you, Edmund; God truly is working in your life. Will Henry and I still see you around eleven?"

"Yes, James and I will be there. Thank you again for calling me so quickly."

Edmund hung up the phone and yelled. "JAMES! GET UP HERE. NOW!"

James, who had been aroused from a deep sleep when the phone rang, had laid quietly trying to listen to the conversation upstairs. Unfortunately, he couldn't make out what was going on, though at one time he could tell Edmund was getting frustrated. When he heard Edmund holler at him in such a way, he jumped out of bed, pulled some pants on, and grabbed a shirt on his way up the stairs.

"What? What is it, Edmund?"

"It's Autumn. She called Penny this morning."

James stopped in shock. "What did she say? Where is she? Is she alright? Is she coming home?" James had so many questions, many of which he could not express to Edmund at this time.

Edmund had made it to the kitchen and relayed the information Penny had given him as he started breakfast. James took a seat at the table and listened intently.

Edmund put the plates on the table and sat down across from James. "So. What do I do now? A month ago, I would have pursued Autumn come hell or high water. But now? Now, I feel like I need to respect her wishes and wait. What should I do James? What would God have me to do?"

James sat back at the weight of the dilemma that Edmund was asking him to discern. He wanted to be sure to tread lightly here; whatever advice he gave could be his undoing or his open door. After several minutes of debating with himself, James answered Edmund. "Often, waiting is the hardest thing to do and the most common response I hear from God. What I would advise is prayer. Not so much as to if you should respect Autumn's wishes, but asking God what *His* plan is for this situation. Let the One you confided faith and trust in last night lead you in how to go forward."

Edmund ate his breakfast in silence while he contemplated what James had just said. He saw great wisdom in letting God lead him - that was, after all, a part of the journey forward. However, Edmund also saw James debate how to answer and recognized the somewhat calculated response. *Why is James still so careful in what he says? Is it that he doesn't want to offend a friend who is so newly walking this path of faith, or is there something else behind James' purpose?*

Edmund recognized his need for a more experienced Christian to help him navigate the new journey of walking with God, and he appreciated James' insights from that perspective. However, something still nagged at him whenever the issue of Autumn came up between them. *I have to protect Autumn's inheritance until I can talk to her and make everything clear to her. Whatever she chooses after that, is up to her, but that has to be my focus right now. No matter how much I like James and think he is a good man, my child comes first.*

"I will be praying, and I request you do the same. For today, since it's Christmas, I'll agree to wait. However, if I don't hear from her by Monday, or if God doesn't reveal something different before then, I will go to the police."

James nodded his understanding. He would indeed be in fervent prayer over the next few days - and not just about Autumn. The time was getting close to revealing his purpose for being there.

The next morning as James was preparing to get back to work, he approached Edmund with the need for assistance in vaccinating the few cattle that Edmund kept on the place to keep the pastures down. "Would you like me to try to find one of the neighbors to help? Or just take them to the vet in town?" James never liked to suggest the more costly route, knowing farming was not an overly lucrative business, especially with the current prices. "It should only take a day with the number of cattle we have. Maybe Henry could even help."

"Well, why not ask me? I have worked cattle before you know." Edmund teased him.

James was surprised. Edmund had never offered to help before. "Really? I actually didn't know that. What experience do you have?" James bantered back.

Edmund laughed. "Oh, I have a small farm that I *own* and have worked cattle a few times over the years. I think I'm a suitable help." More seriously, Edmund explained. "Besides, the insurance office is closed for a few days as they renovate the office area. They thought the week between Christmas and New Year's was a good time to do it. So, I'm available."

James went out to get things in order while Edmund did a few things in the house and changed into his farm clothes. Not knowing how well they would work together or if the cattle would cooperate, James figured it would take all day to get the cattle through. As it was, things started off slowly as the two men - who had never worked together before - figured out how to cooperate. Once Edmund stepped back and allowed James to lead the process, things started moving more smoothly. It was a valuable learning experience for them both.

The two men stopped only long enough to eat the cold lunch Edmund had made and a glimpse at the weather; there were some ominous clouds to the west, and the cattle could sense the change coming. As the day progressed, and the storm grew closer, the men were getting tired and a bit irritated at the stubborn cattle.

"I thought we'd be done by now. If these stupid cows would just cooperate, we could make it inside before that storm hits." James grumbled.

Edmund nodded his agreement and climbed into the narrow alleyway to persuade the current two stubborn cows to go forward into the chute. James was at the headgate waiting to administer the vaccinations when thunder cracked above. Winter thunderstorms were so rare, it caught everyone by surprise.

Three things then happened simultaneously: Being spooked by the thunder and the oncoming weather, one of the cows finally managed to get unstuck in the chute. Unfortunately, the cow was facing Edmund when she charged. In trying to get out of the way, Edmund erred in stepping behind the other cow, who, now having more room, suddenly pivoted, knocking Edmund against the far chute wall. And James, seeing Edmund go down under trampling cattle, jumped over the chute wall yelling, "DAD!".

In a matter of seconds, James realized he had to get the cattle out of the chute before the cows trampled Edmund further. Having fallen to the ground, Edmund was still unmoving. This panicked the livestock and James further. James went to the alley gate and flung it open with all his might. Then he protectively stood over Edmund until the cows were out, so they couldn't inflict more vengeance. It worked; the cows seeing the gate open, followed the far wall to the opening and exited. Unfortunately, the damage was already done in the two previous passes of trampling.

Now at Edmund's side, James tried to assess the damage without moving him. Edmund lay unconscious. It looked like a head wound and maybe a broken leg. Not having anyone else to send for help, James was forced to leave Edmund unattended to call for help.

Assuring the gate was securely closed behind him, James quickly ran to the house to call for an ambulance.

He also made a quick call to the Bogarts before rushing back to Edmund's side. Henry found him there moments later, ardent in one prayer: "Please don't die, please don't die, please don't die."

Edmund was rushed to the hospital, where it was determined that he did indeed have a severe head injury causing him to be in an extended unconscious state or a light coma. He also suffered from a broken tibia and several cracked ribs. The bone injuries were nothing of real concern to the doctor, though the coma was to be watched diligently.

To James' horror, upon arriving at the hospital behind the ambulance, the hospital refused to disclose any information to him. "I'm sorry sir, the patient you are referring to is currently unable to give us permission to speak with you." He tried for nearly an hour to get them to waive their policy because he was the only link to Edmund's daughter but they insisted. "I'm sorry, sir. Due to HIPPA regulations, we can only speak to the next of kin."

The Bogarts had been with him this whole time, following the ambulance themselves. "He's at least here, James, where he can get the help he needs." Penny tried to comfort him.

"No. That's not good enough. You don't understand. I have to be with him. He doesn't know." James abruptly turned and left the hospital.

Penny and Henry stood there looking at each other wondering what they were supposed to do now. They asked the nurse if they could wait for a while in case Edmund woke up and gave permission for them to see him.

About forty-five minutes later, James came running back into the hospital, slapping a paper down on the counter. "There, proof that I'm next of kin. NOW, can I see him?"

The Bogart's had just been thinking of leaving when they saw James return and joined him at the desk. Seeing the birth certificate on the counter, they exchanged a shocked glance.

The nurse looked at the birth certificate and asked for his ID. "Mr. DeBlue has been moved to the ICU. Third floor, Room 310." Glancing at the Bogarts, she explained. "Only family is allowed inside, I'm sorry." Printing out a bracelet from her computer, she extended it to James. "This will allow you to come and go into the ICU. Once up there, check in at the nurse's station and they will give you an update on Mr. DeBlue's condition."

"Thank you." James exhaled. Not waiting to see if the Bogarts followed, James headed for the elevators. *I hope that was not the biggest mistake of my life. But I know, if he dies without me telling him, I will definitely regret it.*

After checking in with the nurses and seeing that Edmund was still unconscious, James returned to the ICU waiting room to speak with the Bogarts. "Thanks for waiting." Rubbing the back of his neck, he tried to think of how to explain the situation.

Before he could though, Henry put his hand on his shoulder. "You don't have to explain anything to us. We're here for whatever you need."

James nodded in appreciation. "I want to stay here with him, but the chores need tending to."

"I can take care of the chores. Just tell me what needs to be done."

James blew out his breath. "Thanks, Henry."

After explaining what needed to be done with the chores, the Bogarts prepared to leave. Penny gave James a hug. "We called the prayer chain. Everyone is praying. I'll go with Henry now, but I'll be back in a little bit with a change of clothes. Is there anything else you need?"

James had not even thought about his appearance. On second thought, it was amazing they let him in the ICU as filthy as he was. "A change of clothes would be greatly appreciated, thank you."

Henry added. "And don't worry. Your secret is safe with us."

James just nodded. *And if Edmund dies, or never comes to, it may have to stay that way.*

James took up vigil at the hospital, keeping the Bogarts and the prayer chain updated as events happened. All through the next day, Edmund's condition did not change. The battle Edmund fought for his conscious life was nothing compared to the battle James was fighting at his side.

At first, James was occupied by the havoc around Edmund - stabilizing him and checking his vitals. However, by the next day, things had settled into a routine, and that's when the assault started. *This is my fault. I've killed my father. It was foolish to agree to let him help me. I should have known better. I should have been the one inside that chute. We should have stopped sooner.*

Thoughts bombarded him like a tumult against the silence of the hospital room. Under such assault, James was blinded to the enemy's tactics of keeping him from prayer or even rational thinking. Being weakened by the sudden revelation of his secret, he succumbed to the torture. *Why was I waiting to tell him? Maybe it wasn't God telling me to wait, but my own fears? I should have told him. Now I will never get the chance. The family won't recognize me as his son - even with the birth certificate. Sue said no one knew I was born. And what about Autumn?*

At the thought of Autumn, another barrage hit. *I'll never know my sister, my only living relative and she'll shun me for sure. She'll think I am trying to steal what belongs to her. My dreams of a family are hopeless now. I'll be alone forever.*

James was in such despair and selfish foreboding that he did not notice Edmund's slight eye or finger movements. It was only the nurse coming to check Edmund's vitals that interrupted James' thoughts.

"Your prayers must be working."

James was dumbfounded at the nurse's response. He knew he had *not* been praying. "Why?"

"He is starting to come to."

Immediately, James was on his feet looking at Edmund. He didn't see anything. "Are you sure?"

Giving James an indignant look, she quietly stepped out to summon the doctor. A few moments later, the doctor came in to examine Edmund. "Sometimes it takes a while for full consciousness to happen but his vitals are strong, and we see increased movement - all good signs. With the brain not swelling, I would guess that he'll be awake within the next 24 hours. We will need to keep him for several days yet, as there can be other complications with a head injury like his. We'll have to ascertain that when the time comes."

James was in awe. "Thank you, doctor." The nurse smirked as she left with the doctor.

As they left, James realized he had been trapped in a cycle of despair by the enemy and his own guilt. Falling to his knees beside Edmunds bed, he took his hand and cried out to his Heavenly Father. "Lord God, I have been foolishly listening to the lies of the enemy, and I confess that I almost conceded to them. I ask you to forgive me for not standing solidly on the Rock in this crisis. I thank you for not only preserving my life and faith in you but delivering my earthly father, Edmund, from this coma. I beseech you now for a full recovery. Please strengthen us both and enable me to follow Your will. Amen."

Edmund squeezed James' hand. Startled, James looked up at him, but Edmund's eyes were still closed. *How alert is he? Did he hear me call him my earthly father? Does he know?* There was no way to find out, except wait until Edmund woke up completely.

It was two in the morning when Edmund regained consciousness. James was sleeping in the recliner chair with the blankets the nurses had offered him. It wasn't restful by any means; still, James could not leave until he knew Edmund was out of the woods.

He was glad, exceedingly thankful, that he had not left when he heard Edmund's weak voice. "James? James are you here?"

Immediately, James was out of the chair and by the bed. Edmund opened his eyes just a little but did not move his head or his arms. "Yes Edmund, I'm here. I'll call the nurse."

"Wait." James paused, heart pounding in his chest. "Who are you?"

*Did he lose his memory? No. He was just asking for me. Why is he asking who I am then? He must have heard my prayer. Maybe I should just pretend not to understand? No, this may be my one opportunity. What am I supposed to do?*

Before he could make up his mind, Edmund said. "You called me Dad. Why?"

*He heard that?* "It is a long story Edmund; you need to get well first." James was trying to buy time.

"No time. I must know, now."

James went white. *What did he mean 'no time'?* James breath quickened as he realized the window of opportunity may be closing. "Edmund, I am your son."

"How can that be? My wife was only pregnant twice. One ended in abortion, the other was Autumn. I have never known anyone else. How can you be my son?" Edmund was calm and laid perfectly still while clasping James' hand.

James could tell Edmund was tired and thought about insisting on waiting, but that sense of urgency inside of him demanded he tell the truth. "You may have ordered Sue to have an abortion; however, she could not follow through with it. Do you remember how she moved to Colorado for a time?"

Edmund, still motionless, gripped James' hand a bit tighter. "Yes. It was the worst two years of my life."

"Well, it was the best two of mine. Sue found a family in Colorado who wanted to adopt a newborn. She agreed to the adoption as long as they paid for her care and delivery. She actually lived with my adoptive parents until I was born. However, due to a fall Sue had, I was born prematurely. My parents were advised that the best thing for me was time, touch, and breast milk. So, Sue offered to stay on at her own expense and pump milk for me. My adoptive parents thought it would be better if Sue actually nursed me so that I had both touch and milk. Sue ended up staying on with my adoptive parents as my wet nurse and then as my nanny until I was eighteen months old."

Edmund remained still, though the grip on James' hand grew tighter. "What proof do you have?"

James' heart sunk. *He didn't believe me? How could I make a story like that up?* "My birth certificate states my mother to be Sue Barker and my father to be Edmund DeBlue. Sue also kept in contact with my parents. When I was eighteen I was told of my adoption and that Sue would like to know me as an adult if I was willing. I vaguely remembered her from pictures when I was small. I met with her, and she explained to me the circumstances behind my adoption and that she had, eventually, married you. I asked to meet you; however, she didn't think you'd be receptive. We kept in contact after that until she got too sick. I didn't know she died until my parents heard about it through a mutual acquaintance and then they told me."

"And your job with me, how did you come to find out about that?"

"Truly, I felt it was ordained by God. I moved into the area three years ago after I heard of Sue's death in an attempt to find my roots. I wanted to meet you but didn't really know how to go about it. I started to work various jobs in the area to pay my way while I tried to figure out how to approach you and looked into my history. One day as I was looking at the want ads and I couldn't believe it - there was your ad for help. I figured it was God's way of opening the door."

"Why didn't you tell me sooner?"

"At first, I wanted to feel you out. Sue seemed to think you'd be unreceptive to the truth and I had heard from her before she died that you were very anti-Christian. Provided the opportunity I had, I wanted to see if she was right. Then as I got to know you and we became friends, I wanted to tell you many times; however, with everything going on between Autumn and your curiosity about God, I felt Him telling me to wait. So, I tried to be obedient. I told you - waiting is the most common response I get from God." James tried to inject a bit of humor into the conversation.

However, Edmund did not laugh. In fact, there was no response from Edmund at all. James leaned closer in an attempt to see if Edmund was still okay. He was breathing soundly. James didn't want to wake him if he was sleeping, so he tried to ease his hand out of Edmunds.

Edmund gripped James' hand tighter, not wanting to let go. *I have a son. A son! Thank you, God. I thought I had killed my child, but, you, in your graciousness, spared his life and brought him back to me for a season. Thank you. Thank you. I have a son.* Tears began to stream down Edmund's face.

James saw the tears. "Edmund? Are you okay? Do I need to get the nurse?" Concern gripped James' heart.

Edmund managed a small shake of his head, though that little movement caused him to wince. "No. I'm just so thankful. I have a son." That was all that needed to be said. The two men sat in silence, tears streaming down their faces.

Hours later, the doctor came in for his early morning rounds to find Edmund's eyes opened, partially sitting, and cognitive. There were obvious restrictions in his limbs, and his ribs and head were painful when he moved; however, the doctor said everything looked hopeful for a full recovery - in time.

Unfortunately, Edmund did not like that verdict. "How long do I have to stay here? When can I go home? I've got some things that need to be done."

"I'm sorry, Mr. DeBlue, but you need time to heal. You are looking at being here for another week, if not more. Though you could possibly get around with crutches, your brain needs time to heal."

After the doctor left, Edmund turned to James. "What day is it?"

"Monday. Why?"

"Have you heard anything regarding Autumn?"

"Autumn? No, I haven't been to the house since the accident."

"Not *from* her, *about* her. Are we to pursue the lead or wait for her to contact us?"

James was ashamed. He truly had not thought or prayed about Autumn for days. He had been so distracted by his own thoughts and issues, Autumn had not really been a concern. *Except whether or not I'd ever get to meet her or whether she'd accept me as a brother.*

Edmund saw his shame and tried to ease his guilt. "It's okay, son; there has been a lot going on. I haven't really been praying either." Edmund tried to banter. Still, he really did need to know. "So, what do you want to do going forward?"

It warmed James to hear Edmund call him 'son.' "What do you mean?"

"How am I going to explain you to Autumn? Do you want an active role in her life? Do you want a share of the inheritance? What is it that you hoped for when you decided to move here?"

"I don't really know. When I moved here, I simply wanted to know my father and possibly find out a bit about my family history. Sue had, of course, told me about Autumn, but I never really expected to meet her. I guess, now though, I really would like to know my sister. Do you think she'll accept me as her brother?"

"I think it will be a shock and we will both have to work hard to make things right. Though, knowing Autumn is a Christian now, gives me hope that we can work this all out. What about the inheritance? You didn't say."

"I don't care about any inheritance. My parents...adoptive parents are well off. I don't need Autumn's money or whatever the inheritance is. I just want to know my family."

"Okay. Well then, I think we should give Autumn time to call back. Especially since I'm stuck here. But, if we don't hear from her after the new year, or if God doesn't show us something different before then, we need to find her. Though, if she did call, it would be at the house."

James anticipated the request before it came. "Now that you are doing better, I can return to the house. Henry was doing chores for us, but I still need to deal with those last few cows."

"You are a good man, son. Be careful."

Later the next day, Edmund had had enough of the hospital. He felt fine - other than his ribs, which hurt when he used the crutches. Still, he had been up and around without difficulty. Besides, bones could heal just as well at home. Therefore, against doctor's orders, he discharged himself from the hospital signing the AMA waiver. He called James from the lobby to come to get him.

# ♥ 22 ♥

The week after Christmas was a flurry of activity in cleaning up from Christmas and preparing for the New Year. After her experience at the Christmas Ball, Autumn had all types of new ideas she wanted to implement, and Lady Cannon was pleased with her enthusiasm.

Several of the guests would stay on to continue the holidays with Lady Cannon; however, the vast majority of them left to attend to other business. Some would return in a week and others would not; replaced with new names on the guest list.

Not only did Autumn have the pressures of planning the next ball, tending to Summer, and a few newly appointed responsibilities that Lady Cannon had bestowed upon her, Landon was now making it a regular practice to call on her.

The day after Christmas, Landon sent Autumn a dozen yellow roses. The card read: MY BELOVED CHATELAINE, I LOOK FORWARD TO WHAT LIES AHEAD. FOREVER YOURS, LANDON

Lady Cannon was apprised of the roses immediately upon delivery, and only moments later, Autumn received a knock at her door.

"Chatelaine, our Lady desires your company in her great room."

Autumn glanced back at Ménage Eleanor, who was smiling grandly, as she situated the flowers on the table in the corner. "Of course. Eleanor, I have several correspondences on my desk that need return addresses and stamps. Please finish them and send them down for delivery while I visit with our Lady."

Eleanor curtsied in acknowledgment of her orders, and Autumn followed LeDare Anton to Lady Cannon's suites.

"Our Lady, as you have requested, the Chatelaine."

Lady Cannon nodded. "Thank you for coming so quickly, my dear. I know you have much to do; nonetheless, I feel this is a significant issue that needs to be addressed." Lady Cannon gestured for Autumn to join her on the couch as she finished her stitch of cross work.

Autumn faithfully obeyed, yet did not wait to hear what Lady Cannon would say. "My Lady, I want to make it clear that I did not encourage Lord Michaels attentions. In fact, I reminded him of the marriage clause very plainly. I have no intention of going against our agreement or pursuing a relationship with him." Autumn nodded as if that made her statement final.

"I see. Do you not realize that by accepting Lord Michaels' *very* nice gift, that you have already encouraged him and stated that you would be open to receiving further attention from him? And do you not have any affection or feelings for Lord Michaels?"

"Yes, my Lady, I realize that is a possibility. However, I was more concerned that refusal of such a token could reflect poorly upon my Lady."

Lady Cannon's ceased stitching and looked up at Autumn. "How so?"

"If I refused Lord Michaels' token **of friendship**, it may appear to him that someone was seeking amusement of him and trifling with his feelings. Especially after receiving permission to be so casual and attentive in association just yesterday."

"That is very perceptive of you. Is that the only reason you accepted Lord Michaels' gift? Do you not have any similar feelings of affection for him?"

At Autumn's silence, Lady Cannon took her hand. "Dear Chatelaine, I actually called you here to let you know that I am not opposed to you gaining Lord Michaels affections if you are so inclined. I only fear I have trained you to be a lady and neglected to arm you with the knowledge of how powerful a lady can be in matters of the heart - especially a young beauty as yourself."

Autumn did not understand, although Lady Cannon already knew that. "Let me explain…" Lady Cannon took the next hour to talk to Autumn about how a lady can use certain charms - known or unknown by her - to influence a man. Lady Cannon was very careful to instruct Autumn properly to use her influence and strictly charged her to avoid the folly of misusing it. "God created women with beauty and intellect. It is our responsibility to use it only to glorify Him."

When Lady Cannon felt that Autumn had a good understanding of all that she shared, she again returned to the situation with Lord Michaels. "Now, my dear, tell me. Do you return Lord Michaels feelings of affection?"

"I don't know." Autumn shrugged her shoulders in confusion. "I don't really know the man, and though my feelings are stirred like never before, I'm not sure what exactly I do feel. And, even if I did feel affection for him, I would not act on them. I made an agreement with you, and I will follow through with that commitment. You and Summer are my family. I will not risk losing either of you, even for the affections of Lord Michaels."

"I see." Lady Cannon frowned. "This is what I was afraid of."

"I don't understand. Why are you encouraging this after you had such grave concerns regarding marriage in the first place?"

"Because I have known, from our first conversation regarding this issue, that you would one day marry. You are young, naive, and not impervious to temptation. That is why I was so hesitant to add the marriage clause, despite my concerns. The only true concern that I have is to **whom** you will marry. Strictly for my own selfish reasons, I wanted to have control over whom you chose, to assure Summer would be taken care of.

"I know it was not right for me, and I do beg your forgiveness. I should never have allowed that clause to be added. Nevertheless, in regards to Lord Michaels, he would be a perfect match for you in many ways. He has a strong faith, is very loyal and very committed. He knows our situation, he would never take you from us, and in fact, would probably reinforce your commitment to Summer. Also, I am certain that when he chooses to love, he will love for the rest of his life. He's just that sort of man.

"Furthermore, I'm not at all uncertain that God does not have His hand in this. I have never seen Lord Michaels behave in such a manner - and I have known him for many years. If God is for this, who am I to stand against it?"

Autumn was very confused. *She knew she had an attraction to Landon, though she didn't understand it. And she would never have even thought to ask Lady Cannon to approve of a relationship between her companion and her lawyer. Therefore, to have her encouraging it was just so unbelievable - despite how much her heart wanted it.* "So...you **want** me to pursue Lord Michaels?"

"Oh heavens, no! A lady does not pursue a man. No. I'm simply saying that if you return his affections, I am in favor of **him** pursuing you." Lady Cannon looked like the cat who got the cream.

"Okay. So what happens now? What about the marriage agreement?" There was a small thread of hope that began to uncurl in Autumn's heart.

"My dear, you can rest assured that Lord Michaels is fully capable of handling that marriage agreement if he so chooses. Therefore, I would recommend that you let him. When the time is right, he will make his intentions known, and you will have my blessing. Nevertheless, have no doubt, I will not make it easy on him and neither should you. You are a precious jewel, and I will insist on you being treated like one." Lady Cannon winked.

*She winked. Actually winked. I've never seen Lady Cannon so giddy. Maybe there is hope yet. Maybe things will work out with Landon. God, is this you? Is this your will? I wish I knew. I wish I knew more about how to walk this path with you. Please God, show me your way.* Peace came over Autumn's heart, and she knew - not the future, but that God was in control and she could trust in Him.

It wasn't long after the roses arrived that Lord Michaels requested an audience with Lady Cannon. Ménage Eleanor informed Autumn immediately that he had arrived. Still, they did not know if it was business or personally related.

All Landon really wanted was to see Autumn, yet he knew that was the wrong course of action to lead with. So, he requested to meet with Lady Cannon to discuss the issues at hand.

The first thing they discussed was the situation with Autumn's father. It was Landon's opinion - and heavily biased - that Autumn should not divulge her whereabouts until she was of age in Nebraska. "It is my understanding that since she is eighteen, and Michigan acknowledges her as an adult, that she can stay here without threat of consequence from her father. However, my knowledge is limited as to Nebraska law, and I'm still looking into it." Since they did not know what light Mr. DeBlue's newly confessed faith in Christ would bring on the situation, it was unanimously agreed to proceed with caution over risking Autumn's forced departure.

"I understand what you are saying, Lord Michaels, and I do not want to lose Autumn. Still, I feel very strongly that Autumn needs to talk to her father directly. We cannot be seen as keeping her from him."

Lord Michaels agreed that it would bode well to have her contact him regularly. "If, however, he pressed for her location, the conversation should be ended. Better to avoid the issue than outright lie about it."

"Better to trust that God is in control than to avoid a difficult situation. I know your heart might be slightly clouded in regards to my Chatelaine. Still, we do need to keep in mind that God's plan is ultimately the best and what we seek."

*What does she mean my heart is clouded? Am I not being good counsel? Have I let my convictions slip in place of the influence of my heart?* Brushing aside these thoughts, Landon felt he needed to get back to business. "I have looked into the situation of you aiding the Chatelaine in running away to Michigan, which - I would like to remind you - was kept from me. I do not believe your aide can be construed as kidnapping, even in Nebraska, as you were not physically a part of helping her leave. And as far as the contract is concerned, Michigan recognizes the Chatelaine as an adult, so the contract remains binding. However, I do agree that it would be wise to postpone the announcement of her promotion until she is nineteen and there is no further doubt of complications from her father."

"As much as I'd like to have the matter settled, I thought it best to wait as well. I trust the Chatelaine and know she does not want to leave us. However, only God knows what the future holds. We will hold off on the announcement."

Landon stood uncomfortably, trying to figure out how to broach the next subject. It was not the ideal timing, but he felt the need to clear the air and make his intentions known. Therefore, as Lady Cannon eyed him suspiciously, he took a deep breath and laid his heart out on the table. "I also had a secondary reason for coming today….I would...um...I would like to ask you for permission to court Autumn...the Chatelaine." *There, it's out there. What will she think of that? Will she reject it? I really hope this doesn't mess up relations between us. I value Lady Cannon - not to mention my father would kill me if I lost their account. But this isn't about business. This is personal.* "I acknowledge that I am in the same boat as you are regarding her situation with her father, though mine may be a bit more precarious because of our age difference. Still, I intend to court her slowly under chaperoned encounters until she is more comfortable with the idea. Then, I would like to pursue her in full courtship style for her hand in marriage. I would request your approval in this endeavor, as I believe this arrangement benefits everyone." He hoped to make the offer irrefutable.

Lady Cannon listened to Lord Michaels' well-prepared speech in amusement. She had never experienced a conversation with Lord Michaels where he stumbled over his words and presented them with such hesitation. Still, she couldn't give in to him immediately; it would do him good to squirm a bit. Therefore, her response was slow and deliberate. "As you know…the Chatelaine has many things going on in her life right now." She paused as if debating. "She needs to grow in her new faith, Summer requires a lot of attention, and then, there is this issue regarding her father."

She made herself pause again, this time taking longer before continuing. Lord Michaels shifted from foot to foot as if he was preparing his arguments in his head and couldn't wait to get them out. Lady Cannon finally decided he'd suffered enough. "That being said, you do have  *my*  permission to court her slowly and carefully. However, I would like to make sure that we are both on the same page. Therefore, if I catch even a hint of impropriety, abuse of privilege, or folly on your more mature and responsible part, there will be serious consequences both personally and with the firm. Am I clear?"

Landon let out an audible sigh. *I can't believe it. Did she really just say yes? For a moment there, I thought I'd have to argue all the benefits of a union between us, but I didn't.* Landon squinted his eyes as he studied Lady Cannon. *I think she was playing with me. She's more in favor of this than she was letting on. That shrewd woman.*

Nodding his head in agreement with his own thoughts, as well as, duly noting the warning, Landon graciously bowed. "I am in complete agreement with you, my Lady. Now, if you will allow, may I take Autumn out to the garden for a private word?"

"Take Ménage Eleanor with you. She can stand at a distance and chaperone." Lady Cannon winked.

*She winked. Lady Cannon winked at me. I have never seen her wink ever, and especially not at me. I knew it, she is more in favor of a match between us than she is letting on.*

Leaving Lady Cannon's suites, Landon nearly ran to Autumn's doors. Pausing only long enough to gain his composure, he gently knocked. He thought he heard bidding to enter, so he opened the door accordingly.

Autumn sat at her desk writing correspondence of thanks to all those who assisted in making the Christmas Ball successful and soliciting others for assistance in the New Year's Eve Ball. She had been expecting LeDare Anton with a delivery and thought it was him, so she did not glance up immediately.

Landon stood in the doorway cautiously searching the room for her - seeing the roses on the table, he smiled to himself. At first glance, he did not see anyone and wondered if he had misheard. It would not bode well with Lady Cannon if he entered Autumn's suite unsupervised and uninvited.

Noting no movement from the door, nor greeting from LeDare Anton, Autumn finally glanced up from her desk and was surprised. "Landon! I was not expecting you, pardon my delay in attending you."

Turning to her voice and seeing her stately situated behind her desk, his heart thundered in his chest. "Ah, Chatelaine, there you are. No pardon necessary. Would you be available to join me for a brief walk in the garden?"

"A walk? Now? Is it not bitter outside?"

Landon took a few steps closer to her away from the doors, leaving them open as they were alone. "Actually, the sun has come out, and it is warming nicely. It may be brisk, but I believe, pleasant as well. It will be only for a moment; I must get back to the office. However, I have something very important to discuss with you."

Autumn's heart leaped in anticipation of what could be so important that he'd take time away from his work to seek her out. "Of course, I'll have Ménage Eleanor meet us in the vestibule with my jacket." Autumn picked up the phone to call Eleanor.

"Have her bring hers as well; we will need to be chaperoned."

Autumn raised her brows at this but did as he instructed.

Once outside, Landon led her through the only garden path scooped of snow to a small bench. Eleanor followed curiously but stood a few feet away in full view. He gestured for Autumn to sit and then took her hand in his.

With a deep breath of what *was* bitter cold air, Landon launched into a presentation of his intentions. "I acknowledge that we do not know each other very well - I, of course, know more about you than you do of me. I also know that there is a gap in our ages that some would consider significant - though I do not see that as an issue. I also would like you to know that I have spoken to Lady Cannon and received her permission to not only speak with you today but to proceed if you are in agreement. That all being said, I would like to ask you if I may court you?"

Autumn glanced over to where Eleanor was trying not to listen. "Court me? What does that mean?"

Landon smiled. *At least it was not an immediate no. There is hope.* "Courting is a more restrictive and committed form of dating. When a man courts a woman, he agrees to solely be committed to her with the full intent of marriage at the end of the courting time frame.

When a woman is being courted, she agrees to solely be pursued by that man, with the full intent that in the end, she will marry him. Some decide during courting that it will not work out, but many find that by going through the slower steps of courting, the temptations that drive other relationships apart are not present. Plus, the relationship starts with commitment, which is key to keeping any marriage on solid ground."

"So, we will be exclusively committed to each other while we spend time getting to know each other. Is that correct?"

"Yes. The biggest difference in courting as opposed to dating is the commitment to each other with the intent of marriage being the end result. Dating does not have those elements. If you say yes, we will move forward very slowly - eating meals together when it works out for everyone, spending time - chaperoned," Landon gestured to Ménage Eleanor. "until you are comfortable with me." He nervously chuckled, and the dimple in his cheek caught Autumn's attention.

*He is so handsome. And he is choosing me! He wants to pursue me. He knows all there is to know about me and my past, and he is not running from me. Still, though, he is correct. I don't know much about him. Everyone says he's a good man, but how do I know we will get along? We obviously have a connection, but is that enough? I've never liked the idea of dating and messing around. Courting sounds much more refined and promising.*

Landon started talking again. "Once we have built a solid foundation in our friendship, we will move to the next step of getting engaged. That usually lasts a season of time where we will have more time together without the chaperones. After that, we will set a date to get married." Squeezing her hand, he emphasized. "Autumn, I want to be clear and honest with you. I am asking to court you slowly because I feel that you need time. Time to get to know me, time to grow in your faith, and time to adjust to changes in your position with Lady Cannon." He smiled again. "However, I want you to be my wife. I have no doubt about it. Therefore, as far as I am concerned if you say yes, I will see you as my wife. That is my commitment to you."

*Wow. That is a very bold statement. He has no doubt? He knows he wants to marry me without a doubt? How can he know this? Am I supposed to know this too? What if I say yes and then it doesn't work out? Am I locking myself into something I can't get myself out of? What am I supposed to do? GOD - are you there? What am I supposed to do?*

Landon could see the thoughts flashing wildly through Autumn's head as they were reflected in her eyes. He saw the doubt, the questions, the panic. "My Beloved. Look at me."

Autumn looked up from studying the hands entwined in her lap. A calm washed over her as she stared into his golden brown eyes.

"Autumn. I am not asking you to make the same statement that I just made. I know you need time. All I am asking you right now, is if you are willing to allow me the great privilege of courting you? Will you agree to commit to the process of walking this path with me?" Landon held his breath.

*There was such peace in his eyes. Such strength. Yes. Yes, she could commit to what he was asking right now.* "Yes. I am willing to walk this path with you."

Landon could not contain his elation at hearing those beautiful words. He jumped straight up off the bench hooting and hollering like an Indian warrior after victory in battle. Noting both Autumn and Ménage Eleanor's amusement, he gained control of himself and gently lifted Autumn from the bench and wrapped his arms affably around her. In this embrace, Autumn could feel his chest throbbing for air from his previously wild display.

For a long moment, Landon held Autumn taking in her presence, and she thought he was going to kiss her. But instead, he released her and reached into his pocket to produce a small square blue box.

Autumn gasped as he opened it to reveal an intricately designed silver ring with miniature pearls strewn throughout the top half of the band.

"I noticed your other ring was silver, so I had this one made of the same. I hope you like it."

The expression on Autumn's face should have shown him she did; however, her words did not. "Landon, I cannot accept such a gift. It is too much."

This surprised him. He had never had a gift refused before. "It is a **small** token of the love I am pledging to you and a reminder to us both of our commitment. I would be greatly offended if you refused my token after accepting my offer." He teased her.

Autumn blushed and bowed her head in shame of her misstep and completely missed his smile. "Forgive me, my Lord, in no way did I mean to offend. I was simply…"

Landon raised his finger to her lips to hush her, electricity sparking between them at the intimate touch. Lifting her eyes to meet his, she saw such compassion. "No explanation needed. Will you accept my token? It would honor me greatly to see you wearing my gift."

Completely taken in by his eyes, she nodded. "Yes." Landon took the ring and placed it on her left hand, pledging his commitment and love. Then he turned her hand up and kissed her palm. Autumn had never experienced such a passionate and intimate exploit on her behalf, and it warmed her from head to foot.

Noting Autumn's hands were rather cold, he escorted her back to the house. Upon seeing her safely tended to in the vestibule by the fire, he excused himself to return to his office elated and with promises of another visit later on.

After Landon's departure, Autumn immediately went to Lady Cannon and informed her of everything. In hearing about the presentation of a token, Lady Cannon commented with a smile. "He is definitely efficient."

# ♥ 23 ♥

James was not happy with Edmund. Still, he obediently picked him up from the hospital and brought him home.

Edmund did not waste any time. Once home, he set to the task of reviewing his wife's will and the status of his estate. There were so many things that made sense after the revelation of James. Sue actually made allowance for him *if* he were to go against her wishes and make himself known.

Edmund made sure all the papers were in order and clearly identified James as their son. He made a copy of James' birth certificate and put it with the estate papers as proof of James' claim. When he thought he had everything in order, Edmund did as his wife had requested and sealed everything in the ornate box she had specified. He then took the letter explaining the box and put them in Autumn's room.

Edmund did not know why he felt so compelled to finally put this all together, but it was hard pressed upon him. After placing the box in Autumn's room, he told James if anything ever happened to him again, he was to find Autumn at all costs and give her the letter on top. It would explain everything else.

James was confused and unsettled by Edmund's intensity in the explaining of the instructions yet listened attentively. *It's as if he knows something the rest of us do not. What is going on?*

"Why are you so intent on getting this all figured out now? Sue has been gone for a while, and you've never done anything with her will before now."

Edmund simply shook his head. He couldn't explain the bone-deep need to get everything put together for Autumn's return.

The next day, James found Edmund on the floor unconscious. Edmund had mentioned he did not feel well that morning, though he insisted it was just a winter cold. James immediately called the ambulance once again - as well as the Bogarts.

The assaults of the enemy hit hard as James waited for the ambulance for the second time in a week. *Why did I agree to get him from the hospital? I should have found a way to make him stay. Why didn't I insist he check in with the doctor this morning? He said he wasn't feeling well. I should have known something was wrong. I didn't get much time with him - only a few days of being called his son. What am I going to do if I lose him now?*

James sat next to his father as he waited for the ambulance again. This time though, he recognized the attack against him and he took his thoughts captive. Giving praise to God for the time he had with Edmund and praying for his safety as he surrendered to God, peace and assurance came over him. God had opened so many doors to allow James to get to know his father, to aide in his salvation, and to have several days of being acknowledged as his son. With that fresh in his mind, James continued to silence the attacks against him as he petitioned God for one more miracle – to bring Autumn home.

After waiting long hours in the waiting room while tests were run, the doctor finally approached James - and the Bogarts - with the news. Edmund's brain had been infected with meningitis, a complication of the previous head trauma. They put him on antibiotics immediately and were waiting for confirmation that this was the only complication. However, the diagnosis did not look good from what was ascertained on the CAT scan. The doctor advised notification of all family, immediately. "It will be a miracle if he lives more than a week at the level of infection in his brain."

All the color drained from James' face. *No. He could not be losing his father now. This could not be happening. What was he going to do now?* James shot glances at the Bogarts who looked almost as stricken by the news as James himself.

"Is he conscious? Will he regain consciousness?"

"He is in a deeper level of a coma than before. It is not certain at this time if he will regain consciousness, and if so, for how long. We are doing everything we can, but with the level of infection, the situation is very unpredictable. Meningitis is a nasty disease in the brain; it usually advances rapidly shutting down various parts of the body. There is no way of knowing which parts it will attack first; however, usually, once meningitis is in the brain, the patient has a week to 10 days. In Edmund's case, we are pretty sure there had to be some evidence of the illness in his system before the accident."

James hung his head. He couldn't find Autumn that fast - even if he went to the police. James thanked the doctor and started pacing. The Bogarts stood to the side in support, yet said nothing. James began talking the dilemma through, out loud, hoping it would give him clarity.

Suddenly, Penny spoke up. "Why can't you call her?"

James stopped in his tracks. "What do you mean? We don't know where she is. How can I call her?"

"When Autumn called on Christmas Day, I gave Edmund the number from my caller ID. Why not at least *try* to reach her through the same number?"

"I don't know where it is? He never showed it to me. I guess I could go search the house."

Mr. Bogart then spoke up. "I bet we still have it. We never delete those numbers; it might still be on the phone."

"Yes, it may still be there. Henry, why don't you and James see if you can find it? I'll stay here to keep an eye on Edmund. But, hurry!"

James and Henry ran for the doors of the hospital.

At the Bogarts, they began sifting through the phone numbers on the caller ID. The last number said "Michigan CALL," and they knew they had found it. Had one more call came in, it would have been erased. Saying a prayer of thanks, James started to leave.

"Where are you going?"

"Back to the house."

"Why not call from here? If Autumn has caller ID, she may be more willing to answer the call from us than from her father's house."

James had not thought of that. "I'll reimburse you for the call."

"Don't worry about it. Just make the call and get Autumn here."

It was the night before the New Year's Eve Ball, and Autumn was feeling good about what she had accomplished.

Around seven that evening, there was a knock on her door. When she opened it, she found Landon holding a movie and popcorn. At first she hesitated, *they would be together all evening at the ball tomorrow,* yet, in all honesty, she welcomed the distraction from the mayhem in her mind.

"Ménage Eleanor is on her way. LeDare Anton summoned her for us. I'll wait here in the hall until she gets here."

Autumn leaned up against the door. "You are very persistent in your attention, my Lord." She smiled teasingly at him.

Landon leaned in. "Are you complaining?"

"No." Autumn blushed.

"Good." Landon leaned on the outside of the door, a few inches away from her. "Because it has been a very long day, and all I want to do is simply veg out with you beside me for a few hours of downtime. If, that is okay?"

Autumn nodded. She completely understood. And truly, felt honored that it was her he wanted to spend time with.

Ménage Eleanor showed up, and they all made themselves comfortable around the sitting area in the great room. Autumn had insisted that if Eleanor was going to have to be there anyway, she was going to join them as a friend. Landon had understood, and accepted this - in fact, the three of them had had many enjoyable evenings over the last week.

The movie had just begun when Autumn's phone rang. This was rather unusual, as few people had her direct line and most of them were businesses; therefore, her phone never rang after five.

Autumn thought about ignoring it; nevertheless, something inside of her nudged her to answer. She nodded to Ménage Eleanor who ran to the phone on the fourth ring. With nerves in the pit of her stomach, Autumn watched as Eleanor answered the phone. "Chatelaine Autumn DeBlue's suite."

James was starting to think that he wasn't going to get through when a lovely woman's voice answered. *Could this be his sister?* Caught off guard by this thought, the greeting, and not being prepared with what to say, James stood silent.

Henry nudged him, and James came to. "Um, yes, this is James McCurry, I am looking for Autumn. There is an emergency regarding her father. He's dying, and I need to speak with her right away." James wanted to make his point clear so she wouldn't deny the call.

Eleanor turned white as what the man said registered in her mind. "One moment please, and I'll see if the Chatelaine is available to take your call."

Seeing Eleanor's reaction, Autumn moved toward her, with Landon staying by her side in his usual protective stance. Autumn heard a man's voice on the other end of the line. "Please tell her that it's critical."

James was not sure if the woman on the other end heard him, so he waited and prayed.

Eleanor put the line on hold and turned ashen to Autumn. "It's a man named James McCurry. He is quite emphatic that it is critical for him to speak with you regarding your father. He said..." She paused not wanting to say the words. "He said – your father is dying."

Autumn's face went blank, her heart sank, and the room began to spin. Landon's hand which was at the small of her back quickly encircled her waist, pulling her to him, bringing her warmth and security. He then took charge of the situation.

"Go tell our Lady she is needed at once. My Love, take the call but do not indicate where you are. Get as much information as you can so that we can verify it."

Eleanor left at a run, and Autumn went to the phone. "How did he get this number?"

Landon shrugged. "Caller ID."

*Why had she not thought of that before she called Mrs. Bogart?* Though Lady Cannon's house did not have it, caller ID was growing more popular everywhere. Taking a deep breath, she exhaled and answered the phone.

Relief and excitement came over James at the same time when he heard Autumn answer. He had done it: he had found his sister. "Hi Autumn, this is James, your..." He wanted to say, brother, then decided now was not the time for introductions, "father's employee."

"Yes, Mr. McCurry, Mrs. Bogart told me of you, please inform me as to what has happened with my father."

Autumn sounded so calm, so poised in her request - though her hands were shaking and her skin was pale. Landon marveled at her demeanor even though he knew she was terrified.

James told Autumn about the trampling, the coma, and now the diagnosis of meningitis. He relayed what the doctor told him about immediately notifying family as it could be any time. As she was listening to James, Lady Cannon entered quite alarmed as Ménage Eleanor had filled her in.

Landon held his finger up to his lips indicating she should not speak. He did not want to take the chance that this was a ploy of some sort to lure Autumn back to Nebraska or give away her location. He fought the panic growing in his heart. *I finally find a woman that I can love and have a hope of a future with when it is all threatened to be taken away. Lord, please help me put this in your hands, and if this woman truly is my future, help us to work it out. Please protect us both.* Landon turned his attention back to what Autumn was saying.

"I see, so he is in the hospital now? Do you know his room number?" Autumn inquired.

James was uncertain why she needed to know so many details, but didn't want to lose his connection with her, so he answered them.

"Edmund had a Release of Information form completed after his first time at the hospital, so you are listed as next of kin and shouldn't have any trouble getting information when you arrive."

Suddenly, Autumn realized he was expecting her to come back to Nebraska. Up until that moment, she was just gaining information. It had never crossed her mind that she would actually go back - even with the information that her father was dying. *Does that make me a horrible daughter? Shouldn't I be there if he truly is dying? I was there with mom. I watched her die. Do I really want to do that with my father?*

"Can I place you on hold for a moment, while I look into the situation from here?"

James reluctantly agreed. *Look into the situation? Does she think I'm lying? Doesn't she understand that her father is dying! What happened between these two that she wouldn't come running? I simply don't understand.* James wanted to keep talking to his sister and was afraid of losing this one connection he had. *But I guess I've got the number now. I can call back. And if they change the number or restrict the call, I'll hire a detective if I need to trace the number down. I* will not *lose this lead. Autumn will come home again.*

With hands shaking Autumn put Mr. McCurry on hold and turned to Landon. "He wants me to come immediately. What do I tell him?"

Landon was busy verifying the story with the hospital through the numbers Mr. McCurry had provided. It was confirmed - once Autumn gave them her name and verified who she was - Edmund DeBlue was in the hospital and he was on the second floor. His condition was critical, and he was not expected to live past a week. Landon's heart sank.

With Mr. McCurry still on hold, everyone was brought up to speed. It was Lady Cannon who spoke first. "You must go to him." Landon watched while Autumn's eyes widened in horror at the proclamation. "My dear, if your father is dying, you need to at least attempt to make peace with him. If you don't, you'll have to live with that regret the rest of your life. You must at least try."

Landon hesitantly agreed, though did not like sending her alone. "What if this is a ruse? I don't want to take for granted that Mr. DeBlue's status is critical; however, we cannot ignore the possibility that this McCurry fellow is up to no good - taking advantage of what he considers a naive minor in a bad situation. We know nothing about him."

"Then I charge you, Lord Michaels, to accompany the Chatelaine to see her father and aide her in any way she needs. I also charge you to protect the interests of the estate you have been hired to protect by being legal counsel to our Chatelaine in this time of possible death. If it is discovered to be a ruse, I charge you to use your cunning and way with words to secure her return, at whatever time it can be arranged."

Landon swelled with gratitude for Lady Cannon and gently took her hand to kiss it. He then turned to Autumn, who was still white with shock at what she was hearing. "Reply that you will come immediately, as soon as arrangements can be made with your accompaniment."

James could not imagine what was taking so long, but he could not hang up either. After what seemed like hours, though it was just several minutes, Autumn came back on the line, and to the best of his understanding, said she was coming immediately.

James hung up the phone and embraced Henry out of relief and gratitude. "I'm sorry that took so long. She's coming - at least I think that was what she meant. I really will reimburse you for that call."

Henry dismissed the offer again, and they headed back to the hospital to wait for Autumn and word on Edmund.

After updating Penny on how the call went, she asked. "Are you going to tell Autumn you are her brother?"

James shook his head. "How can I drop a bombshell like that on her with Edmund lying on his deathbed? No, it would all be too much of a shock. Besides, I don't want her thinking I'm here only to claim some part of her inheritance or something."

Penny disagreed. "Autumn has been dealing with lies and neglect for far too long. She needs the truth up front. However, it is your call as the eldest, and I will simply pray about it while we wait."

James nodded his appreciation.

Lady Cannon summoned LeDare Anton and inquiries were immediately made as to flights and travel arrangements. It was determined the best flight would be at nine that evening. It did not allow for much time to prepare, yet Lady Cannon felt that time was of the essence.

Landon left immediately to prepare for the trip.

Eleanor was informed that she would be accompanying the Chatelaine on this trip as well with Lady Cannon giving her specific instructions. "You are to prepare the Chatelaine's best daily attire. I will not suffer her to be presented as anything less than the lady she has become. You are also going as a chaperone for Lord Michaels and the Chatelaine. I trust Lord Michaels completely; nonetheless, I am not blinded by the fact that he is completely smitten with our

Chatelaine. There may be a time when you are needed. I trust you to keep a clear head and inform me of any difficulties."

Eleanor smiled. She was honored to be entrusted with the responsibility of not only presenting the Chatelaine appropriately but also with looking out for the well-being of her friend.

Autumn immediately busied herself by delegating the final details of the ball to the house staff. She felt grieved and anxious about having to leave at such a crucial time. With so many guests and activities she had planned to administer, it seemed incomprehensible she would be leaving. Fortunately, she had been organized in her preparations, and when she finally felt satisfied with everyone's comprehension of her plans, Autumn headed down the east corridor to face something even worse than leaving the ball – Summer. She dreaded facing her more than returning to Nebraska.

Autumn had no idea what lay ahead of her. *Would her father die, and if so, what would she do with the farm and land? Was this a ruse to get her back? Landon thought it possible. How long would she need to be gone?* All the uncertainty would make it all the harder to explain to Summer.

Autumn gently knocked on the doors as she ever so slightly opened them - it was almost Summer's curfew, and Autumn wasn't sure if she would already be in bed. Summer was in her pajamas and sitting on the floor playing with her dolls. Autumn entered and joined her on the floor.

"Summer, I have something really important to tell you." Autumn was trying to be ginger and careful as to not upset her too much. The last thing Autumn wanted was for Summer to think she was abandoning her.

"Sounds serious." Summer still focused on her dolls.

"It is." Autumn pulled Summer toward her to sit on her lap. "Summer, I am going to take a little trip tonight."

Summer stood up and turned facing her. "A trip? Where? Tonight? Do I get to come?" There was a hint of excitement mixed with concern in her tone.

"Yes, a trip. Lord Michaels and I are going to Nebraska to see my father - he is very sick and might die."

"Nebraska! No, you can't!" Summer stamped her foot and threw her doll down crossing her arms in front of her. After a few minutes, when she saw Autumn was not going to change her mind, her countenance changed, and she begged. "You…you can't leave us, Autumn!" Summer threw herself into Autumn's lap. "*This* is your home now; you said so yourself. Please don't leave, Autumn…if you go…I know you'll never return…why, Autumn, why are you going away?" The anguish in Summer's voice broke Autumn's heart.

Autumn knew it was going to be hard to accept; nevertheless, the severity of Summer's words and actions were definitely unexpected. "Oh Summer, you're right, this is my home. And I am not going away for good, just for a little while to see my father."

"How long is a little while?"

"Oh, my sweet one, I don't really know. There are too many uncertain circumstances. I….I need to go to say goodbye to my father before he is too sick or dies without hearing me say it. Can you understand that?"

Summer looked like she might understand, though Autumn was not sure. Either way, Summer remained utterly silent.

"Summer, please try to understand. I cannot control the circumstances. I do not know how long my father will live, or how long it will take to settle things. I have to be there and make peace with the past so that I *can* be free to live here and take care of you and Granny."

"But what are we to do without you?" Tears streamed down her face.

Once again, Autumn pulled Summer to her lap and brushed the tears away. "I have made arrangements for Becca to take you ice skating and to the museum while I'm gone. I have also made a list of all the fun things we like to do so you can do them with her. You have been doing so well without the carriage; however, just in case you need it, I told Becca where the elf maiden lives. She has agreed to go get it from her if you want it. I won't be gone long, and when I come home we'll celebrate with something very special, okay?"

"No, it's not okay. I don't want you to go. I want you to stay!" Summer cried as she threw her arms around Autumn's neck. Then her tone changed. "Can't I go with you, please Autumn, just let me go with you! That would make it all better, please?"

"What about Granny? Would you want to leave Granny here all by herself? She needs you to help with the ball tomorrow and all the guest that are coming. Would you really want to leave Granny alone to handle all this by herself?"

Autumn knew it wasn't even an option to ponder. She wanted to promise she'd return; however, knowing the history with Summer's parents, she was very careful not to say anything like that.

Summer still seemed to be struggling, yet she at least stopped crying. As Autumn sat there holding Summer in her lap, deep within her heart, she heard: *Locket*. Immediately, she knew what it meant. Ever since Summer had heard the story of her locket, she eyed it longingly. Summer understood the preciousness of such an item.

Taking the necklace from around her own neck, Autumn placed it around Summer's. "I want you to hold this for safekeeping until I return, okay?"

Taken back by such an offer, Summer fingered the locket. "But this was your mother's, why are you giving it to me?"

"I'm not giving it to you. I just want you to keep it safe until I come back to get it? Do you understand? Can you keep it safe for me?" A huge smile came over her face and Summer's whole countenance changed.

A knock came from the door, and Lord Michaels stood next to Lady Cannon.

Landon hesitated to interrupt; however, time was running out. "Chatelaine, it is time."

Summer stood and marched over to Lord Michaels gesturing for him to bend down. In like manner to her grandmother, Summer shook her finger and said as sternly as she could. "I charge you to bring her back!"

Landon had every intention of doing just that, though he wondered when it would happen. He tried not to smile. "I want her to return too." He had no doubt Autumn would come back with him at some point; however, if her father recovered or worse yet, died, he was sure it would be after her nineteenth birthday.

Autumn came to Lady Cannon and curtsied. As soon as she was done, Lady Cannon embraced her with a hug so telling, that Autumn had to fight back the tears. Lady Cannon placed an envelope in Autumn's hand. It read: MRS. BOGART. Autumn immediately knew what it was. She hugged Lady Cannon again and thanked her from the bottom of her heart.

Autumn then turned to Summer again with a few last encouraging words. Fighting tears and fear, Autumn took Landon's arm as he escorted her down the stairs.

Lady Cannon marveled at the changes in Autumn and her granddaughter yet again. She knelt down beside Summer as the couple left. "Let's say a prayer for a safe journey and quick return."

Summer immediately bowed her head.

# 24

The trip back to Nebraska was very different than the one away from it less than a year ago. This time, she was escorted by Landon, her betrothed, a wealthy man of class and stature, and Ménage Eleanor, her attendant, who was also her best friend, and they were riding in limousines and flying first class.

The flight took no time at all being the later hour. Still, the drive to the hospital was tedious in the traffic being a holiday weekend night - especially in a limousine. As they pulled up to the hospital doors, Autumn's heart began to race, and all color drained from her face. It was late, and she was tired. For a brief moment, she debated waiting until morning to face what was ahead. Sensing her hesitation, Landon put his arm around her and pulled her to him in reassurance.

Holding her hand, he kissed it gently. "I'm not leaving. I'll be here with you every step of the way. As will Eleanor."

After instructing the driver to find a place to park and wait, all three of them exited - Landon first, followed by Autumn with Eleanor behind. They entered the doors and proceeded to her father's room on the second floor. As the elevator doors opened, Autumn was filled with relief to see Mrs. Bogart standing in the waiting area.

Hearing the elevator doors, Penny glanced at them out of habit. At first, all she saw was a very elegantly dressed man and woman standing side by side with another well-dressed woman standing slightly behind. But what caught Penny's attention was the way the first woman fixated on her; it was as if the woman knew her. She looked harder and realized - it was Autumn.

Penny stood in total disbelief at the transformation of the beautiful woman before her. "Autumn?"

Autumn nodded her head in acknowledgment, yet was too choked up to say anything. Penny flung her arms around her, embracing her like a mother would a child. Landon and Eleanor stood to the side watching the welcome Autumn received.

Finally, Autumn was able to get words out. "Mrs. Bogart, it is good to see you. Where is my father?"

"Come, he is worsening despite the antibiotics. It will do him good to hear your voice."

"Are you sure about that?" Autumn could imagine him being so furious that he'd come to just to reprimand her and then die from the exertion, leaving her even more distraught.

"Yes, child, very." Without a glance to either of the other two people with Autumn, Penny took Autumn by the arm and led her down the hall.

It bothered Landon greatly that they were ignored and that this woman treated Autumn like a child. What made it worse was Autumn allowing it. He reasoned with himself that this was a trying situation, and this woman probably only knew Autumn as a child and not the young woman she had become. He needed to have patience with what lies ahead; nonetheless, he was not going to let Autumn out of his sight, so he gestured to Eleanor who followed.

Thankfully, Edmund was not in the ICU, and everyone could go to his room. They approached a room where Autumn could see her father, ashen and grey, on the bed. A man was sitting by his side, gently holding his hand, head bowed. Hearing commotion at the door the man looked up.

"James, this is your…" Catching herself at James' glare, Penny changed her statement. "your boss' daughter, Autumn."

Rising, James looked Autumn over from head to toe. He had seen pictures of a girl and had not anticipated a young woman. Even with the hints from Penny that Autumn had changed, he in no way imagined such a beautiful young woman as his sister. Further study revealed the definite characteristics and traits he remembered in Sue - their mother.

James' thorough intake of Autumn infuriated Landon to the point that he could take it no longer. "I beg your pardon, sir. We do not take kindly to men gawking at our Chatelaine." He wanted to say, 'and my wife' yet dare not give away too much information too quickly - after all, she was still a minor in Nebraska, and her father was lying in that bed.

James eyes immediately shifted to the finely dressed man who had stepped to his sister's side and slightly in front of her in a clearly marked and guarded manner. Ever so slightly James inclined his head, in a slight bow, though he did not know why - the man's presence just seemed to demand it. "I beg your pardon, *sir*." Reusing the same terms used to address him. "I have only seen pictures of a young girl as Edmund's daughter, and was taken back by seeing such a fine young woman."

Accepting this explanation as probable, though not acceptable, Landon hesitantly nodded and allowed Autumn to enter the room staying by her side.

"James, it is a pleasure to meet you. Mrs. Bogart speaks highly of you." She slightly curtsied out of respect then gestured to Landon and Eleanor. "This is Lord Michaels, my Lady's counselor and legal aid and this is my personal attendant, Ménage Eleanor. I ask that you, please pardon Lord Michaels as he has been charged strictly by my Lady regarding my safety."

"Your Lady, as you refer to her, must not be very trusting to send such dubious attendants to guard you at your father's deathbed," James said this snidely and accusatory. Then catching Penny's glance, realized things were not going well for him. "But I am grateful to her for delivering you safely back home."

Autumn's heart dropped, and Lord Michaels stiffened. "I do not know what difference my safety is to you, Mr. McCurry, but I do not feel the tone of this conversation is appropriate over my father's deathbed, as you so astutely noted. Now, if everyone will excuse me, I'd like some time alone with my father."

Landon stood his ground, waiting to assure James was leaving before he budged from his place next to Autumn. Seeing this, James made the first move, bending down to whisper in Edmund's ear.

Then coming to the bed, he stopped before Autumn. "You should know, the doctors said it is good to talk to him as if he can hear. There is no telling if he is conscious and simply cannot respond or if he is completely unconscious. I know from personal experience he can, at times, hear as he has squeezed my hand in response."

Noting the deep regard, James bore for her father, she put a hand gently on his arm and thanked him. Then she moved around the bed to where he had stood, and she looked down at her father. Seeing this, everyone began to leave.

"My love…" Seeing James watching him, Landon altered what he was going to say. "…ly Chatelaine, if you need anything I will be right outside the door. Take as much time as you need and feel free to summon me at any time."

She nodded and looked back to her father.

Autumn sat for what seemed like hours praying over her father, yet not speaking a word. She had no idea of the time. Still, she knew it was late. Finally, having enough strength and courage, she reached out to take his hand. It seemed so lifeless at first, but as she sat there, she felt him squeeze it ever so slightly.

Autumn had sudden hope that he could hear her. "Papa, it's me - Autumn, I'm here. I am so sorry I hurt you, and for all the years I struggled against you. I know I was wrong in many things. Can you forgive me, Papa?" In the midst of all the emotions she was struggling with, Autumn unknowingly reverted to using the nickname that she had used when she was very young before her mother had gotten sick.

Feeling compelled to make him understand her new life, in the hope that he would not detain her if he did recover, or be free to let go if he didn't, she went on to explain. "I want you to know, that even though how I left was not right, I have found a good life. I am living in Michigan with a very wealthy woman named Lady Cannon. She has a beautiful five-year-old granddaughter named Summer whom I have grown to love very much. Lady Cannon has been so good to me Papa; she has given me an education - something I know mom would be happy about. Eventually, I will be given guardianship of Summer. She is such an amazing little girl, I wish you could meet her. God has blessed me so much. I would like very much to have your blessing, Papa, though I know I have not done much from your perspective to earn it. Is it even possible?"

Autumn gasped as her father squeezed her hand again, this time tighter. She looked up at him and saw his eyes were open and looking at her. "Are you a dream or really my daughter all grown up?"

"Oh, Papa, it is me. I have changed so much and learned so much, but most importantly, I have learned to forgive and to seek forgiveness. Can you forgive me, Papa?"

"Yes, I can forgive you. I already have, but the real question is can you forgive me - for my neglect and wrongful treatment of you? I was so selfish when your mother was sick and after she died. I didn't realize how much I wronged you until I thought I had lost you forever. God led me to despair to open my eyes. It was His will you went away. I am thankful you have been treated well, and I am relieved you have come home. Can you find it in your heart to forgive me for all those awful years?"

Autumn could tell it took a lot of his strength to talk and so she did not press the issue of her not staying. "Yes, Papa. God has been good to both of us, hasn't he? Now save your strength to get better."

"God is good, dear daughter, beyond what you know. But - my time has come. It's ok, I'm at peace, and know I will soon get to see your mother again. It is good." Autumn went white and thought she would pass out at his declaration, but then, he shocked her back to the moment. "Is James here?"

"No, he stepped out so I could have time alone with you."

"Please get him. I need to talk to you both."

Autumn was stunned. *Why would he need to talk to his employee and her together now? He just said he was dying.* Obediently though, she went over to the door and opened it, gaining the attention of everyone gathered around. "James, he is asking for you and time is short."

Immediately, James rushed to his side. "Edmund, I am here, it's James."

Autumn followed back to the bed and stood by Edmund's other side; Lord Michaels stepped inside as well - since Autumn left the door open - as did Ménage Eleanor and Mrs. Bogart.

"James, does she know?"

"No."

"Autumn let me have your hand."

Autumn gave her hand to her father.

"James, your hand."

James gave Edmund his hand as well.

With all that was left in him, he brought their hands together. "Daughter, I know you have a new life that is good to you, and I'm sure you want to return. I wish I had more time to make this easier; however, I'm being called home. Autumn, we have made our peace, receive it and do not fret over the past any longer. James - know all is well with us. Please heed your father's dying wish to work together for the betterment of the family. And Autumn, I ask you specifically to listen to James. He has some very important things to tell you. I affirm now what he says is the truth. Therefore, until you come of age, Autumn, I give you into the hands of your brother, James, my son."

Landon cringed as his heart sank.

Autumn shot a look of unbelief at James.

Squeezing James' hand, unaware to Autumn, Edmund finished. "My son, do my will." And with that, the hands that held theirs together collapsed.

Edmund was gone.

Autumn stood for several moments, staring at the man across the bed from her in whom her father had just declared to be his son. The stranger he entrusted to look after her. James looked at her in return, tears pouring down his cheeks and their eyes met for a brief moment.

Recognition stirred deep within her. *James looks just like my father.*

In that instant, Landon rushed to her side, just in time to catch her as she fainted.

# ♥ 25 ♥

When Autumn fainted after Edmund's death, things got very crazy. The hospital staff was there immediately as the monitors started sounding; Lord Michaels - who was cradling Autumn in his arms - was saying he'd take "the Chatelaine" to a hotel; and James' emotions were crashing around him at the enormity of what had just transpired.

Somehow, God gave him the strength to pull his thoughts together as they were rushed out of the room by hospital staff. Taking charge, he clearly declared. "I'm sorry, Lord Michaels, but my sister is **not** going to a hotel with any man - even supervised by a maid - especially when she has a home a few miles away. Mrs. Bogart, thank you and Henry for being here. You have been such a blessing to our family. Would you be willing to help again by taking Autumn - and her guests if they so wish - back home to the farm? The familiar surroundings may be comforting during this time of loss." *Or so he hoped. If not, he'd have her at the house where he could convince her to stay and not disappear...again - so he hoped.*

Penny simply nodded her agreement and gave him a hug. Tears threatened, but he would not yield to them yet - too much still needed to be done. Bracing himself for the argument he thought was coming, he turned to Lord Michaels.

"The Chatelaine's well-being is our only concern here. She obviously needs some sleep and time to recover from the shocks of this night. Thank you for offering her a bed." Lord Michaels then nodded as he turned and followed Mrs. Bogart out the door, still cradling Autumn in his arms.

*That was a shock. No argument. No snide comment? Maybe I misjudged. It's obvious this Lord Michaels cares for my sister; the question is: how much? The maid - what was her name - she cares a great deal too.*

*Autumn came to know Jesus while in Michigan - are these people all believers? Does Lord Michaels fear God? Would he take advantage of my sister? At least Mrs. Bogart is with them; that's some reassurance she'll be okay. He said his only concern was Autumn - so what is his true purpose here? Why would this Lady Cannon send a lawyer? Is she expecting a legal battle of some sort? So many questions and so few answers.*

*Whatever the answers are, it's obvious Autumn cares about these people. So, if I want to keep my sister here without a fight, I should probably do my best to get along with them.*

By the time James had arrived back at the farm, it was the middle of the night, and all good-willed intentions were gone. He was exhausted - emotionally and physically. As he walked into the dark house, thankfulness warred with concern. Thankfulness that Lord Michaels was not there and concern whether or not Autumn was. James headed straight for Autumn's room. Quietly, he cracked the door open to see if she was inside. Seeing her on the bed, he let out the breath he'd been holding. Softly, he shut the door again and turned to leave.

"May I help you with something, Mr. McCurry?"

James jumped straight into the air, heart racing. He might have yelped, but he wasn't sure as the beating in his ears drowned out everything else. Reaching for the light switch in the hall, James flicked it on. There stood the most beautiful woman he had ever seen: soft, curvy, slightly tousled hair, and completely covered in the most modest sleeping robe he'd ever seen. Still, he was completely struck dumb.

"Mr. McCurry? Are you alright? I didn't mean to startle you. Mr. McCurry? Do you need something? I can wake the Chatelaine if you need her."

The words finally started to sink in. Trying to pull himself together one more time that night, he attempted to speak. "No...I'm...don't...where?...Um...Who..."

Taking pity on him, the woman before him explained. "I'm Ménage Eleanor, a personal attendant to the Chatelaine - Autumn, as you call her. Mrs. Bogart offered Lord Michaels a guest room so that he could be close by. Since there are so few rooms here, I'm staying on the couch - if that is okay with you. I can also sleep on the floor in the Chatelaine's room if you'd prefer."

*Sleep on the floor? No, this angel should not be sleeping on the floor.* "No...that's fine...the couch...I'm downstairs." Words were still escaping him.

"You must be so exhausted. Is there anything I can assist you with? Have you eaten anything today? Mrs. Bogart said she'd bring breakfast over around 10 tomorrow morning...or I guess this morning now...they figured everyone would like to sleep in a bit before having to deal with the funeral arrangements."

James just nodded, figuring it was easier than trying to talk again.

"So, would you like something to eat? Or do you just need to get some sleep?"

James stared blankly for a minute then shook himself. "Sleep. Shower and sleep. Yes. That's what I need." Not meaning to be rude, yet still completely at a loss, he simply walked past the angel and down the stairs to his rooms.

Autumn awoke late the next morning in a dazed remembrance of her father dying and his shocking proclamation. She lay still with her eyes closed as she recalled looking at James and the recognition she received of him being her brother. Vaguely, she remembered Landon carrying her out of the hospital and the ride to wherever she was now. *Did they go to a hotel? Did James take her back to the farmhouse? Where are Landon and Eleanor? What am I supposed to do now?* Carefully, Autumn opened her eyes and looked around. Immediately, she recognized her room at her father's house.

The familiarity of it warred within her. She glanced around and found her father had left it exactly the same. Slowly, she got up noting she was still dressed in yesterday's attire. She started to go look for Eleanor when she noticed the carousel her grandmother had left her and the doll given to her by her mother sitting on the chest where she had left them. Forgetting all about getting dressed, her heart lifted as she would now be able to reclaim her prized possessions and take them with her to Michigan. Then she remembered her father's charge to James.

*Will he prohibit me from leaving? I wonder if I can convince him to stay on the farm and let me leave. He is a stranger to me. We may be brother and sister, but we don't have any connection. Surely, he won't make me stay against my will. Landon will know what to do. I need to go find him.*

As she gazed around and thought about this house, she was surprised to realize she had no desire for anything else in the house. On second thought, maybe a few pictures for the historian to put into a book – one like Lady Cannon had done for Summer. Yes, she wanted a few of the pictures, but other than that, there was nothing left for her here. Not even the revelation of a brother could keep her here.

Walking around her room, Autumn saw that there was one change. There was an ornate box sitting on her dresser with a letter on top. She had not seen it before. Curiously, she picked up the letter and saw the envelope was addressed to her. Opening it, she read the first page.

My Dearest Daughter: If you are reading this, then you know that I am gone. I hope that we were able to find you before I passed on but if not, please know that I hold no ill will against you. I truly understand that it was my neglect of you that forced a wedge between us, and eventually, away from me. Even though I am gone, I seek your forgiveness.

In the pages that follow this letter, you will find detailed instructions for your inheritance. I kept your inheritance from you because there were things that did not make sense, and in your rebellious state, I did not feel it beneficial. Your mother had a few surprises for me at her death and only in recent days have they fully come to light.

The first thing you should know if I did not have a chance to tell you myself, is that before your mother and I were married, we had a son. I have asked James to explain the story to you, and I want you to listen to him. God has forgiven me for my mistakes and James has too. I ask that you also forgive me for preventing you from knowing your brother.

Though he rightfully has claim to it, James has made it clear he has no desire for any part of your inheritance. Therefore, I ask that you review your mother's wishes and deal kindly with him out of the

GOODNESS OF YOUR HEART AND WITH GOD'S LEADING. PROOF OF HIS LEGITIMACY AND BIRTH ARE WITH THE ESTATE PAPERS IN THE ORNATE BOX AS YOUR MOTHER DIRECTS IN HER LETTER.

THE SECOND THING YOU SHOULD KNOW IS THAT I SAVED ALL THE MONEY YOU PAID ME IN RENT OVER THE YEARS. IT IS IN A SAVINGS ACCOUNT BEARING YOUR NAME AT THE BANK. I KEPT IT FOR YOU IN CASE YOU WANTED TO ATTEND COLLEGE. I HOPE YOU WILL CONSIDER FURTHERING YOUR EDUCATION.

AUTUMN, I AM SURE WITH MY DEATH, NEWS OF MY SALVATION, AND THE REVELATION OF AN UNKNOWN BROTHER; YOU ARE HAVING A HARD TIME ABSORBING IT ALL. I DO NOT CLAIM TO UNDERSTAND GOD'S WORKING, YET I KNOW HE HAS A PLAN FOR YOU – LEAN ON HIM. I LOVE YOU, DEAR DAUGHTER, I HOPE SOMEDAY YOU CAN REALIZE HOW MUCH! - YOUR FATHER, EDMUND

Autumn sat on the bed in utter astonishment. *It **was** a lot to absorb – the death of her father, the revelation of a brother, and what was this about an inheritance? She knew about the land and house, but those would not have to be explained by her mother. What would her mother have left her that she did not already know?*

With that question running through her mind, she started reading her mother's letter.

*My sweet Autumn,*

*By the time you read this letter, I will have been gone for quite a while I would assume. I wish I could be there to explain all of this to you in person, but that was not what God had planned for us. So, let me tell you about your inheritance.*

*You probably know about the farmland and the house already. What you don't know is that around fifty years ago - give or take a few years by the time you get this - your grandmother used the money from her dowry to purchase stock in the railroad as an investment for the future generations. With the growth of the railroad, combined with various economic developments, it has become a lucrative investment.*

*Your grandmother gave me the stocks as a dowry when I married your father. To my shame, I never told him about them. We had too many secrets and hurts between us before getting married. My sweet Autumn, if the time ever comes that you should wish to marry - my one piece of advice is to put God at the center and be honest with each other. Secrets can destroy what God has brought together.*

*I intended to pass on the stocks to you as a dowry as well. Unfortunately, I will not be there for your wedding, so I have asked your father to give you this letter when you are nineteen. I pray that you will use the inheritance wisely, and keeping with tradition, put some aside for the future generations.*

The letter went on to give the specifics of how to claim the inheritance: the stock certificates were located in a safety deposit box at the bank; the key was taped to the inside of the ornate box; Autumn would need to present the key *and* a token of the legitimate right to the bank.

*Your father should have given you the token after my death. It is also the key to opening the ornate box which holds the bank key, deeds to the land, house, and my official will.*

Autumn paused to think. *What had her father ever given her? Oh no! The locket - the key was the locket I left in Michigan. Well, at least I know I will have to go back to get it.* Autumn smiled.

Autumn finished reading the letter.

*There is one last thing I wish to ask you. In the future, there may be a time when you meet someone who reminds you of your father. Someone who shares the same color of eyes, the same smile when they smirk, the same tone of voice, the same laugh. If that person should ever come to you, I'd ask, my sweet Autumn, for you to be kind and generous with him. He holds secrets I cannot share, but I hope you will embrace.*

*I love you so very much Autumn. And I pray that one day, you will come to know the same saving grace in Jesus Christ that I have so that we can see each other again in heaven.*

*With all my love, your mother.*

Autumn sat on the bed, tears staining her cheeks. *How she missed her mother. How she wished she could have had this letter sooner. Not for the inheritance but simply to hear her mother's voice through it.* Autumn smiled again. *But I did find Jesus, and I did accept Him as my Savior so we will have heaven - with Papa too.*

As Autumn left her room, her stomach was nauseated from lack of food - she hadn't eaten since lunch yesterday and now it was nearly noon, plus she was riveted with anxiety; she stood in the doorway bracing herself again. In the living room, she could see James and Landon deep in discussion.

Forgetting about feeling faint, Autumn watched James intently. *This was her brother. Brother! She was **not** an only child. She was **not** alone. She had a family.* She could now see it in his mannerisms and even in his look; he was so much like her father. *I wonder if he has Papa's temper too?* Her thoughts were interrupted as James noticed her leaning in the doorway. His glance alerted Landon, and they both stood.

Landon was the first to move, concern etched in his handsome face. "Are you well, Chatelaine?"

"A bit hungry, a little faint, though truly I am fine. Where is Ménage Eleanor?" *I so dislike having to be so formal. I'd really rather have him hold me.*

"She is in the kitchen helping Mrs. Bogart prepare lunch; shall I summon her to attend to you?"

"No. Let her finish as that is the more pressing need I think. Then I will freshen up and prepare for the day - or what's left of it. I apologize for being so lazy today, I was...distracted. I assume we have much to do in the wake of my..." She paused as she looked at James. "I mean, *our* father's death."

James smiled warmly at her. However, it was Landon who answered. "Yes, and if I may request a moment, Chatelaine, I think we have a few things we need to discuss privately as well."

As much as he didn't like to admit it, James nodded his approval because, at this point, Autumn would probably trust Lord Michaels more than she would him. That hurt, still, he knew it was the truth. He'd have to work hard at building a relationship with his sister.

Since James did not object, Landon took Autumn's hand and escorted her back to her room shutting the door behind him.

"Chatelaine, our Lady, sent me here to aid you, please hear my counsel. I have had a chance to speak with James thoroughly while you rested. I think our first impressions were false. He is a decent God-fearing man, who loved your father."

Autumn listened to him intently as he was so formal and proper. *Which first impression had been false - the idea that there was a ruse or that James had nefarious intentions - I assume Landon means the way James looked at me when we first met, but I'm not sure.* Autumn now understood his intense evaluation of her better - it was the first time he was seeing his sister.

"I truly believe he wants what is best for you, and we do not want to risk his displeasure. Your father gave him charge over you in a dying sentiment with witnesses to verify; I can do nothing legally to prohibit this charge while you are here in Nebraska. Hopefully, if we show him respect and indicate you have been well taken care of with our Lady, he will determine it is best for you to go back with me once the funeral is over."

Forgetting about the letters, for the time being, Autumn turned her attention back to what Landon was saying. "And what if he doesn't?"

Landon softened, and he took her hands in his. "My love, in the worst case scenario, I believe, he could only detain you until your nineteenth birthday. Once you are of legal age, you are free to make your own decisions. If you would choose at that time to come back to us and he tried to restrain you, I would fight to my last breath to regain your hand, but let's not get ahead of ourselves. Let's give him a chance and see what happens first."

Autumn was moved by his intensity in stating his defense of her hand, yet was troubled at the thought of having to stay. Nausea and weakness came over her again as she silently nodded in agreement with what Landon suggested.

"Come, James wishes to discuss funeral arrangements. There is much to do."

It really was all too much to comprehend. Autumn stood shaking and in need of some security, something stable to hold on to in facing the days ahead of her. With her faith so new and being in the old familiar house, Autumn did not think of turning to God. In fact, the only thing she could think of at the moment was Landon, with a new awareness of his hands holding hers, she slipped her arms around him.

As Autumn reached out to him, Landon suddenly became aware of the toll the last twenty-four hours had taken on the beautiful woman now in his arms. She seemed pale and fragile. His heart cried out to be able to provide her comfort and protection, yet he had to tread gently as he now saw what James had seen - her youth. He held her for several minutes as neither wanted to let go.

Still standing in their embrace, a knock sounded on the door and without bidding entrance, the door opened - it was James.

James didn't know what to make of the sight before him. *Was this just an act of comfort to someone who just suffered a loss or was there something more to it?* James' protective instinct rose within him at the thought of his younger sister embracing an older man for any other reason but sorrow. What really grated him was that he hadn't had the foresight to insist the two of them not go behind closed doors alone. He would remember that for the future. "Lunch is ready."

Autumn and Landon separated.

"Thank you, James." When Autumn got close enough to him, she put her arms around James in a sisterly embrace. "I can see him in you. Later, will you tell me the story?" She was hoping to disarm the stern look in his eyes.

James looked at Lord Michaels, and then back at his sister, who was now in **his** protective embrace and squeezed her slightly. "Yes, there is a lot for us to discuss."

James led Autumn in his arms to the kitchen where lunch was being served. It seemed so odd to be in the house without Edmund.

Noting Autumn's apprehension to her surroundings, James wondered what caused that reaction in her. *What happened? Why is she so anxious to get away? Does she just have so many bad memories? What are those bad memories? Could Edmund really have been as bad as Mrs. Bogart had first thought? What if Autumn won't stay? Edmund couldn't get her to stay. How will I convince her to? I don't want to lose my sister now that I just found her. God, what am I supposed to do?*

As soon as Eleanor saw Autumn still wearing the same dress as yesterday, she approached her and curtsied. "Chatelaine, please excuse my lack of attention to you, especially in this time of loss. My actions are unforgivable."

Penny and James - who were not accustomed to this type of protocol - watched intrigued. James especially seemed to dislike Eleanor being submissive to anyone.

Autumn, inclined her head in acknowledgment. "My dear Eleanor, you have not been neglectful in your duties to me, I desired your assistance with lunch first. Otherwise, I would have summoned you. You are not in any error on my part; please do not think of it again."

Eleanor curtsied again gratefully.

"I will, however, desire to change after I have eaten something. I fear I'm a bit faint from everything."

Eleanor nodded. "I'll go prepare your dress while you eat, Chatelaine." She curtsied again and left the kitchen.

James watched her go.

Autumn made a note of the interest, yet was distracted by the food that Mrs. Bogart was placing on the table.

Once everyone else was seated, Penny asked. "Will you tell us what happened after you ran away? How did you end up in Michigan with Lady Cannon?"

Glancing at Landon, who gave her an approving nod, Autumn told Mrs. Bogart all that had happened from arriving at her house to ask for help, to the train ride and the encounter with the police, then arriving at Kalamazoo to wait for the chauffeur, and finally, arriving at Lady Cannon's estate.

Looking at Landon, she added. "Please do not mention Master Philips tardiness to Lady Cannon. I promised I would say nothing as it was not a big delay."

Landon nodded his agreement.

Autumn then told them of the house and all the wonders there, including being offered the position as a companion, and all that led to her salvation on Christmas Eve. Autumn tried to emphasize how well Lady Cannon treated her in hopes James would take note.

Landon sat attentively listening as Autumn relayed her story. He knew the general events; however, to hear the whole story with details, he marveled all the more at what she had accomplished on her own.

James also listened intently, and he did not miss the hints and pointed remarks that Autumn was giving him. *She doesn't want to stay. She's hoping I will see how good it is in Michigan and let her go. But I can't. I have a duty to our father to keep her safe. To keep her here. That was what he wanted me to do. I can't let her go.*

When Autumn was done with her story, James suggested they discuss the funeral plans as the mortuary was waiting for his call. Though Autumn wanted to freshen up before the day got too much farther gone, she felt she needed to honor his request. Mrs. Bogart and Lord Michaels continued to sit with them as James went over the questions from the mortuary and the instructions Edmund had left him.

Whenever Autumn was unsure about something, she would refer to Lord Michaels who replied with his opinion. Autumn soon found James heeded his suggestions and was encouraged in this. *Maybe James would also heed him in letting me go back to Michigan.*

Finally, James finished with all of his questions. "There are still things we need to do, but they can wait until later. I need to get some chores done before the visitors start arriving."

"What visitors?" Autumn looked alarmed.

"From the church. Some are bringing food, and some are coming to offer support. I asked them to hold off until this evening to give us some time to discuss things, but we should be prepared for a busy evening."

"Why would these people from a church Papa hated be coming here? He'd roll over in his grave if he were buried yet."

Penny exchanged a look with James that Autumn didn't understand - it seemed to say "I told you so." Then Penny took Autumn's hand and explained. "Honey, your father changed a lot before he died. He was going to church and bible study group regularly; even before he accepted Jesus as his Savior, he was seeking answers. Plus, James has been a member of our congregation for several years. The church will want to support him too."

*Of course. There was much Autumn did not know and had missed out on. Had not she also been attending church? Yet, the idea of her father - even knowing he had accepted Christ as Savior - going to church seemed so foreign.* She blushed, embarrassed that she hadn't thought of these things before speaking. "I suppose I'd better go get ready to receive guests then. I apologize for my blunt speaking; it's still so unfamiliar that he changed that much."

Without waiting for a reply, Autumn got up and left the table in a hurry to be away from all the concerned and curious eyes.

After freshening up with Ménage Eleanor's assistance, Autumn still didn't feel able to face James again. *He wants to ask me questions I don't want to answer. I don't want to relive all those years. I just want to move forward, leaving the past where it is.* In her desire to avoid everything, Autumn laid down on the bed and slept.

When Autumn finally woke again, she lay staring at the ceiling not wanting to get up. As she did so, it dawned on her that if she were in Michigan, she would be preparing for the ball right now. Sinking further into her bed, she let the tears finally come. When she was all cried out, she said a quiet prayer for Lady Cannon and all the activities of the evening.

That night in Nebraska, there would be no celebrations, no ball. Only quiet contemplation as Autumn, Eleanor, James, and Landon watched the ball drop into a new year.

# ❦ 26 ❦

For the next three days, while waiting for the funeral, James kept up the chores and business of the farm while Autumn was left to entertain visitors with condolences - most of whom she did not know. When he was around, Autumn made a point of introducing James as her brother, son of Edmund and Sue. She felt it only right to acknowledge him as a family member as it would have pleased her mother.

Autumn read the letters from her parents daily, though she had not shared them with anyone else yet. Autumn knew instinctively that her mother had longed for James to be a part of their family. Therefore, out of respect for her mother, Autumn tried with James, but it was not easy.

Autumn felt she had lost all control of her life and James was dictating to her at every turn. She tried to keep up the appearance that everything was okay; however, she continually fought the dictatorial hold of James within herself - just as she had with her father. James' house rules prohibited any time with Landon in anything other than supervised business like conversations. Landon had been so caring and gentle with her in his affections, the aloofness they were forced to participate in left her aching for the freedom she knew in Michigan all the more.

Landon longed to be close to Autumn to comfort her and be an arm of security in this time of loss. He saw more and more each day that she stayed in that house that the memories there weighed her down. He would often find her in tears, which he was certain were not related to the loss of her father, as she sat by herself trying to avoid everyone.

There was so much she was facing, and he longed to be the one there for her. It broke his heart to know he could do nothing. James had strictly forbidden any contact between them after finding them embracing that first day. Landon had debated declaring his intentions; however, Mrs. Bogart had made it clear in one of her not-so-subtle comments that James had no intention of letting Autumn marry anytime soon - especially not to an older man.

Without being able to speak privately with her, Landon was left with what he could observe, which was that Autumn was struggling and James was oblivious to how this place was affecting her. Plus, she seemed to revere her new brother. *Could James possibly use his new influence over her to turn her against him?* This thought paralyzed him so much so that Landon stepped aside time and again instead of fighting for what he wanted. This resulted in him constantly feeling like he was losing control of his life and his love - a very unfamiliar sense.

The evening before the funeral, Autumn found herself thinking of Michigan: Lady Cannon, Summer, and all that awaited her at home – for that was what Michigan had become, *home*. She was anxious to get the funeral over with and be on her way. *I'm not staying here. As soon as I can leave, I have to get out of here. I cannot stay here.*

Suddenly, Autumn was swept away in her thoughts. She was pulled back in memory to the days after her mother died, when she was stripped of all she was familiar with. Her stomach was painfully cramped with the thought. She tried to pray through it; however, it seemed the heavens were shut up to her. She was once again alone and fighting for her very life. *Would James do the very thing her father had? Would she have to suffer under the selfish acts of another man who had authority over her? How much pain would James inflict upon her?* The memories caused such panic to hit her that she collapsed during the last portion of the viewing.

James was looking for Autumn. She had been here just a few moments ago, but now he couldn't find her. What concerned him most was that Lord Michaels was missing as well. *Did they run off together? What do I do if he takes off with her? Autumn seems to be growing more and more distant? What is wrong with her?*

At first, James had been appreciative of Autumn's readiness to introduce him as her brother - he thought it was acceptance of who he was and the authority he now had. It had encouraged him when she had sought him out to talk about Edmund's last days, the times he had shared with their mother, and about his adoptive family. He had hoped her acceptance of him would help when he told her he had no intention of letting her leave after the funeral. But now, he didn't think she'd stay or that he could make her.

Still, the funeral wasn't over, and though he doubted Lord Michaels' intentions, he didn't think he would run off with her before the funeral was over. Then he saw Ménage Eleanor. *They wouldn't leave without her, so they have to be here somewhere.*

Once Eleanor saw James, she headed straight for him - concern etched on her face. Even still, she was an angel, and he struggled to regulate his beating heart and keep his mental functions.

Once she was within whispering distance, she leaned in, sending a wave of the vanilla scent he'd come to associate with her. "Have you seen the Chatelaine - Autumn - I can't find her anywhere."

That cleared James' mind. "Where is Lord Michaels?"

"He is outside getting some fresh air. I just spoke to him. He hasn't seen Autumn since she went to the restroom a little while ago. But I checked, and she's not there."

Now James was seriously concerned. "Get Lord Michaels. I'll get Mrs. Bogart. We'll start searching."

It was only fifteen minutes later that James found Autumn unconscious in a side room off the main sanctuary. *Not again, not again!* James yelled for help and rushed to her side. Within moments Lord Michaels was at his side.

"I'm taking her to the ER. You stay here and deal with the people." Landon didn't wait for permission or approval, he simply scooped Autumn up and walked out the door talking to Ménage Eleanor as he did.

James was furious. "Stop! You can't just take her. She's *my* sister and *my* responsibility."

Landon swung around the blood pumping through his veins. *I've had enough. No more.* "This is not the place nor the time - however, we *will* have words. Right now, Chatelaine Autumn needs attention, and *she* is my *only* priority here."

Sensing things were going to get out of hand, both Mrs. Bogart and Ménage Eleanor stepped between the men.

Penny addressed James. "You have a room full of people. They need your attention. Let Lord Michaels help with Autumn."

Eleanor addressed Lord Michaels. "Sir, remember, she is not of age yet. You don't want to go against him."

Landon didn't care anymore. Autumn needed to be away from here. So he simply turned and walked out.

James heard what Mrs. Bogart said and knew she was correct. Yet, how could he just let Autumn walk out that door? Seeing Eleanor wavering on what to do, he quickly took a funeral folder and scribbled a release on the back and handed it to her.

She read it, nodded, and ran after Lord Michaels.

Three hours later, James walked into the farmhouse.

Lord Michaels was there.

"Where is Autumn?"

"She came to on the way to the hospital. She didn't want to go. Still, I didn't give her a choice. She confessed to not eating or sleeping well. The doctor said she is suffering from stress. She needs to be in a peaceful place."

"Then it's good that she's here. Thank you for taking care of her."

"Don't thank me. Because Autumn is not staying here. Ménage Eleanor is packing as we speak."

"What! She's *not* leaving with you. She is staying here - with me - where she belongs. I have the authority here - or do I need to remind you that she is still a minor."

"You *DON'T* have to remind me. I'm fully aware of both her age and your so-called authority. I'm also *FULLY AWARE* of your lack of attention and blindness to how this house is affecting her. It's killing her - if not physically than emotionally. She *HATES* it here. *HATES IT!* And I *WILL NOT* stand by and watch you *DESTROY* her for your own selfish reasons."

James stood there stunned. *Was he destroying her with his own selfish motives? Was it this house that was causing Autumn to be so distant? Could what he was saying be true? Lord, I don't want to harm her. I want to know her. What am I supposed to do?*

The silence between them hung heavy in the room.

Finally, James broke the silence. "I don't want her leaving. I want time with my sister. What do you suggest?"

Landon ran his fingers through his hair. He didn't want her to stay; however, he knew he had no grounds to take her with him. "Perhaps Mrs. Bogart would be willing to allow Autumn to stay with her for a while. She'd be close by, yet not under this oppressive roof."

"What is it about this house that is so oppressive? I don't understand. This was her home her whole life."

"Honestly, I don't know either. I just see the effects it's having on her. She wouldn't talk about it before, and I haven't had the opportunity to ask her since we got here." Landon gave James a pointed look that placed the blame for that solely at his feet.

James rubbed his face - he was exhausted. *I don't like it, yet I suppose it's the best I can hope for. At least he isn't running away with her. And she will only be a few miles down the road. If it keeps her close by, I should probably agree to the compromise.*

Just as he was about to agree, Autumn walked in, leaning heavily on the door jam. She had heard Landon's reprimand and declaration, as well as James' defeat. "I'm staying here tonight. And then the day after tomorrow I am going back to Michigan - one way or another." With that declaration, she walked unsteadily past them both and into her room.

Eleanor had stopped packing when she heard the two men arguing. Listening to the conversation, she was torn between her allegiances. On the one hand, she knew the Chatelaine, and Lord Michaels had a growing fondness towards each other, and this last week had been torture for them. She had likewise seen the effects on Autumn of being here in Nebraska and didn't understand it as well. However, she could additionally sympathize with James and his desire to hold on to the only family he had left. When the Chatelaine walked into the room and collapsed on the bed, Eleanor knew where her heart lay. The question was, what was she going to do about it.

The next day at the funeral James insisted on being at Autumn's side. Landon, in turn, did the same, and Autumn felt she was being suffocated between the two. It was a well-attended funeral due to Edmund's line of work and the family's years in the community.

Autumn and James stood for hours receiving more condolences - some multiple times from the same people - which drained Autumn all the more of what little energy she had. Her ability to keep the appearance of a dutifully grieving daughter was waning fast, yet this time, both men noticed.

The more people she greeted, the more she wanted to get home to Lady Cannon. It did lift her spirits to see that Lady Cannon had sent a beautiful arrangement on behalf of the entire household. Still, she would rather have Lady Cannon in person than an arrangement.

When the house was finally cleared of guests and family, Autumn took the letters from her parents and went for a walk. She needed some time alone to rejuvenate her spirit and optimism in returning home. She also hoped by getting away she could find God and be strengthened by Him.

When she was younger, she loved to walk through the small pasture to the creek that ran through it. The stream had a small cove plush with grass in the spring, though it would be barren now. It wasn't too far from the house so she could hear if someone called her, so she didn't tell anyone she was leaving. She loved the cove because, though it was close, it was also secluded. Since it was winter now, she would not be able to sit and truly enjoy herself, yet she wanted to see it nonetheless.

She had been at the creek for nearly a half hour when, as she stood watching the water run under the frozen top layer of the stream, she heard someone approaching. She turned to see Landon coming over the rise and beckoned him to join her. He did so willingly, taking her hand to kiss her palm. His passionate kiss told her he was feeling the strains of not being able to spend time with her or comfort her in these last few days. Concern was etched around his eyes, and it made him look so much older. "What is worrying you so?"

"I am afraid of losing you." His entire countenance fell at the admission, and she swore his eyes glistened with unshed tears.

Autumn was rocked by his confession. "Losing me? Are we not still courting? Do we not still share a commitment to each other?" She took the hand with his ring on it and gently put it on his cold cheek.

Landon quickly put his hand over hers, taking pleasure in her touch. Still, his heart sank. "Autumn...I am as committed as ever, but James is not going to allow you to return with me tomorrow or any other day soon. And if I help you leave in any way: money, transportation, anything, he can press charges against me. And...I fear...what we have shared to this point is so new and untested it will grow cold in our separation. I will stay as long as I can; however, I'm not even certain James will permit that." He didn't want to admit it, yet it was true. "I feel like your affections have been stolen from me - by your brother, your father's death, and this place."

Autumn didn't know what to say. She stood stock still, pondering his confession. *James' house rules had separated them, and this not only affected her but had shaken Landon's confidence in her returned affections. She had been so focused on herself, and what she was going through, she had not thought about how Landon was dealing with things. He was correct in a way, her focus had been shifted, but her affections had not.* Autumn slid her hands from his cheeks to around his waist, drawing him closer. "Landon, I am just as committed as well. James may be able to keep us physically apart for a time; nevertheless, he cannot change the matters of the heart."

Landon put his arms around her, wishing he would never have to let go, as he gazed into her eyes. He had been wrong, matters of the heart were still stronger than circumstances. James had not severed any of Autumn's affections for him, or Lady Cannon, this was now clear to him. "Forgive me for doubting?"

Autumn nodded.

"I see these last few days have been hard on both of us. I was wrong to let my mind carry me away with fears of losing you. Especially, when you have had many more difficult matters to deal with. It was selfish of me; please forgive me."

Autumn smiled up at him. There was an assurance within her; Landon would never take her for granted or force his own selfishness on her like her father had. "I forgive you, again. And again, and again. I love you, Landon."

Landon was so moved by the trust being given him, the tears that threatened earlier fell. "I will cherish you and protect you for the rest of my life. And, I will not doubt your affections again." He took her hand and kissed her palm again.

Settling her head on his chest, she relished his presence and strength. She came to the creek to seek strength, hope, and rejuvenation, and she felt God had answered her searching by bringing Landon to her. As they stood in this embrace, Autumn began thinking of assurance, remembering the assurance she received the night of her salvation. *Even if I am never again able to be together with those I have come to love here on earth, we will have all of eternity together. I have to remember that. And above all, that God will never leave me even if people do.* However, the more she thought about this, it did not bring her comfort, but made her realize Landon was right: James was not going to let her go. A shiver ran through her, and she clung to Landon all the harder.

Landon sensed her growing anxiety. He was about to inquire if she wanted to share when James came over the ridge and saw them embracing.

James was infuriated.

He had seen Lord Michaels walking in the pasture, and decided to follow his tracks in hopes of finding Autumn. He did ***not*** expect to see them in such an intimate embrace, especially after he had strictly forbidden it. *How dare they sneak off to secretly embrace? He was in charge of Autumn now, not Lord Michaels, and I will make my point clear. I will be obeyed in this.* He marched down to where they stood - now separated, Autumn's back to him - and grabbed her by the arm. "You are coming with me, now!"

Landon seeing James' fury, let her go as to not provoke him further, unsure of what he'd do. Yet, he kept a close enough proximity in case James tried to hurt Autumn.

Autumn on the other hand deftly maneuvered out of his grip with shocking speed and obviously well-practiced maneuvering. "Let me go. You will not hurt me again. ***NEVER*** again!"

In his fury, James did not register what she said. "You are ***my*** charge and ***my*** sister. I will not allow you to be prey to this man who is clearly taking advantage of your need for comfort to fulfill some sick desire of his own." James blindly retorted, his fury continuing to build.

"I belong to ***NO ONE***...least of all ***YOU***! I ran from you...so you could ***never*** hurt me again." Autumn collapsed on the ground, sobbing. "I...I won't l...let you h...hurt me a...again."

James stood dumb. The words finally sinking in. *Run from me? Hurt her again? He'd never hurt her. What was she talking about?*

Understanding slammed into him as he realized that he looked enough like their father and by grabbing her, he had triggered something within her.

Landon was on the ground with her, soothing and cradling her in his arms once again.

Squatting down next to her, James reached out his hand toward her. She flinched away from him and burrowed further into Lord Michaels' embrace. Lord Michaels looked at him with pity; James pulled his hand back. "Autumn, I'm so sorry. I had no idea. I promise I won't grab you again. I...I'm sorry."

They all remained stationary while Autumn slowly regained her composure as she clung to Landon. She couldn't believe she had fallen apart like that. It was her secret. No one knew. But now, they would all question.

Seeing Autumn calming down, James tried to apologize again. "I am sorry I grabbed you, Autumn. When I came to the bank and saw you, I lost control. Our father charged me with your care while you are a minor, and I take that charge very seriously. You are young and naïve, and I ask that you respect our father's wishes and yield to my rules. They are for your own protection."

Though Autumn had been in the midst of a panic attack, she had not missed James' earlier accusations, and now this. *For my own protection? How many times have I heard that same excuse from Papa? It's nothing but justification for pushing their own selfish desires. Why do these people keep thinking they are the only ones who know what is best – especially without even consulting me? And how dare he make accusations against Landon, when he knows nothing about the situation between us?* She let the simmering anger have full control now - it was better than feeling weak. *This is why Papa yielded to his anger. It makes you feel in control, powerful.*

Even though these thoughts went through her head, their meaning did not fully register. Therefore, she continued to let her anger fuel her. Propelling herself out of Landon's arms and onto her feet, she knocked James backward as she yelled. "You know nothing of Landon or his care for me. I have treated you with respect and dignity, I have embraced you as my brother, and yet you treat me like a naive child who can't think for herself. Well, guess what…I may be young, but I am still fully capable of taking care of myself. I've been doing it for years…*years*…I don't need you or anyone else to start doing it now.

"Besides, you don't truly want what is best for *me*. You're just like your father: selfish and controlling. I won't stand by idly and be subjected to the brutality of being robbed of everything dear to me again just because of close-minded selfishness. You have prohibited me from receiving any comfort during these trying days of being here stripped from my home. Our father may have given you a temporary charge over me, but you cannot control my life forever. If that is the brother you chose to be, you can be guaranteed as soon as I can get away from you, I'll be gone for good!" Autumn turned and stomped back up the bank towards the house.

James stood there as if he'd been slapped; he didn't understand all she said, yet, the words stung deep in his chest. *Were they true? Was he being selfish?* That was what stung the worst. Trying to understand, he followed in hopes of stopping her; he was careful not to grab her. "You are not being stripped of your home. Sure, I'd like to stay and run the farm; however, you can do as you wish. I am not selfish or close-minded in the matter. As far as receiving comfort, you have Ménage Eleanor and Mrs. Bogart; you don't need comfort from Lord Michaels."

Autumn stopped for a moment in utter disbelief at what she just heard. "Really James! Oh, thank you, thank you." Autumn turned and threw her arms around him in a huge hug.

James stood stock still in shock. *What had he said to make her turn so quickly?* Autumn was rattling on when James finally heard her say, "Can we leave first thing tomorrow?"

Autumn was looking at Landon with such hope; it crushed him to realize that whatever Autumn thought James had said, was not what he had meant. Not knowing how to answer or what to say with the vast swing of emotions going on before him, Landon stood silently waiting for James' lead.

Landon had not been wrong. James' look turned to iron. "Leaving? I said nothing about leaving, what are you talking about?"

Autumn halted and turned from Landon to James. "You just said, you'd stay with the farm, and I can do as I wish. I wish to go home…to Michigan."

"Michigan! You're not going back to Michigan. **This** is your home. You're staying **here** with **me**!"

Autumn's anger started building again. "But you said…"

James interrupted her - it was getting cold, and he wanted to make his point clear. "I don't care what you **thought** I said. What I meant, was that I'm not taking the farm from you - your home! You will be staying here with me. End of subject. Now…it's getting cold. Let's go to the house." He stretched his hand out toward her slowly.

Autumn ignored his hand and looked at Landon. *He wasn't going to fight it. James had the legal claim, and she knew Landon's character would not allow him to go against it. It was over. She was stuck for the time being.* Defeated, and with despair settling over her, she turned for the house without another word. Upon entering, Autumn ordered a warm bath and got ready for bed; speaking only the bare necessities as she did not want to see or talk to anyone else.

She was done hoping and fighting.

James and Landon followed Autumn to the house in silence. Once outside the house, James stopped Lord Michaels. "I don't know what your intentions with my sister were out there, but I want to make myself very clear. She will not be leaving with you, and, if I see you touch her again, I'll have charges brought up against you. She is still a minor, and despite what she thinks, I *do* have that control."

Landon nodded gravely and entered the house to let Autumn know he was going back to the Bogart's for the night. However, when he spoke to Ménage Eleanor, she informed him the Chatelaine had retired for the night and wished not to be disturbed.

"Please tell the Chatelaine that I will be back tomorrow morning with news from Lady Cannon. I hope she will see me then."

Eleanor nodded, though she looked grave and worried.

After returning to the Bogarts, Landon called Lady Cannon to convey the latest happenings. He was once again struggling with feeling defeated.

Lady Cannon listened to everything Lord Michaels related to her and heaved a great sigh of distress. Several silent minutes passed between them. "I know you are not going to like this, Lord Michaels; nonetheless, I think the best thing to do is have you return immediately."

Landon exhaled heavily. "You're right. I don't like it."

"Leave Ménage Eleanor there to attend to the Chatelaine, and you come home. I'll make arrangements for you to fly out first thing tomorrow morning. Let's give James time to cool off. We'll have to come up with a plan to come back for her after her birthday. That is if you think she still wants to come?"

"I have no doubt she wants to come back, my Lady. That part I am clear on. However, what I am unclear on is what to tell the Chatelaine? I don't feel comfortable leaving her here, this place has a very negative effect on her."

"Tell her the truth, Lord Michaels. Ménage Eleanor will stay with her while you return to tend to business, and I will be in contact after her birthday."

Landon did not like the idea at all. Still, he did as he was instructed. Lady Cannon made arrangements for him to leave on the eight o'clock flight the next morning.

Autumn had shut herself in her room and would not speak to anyone - not even Eleanor. James even called Mrs. Bogart to come over and try to coax her to come out of her room or even talk to them. Nothing. They knew she was in there - James had peaked through her window to make sure.

She refused to come out to eat - or even open her door for food. She *was* acting very childish, and she knew it. Still, she couldn't bear it – her heart was breaking, and she had lost all hope.

Landon deliberated what he should do and reasoned it would be near impossible for him to speak through the door without provoking James' wrath. Therefore, with a heavy heart, he prepared to leave without speaking with her.

When Lord Michaels had arrived to try to coax Autumn out of her room, James had retired to the basement to gather his thoughts and pray – something he had been lacking in doing since Edmund's death. Hearing commotion upstairs, he went back up to see what was going on.

Lord Michaels was in the kitchen explaining to Ménage Eleanor that he had been summoned to Michigan by Lady Cannon. She was to stay and attend the Chatelaine and try her best to comfort her. "If you have to knock down the door, do so. Lady Cannon will pay for the repairs. I know the Chatelaine is struggling right now. Still, we are hopeful she will eventually come to her senses."

Eleanor nodded in understanding and sympathy. This was such a difficult situation.

James' brow creased with concern as he listened to Lord Michaels.

Seeing this, Landon inquired. "What's wrong? I assumed you'd be relieved to be rid of me so you can have her to yourself." He couldn't help the bite that came out in his tone.

"I am. Though I'm also concerned that if you leave, Autumn will follow. At least while you were here, I knew she would be too. Though I don't approve of your familiarity with my sister, having you close by kept me from having to track her down, should she run away."

Landon nodded. "I have personally instructed Ménage Eleanor to keep an eye on her. To lessen the appeal of running, here are the address and phone numbers for myself and Lady Cannon. I will have the Chatelaine informed that you possess this information. The appeal to run should be curbed by this, as you would be able to easily locate her. I doubt she will run anywhere else."

"Why are you doing this? Why are you helping me keep her here?"

"Despite what you may think, Lady Cannon has no desire to go against you. She loves the Chatelaine dearly - as a daughter even - and desires for her to return. However, she acknowledges and respects the authority given to you by Mr. DeBlue. It is Lady Cannon's hope by showing you her willingness to respect your authority now, you will not prohibit her from communicating with the Chatelaine in the weeks to come."

James acknowledged this. "I do not have a problem with Lady Cannon contacting Autumn as long as she does not encourage her to run away."

Landon nodded his understanding.

"How long is Eleanor to stay?"

Landon noted the familiar reference but didn't mention it as he responded. "Ménage Eleanor is the Chatelaine's attendant until the Chatelaine dismisses her. Though Autumn may be staying here, Lady Cannon refuses to acknowledge she is anything less than the lady-in-waiting that she has been trained to be. Therefore, Lady Cannon will send monthly provisions to the Chatelaine to assist in her care as per their agreement and will cover the cost of Ménage Eleanor's wages as well for the duration of the Chatelaine's stay."

With everything settled, Landon had no other reason to tarry since Autumn still refused to see him. As the car pulled out of the driveway, Landon glanced back at Autumn's window and saw her standing there, tears streaking her beautiful face.

# 27

Autumn's heart sank as she watched the car pull away with Landon in it. *What was she going to do now? It felt as if everything was crumbling down around her: her strength, her security, her future.*

Autumn sank to her knees and cried out. "Lord, why have you forsaken me? Why have you brought me here to abandon me in my need? Why have you taken everything from me that you had once given so richly?"

There was no still voice; there was no reassurance.

She rose from the floor and threw herself on the bed. Despair completely taking over her as Eleanor knocked one more time. "Autumn!"

Nothing.

"Answer me."

Nothing. Though Eleanor thought she heard sobs.

"You do realize you are acting very childish, correct? Lady Cannon would not be pleased. You need to grow up. I'll be here when you do, but until then, don't expect me to be begging at your door."

Since being in Nebraska, Eleanor had gotten accustomed to everyone there addressing Autumn by her first name without the title. She had also started taking a more personal tone with Autumn, a bit less respectful, but nothing so bold as what just came through the door.

Autumn was stunned. She did know Lady Cannon would not be pleased. However, if James wanted to treat her like a child and control her life, he'd find out just how difficult she could be. After all, she had years of practice.

For the next several days, Autumn did not venture out of her room other than to use the restroom or to sneak food in the middle of the night; though she did, eventually, allow Mrs. Bogart to come in and visit.

Eleanor seemed to disappear quite frequently, and Autumn didn't mind or take much notice of what she did.

Autumn missed Lady Cannon, Landon and Summer greatly. She wondered how Summer took it when Landon came back without her. She tried to comfort herself with the idea that it would only be a few weeks and she could leave. Unfortunately, without knowing how she would get back, it didn't really encourage her much.

She continued to struggle inside wondering where God had gone. She knew he was not limited to working in Michigan, yet He didn't seem to be responding to her in Nebraska. She spoke with Mrs. Bogart about it, and her best advice was to read His Word and continue to pray, being faithful even if it didn't seem He was hearing her at the time. Mrs. Bogart also gave Autumn several scriptures to start memorizing.

A week went by, and Autumn's despair was growing. She felt more alone than ever before in her life, and she began wondering if everything in Michigan was only a dream or farce. Still, she kept praying and reading as Mrs. Bogart had instructed and one night, she received a phone call.

James had decided to just give Autumn her space, hoping her tantrum would eventually get old. However, he was starting to despair of his plan when the phone rang one evening. On the other end of the line was a sweet little girl's voice asking for Autumn.

He knocked and then spoke through the door - his only way of communicating with her. "Autumn, there is a little girl on the phone for you. Will you come out to speak with her?"

Autumn flew from the room faster than James had ever seen her move.

"Summer? Oh, my sweet Summer, is that really you?"

James stood by protectively as they talked. He could see the obvious care and love his sister had for the girl, and he began to wonder if he was doing the right thing by making her stay. Eventually, he decided it was wrong for him to stand by so protectively, eavesdropping, and left Autumn to converse alone, first with Summer and then Lady Cannon.

By the time Landon got on the phone, no one was around to listen. Once she heard his voice, all hopelessness left her, and she pleaded with him. "Oh, Landon, please forgive me for refusing to see you before you left. I was in such despair. I know it was childish, but I just couldn't see you. It hurt too much to say goodbye. Still, I should never have refused to see you. Can you ever forgive me?"

"Of course, my love. It...it was a hard situation. I hated to leave you, yet I think it was probably best. We couldn't have said a proper goodbye anyway, though I so ached to see you crying in the window."

"Will we ever be together again this side of heaven?" Autumn betrayed her despair and short-sightedness in the question.

Landon sensed her hopelessness and tried to reassure her. "Of course we will. Lady Cannon and I are making plans to come for you after you turn nineteen. I thought I made that clear to Ménage Eleanor. Did she not tell you?"

"She might have...I don't remember...the days have been so dark...it's just…what if James protests again?"

"I am looking into that, just to be sure; however, from what I have discovered, he will have no say. Once you are of legal age, he cannot force you to stay."

Hope began to spring up. "My birthday is only two and a half weeks away. When will you come?"

"I will be there the day after. Autumn, listen to me. Though James cannot make you stay, he can do other things that would make it difficult for you to leave. The estate is not settled, and if there is a debate in the courts, he could..."

Autumn interrupted him. "There is no debate. It's all mine. Everything was given to me."

"What do you mean? James told me before Edmund died he set all the papers straight indicating James as his son."

"He did, but from what the letters say, everything was still given to me, and I am simply instructed to share with him. I don't know what the actual will says, but that is what the letters say."

"What letters? Why haven't you seen the will yet? Is James not settling the estate?"

"My parents each left me a letter when they died. I found them in my room. The will is actually locked in a box, and the key is there in Michigan, so I haven't been able to open it or see it. James can't settle the estate and neither can I without the will, besides, my legal counsel is in Michigan." She replied with a smile.

"Where is the key? I'll get it and send it to you. Then I'll make arrangements for a colleague to contact you regarding Nebraska estate law."

"It isn't that easy. The key is the locket I gave to Summer to hold for me. She isn't going to easily give that up."

"I see, you are right about that. Heiress Summer has been very upset with me for not returning you to her. I will have to contact my friend and get back to you. Meanwhile, I'll speak with Lady Cannon and see what we can do about the locket."

Autumn did not want to hang up but knew she had to. Whatever hope she had during the call quickly vanished as she thought about all the obstacles that lay ahead of her.

That night Autumn had a dream about her mother and father. They were sitting in a beautiful grassy area that looked like a park and was surrounded by all kinds of beautiful things, but they were crying.

She walked up to them, but they did not look at her as they were weeping. "Why are you crying? It's beautiful here. There are so many good things, why are you weeping?"

Her mother looked at her then. "My children will not get along. I waited years for them to meet and they only want to fight. It grieves my mother's heart."

At the end of her dream, as the picture of her parents was fading, Autumn heard the still small voice inside her. *A new command I give to you: Love one another. As I have loved you, so you must love one another.*

Autumn woke and laid there staring, at the ceiling as she had become accustomed to doing when she needed to think. She had accused James of being selfish, yet she realized he had not been the only one. *How many times am I going to have to say I'm sorry to the people in my life. Probably a lot, since I am just learning to grow and walk.* Quietly, she sank to her knees on the side of her bed and asked God for forgiveness for being selfish. She also asked Him to show her how she could show James love as He commanded her.

When Eleanor entered to find Autumn dressed in the old clothes she had left at the house, Eleanor was stunned.

"I am going to see if James will let me join him on the farm today. I didn't want to get my good dresses dirty, so I dug around in my drawers."

Eleanor was speechless.

"Has breakfast been made yet, I thought maybe I'd make my father's favorite potatoes and bacon as James had indicated he'd like to try it."

"No. Breakfast isn't done yet. We've gone to a simple cold breakfast since you weren't eating and James has to get out so early."

Autumn noted the casual reference to her brother, yet simply tucked it away for later consideration. Approaching Eleanor, Autumn took her hands. "Eleanor, I need to apologize for my attitude and actions of late. You were correct. I've been behaving very wrongly, and it is not pleasing to anyone. I hope you can forgive me and that we can be on friendly terms again."

Eleanor smiled broadly and embraced Autumn in a huge hug. "Welcome back to the world of reality. I'm so glad you came around."

Autumn laughed, and the two friends went to the kitchen where Autumn showed Eleanor how she used to prepare breakfast.

When James came in from chores a while later, he was amazed to see Autumn and Eleanor working side by side in the kitchen. Though he had to confess, to himself only, he was also a bit disappointed; he had gotten used to having morning coffee with Eleanor alone.

When Autumn saw him, she approached him as she had Eleanor. "James, I have come to realize that *I* have been very wrong and selfish. Will you please forgive me and give me a chance to make it right?"

James looked at Eleanor with a questioning glance, and then back to Autumn. *Had his prayers been answered? Or was this another ploy to disarm him? He wasn't sure, but he decided to go with the flow.* "Yes, I can forgive you. Can you forgive me for not being sensitive to what you have faced in the past? I had no idea our father was abusive."

Autumn cringed. She had hoped that was forgotten. "Yes, I think it best if we can simply put this whole situation behind us. In regards to Papa, I'm not ready to discuss what happened there. I really want to leave the past where it is. Nevertheless, we have a future that is still unknown. I'd like to get to know you, and try to have a relationship going forward."

James seemed to accept that for now.

"So, I made breakfast - like Papa used to like - and I hope you will allow me to come along with you for a bit this morning?"

James agreed, and this started a daily routine with them where Autumn would spend the mornings with James and the afternoons with Mrs. Bogart.

Once she came out of her room, Autumn soon found out what Eleanor had been doing while she had been wallowing. Eleanor had been accompanying James around the farm, and the two of them had grown rather fond of each other.

Autumn soon grew to admire and love James as her brother, and she noticed Eleanor grew to love him as a man. Their evenings were filled with stories, games, and conversations. After James retired for the night, Autumn would stay up late with Eleanor and giggle like school girls once again - only this time regarding James instead of Landon. And something healed inside of her as she felt like she had been given her teenage years back.

Lady Cannon began calling twice a week, and she always had Landon there with her. James soon figured out who Autumn was talking to, yet did not protest since he was miles away. Plus, most of the time he heard them talking about what seemed like business.

Landon had discovered after speaking with his friend, that there had to be a thirty day published notice before they could close the estate or deal with any claims that came in. Autumn met with the lawyer Landon had recommended, and it was determined that they could proceed with publishing intent to settle without the actual will. Though it would have to be presented at the time of the hearing. So Autumn told them to proceed.

A couple of days later, James pounded on her bedroom door, clearly upset. "Autumn, we need to talk. Please come to the kitchen."

Autumn was startled by his tone but willingly followed him to the table where he had the paper laid out.

He pointed to the published notice. "What is this?"

"Notice of Settling of Estate." Autumn simply read the title.

"I see that. What I mean is what are you doing?" He raised his voice in frustration.

Autumn blanched at his tone but thankfully didn't cower. She wasn't exactly sure what he was mad about, though, he was definitely upset. So she trod carefully in her response. "I have been advised to go ahead with trying to tie up our parents' estate by taking the first step in publishing the notice which has to run for thirty days."

"And who advised you to do this?"

"Lord Michaels and an associate here in town."

"Why have you not mentioned anything to me about this? When did you do this?"

"A couple days ago. You and Eleanor were out checking cows. You said you didn't care about the inheritance, and you never mentioned settling the estate. Nothing will officially be done until after I'm nineteen, and of legal age to make my own decisions. I didn't think it really mattered to you. Was I wrong?"

James shook his head. Things had gotten so messed up between them at the beginning. "Autumn, I don't care about the money or the inheritance per say, but I *do* care about you and about the choices you make. I *do* care about what you intend to do with the farm, and I *do* care that the money is running out in the account our father left us." Silence weighed heavy between them for several minutes. "I guess what I'm trying to say is that I want to be a good provider for you, but my hands are tied."

With the door open, and in light of their recent bonding, Autumn decided to leap forward with an olive branch. "I don't want your hands tied, and I don't want to keep secrets from you. So, how can we make this work?"

James exhaled. *Maybe they could actually talk this out without ranting and fighting. Maybe if I treat her as an equal instead of a kid, we can build a relationship with respect as the foundation.* "Why don't we start by you telling me what you know of your inheritance and the plans you have made, and I will tell you of the needs on the farm?"

Autumn agreed, and they sat down to discuss the situation. She told him of the letters, the savings account from her rent, and how everything else was locked in the box. He expressed the need for operating cash, and if they did not have cash, then he needed to sell some cattle to get some. Autumn called the bank, and it was determined it would be sufficient to keep them going until the estate could be settled in a month, so she transferred the money to the farm account.

"Hopefully, we can get the estate settled before this runs out and go from there."

James nodded and smiled. "We actually work well together - when we aren't fighting."

Autumn laughed. "Let's try doing this more often then." She winked at him. Since things were going so well, Autumn decided to venture into a tender subject. "James...I have no interest in the farm or in staying here on it. I hope you understand that. I am here now out of respect for you and our parents, but I will not stay here forever. I simply can't."

"Can you tell me why?"

Autumn took a deep breath. "Frankly, it holds too many sad, painful, and unhappy memories for me. I don't want to relive those every day. I can't go into our parent's room without seeing mom dying on the bed, alone except for me. I can't sit at this table without remembering how many times Papa would make me lay across it and whoop me for not fixing the right thing for supper. I can't go outside without seeing the tree that Papa tied me to when I forgot to do chores or didn't get them done when he thought they should be. I can't sit in the living room without remembering the months on end that Papa would not even acknowledge I was there."

Shaking her head, she confessed. "I could never decide which was worse, him noticing me when he was drunk and beating me, or when he was sober and wouldn't speak or acknowledge me for weeks."

They sat quietly, each with their own thoughts.

Autumn finally continued. "I've found a good thing in Michigan. I know it seems far away; however, I'm happy there. I enjoy the work given to me, and I love the people. I'm needed, and I feel like I have a purpose and a future there. I don't want to lose connection with you, and I'm not running away. I simply don't want to stay stuck in the past here on the farm, and I do want to live in hope there in Michigan."

James absorbed all of this and sat quietly debating. "So are you going to sell the farm?"

Autumn looked at him in surprise. "No, why would I sell the farm?"

"Why would you keep it? If you don't want to stay on it, and it holds so much misery for you, it would make sense to sell it.

"Don't you want to stay on the farm and run it?"

"Are you offering to let me run the farm for you?"

"No, I was offering you the farm - to own." Autumn turned to him and smiled.

James looked down in shame. "Unfortunately, I don't have the capital to make such a purchase. My adoptive parents are well off, but I won't ask them for the money to purchase the farm."

Realizing he wasn't getting the gist of what she was trying to say, she tried again. "Oh, well... let's say you suddenly came into some capital. Would you want to own the farm?"

James looked at her skeptically. "Don't even think it; whatever cash is in the estate is yours. I will not take it from you."

She held her hands up in surrender. "Okay, okay. I promise I won't give you any cash from the estate, but you didn't answer my question. If you miraculously came into some money, would you buy the farm?"

James shook his head at her persistence. "In a heartbeat."

That settled it in Autumn's mind. James would get the farm.

# ❦ *28* ❦

The weeks actually flew by.

Autumn's birthday was rapidly approaching, and James wanted to throw her a big party; however, there wasn't the money or the people. He spoke to Eleanor about what he could do for her, and she frankly told him. "The best thing you could possibly do for Autumn is to invite Lady Cannon to come here. She misses them dreadfully."

He debated this for several days and finally decided he'd do it. It was an awkward call, but Lady Cannon was gracious and agreed to come.

The morning of her birthday, Eleanor woke her early.

"What in the world? Why are you getting me up so early and wanting to dress me? It's not like we have any place to go, and the cows won't care. I promise."

Eleanor chuckled. "Trust me; you want to do this."

So Autumn agreed and let her put the extra effort toward readying Autumn for the day.

Finally, James knocked on the door. "Are you two about ready yet? My surprise can't wait much longer?"

"Surprise. What surprise?"

"Well, finish getting ready, and I'll show you." James teased.

Eleanor smiled as she produced a blindfold and escorted Autumn to the living room.

"Sister, I wanted to do something very special for you on your nineteenth birthday. With help from Eleanor, this is what I am giving you…" He removed the blindfold and standing before her was Lady Cannon, Summer, and Landon.

Autumn was so taken back she stood stupefied for several minutes, and then she flung her arms around James and wept.

When Autumn finally let go of James, Summer came running to her and threw her arms around Autumn in an unyielding embrace. James stood back and watched in awe at the love between them. Autumn pried Summer from her and approached Lady Cannon. She curtsied, and Lady Cannon reached out to embrace her as well.

Finally, Autumn looked at Landon who in turn looked at James – who eyed him with an upraised brow. Every so gently, Landon took her hand and kissed the top of it. She understood that was the best he could do under the watchful eyes of her brother. James nodded in appreciation for the respect shown.

Autumn was also pleased to see the Bogarts and quickly introduced Lady Cannon and Mrs. Bogart.

Penny had never met a statelier or more elegant woman as Lady Cannon. It was clear that the woman who had taken Autumn under her wing was indeed very wealthy. Still, Lady Cannon had a gentleness about her that only aided in Penny's desire to know her.

Lady Cannon was thrilled to finally meet the woman who had laid the foundation for Autumn's salvation. In Lady Cannon style, she thanked Mrs. Bogart for all she had done for Autumn in such a way that Mrs. Bogart soon felt honored and elevated by Lady Cannon's praise.

The whole group enjoyed a wonderful day together with Summer never leaving Autumn's side. Unfortunately, Lady Cannon, Summer, and even Landon could not stay, and Autumn could not leave, though she was *now* of legal age. Autumn knew she needed to stay and finish the estate work. Just seeing them warmed Autumn's heart back to life – and now she could withstand the wait.

As they were getting ready to leave that evening, Autumn suddenly remembered the locket. "Summer, do you have my mother's locket?"

Summer carefully pulled it out from under her collar. Looking at Summer's eyes, Autumn knew she was afraid Autumn was going to ask her to relinquish it; however, Autumn had another idea. Quickly, she went to her room and got the doll her mother had left her. Bending down again before Summer, Autumn explained. "Do you remember me telling you about my mother's doll? And how sad I was to have to leave it in Nebraska?"

Summer nodded.

"Would you be willing to take it back to Michigan for me? It can ride in the airplane with you, and I know you'd keep it safe."

Summer nodded again, afraid to talk knowing it was getting time to leave.

"Oh, no." Autumn looked sad. "If I give you the doll, then I will have nothing to remind me of my mother. I know, would you be willing to trade me the locket for the doll? Then I can have one thing, and you can hold one thing for me. How does that sound?"

Summer thought about it for a moment and looked over the doll very carefully. It was a beautiful doll.

"Remember, I am not giving you the doll; I just want you to keep her for me and make sure she gets to Michigan safely so I can have her there when I return. Okay?"

Summer agreed and traded. Autumn breathed a sigh of relief.

Hugging Lady Cannon before they left, Autumn whispered in her ear. Lady Cannon looked at Ménage Eleanor standing by James and nodded her agreement. Autumn knew it was a sacrifice for them all to make a one day trip to Nebraska just for her and as they left, tears streamed down her cheeks.

James came to her side and hugged her. "They are good people."

Autumn nodded.

"You love them deeply, don't you?" Tears began to well up in *his* eyes.

Autumn turned to him.

"You can go with them."

Autumn hugged her brother. "I know I can, but now is not the time. I must wait a few more weeks to settle the estate and say goodbye. Landon will be returning for me then."

James was astounded by his sister's bold proclamation and sudden air of authority – like that of when he first saw her – and his heart grieved for her leaving, but knew he was not losing her.

In those last weeks, Autumn made every effort to spend as much time as possible with James, while also making time for Eleanor to do the same. Autumn also sought out Mrs. Bogart to continue learning more from her about Bible study, and to discuss the relationship between James and Eleanor. Autumn had already decided what she was going to do, though she needed to make the appropriate arrangements before she told either of the parties involved.

As the time grew closer for Landon to return to assist in the closing of the estate, Autumn became more excited, and Eleanor became more anxious. Finally, Autumn could not let them suffer any longer. As James and Eleanor were watching a movie, Autumn came in and sat down directly in front of them blocking the view to the television.

James stopped the movie. "What are you doing?"

Looking at him squarely in the eye, she asked him. "James, I need to know - do you love Eleanor?"

James was speechless. He never expected Autumn to ask such an audacious question, and especially not in front of Eleanor. But, looking at her, he could not deny it. "Yes, I love her."

"And what are your intentions towards her?"

Again caught off guard, it took him a moment to reply. "Well...I'd like to marry her, but I don't have a reliable future, and she will be leaving in a few days. So, I guess I don't know."

Nodding in understanding, Autumn then turned to Eleanor. "Eleanor, dear friend, do you love my brother?"

Not sure where Autumn was going with this, as Eleanor had repeatedly confessed her feelings to Autumn, she replied truthfully. "You know I do."

"And does it bother you that James is poor and has nothing to really offer you for a future?"

Eleanor laughed. "You know it doesn't. I just want to be with him."

James smiled at her and was about to object when Autumn stood. "Perfect. Then, with authority given to me by Lady Cannon, I release you from the duty to myself and Lady Cannon. You are free to stay here and pursue whatever may come from your mutual love. You are not required to return with me to Michigan. I have made arrangements with Mrs. Bogart for you to stay in her basement apartment in exchange for help with house cleaning if you desire. And, I can have whatever you need from your room in Michigan sent to you there."

James and Eleanor looked at each other in awe, and then in mutual consent, they tackled Autumn to the floor, laughing and hugging. The whole scene would have made the most scrupulous person smile.

In her joy, Eleanor proclaimed. "Oh thank you, Chatelaine, I will miss you so, but thank you!"

"Well, it is the least I can do, after all, your kindnesses to me, I only have one request."

"Anything." Eleanor would have given Autumn the moon if she could have.

"Bring my brother to see me, okay?"

"Most definitely." There was another round of hugs and James even kissed Eleanor.

Autumn blushed. "If you are going to show such forward intentions, I expect an invitation to a wedding *very* soon."

James smiled at her and winked.

Two days later, Landon arrived.

Seeing Landon exit the car, Autumn flew from the house and threw her arms around him, as Summer would have done. Landon saw her coming and braced himself for the impact, pleased with her enthusiasm to see him. Seeing James standing in the doorway watching, he didn't know how to fully respond – everything inside of him wanted to envelop her in his arms and passionately kiss her. However, considering the restrictions he'd placed on himself regarding their courting, and his resolve not to offend James further, he stood stiffly - hands barely touching her - so that he was not totally rejecting her either.

Seeing the commotion Autumn caused and the concern on Lord Michaels' face, James purposely marched up to them stoically - a look of what Landon interpreted to be fury in his eyes.

Immediately, Landon started planning his defense and rationale – as to not be deprived of Autumn again.

"Lord Michaels, tell me..."

When he hesitated, Landon withdrew from Autumn – hands in the air. Landon tried to look innocently at James buying time to finalize his defense, as Autumn turned to James with almost a warning in her glare.

But when she saw he was trying to contain a smile, Autumn relaxed as James proceeded. "Do you love my sister?"

Landon did not see Autumn smiling as he was transfixed on James. Not being aware of the previous events using those same words Landon was shocked into dumbness – he was not prepared for *that* question. As Autumn nestled herself in his arms again, Landon perceived an unexplained change in circumstances and therefore responded honestly. "Yes, very much."

"Sister, do you love Lord Michaels?"

"No." Autumn looked up at Landon as the shock hit him.

"What?" James stared at her in shock as well.

"Lord Michaels is a fine attorney and an honorable man, but I love Landon Ray Michaels, the man, all on his own." She turned her head upwards to Landon, and his knees about buckled at the love in her eyes.

James could no longer contain his smile. "Whoa. You had me going there for a minute. And I'm certain Lord Michaels about had a heart attack. However, since Lord Michaels and Landon are one in the same, I release you from my previous restrictions, as long as you promise to invite me to the wedding."

Landon stood stunned and utterly confused as Eleanor came to James' side and put her arms around him. The three who had knowledge of the previous conversation laughed. Sensing Landon's stiffening under her arms, Autumn quickly explained so that he knew they were not laughing at him. Upon understanding, Landon relaxed considerably and eagerly took Autumn's palm and passionately kissed it. The rest of the evening was spent joyously laughing, making plans, and discussing the future ahead of each of them. It was a totally different environment from when Landon was there before.

The next morning, the four of them went to the courthouse to close out the estate of Edmund and Sue DeBlue. All bills and claims to the estate were settled, and Autumn left knowing whatever remained was hers, free and clear. James still refused to accept any part of the inheritance from her – he was content to run the farm in her absence knowing he'd be doing it for his sister and she'd compensate him well enough for his labor.

While in town, Autumn decided to take the key to the safety deposit box at the bank and discover the secrets inside. After discussing bank policy with the manager, it was determined that Landon would accompany Autumn inside, while James and Eleanor waited in the lobby. Autumn produced the key, locket, and will - just to be safe - and the manager took them back to a viewing room after signing the registration cards.

When they were finally alone, Autumn opened the box. Inside was a letter from her grandmother to her mother explaining the stocks and why she purchased them. Under that was one hundred stock certificates each worth one hundred shares. That was ten *thousand* shares. What was more shocking was that the railroad that her grandmother had invested in was *the* number one railroad in the nation.

Prior to coming back to Nebraska, Landon had researched the top five railroad share values in hopes of being able to counsel Autumn on how to proceed. Therefore, based on the preliminary numbers he found and their rough calculations, the stocks were worth well over one hundred thousand dollars. Being so stunned, Autumn had to sit down to contemplate her choices.

Her mother had asked her to save some back for future inheritance. She knew James needed operating capital, and then there was Mrs. Bogart - whom she had forgotten to pay back with Lady Cannon's envelope. Strangely, Autumn never even considered taking some of it for herself, she had everything she needed between Lady Cannon and a future with Landon. Not wanting to take her future with Landon for granted, she discussed all her options with him including their future plans. In the end, Autumn wrote a note to James, and left it with all but ten thousand dollars' worth of stock certificates in the box and closed it.

When Autumn got back to the farm, she took the stock certificates that they had taken from the safety deposit box and sat down to write Mrs. Bogart a note.

DEAR MRS. BOGART, YOU WERE FAITHFUL TO SEW THE SEED OF GOD'S WORD, AND IN LIKE MANNER, HE HAS BEEN FAITHFUL TO FULFILL HIS WORD: '*Still other seed fell on good soil. It came up, grew and produced a crop, multiplying thirty, sixty, or even a hundred times.*' IN REPAYMENT OF MY IOU.

Autumn then gave the envelope to Eleanor with strict instructions to present it to Mrs. Bogart after she had left.

The rest of the afternoon was rather solemn as Eleanor helped Autumn pack her things, including the carousel, which was packed very carefully in a separate box and shipped ahead. Then, Autumn helped Eleanor pack her things, and they went over to Mrs. Bogart's to settle Eleanor into her rooms. The somber atmosphere continued into dinner that night as James and Eleanor's faces were cast with sorrow and Autumn and Landon respectfully restrained their excitement. Finally, Autumn couldn't take the gloom anymore, and she picked up her glass of water and flung the contents at James.

Sitting in shock, he stared at her – *what was she thinking!*

"Oh, come on, I don't want to leave on such a sour note."

With understanding, and remembrance of the fun times they had shared over the last several weeks, he picked up his glass and flung the contents at Eleanor. She in return picked up her glass and flung the contents at Landon. Everyone froze as Landon stared blankly at the wall. Not knowing what he would do, Eleanor started to apologize.

Slowly, he looked at Eleanor, then quickly grabbed the pitcher of water off the table, and poured the entire contents over Autumn's head while keeping a completely stoic face. As Autumn jumped up sopping wet, everyone bust out laughing and Autumn knew things would turn out alright.

The next morning, Autumn sat contentedly beside Landon as the limousine drove off. She was on her way back home. James and Eleanor stood, arms around each other, in the driveway of the old farmhouse. Inside on the table, they would find the title of the house, land and all it contained, given to James – something Autumn and Landon had accomplished over the last few days. They would also find the key to the safety deposit box with a note that said:

**TO MY BROTHER,**

**AS PROMISED, NO CASH FROM THE ESTATE.**

**WELCOME TO THE FAMILY!**

**YOUR LOVING SISTER**

# ❤ Acknowledgements ❤

*Thank you* first and foremost to my Heavenly Father for the talent and ability to write. Without His creativity flowing through me, things like this book would not be possible.

The next thank you goes to my husband - lovingly known by me as the Farmer. He is my best and worst, critic. He constantly reminds me to be humble and that there is "no such thing as good writing, only good rewriting." Thank you for being patient with me, making me get some sleep now and then, and for supporting me in your own ways.

Thank you to my sister and Dot's House for providing me with a way to finally get this book on the shelf and out into the world beyond my computer. Your editing, ideas, and support are invaluable to me. Truly, you are a gift to me, and I thank God nearly every day that I have you!

I also need to say thank you to my daughter as she helped me bounce ideas, correct my punctuation, and spelled many words for me. Thanks, sweetie, for all your input.

And finally, I want to thank each and every one of YOU. I am deeply grateful you would join me in making this dream come true. I pray you not only enjoyed the experience of reading this work of fiction but that perhaps you were challenged in some way to walk closer with God.

## May God bless each of you richly

# COMING SOON

## *SEASONS OF THE HEART BOOK TWO - WINTER TUMULT*

Autumn DeBlue returns to Michigan full of hope for the future. However, it isn't long before she realizes that being a guardian is much more difficult than she thought. Faced with having to discipline a growing child, who constantly challenges the boundaries, and step into the authority given to her by a deteriorating Lady Cannon - time with Landon Michaels is put on the back burner.

James and Eleanor come to Michigan to get married. Though it's a joyous event, the time is stressful as old relationships are tested, new relationships are proven, and matters of the heart are confronted.

Landon Michaels is struggling to hold it all together. Between the harsh judgment of his family, the demands of the Cannon Estate, and his new promotion, it's taking everything within him to fight the despair sinking into his soul. Can his faith survive the trials being forced upon it? And what will happen with his commitment to Autumn?

*TRAVANE*

COMING SOON

*Available in eBook*

CherRené Rayna - princess of Travane - is faced with the struggle of her lifetime. Will she do what is expected and marry CherRio Nikélon of the east country - Morat? Or will she go in search of the answers to a dream that won't let her go? A dream that threatens to reveal secrets long ago hidden, yet will change the future for all of Travane.

In the midst of such a monumental struggle, CherRené Rayna is confronted with an even graver thought - is life governed by people and the choices they make or by the Divine whom she's heard about from childhood. Will yielding to the Divine change her circumstances or her heart?

How will the decisions the CherRené makes affect the Land of Travane and the only life she's ever known?

#  Contact M.D. Schlatter 

Follow M.D. Schlatter on her website at

https://mdschlatterbooks.com/

email her at mmschlatter@ruraltel.net

or visit her Dot's Micro-Publishing House page at

https://dotsmicropublishinghouse.com/m-d-schlatter/

Lebanon, Kansas USA